GW00857562

For Charlotte
Loved your story - well
done on winning the competition.
Dream big, live bigger!
R E Lewin
x

CHILDREN OF PISCES

THE TWO PENDANTS

R E Lewin

Matador
Unit E2 Airfield Business Park,
Harrison Road, Market Harborough,
Leicestershire. LE16 7UL
Tel: 0116 279 2299
Email: books@troubador.co.uk
Web: www.troubador.co.uk/matador
Twitter: @matadorbooks

Paperback ISBN 978 1803130 927
Hardback ISBN 978 1803132 297

British Library Cataloguing in Publication Data.
A catalogue record for this book is available from the British Library.

Printed and bound in the UK by TJ Books Limited, Padstow, Cornwall
Typeset in 11pt Minion Pro by Troubador Publishing Ltd, Leicester, UK

Matador is an imprint of Troubador Publishing Ltd

I'd like to dedicate this book to
the following very special souls:

To my son Thomas and daughter Olivia for editing
this with me during lockdown. You amaze me every
day and I'm blessed to be your mother. You can make
your future exactly what you want it to be with enough
determination. You have the power over your life.
I love you tremendously;

To Judith Cutler for inspiring me and spending so much
time guiding me while still working on your own books;

To my Labrador Retriever, Gracie, for being the best earth
angel and changing my entire belief system in 14 years;

To all the teenagers brave enough to dare to be different.

Thank you, all of you.

PROLOGUE

A MOTHER'S PROTECTION

The creature threw back its head as a long howl bellowed through the forest, sending waves of terror through Sarah. It was giving a new set of orders to the rest of the pack. Sarah's legs buckled and she plunged headfirst to the forest floor. She raised her head, spitting leaves and gasping for breath as she looked behind her. The fear made her want to vomit.

'*Get up, Sarah! Get up!*' she told herself.

She'd been on the run for two days and they were very close behind her. Could she outstrip them? Grabbing a tree for support, she hauled herself to her feet, looking around desperately as she caught her breath. She must find somewhere to hide, and hiding from *them* would not be easy. She felt movement and placed her trembling hand over her huge stomach. She must protect her babies.

Grunting with determination, she left the support of the tree and stumbled deeper into the forest, desperately searching as she passed. Then she saw it – so small and hidden she almost missed it – behind a huge and ancient tree was a shallow hole, almost concealed by undergrowth. It was just big enough for her to hide in. She ran past the area, doubled back, and retraced her steps a few times, expertly covering her tracks.

She eased off her rucksack and reached inside. Where was that fire blanket she had taken? It might not look much and was very small, yet it had many special qualities. Would it be soundproof? Would it prevent *them* and their machines from hearing her or her unborn children? She hoped so. She snuggled into position, wrapped the blanket around her and dragged leaves and twigs over the blanket, ensuring the undergrowth covered her completely. Only a small fraction of her face remained uncovered, which she smeared with soil and spit to make a mud mask. With sheer willpower, she slowed her breathing down, placed a reassuring hand on her stomach and waited.

The first two appeared from within the trees so suddenly that Sarah jumped with surprise at not having heard them. She had excellent hearing – they were super silent. They were dressed all in black, just like ninjas, and could have passed for humans except for their large eyes, far more menacing than any human ones. They were black and looked as if they had been plucked from the eye sockets of a seal before being placed into the head of a ghost: bulging and shimmering in the pale grey skin like a dark nightmare whenever the light caught them. Her heart raced and she again felt the sickness rising within her. She heard the footsteps of the others. There were about twenty of them now, scanning the environment for any traces of her existence as they moved through the forest.

They came to a halt a few yards from where Sarah was hiding, looking and listening intently, trying to sense her presence. One was holding a small glowing machine in his hand. This was the machine they used to sense the *unborns* – her babies. They moved back and forth, the machine's colours changing as they went.

And they moved closer to Sarah.

Every instinct told her to run. Instead, she relied on her experience, held her breath and remained hidden. She saw the one holding the machine coming closer and closer to her. Every step he took sent another shiver of fear soaring throughout her trembling limbs. He stopped in front of the tree and looked it up and down until his eyes came to rest on Sarah's hiding place. All she could do was close her eyes and hold her breath. He could not reach her from where he was standing and would have to take a step to his right and launch forward to grab her. Her ears strained for the sound of this movement. She would have a nanosecond to escape his grasp and try to outrun them – impossible in her condition. Despite herself, she felt her lip tremble as the fear intensified and tears for her unborn children welled up.

He was so close she could smell him; a light earthy scent similar to mud. She opened her eyelids just a fraction and peeked through her lashes. His eyes searched the undergrowth until they came to rest on Sarah's face. He was looking right at her now, yet her camouflage was so good he did not know it and his gaze travelled past her face. She daren't breathe – this was too close to risk breathing at this moment. She forced herself to lie as still as a corpse and closed her eyes again.

Then the smell was gone. She had not heard him move away. At first, she was too scared to open her eyes and look. When she did, it was to see the back of them as they left. He had looked right through her. He had the machine almost within reach of the *unborns* yet still he had not detected them – the fire blanket had worked. She watched as he raised his head and let out a long and horrifying howl. A similar reply came from somewhere in the distance. Sarah hated that sound.

He reached for his belt and selected two small gadgets, made of a soft flexible type of metal, which resembled small flying insects – Sarah knew them as *seekers*. He activated the bracelet on his wrist and a 3D holographic photo appeared in the palm of his gloved hand. Sarah gasped as she recognised her image. Each *seeker* acknowledged the image with a click of its internal camera and then flew out into the forest. They circled the area; one whizzed in a circle just above Sarah's head and then they buzzed away in opposite directions. It was essential that she avoided these *seekers* and if luck was on her side, she would remain behind them.

Sarah dropped her head, gasping with relief. Yet even that sound might bring them back. They must be long gone before she allowed herself to move. She counted to one hundred. Two hundred. At last, silently, she uncovered herself, kissed her fire blanket in gratitude before packing it away and got to her feet. Now she needed more than a hiding place; she needed somewhere to spend the night. Was that the very faint sound of a horse in the distance? Could it be? Shrugging – she had nothing but instinct to guide her, after all – she set off towards the sound.

*

It was a horse. Not a great one; small, white, a little plump and in desperate need of a wash. However, it would do the job. Sarah had a way with horses and it wasn't long before she had mounted the horse – somewhat more difficult bareback and pregnant – and was galloping away from the trees and northward over the moors.

After four hours on horseback, taking care to remain out of sight, Sarah found her way to an old friend who now worked as a priest in Ilfracombe, North Devon. He lived in St Nicholas' Chapel, which sat high upon the top of a cliff known as Lantern Hill. For centuries, this beautiful chapel had overlooked the ocean and provided safety to many people. In the past, it had been a lighthouse, then a tourist attraction and now, since the Pisces virus outbreak, it was a sanctuary. Many people owed their lives to this place – she hoped her babies would be safe here too. It felt warm and welcoming as Sarah galloped up the hill. Out of breath, she gasped as she approached the top and was overwhelmed with joy when she saw the outline of the priest standing by the door, arms open to welcome her, a familiar smile spread across his face.

*

On a morning in March 2058, a baby girl was left in a small Moses basket outside an orphan school in London. Sarah gently placed a letter and a small crystal pendant beside the baby in a sealed envelope marked *Tammy, born 16th February 2058*. She tenderly kissed the little girl's cheek, stroked the small birthmark on her upper arm – two circles – and then looked up at the dreary large white building. Sarah felt sick as she rang the bell and then hid in the shadows and watched. Lieutenant Cole, an elderly woman with a hard, cold face, opened the door to find the baby on the step. She looked around, saw no sign of anyone and sighed, reluctantly taking the basket inside.

'Tammy...' Sarah whispered, and sighed deeply.

*

Later that morning, Sarah approached Stephen Terrett's large mansion in Surrey and knocked loudly upon the door. Stephen, a computer whizz-kid turned entrepreneur, opened the door to find no one there. He was just about to slam the door shut when he looked down to see the baby, lying in a Moses basket on his doorstep, staring up at him. He crouched down and took the envelope labelled *Mikie, born 31st January 2058*. It contained a letter and a small pendant made of clear crystal and shaped like a miniature sword. Stephen read the letter, covered his eyes with his hands and sighed heavily.

Then, nodding sorrowfully, he crouched down and gently took hold of the baby's hand. The hand closed around his finger and he moved it back and forth a couple of times, smiling. As he did so, the blanket moved a little, revealing a strange birthmark of two circles on his upper arm.

'How did you get this strange mark, little man?' he asked, expecting no answer.

Then, Stephen scooped up the basket and took the baby inside.

Sarah watched from behind a tree, gently rocking her pram as a tear rolled down her cheek. She fought to hold back the tears and felt the physical pain of her heart breaking.

'Look after him, my dear brother,' she whispered, looking down into her pram at the two remaining babies. She smiled, sadly, as they smiled, unknowingly, up at her. She touched the matching birthmarks on their arms and burst out crying. She almost fainted then, barely grabbing a tree in time to steady her balance. She was so weak now, she didn't have much longer.

'Just you two left,' she said. 'You will also be given wrong birthdates so no one knows you are quadruplets. Forgive me, my loves – my Mina and my Diego – my flesh and my blood, how I shall miss you all.'

Fresh tears fell down her face and she wiped them weakly away.

'Goodbye, Tammy and Mikie,' she sobbed.

She was still too weak to walk away. Resting her hand on the tree again, she took a couple of deep breaths, then raised her chin and forced her weary body to trudge on.

ONE

TAMMY AT THE ORPHAN CAMP

Without shoes was the only way to do it and you had to leave your socks on; otherwise, your feet would stick to the floor and make too much noise – even with a dusting of talcum powder. Tammy had learnt this through trial and error over the years. She was light on her feet and moved silently, like a ghost, behind Lieutenant Cole. It was uncanny how the rain started hitting the windows hard just as Tammy thought rain would help cover her presence. She frowned, telling herself that it was just coincidence, but the truth was this wasn't the first time it had occurred.

Lieutenant Cole remained completely oblivious to Tammy's presence as she rummaged for her keys in her tawdry moss-coloured cardigan, hanging over the smart white military dress she was supposed to officially wear at all times and hidden if anyone of authority came to visit the camp. To call her scruffy was an understatement. She was an obese woman in her late fifties, slouching in misery as she walked, forever hiding her grey hair in a tight bun under her army-style black beret. Her nose and cheeks were cherry-red and shone out from a wrinkled and pinched face. She might not have been so ugly on the outside if she hadn't cultivated such an unpleasant personality over the years. Lieutenant Cole hated children – especially Tammy. Finally finding the keys, she opened her office door and, as she turned to close it, did not see Tammy slip into the office. Once inside, Tammy dropped behind the filing cabinet next to the door. Lieutenant Cole locked the door and then, as if suddenly realising someone was there, quickly looked around.

'Who's there?' she asked, in her usual chilling voice.

Tammy crouched behind the cabinet, out of sight. Lieutenant Cole couldn't see her.

'Huh!' grumbled Lieutenant Cole, and rubbed her forehead to help relieve the headache she felt coming on. 'Those kids are driving me crazy. Will I ever get away from them?'

Just then, the phone rang and startled her for a moment. She walked to her desk, sat down in the chair with a large sigh and lifted the receiver.

'Hello' she said. 'Yes, that would be me. We are indeed. I have made all the travel arrangements and I shall be taking the kids to the safari park in May. No, I was not going to take all of— Yes, if I have to then I'll ensure everyone attends – I don't understand why it's so important…' There was a long silence and Lieutenant Cole lowered her head, rubbing her temples, the headache giving her obvious pain as she listened to the caller.

'Of course I will ensure we take all of the kids, even those that have been naughty, since it is that important. Yes – I understand.' She slammed the phone down and groaned as she slumped over her desk. Tammy watched as she sighed noisily and poured a large spoonful of medicine from a bottle she kept on the corner of her desk. She took a couple of pills from her top drawer and eagerly swallowed them, closing her eyes and waiting for the relief. A few moments later, she opened her eyes and looked towards the cabinet where Tammy was hiding. Tammy ducked back, pressing herself hard against the wall and bit her bottom lip nervously. Frowning, Lieutenant Cole walked over to the cabinet and was about to look behind it, where Tammy was still crouching, when a small grey field mouse came running out towards her.

Lieutenant Cole screamed as the mouse ran past her; she held her hand over her heart and released a long, slow breath.

'I hate mice and I hate this rotten school,' she muttered, trying to regain control of herself. The hate she felt for the rodents rose from her stomach and caused acid to hit her throat. She swallowed with difficulty. Rodents had caused her husband to get infected. She knew that much. She blamed them for spreading the virus rapidly, and the fact that so had several other species didn't seem to matter. Rodents were the problem.

She turned to the top drawer of the cabinet and entered a code – it sprang open. She sifted through the files within and found a folder labelled *Tammy*. She removed the folder and took it over to her desk. She often looked at this file; her hate for the child had turned into an unhealthy obsession

– she couldn't help herself. She sat down and was about to open it when the internal alarm went off three times. That meant a high-level problem.

'Oh, what now?' she grumbled, and stomped out of the office.

Tammy waited for the door to close behind Lieutenant Cole before dashing to the desk and opening the folder. There was a letter inside and a beautiful pendant. Tammy placed them in her pocket. Then she browsed through the rest of the papers within the folder and read of several attempts that had been made for her adoption – each accompanied by Lieutenant Cole's handwriting explaining why she had not allowed the adoptions to take place. Silly reasons: instability, bad behaviour, lack of discipline, inability to follow orders. The excuses were endless and certainly exaggerated – not enough to deprive a child of a real family. Tammy banged her fist on the desk angrily and slammed the folder shut.

She walked to the office door and listened – silence. The mouse ran across the floor and stopped by Tammy's shoe. Tammy smiled, picked it up and slipped it into her pocket, then noiselessly let herself out of the office. She ran quickly to her bedroom, closed the door behind her and breathlessly jumped onto her bed. Her roommate, Sukie, sat nervously on her own bed, watching her. Tammy smiled at her roommate, once again admiring her long dark hair, golden skin and hazel eyes. Sukie was from India originally and Tammy adored how pretty she was. She was less comfortable with her own auburn hair, green eyes and pale skin even though Sukie often told her she was naturally pretty too.

'I went to reception and set off the alarm exactly when you told me to. Did it work? Did you get your file this time?' Sukie asked.

'Yes, it was perfect. She got my file out and left it on the desk this time, just as I'd hoped,' Tammy said with a smile.

'It's about time.' Sukie sighed with relief.

'It was only the fourth attempt,' Tammy said.

'I don't know how you can be so calm. I'm still a bag of nerves.'

'Yes, but I got it and I was right – the old bat has been lying to me.'

'Well, we knew that,' Sukie retorted.

'I needed to know for sure and there have been people who tried to adopt me and she stops it every time. She said I was abandoned here by my mother without so much as a letter, but look what I have.' Tammy pulled the letter and pendant from her pocket.

'She's such a hateful cow! Oh, that's a beautiful pendant,' Sukie said, admiring the pretty crystals. 'I wonder what it is. Read the letter.'

Tammy opened the letter and read it out loud.

To whom it may concern:

I am writing this letter because I am very ill. I do not have long to live and must look to protect my child. Please take good care of my baby, Tammy. Let her know I did not abandon her but loved her dearly. That I am so sorry I couldn't be there to be a mother to her.

Let her know that she is very special and that one day it will all make sense. She should not worry if she feels alone,

THE CHILDREN OF PISCES

since it's meant to be this way and will not last for very long. Her friends will soon become apparent to her.

On her 13th birthday, her father will find her and she will come to understand everything. Until then, please love her and keep her safe.

XXX

Tammy looked up at Sukie, her mouth open in surprise.

'Your father?' Sukie gasped.

'When I'm thirteen? Not long to go now. I can easily take another year here.' Tammy smiled, content that she finally had some information about her past and disappointed that she would probably never see the mother she had always dreamed of.

'Oh Tammy, you are so lucky. Even if you aren't adopted, you'll be out of here within a year. You were right all along to suspect Lieutenant Gremlin.' Sukie giggled as she used their nickname for Lieutenant Cole.

Tammy put the pendant on and fastened it behind her neck, making sure it was hidden beneath her collar. There was no way Lieutenant Cole would find it now.

'Anyway, I wonder why she didn't sign it with her name. I'd like to know my mother's name, but then I guess I'll know in a year. You know what? I heard Lieutenant Cole trying to ban me from the annual visit to the safari park again. I overheard her speaking to someone on the phone and I think I get to go this time after all,' Tammy said.

'That would be great and an extra bonus to celebrate your birthday,' said Sukie, hugging Tammy excitedly. 'Tammy, why does she hate you so much?'

6

'She has never forgiven me for complaining about her in that assessment interview.'

'When a school official asked you questions about our lives here? You were only five years old, weren't you?'

'Yes, I was. Remember how they used to come and interview everyone? Anyway, I was honest and Lieutenant Cole was investigated. There were a few changes. Food was improved and taking meals away as punishment was banned. Also, they banned Lieutenant Cole's favourite punishment in the pond. Now they only select a few of us at random – her random!'

'I heard stories of that from the older kids. She'd make you stand in the icy pond, waist-deep, in all the slime and loads of tadpoles running through your toes – was that it? The older girls still shook as they remembered the ordeal and told me.'

'Yes, that's true. I didn't mind that punishment. The pond animals kept me entertained hour after hour, so I never cried, and Lieutenant Cole didn't let you out until you cried. I was very sick by the time I was allowed out. She hated me for not breaking. You were lucky you weren't here then.'

'So why didn't you just cry?'

'I couldn't – something inside wouldn't let me. The frogs and fish kept me company, though, so it wasn't too bad. However, the review board were shocked. She lost her promotion due to *unnecessary extreme punishment of children in her care* and has always blamed and hated me since.' Tammy shook her head sadly.

'I didn't realise. It was kept very quiet, and even now after all this time?'

'Well, she hated not being able to control me before so this just made it even worse. Lieutenant Cole promised me that she would make me pay and that if she was stuck here against her will, then I'd have to be as well. She made it clear I should never say anything bad about her from that day on, and I knew not to.'

'I'm sorry, Tammy, that's horrible.'

'That's okay, only a year left now. Thanks for helping me, Sukie, for setting off the alarm again. Now I have hope. You are the only one brave enough to be my friend and I thank you for that.'

'Well, I always love a good fight! Besides, it was all worth it in the end, wasn't it? Twelve years you have been here and you should have been given that pendant and letter years ago. At least you know now and in a way it's like a birthday present, eh? Nicer than the chocolates I stole from Lieutenant Cole's desk for you and let's face it – she can afford to skip a few,' Sukie said, giggling.

'Yes, it's the best birthday present for me. I loved your chocolates too. My twelfth birthday is the best one ever. Now I don't care what Lieutenant Gremlin says. I'm going to set Minnie free at the safari park.' Tammy stroked the mouse sitting quietly in her hand.

'You've always wanted to, she'll like it there.'

'Yes, much nicer than here. Minnie should have an easy retirement now she is so old. She deserves it and I get worried about her safety here, since Lieutenant Cole hates mice. It's an effort keeping Minnie away from all the traps.'

'You seem to have trained her very well but you're right, she has earned it. Come on, Tammy, it's getting late. We should head for the canteen.'

It was twenty past six and, despite the new rules against starving the children, the canteen doors closed promptly at six thirty; therefore, anyone late would forego dinner. However, dinner was far from satisfying and consisted of a basic vegetarian diet that was mostly potatoes and bread.

As Tammy and Sukie left their room, they were joined by other children and all formed a neat line in the corridor. The orphan school had a white colour scheme and was very military in both design and outlook. The orphans were raised as army cadets so that if they were not adopted they would be well trained to enter one of the armed forces. It kept them off the streets when they reached teenage years and gave them a family to be part of, should no other family opportunity present itself. There was no choice in the matter; it was a good system and offered the children plenty of opportunities as adults. Once they had completed two years in the forces, they were free to leave if they wished – few chose to leave. They wore white uniforms which made them all look like army scouts in a mental institution and were impossible to keep clean, wasting huge chunks of their time every day. Regardless of their gender, everyone wore white trousers and jackets with black berets. Adult women who worked there could choose between trousers or a dress if they preferred. But not the children.

Quietly, they marched to the canteen, lined up with their trays to receive their plain-looking food and then sat neatly at long wooden tables. To talk over dinner meant immediate dismissal and an early night, followed by various degrees of punishment the following day. It was easy to stay on the right side of authority if you followed the orders, which was something Tammy had repeatedly failed to do.

Minnie was still in Tammy's pocket and a few pieces of bread were sneakily dropped in to keep her company. Sukie was the only person who noticed, and smiled. Tammy smiled back and promptly received a warning look from Lieutenant Cole, who had just walked in. The doors closed with a loud bang and everyone knew to be quiet. Lieutenant Cole walked to the centre of the room; her heels echoed in the silence.

'I have an announcement to make,' she declared coldly. 'Our annual visit to Brunswick Safari Park is scheduled for the end of May. This is a charitable event, as some of you know, whereby Mr Edward Brunswick allows different orphan schools to visit at different times of the year. This is very generous and to avoid taking advantage of such an offer, I have been careful how many of you have attended in previous years.'

Tammy, on occasion, had been the only one left behind, and Sukie gave her a small sympathetic smile. Lieutenant Cole glared unpleasantly at Tammy before continuing.

'However, this time I have been informed that it is essential everyone here attends.' Her eyes remained, disappointedly, on Tammy. 'This is because our board of directors requires a group photo of everyone for some advertising campaign of great significance. You must all be on your best behaviour, needless to say, and anyone falling short of this will be subjected to the appropriate punishment for three months after the visit.'

The children gasped; three months was a long time for the sort of punishments they were used to. Lieutenant Cole abruptly left the canteen. Tammy slowly let out her breath – at last she could go.

'I don't think anyone would be crazy enough to risk behaving badly. You were right, Tammy. You do get to go after all, and the fact is killing Lieutenant Cole,' said Sukie gleefully.

'I bet I end up getting the punishment upon my return no matter what I do.'

'No doubt about it, but it'll be worth it,' Sukie said.

'Tell me again what it's like,' Tammy whispered.

'I've told you lots of times!' Sukie smiled.

'I like hearing the way you describe it, please tell me again.'

'Well,' said Sukie, leaning in closer, 'the story goes like this. Ed Brunswick is this really rich man who lives on a beautiful island and just before the Pisces virus hit us, he turned it into a massive animal sanctuary. When Pisces hit, he was like Noah because he saved all the animals with an island instead of an ark. His island was unaffected by the virus and afterwards he bred animals and then sent them off around the world, repopulating themselves everywhere. Loads of animals would be extinct if it wasn't for him and his wife. I've never met him. Apparently, he's a really big guy and looks like Santa Claus and lives for the animals. He has set loads free in Africa and India and always keeps at least two of everything safe on the island – just like Noah.'

'Two of everything?' Tammy sighed.

'Yeah, at least! It's magical. Plus, there are trees bigger than buildings all around you. Most of the animals live in a natural environment. Even the few in cages are happy, because there is so much space. You can walk on foot alongside the safe animals, see the dangerous ones in their enclosures or up-close in these cute little bus-like vehicles.

To think, Tammy, that before Pisces, everyone could see such animals all the time, as if it was normal. Many children still haven't seen animals, not just you.' Sukie shook her head in wonderment as she remembered her last visit.

'It's probably the only thing that makes us lucky to be orphans. I have to see them,' Tammy responded.

'Then you'll have to make sure you stay right out of Lieutenant Cole's way,' Sukie said.

Tammy almost smiled yet still wouldn't allow herself to believe it until it happened.

*

The day finally arrived when they were all to go to the safari park. Tammy didn't sleep the night before as the excitement welled up inside her. It was a long drive in the school minibus from London to Southampton and a further hour on the hovercraft to get to Vivacity Island, where Brunswick Safari Park was located. The hovercraft was an air-cushioned vehicle that slid over the water gracefully; bright yellow in colour with a smooth round surface, almost egg-shaped. The bottom of the hovercraft barely touched the water's surface, no matter how large or small the waves. Instead, it hovered over a warm level of air, which acted as a cushion and adjusted itself according to how far away it was from the surface of the water. This meant that the hovercraft didn't ride the waves; it stayed level. Instead, it was the air in between the craft and the water that went up and down, completely eliminating motion sickness.

Tammy had watched the waves ripple alongside the hovercraft all the way to the island and felt the salt air in her hair for the very first time in her life. She felt free and excited and tried desperately not to meet the resentful glares from Lieutenant Cole.

It was a short walk from the ferry port to the entrance of the safari park, and the queue seemed to go on forever. Tammy huffed with exasperation. 'How long does it take to get in?'

'You've waited all your life. A few more minutes won't hurt,' Sukie replied.

She could hear the various sounds of the animals and her excitement grew. Tammy, impatient in the queue, stood on tiptoe and tried to peer over everyone's heads. Sukie laughed at her, shaking her head.

Once through the gates, they had to pose for their group photograph. Tammy was too agitated to stand still. She could feel a burning sensation in her stomach that was much stronger than excitement. She could hardly breathe and just wanted to run away from the group and see what it was that was drawing her near. Lieutenant Cole could not see Tammy from where she stood and did not know to whom the photographer was referring when he shouted for them to look at the camera. She had nothing to gain from this photograph so showed no interest at all.

'Please, boys and girls, I have wasted four shots already. I can't just keep shooting all day. All you have to do is look at me all at the same time – just once.' The photographer impatiently ran his fingers through his brown hair in exasperation.

'You, at the back, please look.' He pointed a long finger at Tammy. She smiled and nodded and yet, before he could click his camera, her head had spun around to another noise in the distance. 'Fine. Marvellous. I give up. That'll just have to do,' he muttered miserably, banging his equipment excessively as he packed it all away.

Tammy had no idea and didn't care how little of her face showed in the picture and how lucky she was for that. As they moved as a group along the path, Tammy broke away and raced forward – even Sukie couldn't catch up with her – until she came upon the elephants. Then, Tammy was alone, lost in her own world as the group disappeared from view. The elephants fascinated Tammy and she stared at them for the longest time. She could read them, feel them, understand them, and she thought they could see right through her too. Her fingers tingled, her breath was short and she trembled from head to toe. She had never felt so alive and excited in her life.

*

Upon a hill in the distance, a man stood in his Jeep with his binoculars eagerly pressed against his eyes. He was a large middle-aged man, tall and broad. His white wavy hair and round red cheeks somehow made him look younger than he was, almost ageless. He had been born with white hair and large ice-blue eyes, and it made him different from everyone else. This was probably one of the reasons he always felt more comfortable with animals rather than people. Besides him panted his number one companion, a Labrador retriever called Fudge. She went everywhere with him.

He watched the strange behaviour of his animals. He had first noticed something strange was happening about half an hour earlier. It started with a feeling in his gut – what he called the Brunswick intuition. His dogs and chickens started misbehaving, shortly followed by the rest of the animals – small things that other people wouldn't notice, but he knew his animals and he knew that something was up. He had decided to take a drive about in his Jeep and could hear all sorts of unusual noises coming from the enclosures. He focused his binoculars on the elephants and watched as they all walked together in a line towards the crowd, as if circus trained. It seemed eerie, unnatural, and made Ed curious.

Moving his binoculars further along, he saw the sea lions all lined up at the side of the water, looking through the crowd like excited children searching for their mother. He moved his binoculars along to the monkeys, who were unnaturally still and silent. Ed had never experienced a whole enclosure full of monkeys being so still in his entire life. They were all poised and watching for something, or someone.

He followed their gaze to see what they were watching and found a young girl, no more than eleven or twelve years old, walking alone, mesmerised by the animals. There was no doubt in Ed's mind that this child somehow fascinated all these animals. Of course, he knew no one would believe him; he had spent his life following his instincts and he was fully aware of what he was seeing right in front of his eyes.

'Well I never,' he muttered. 'What have we here? What is it you have that interests them so much?'

Ed sat back down in his Jeep and raced down towards the young girl with a huge and excited smile on his face – could she be the special one that Sarah had mentioned?

*

Having watched Tammy as she walked and the way the animals had behaved, Ed was convinced there was something incredible happening here and he couldn't quite put his finger on what it was. Fudge raced out of the Jeep towards Tammy and he followed. His dog was an excellent judge of character and it would be interesting to see what she made of this girl. Leaning on the wooden fence alongside her, he watched his dog jump up at the girl.

Tammy gasped in delight and bent down to stroke Fudge, whose tail wagged and eyes glistened with happiness. Tammy remained completely unaware of the man's presence until he spoke to her.

'She likes you,' he eventually murmured.

'Oh, hi. She is lovely – she's yours then?'

'Indeed – my best friend, in fact.'

'She's adorable and such a beautiful colour of gold and red.'

'Yes, it's known as fox-red. She is a belle. She's a Labrador retriever, slimmer and less roly-poly than a traditional Lab.'

She licked Tammy's face excitedly.

'It's unusual for her to take such a liking to anyone – she doesn't like many people,' he said.

'Well, Fudge has no reason to dislike me,' Tammy said with a giggle, wiping the saliva from her face.

'How did you know her name?' he asked, puzzled.

'I don't know, you must have said it.'

'No, no, I didn't.'

Tammy continued to stroke Fudge as she watched the elephants.

'Incredible creatures, aren't they?'

'Yes, they are,' she replied, turning to look at him. Usually, she would be alarmed at being spoken to by a stranger, and yet there was something about the man that seemed very familiar.

'My name is Ed Brunswick,' he said.

'You own this place?' Tammy's eyes widened in surprise. That was where she recognised him from, pictures on the hovercraft.

'I do indeed,' he said with a smile.

'It's beautiful, amazing.'

'Yes, it is, thank you. Some very lucky animals here, you know, shouldn't be alive and yet they are. Can I ask your name?'

'My name is Tammy. I can see how happy the animals are to be here. Can I please ask a favour?'

'There is never any harm in asking,' Ed said.

'May I leave a friend here? She will enjoy life here much more than at the orphan school – it's horrible there.'

'Oh, well, who might this friend be?'

Tammy pulled out the small grey mouse from her pocket and showed her to Ed.

'This is Minnie. I know it isn't an original name, but she likes it very much and it suits her. I know you love animals and she is old. It would be lovely if she could retire here, and I think by these elephants she would be really happy and safe,' Tammy explained.

'I have no objections,' Ed said, smiling , relieved it was only a mouse. 'The only problem is that elephants hate mice, so perhaps somewhere else would be better.'

'Oh, they won't hate her – you'll see.' Before Ed could say anything, Tammy had set the mouse down on the floor.

Crouching down, she softly whispered goodbye to Minnie, accepting a little kiss on her lips before she scuffled away. She didn't notice Ed's wide eyes and open mouth as he silently watched.

'You see.' Tammy sighed, happily.

Ed watched this odd little mouse run over to the elephants, who acknowledged Minnie with little interest as she helped herself to some of their fallen grain. Ed frowned, knowing the elephants hated mice and yet also knowing, for some reason, not to question it. 'Well, Tammy, it looks like your friend will be very happy here after all. How do you feel when you look at these elephants? They certainly seem pleased to meet you.'

'How do I feel? Well, I guess... I can't really explain. Tingly. Excited. When I look into their eyes, it's as if I can see more, like I can understand them and know them. Take her...' Tammy pointed to one of the female elephants. 'She had a very hard time when she was young. Somehow I just know that she was beaten.'

Ed raised his eyebrows. 'How could you know something like that?'

'I have no idea. No way to explain it. I just know.'

'When she was very small—'

'Tammy!' Lieutenant Cole shouted from afar, unable to see Ed. 'Get over here with the rest of the group.'

'I have to go. Thank you for letting Minnie stay,' Tammy muttered quickly, and ran away.

Fudge went to follow until Ed called her back. She whimpered sadly at his side as Tammy disappeared. Ed was not impressed with the violent way that this harsh-looking woman dragged Tammy by the shoulder. He rubbed his chin in the way he tended to do when a plan was forming in his mind.

*

The photographer held his briefcase tightly and hurried across the busy London streets of Canary Wharf towards the seventy-two-storey building. Many different businesses operated from this building and he had been told to go to the Institute of Viral Investigations and ask for Dr Lloyd. It had been a long three-month assignment and he was eager to be paid. The money was good for such a strange task and he understood not to ask any questions. There were some very odd people involved; very secretive and scary people who disliked showing their faces, preferring instead to hide behind Dr Lloyd.

He entered the large glass revolving doors and headed for the main reception desk in front of him.

'The Institute of Viral Investigations, please,' he said hurriedly.

'The lifts are on your right. Go to the seventy-second floor, turn right out of the lift and reception is through the second set of doors on your left. Nothing is signposted so don't forget,' he was told.

The photographer followed the instructions and nervously tapped his briefcase as the lift ascended. He checked his watch; he was going to be right on time and everything was as it should be. He reached the institute's reception, facing a creepy, thin man reading a newspaper.

'I'm here to see Dr Lloyd,' he said, a little out of breath.

'Sign in here, take a seat over there,' the man said in a

bored tone. He waited until the photographer had sat down before picking up his phone.

'He's here,' was all he said.

Ten minutes passed and nothing happened. The photographer checked his watch every thirty seconds.

'They're ready for you. Go into that room there,' the receptionist eventually said, pointing to a closed door.

The photographer entered the room. It was large without any windows. There was, however, a large mirror along the wall. At first, the photographer thought it was strange, then he realised there must be people behind the mirror watching him. It gave him the creeps. The room also held a large conference table, and a man was seated opposite him.

'Sit down,' said Dr Lloyd.

He was dressed in a black pinstripe suit and looked more like a banker than a doctor. He was bald, with beady little eyes, and leathery looking, as if he had spent far too much time outside in the sun. His fat, stumpy fingers tapped impatiently on the tabletop.

'I have them here, all of them. Can I get my money now? It's not every day a man has to work for so long without being paid,' the photographer said nervously, placing the briefcase on the table.

'Paid upon completion, as agreed,' said Dr Lloyd, and handed him a large padded envelope.

The photographer smiled and opened his briefcase. He took out several envelopes, A4-sized, and handed them, one at a time, to Dr Lloyd.

'It wasn't easy in some orphan schools, what with all this protective legislation. They don't just let any photographer come and take group photos of children in their care, you know. They're so protective of the children. I had to use my initiative and come up with all sorts of clever stories and sometimes bribes to get people, even those on the board, to cooperate. I would have included expenses in the deal if I had realised.' He looked at the doctor hopefully.

'We stick to the deal – there will be no extra money,' said the doctor bluntly and, unnoticed by the photographer, rolled his eyes in disgust at those hiding behind the mirror.

'That's all of them. Don't mind if I count this, do you?' the photographer asked, after handing over the last envelope.

'Of course, take all the time you want. Then leave,' said the doctor, quickly walking out of the room.

'Oh, right. Okay. Thank you. Er, good doing business with you,' the photographer mumbled as he took out the money and started counting.

Dr Lloyd walked into the room concealed behind the mirror, where he greeted a large male alien. There was another alien standing behind him. They stayed in the darkened corner, barely visible, their heads hidden by ninja-style black headwraps, showing only their glistening black eyes.

'Here you are, gentlemen,' he said, and handed the envelopes over.

'Excellent,' replied one of them, in a deep and chilling voice that was not quite human. 'You have done well again and will be rewarded.'

'Always a pleasure,' said the doctor calmly.

They sifted through the photographs in the envelopes, group pictures from every orphan school in the country.

The two aliens looked closely at the face of each child before moving on to the next photo.

'Are you looking for similar features, or something else?' asked Dr Lloyd.

'A little of both,' muttered one of the aliens. 'I cannot see everyone's face.'

They all looked through the mirror at the photographer, still sitting down counting his money.

'Imbecile!' hissed the doctor.

'I could kill him,' shouted one of the aliens, in a voice that chilled Dr Lloyd as it threw a photograph down onto the floor in a fit of rage.

'He isn't worth the effort,' said the other one with a sneer.

The doctor looked down at the discarded photograph as the aliens continued to sift through the remainder. It was a group of orphans standing outside a safari park and all but one face was looking at the camera. There was no way of identifying her.

'Well, how likely is it that the few not facing the camera are the ones you are looking for?' the doctor suggested reassuringly.

'Let us hope you are right,' said the alien. 'We are running out of time.'

TWO

BRUNSWICK
HOUSE

Mr and Mrs Brunswick sat opposite Lieutenant Cole as they negotiated the adoption of Tammy. Lieutenant Cole was not impressed and was reluctant to let Tammy go for no reason the Brunswicks could understand.

'She is currently being punished for her bad behaviour during the visit? Just what does that mean?' Ed demanded.

'We are very strict on discipline here and Tammy is in isolation for—'

'Isolation? I can guess what sort of punishment you dish out, Lieutenant Cole. I do not understand the problem.' Ed frowned. 'You say she is odd and has a "mean disposition" and yet I have clearly stated I am not in the least bit bothered by your recommendation. We are happy to make up our own minds, and have chosen her, thank you.'

'I'm afraid I can't allow it, Mr Brunswick. It would be very irresponsible of me to allow you to take her,' Lieutenant Cole replied icily.

'Let me handle this.' Jude patted Mr Brunswick's hand reassuringly. Jude had married Ed when they were young.

She had a striking look about her: tall, slim and elegant with her long black hair, and yet down to earth with a positive can-do temperament. However, she also had the fighting spirit of a Rottweiler, as Ed often nicknamed her, and when she turned her focus on to a person, they did what she wanted every single time.

'We want to adopt that child and if you give us any trouble whatsoever you can mark my words that you will be out of a job in less than two weeks and unemployable for the foreseeable future! I know your sort,' Jude said calmly and scarily, leaning in closer as Lieutenant Cole stared back in horror. 'You are an embittered and nasty old woman and enjoy picking on those smaller than you. My husband saw the way you treated that poor girl at the safari park and I won't stand for any more stories about her from you. Your resentment towards that girl only makes us even more determined to take her away from you. We have made up our minds and unless you have a desire to be taken through the complaints process in a painstakingly slow and embarrassing manner, I suggest you learn to cooperate! Would you really like me to have you and your establishment investigated thoroughly?' Jude planned on doing precisely that anyway, but she wouldn't let on just yet.

Lieutenant Cole glared at Jude Brunswick and knew she had met more than her match. She felt her blackened heart sink as she knew, beyond a shadow of a doubt, that she would have to hand Tammy over to them. The thought of Tammy living a rich life with these people sickened her. She was overwhelmed with the feeling that life was so unfair.

'I was just trying to be helpful. If I were you, I wouldn't adopt a child like that when I could have the pick of many

more suitable girls her age. That is all I was trying to advise.'
She shrugged, defeated.

'You are not us and will never be anything like us. Sort
it out – now!' Jude replied sternly.

Lieutenant Cole opened and closed her mouth. No
words came out.

*

'You'll love the house,' Ed said as the Jeep bounced
along the dirt track. 'It's a wonderful old building dating
back centuries and if all you have known is the orphan
school, I'll bet you won't know what to think when you see
it. Are you okay?'

'Yes, this is fun,' Tammy replied, gripping the dashboard
tightly with both hands. Fudge bounced along happily in
the back seat.

'Oh, you'll get used to that. This off-road Jeep can be
much more fun than this when you get used to it. I can go all
over the island, whether there is a track or not. Sometimes
I go too fast when Jude isn't looking. I'll wait until you're
more used to it before I take you on one of those rides.' He
chuckled and gave her a friendly pat on the shoulder. 'The
shape of the Jeep is a little slicker in design than it used
to be, and uses Jatropha plant biofuel, to be economically
friendly. It's fantastic. Like it?'

'I love it. So, it runs on plant fuel?'

'Yes, like most things nowadays. Anything that doesn't
run on plant fuel, easily grown of course, is run by solar,
water or wind-generated electricity. It's quite amazing what
you can use with simple and natural things.'

'So, what produces the electricity at the orphan school and here?'

'The school, being based in London, will have combined solar and wind generators on the rooftops. London is a city that doesn't get much sunlight and you can never rely completely on the wind to blow just when you want it to.'

'Of course not, everyone knows that.'

'Of course, so most places in London, including your school, will use both solar and wind, which is sufficient and can be stored. Here, we have a giant hydropower plant built alongside the island.'

'What's that?'

'It's a large water dam that collects water from a river that runs across the island and uses it to generate electricity. Coal, gas and oil were ruining our planet, causing irreparable damage. We had to switch to friendlier substances. It is just sad that it took us so long to get rid of large businesses in power so that we could use natural and cheap resources. I hate politics, Tammy, it's the worst part of my job,' he said with a sigh.

'Well, the island is really beautiful. I didn't know trees could be so big,' said Tammy.

'My ancestors invested a lot of time over the centuries importing trees from all over the world. The ones from South America are the most impressive. I'll teach you all about them and all the different species of birds that inhabit them. Without intending it, the island has become representative of the entire world's flora, plant and animal species. It wasn't until the Pisces virus outbreak that I really came to understand what the island was. It's as if it grew itself. Look straight ahead, Tammy. We'll see the house any minute now. I wouldn't want you to miss this view.'

Brunswick House appeared from behind the trees and left Tammy speechless. It was massive; a lovely Elizabethan mansion, surrounded by beautiful parks and a huge pond. It towered high above the mighty trees, the sun reflecting off the pale yellow-coloured stone walls, making it shine. The front driveway was pebbled and surrounded by beautifully shaped bushes and flowers. Wide marble steps led from the driveway to the extravagant pillars surrounding the front entrance – it was incredible.

The door opened as they approached and more Labradors raced towards the Jeep, one black and one golden, competing with Fudge to get the closest to Tammy's legs. Tammy felt the butterflies in her stomach as Jude walked towards them. She had met Jude only briefly at the orphan school and she was now her adoptive mother.

Tammy stared at the silky long black hair that hadn't greyed with age and marvelled at how it contrasted magnificently with Ed's white wavy hair. Her hazel eyes glimmered and emanated a warmth from within her. They were both dressed casually, safari-style khaki shorts and T-shirt, prepared for the outdoors lifestyle they enjoyed. Conscious of her tattered grey dress, which she had considered the smartest of her limited wardrobe until now, Tammy was suddenly aware of how poor she actually was. Her eyes began to water and her lip trembled unexpectedly.

'Hello, Tammy, are you all right?' Jude asked with concern.

'I feel a little like Cinderella must have felt when at the prince's palace. At least Cinderella had a nice dress to wear, even if just for a moment.' She tried to smile; the poverty and sadness of her life until now suddenly overcame Tammy and she bit her lip to stop the trembling. She also felt guilty about hiding the fact that her father was supposed to come looking for her in a year's time. However, she despised living at the orphan school and to have the opportunity to live here with the animals was far too tempting to resist. If she told them about her father, they might change their minds about adopting her. Tammy was too scared to risk that; scared of never seeing the animals again, scared of what Lieutenant Cole might do.

'It feels like a terrible mistake has been made and I shouldn't be here. It had all felt like a dream until now and I feel very out of place, as if I don't belong here. I don't want to go back to the orphan school either.' Tammy couldn't stop herself from talking, knowing that she could ruin this entire opportunity and end up back at the orphanage, but struggling with not being completely honest with these kind people.

'You don't have to. Tammy, we are so excited to have you here,' Jude said warmly, embracing her, holding her tightly. 'I know this must all feel so sudden and strange to you and I promise that very soon you will feel completely at ease and come to see this as your home. I, too, was adopted and do understand how you feel. You are so welcome here and we have been looking forward to having you.'

'There is definitely no mistake, and you will never have to go back to any orphan school again. Jude was very determined to get you here as soon as possible,' Ed added. 'I knew you were meant to be here from the moment I saw you by the elephants. The animals know you belong here,

Tammy, and so do we. You'll feel that way too, soon, just like Jude says. Oh, and I saw Minnie again yesterday. She's settled in nicely, so you see, you already have someone here that you know.'

'Come, let me show you around the house a little,' Jude said, stroking Tammy's hair.

Tammy smiled and watched the dogs bounce excitedly around them, brushing alongside her legs and insisting on being petted. They closed the front door and walked down a large hallway, past spectacular large paintings hung on the high walls. 'Let's show Tammy the library first,' Ed said excitedly. 'My great-great-grandfather William started this library by collecting rare and ancient books. It was really Great-uncle Harry who collected all the best examples. He was an adventurer, travelling the world and bringing back many of the fascinating items we have here today. He collected maps and encyclopaedias and had them translated. Of course, some of them are in the museum at the safari park now so visitors can see them. I keep a few here just for us.'

The heavy wooden door groaned open, sending a waft of musty air into their faces. The walls were a mass of book-filled shelves. A dark green rug lay across the wooden floor, almost covering it completely. There was an open fireplace with a pair of green leather chairs set at either side. At the far end of the room was a large window with heavy green curtains pulled across, blocking out all the natural light. The ceiling was dotted with tiny star-like lights, and lampshades were carefully placed next to two small tables. The result was a very cosy, dimly lit room.

The living room was just as spectacular. It too had a large fireplace, this time with red leather chairs at either side. There was a thick red carpet speckled with dark brown diamond shapes. Two large crystal chandeliers hung from the ceiling and thick red velvet curtains were draped across glass doors leading outside onto a patio. Tammy walked over to the glass doors and looked outside to see that the patio overlooked the most beautiful pond she could ever have hoped to see. Several chickens were pecking at the grass edges of the pond and large fish nosily popped their heads to the surface every now and then to have a good look around.

'Jude's pets,' Ed said, coming to stand at her side. 'You'll notice with time how they get more attention than I do.'

'Oh, stop going on about that,' Jude said, laughing. 'You don't know a good thing when you have it.'

'If that were true, I wouldn't miss it when your pets come before me now, would I?' he teased.

'You're a fine one to talk with all those dogs of yours!' Jude retorted.

Tammy smiled at how they spoke to each other and how comfortable it made her feel. She felt herself relaxing.

Of all the rooms, what was going to be Tammy's bedroom was the most breathtaking. It was at least three times the size of her old shared bedroom in London. The walls were artistically decorated with animals, a jungle scene that went around the entire bedroom. There was a pride of lions sunbathing at the head of the bed, monkeys swung from the trees, zebras ate grass by her wardrobe and a large elephant and its baby squirted a fountain of water over the sink next to the dressing table.

'Wow!' Tammy exclaimed, obviously impressed.

Ed and Jude smiled.

'Look up,' Jude said.

Looking up, she could see a flock of flamingos flying over her head. She could only see the undersides of the birds, which made them look incredibly real. The whole ceiling was a mass of pink. It was amazing. She turned around, looking in every direction, taking it all in. They had been painted so realistically they seemed almost alive.

'Do you like it, Tammy? If it's too much, we can always change it. You can do whatever you like. It's your room now,' Jude said.

'I… It's…' Tammy stumbled.

'I think she likes it,' Ed said, smiling.

'I do, I really do.' Tammy laughed.

'Excellent.' Jude clasped her hands together in relief and smiled.

'We took the liberty of getting you some new clothes, since most of your city outfits won't be appropriate for here,' Ed explained, as Jude opened up the wardrobe.

Tammy looked down at her dress in shame and couldn't quite bring herself to look back up at Ed. *Most of your city outfits won't be appropriate for here*, he had said. Tammy thought this was a rather kind way of putting it and silently thanked him for it.

'Why don't I run you a nice bath and you can try these on afterwards?' Jude said, taking out a pair of blue jeans and a green jumper. 'It's been many years since I have seen such lovely auburn hair. I think this jumper will bring out that luscious red colour.'

Tammy looked up and smiled. 'Do you think so?'

'Of course, I wouldn't say so otherwise. You have such a pretty face, there is something quite remarkable about you,' she said with a smile.

'It's your eyes,' Ed added, bending down to take a closer look. 'They are an amazing green colour. Jude, you have a lovely emerald necklace the same colour as Tammy's eyes, they sparkle in the same way as that emerald. Yet there is something else in your eyes too, like a sparkle of gold light. Just as you try to see it, the sparkle disappears so you can't be sure what colour it is. Beautiful.'

'Really?' Tammy blushed.

'Yes, really. I can't shake the feeling that they remind me of someone. Jude, do we know anyone with eyes like Tammy's?'

'No one comes to mind,' Jude answered.

'I'm sure it'll come to me.'

'Well, when we get you dressed up for dinner one night you can wear my emeralds, Tammy, and we'll compare the colour with your eyes.' Jude beamed. 'It is just so nice to have a pretty young girl about the house.'

'I'll leave you ladies to get dressed. I'll be downstairs when you're done,' Ed said, and left the room.

Jude ran the bath while Tammy undressed and wrapped herself in a towelling robe that had been placed on her bed. As she pulled the towelling robe on, Jude noticed a mark on Tammy's arm. It was a strange mark, more like a tattoo than a scar. It was slightly blue in colour and was shaped like two circles overlapping each other. She couldn't imagine how Tammy had got it.

'What is that?' Jude asked, pointing to the mark.

'It's been there since I was born,' said Tammy with a shrug.

'Really? Do you have any idea where it came from, who put it there?'

'Nope. Lieutenant Grem… Lieutenant Cole… said it's the devil's mark and it gave her the spooks all these years. She said I had it when I was left and it says that in my records,' Tammy replied.

'How very bizarre,' Jude exclaimed as she ran her fingers over the mark. It was slightly bumpy, as if it was glued onto her skin.

'It's almost as if you have been branded, in the same way animals used to be, although I cannot for the life of me think of anything that would create such a mark. So smooth, so… How very bizarre, certainly peculiar for a birthmark,' Jude said, and then she noticed the pendant around Tammy's neck.

'Now this is very pretty. What is it?' she asked.

'My mother left it with me at the orphan school. This and a letter were the only things left with me as a baby. I found them a little while ago in Lieutenant Cole's files.'

'Did she not tell you about them herself?'

'No, she wasn't very nice. You won't tell her I took them, will you?' Tammy asked.

'Of course I won't. You and I both agree on how we feel about this Mrs Cole. She really is a monster, so you have nothing to fear there. I remember her looking puzzled when she couldn't find something in her office and that must have been why. No harm done. They are with the rightful owner after all. May I?'

'Yes.'

Jude touched the pendant and turned it around in her hand. It was a strange type of crystal with small stones around it with a grainy texture. It was held within two overlapping circles, just like the mark on Tammy's arm, made from gold, which hung from a necklace made of leather cord. She had never seen anything similar before.

'Do you know what it is?' Jude asked.

'I don't know what it is exactly. It changes colour sometimes,' Tammy replied.

'Really? When does it change colour?'

'I don't know, I just notice it sometimes. It's strange and yet pretty, don't you think?'

'Yes. Yes, it is,' Jude mused. 'We'll have to find out what kind of crystal and stone they are.'

'Can we? I don't like taking it off and sometimes it feels really heavy. It would be great to know what it is made of.'

'Well, some crystals do that, I believe, but I've never heard of rocks or stones getting heavy. We'll put it on our growing list of things to do. Now, these clothes look like they've been to hell and back.' Jude chuckled as she went to place them in the laundry chute. 'This is how you do the laundry here. Open this chute, every wardrobe has one attached to the side, and drop in dirty clothes. They sink down to the bottom floor and are picked up to be dry-cleaned – it's all done in-house, here. Once clean, the item is sent back up to the wardrobe to hang automatically where it once was. Folded items will appear in the drawers instead. It's all automated now.'

'We used to have to wash our own uniforms.'

'I remember having to do that too, before I was adopted, so I know you'll appreciate this even more. Mind you, these clothes looked much better on you than off. Do you mind if I throw them away, or would you prefer to keep them? I have plenty of clothes for you and thought I could take you shopping for some more next week if you like.'

'Please throw them away,' Tammy said, feeling a large wave of relief pass over her. 'I would much prefer to have nicer clothes.'

'Well, why don't you do that then, in this bin here? It might make you feel better to throw away something you don't like and help you look forward to a fresh start. All any woman needs are new clothes, and life already begins to feel better.'

Wearing a big smile on her face, Tammy took the clothes from Jude, held them up high and dropped them into the bin.

'Well done,' Jude exclaimed. 'I like your attitude.'

Tammy went into her en suite, painted as if it were a watering hole in Africa surrounded by animals drinking. Tammy sighed as she sank into the warm bubbles of her very first bath. She felt her old life washing away and laughed aloud at her wonderful surroundings. She felt much more comfortable with her new clothes, and Jude was right; life did feel better even for that reason alone.

*

That night, Tammy lay in bed exhausted yet unable to fall asleep. She rested her hand under her pillow, stroking her mother's letter tenderly as she twirled the pendant in her other hand. She could hear the noise of the animals from the safari park and it was keeping her awake. Brunswick House was at the opposite end of the island, yet the animals sounded as though they were just outside the bedroom door. She tried to guess what noise went with each animal. She recognised instantly the roar of the lions and the trumpet of the elephants. Her anticipation at seeing the animals more closely than on her last visit kept her awake until late, despite how tired she was. When she finally fell into a deep sleep, she dreamt of an array of wonderful animals gathering all around her. Tammy slept, completely unaware of the green glow emanating from her pendant, pulsating as if it were alive.

THREE

Mikie stared at the kids playing on their skateboards as they darted across the path next to the man-made lake at the park. The sun shone on the water and the sky was clear. Ducks floated effortlessly and people walked their dogs. It was a beautiful day. Mikie felt detached, as he always did, listening in on the thoughts and decisions of those he analysed. Most people did not have many interesting thoughts and were frankly pretty mean in spirit but occasionally someone surprised him or made him smile. It could go either way when you read people's minds. Sometimes you could smile, or be forced to hide a laugh, but other times you could be haunted or traumatised by what you discovered.

Today had been pretty much uneventful and Mikie was about to turn and leave to head home when he caught something that stopped him. It was a young girl, slightly older than Mikie, aged fourteen, with the most beautiful almond-coloured skin he had ever seen. She wore her dark hair in a wild ponytail and stood pensively near the lake watching the ducks. She was truly the most beautiful girl he had ever seen but hanging over her was such a dark cloud and her entire body was surrounded by an aura of melancholy. Mikie couldn't help but be transfixed by her. She looked so stunningly beautiful and yet at the same time so miserable. There was something bothering him, and he was reluctant to go digging in her mind because he knew it held dark things.

He was wondering whether to approach her and ask if she was all right when a man walked over to her. He was blond and skinny, older, and looked as if he drank too much. He looked mean. Mikie could detect mean people just by their posture. The young girl didn't realise he was there until he was right on top of her and he made her jump. As she looked at him, she gasped, clearly unhappy to see him, and Mikie could see her quiver with fear. It made his hackles rise and made him feel protective. The man grabbed her arm painfully, squeezed it, and he could tell the girl was in pain, but she hid it well. Unable to resist, he entered her mind. Mikie read the history and fear in the girl's mind. How this man, Jared, was her mother's new husband and for months he had been hitting her and bruising her whenever her mother wasn't around. He was a horrid person. More than a bully, he was a spiteful man who was waiting for the opportunity to take things further and the girl knew it. Kate. That was her name. Kate knew it was going to get far worse. The beatings and the emotional abuse were a pleasure to him and he often forced her to eat things she did not want to eat, or starved her. Her mother was about to go away for a few days for work and she would be left alone with this man, and Kate knew it was going to end badly.

Mikie exhaled a long sad breath. He hated mind readings like this. He couldn't do anything about it. He had to remain hidden and discreet, so there was nothing he could do even when he knew things, and who could he even tell? Who would believe him? He couldn't risk exposing his power. Not for anyone. But there was something captivating about her – about Kate – that Mikie found hard to ignore. She had a hidden strength. He was about to dig deeper when a tall red-headed woman arrived. She started talking to the man and then to Kate. It soon became clear this was her mother. Surprisingly, because there was no similarity between the tall redhead and the almond-skinned trendy young girl. Mikie couldn't help but intrude on their thoughts and conversation to gather as much information as he could. As usual, the conversation did not match the thoughts.

'Hello, sweetheart, good day? All well at school?' said her mother, pecking her cheek without feeling or even caring about her daughter's day. It was all for show. But the mother's thoughts raged with what an inconvenience this spoiled brat was and how she wouldn't get child maintenance from the rich football player father for much longer, so how could she then get rid of this freeloader before she became even more of a burden? Mikie slowly released a breath of air to keep calm. It was not the first time he had observed such heartlessness from a mother towards a child and it was always a shock to see.

Having been abandoned by his mum as a baby – not out of spite, out of necessity – he found it hard to comprehend. His mother left him with Stephen out of love and desperation. Wasn't it guaranteed that a mother should love her child? But clearly this woman cared only for herself and her own wants and needs. That much was clear. Feeling sad but deciding there was nothing he could do about it and it was none of his business, Mikie went to turn away and leave. That was when it hit him.

The depths of her despair and her sheer determination to do something about it were far heavier than anything he had ever anticipated. Kate calmly removed her arm from the man's grasp, the pain he had inflicted was obvious to any keen observer, but not to her mother. Kate turned to her mother, who was saying that she should head home to pack, as it was getting late. She was calm and collected and numb with depression and pain.

'You go ahead, Mum. I'm going to walk along the park and will be home to make dinner and wash up soon.'

'Oh, that's a lovely thought,' said her mother. 'It's about time you attempted to do something worthwhile and pay your way even though I cannot begin to imagine what vile filth you might throw together and try to call a meal... But that's okay. Jared and I can go out to dinner if it's that vile.'

'I will do my best,' Kate replied despondently. She cooked almost every night for them both and was never allowed to eat at the table with them. They always complained about what she made.

Mikie knew she had no intention of going home this time.

'Fine, see you at the house then, Kate.'

Not home. The house. Mikie could feel how cold that house was for Kate. Cold and terrifying. Mikie's watch beeped with a short video message from his Uncle Stephen that appeared in holographic form above the watch face.

'Hurry up, mate, I'm seriously going to kick your rear end if you don't get here with the shopping in the next twenty minutes!'

But Stephen would never really do that and Mikie realised he had completely forgotten to get the shopping. Stephen would most likely just order in pizza anyway. He didn't have to worry, like Kate did. Stephen could never be anything like Kate's new dad. And with her mother as cold as ice, she was certainly unlucky. Stephen was a martial arts instructor and had taught Mikie to defend himself well, but he never laid a hand on him outside the lessons and never in anger. Mikie took a step to head home then paused. He looked back at Kate for one last time as she walked away from her mother. He knew what was going on in her mind. It was both a gift and a curse. He knew what she intended to do, and it was extremely hard to walk away from that. Stephen had warned him not to try and fix people. 'Walk away,' he repeatedly told Mikie.

Just go home he told himself, but he was frozen to the spot and his feet didn't move. 'Oh no…!' he muttered angrily and rolled his eyes in annoyance as he turned to follow Kate.

Head bowed low, Kate walked along the park, completely unaware that she was being followed. She cared nothing for her own safety; she just wanted the fear and pain to be gone, no matter what the price. Mikie tried not to listen to her depressing and morbid thoughts; he didn't want them to drag him down too, but it was very hard to cut off. Negative thoughts grabbed you and were more powerful than positive thoughts, but he never understood why. It was just the way it worked. Mikie hated other people's miserable energy polluting his own body. It was hard to shift and clear away later on. But Mikie couldn't turn his back on this poor girl. He couldn't abandon her now.

Kate turned out of the park and started walking up the steep hill. She walked sluggishly, defeated, beaten. Mikie felt terrible for her. How awful to feel unloved and unwanted and on top of that beaten and abused regularly. He couldn't imagine it and he couldn't let Kate do what she planned to do.

It's none of your business – just walk away he told himself again, but he knew he couldn't. Wouldn't. It was unfair to have the ability to see things and just have to turn your back on people in need. He could not always do it.

Another message from Stephen appeared.

'Seriously, where are you?'

'Delayed, back soon, get pizza because I failed again.' Mikie recorded his reply with his cutest and cheekiest smile as he walked.

Kate turned into the car park at the top of the hill and marched towards the edge. She suddenly stopped, abruptly turned and frowned as she looked around. Mikie jumped behind a bush and hid. Cursing himself for not just walking casually on like any other normal stranger and now looking like some creepy peeping Tom! Kate didn't spot him and turned to carry on. Mikie got up and followed her to the edge of the hill. It was a hanging cliff, high above the grassy rocks below, and no one could survive such a fall. It was an exceptionally long drop to the bottom.

Kate stepped close to the edge, took a deep breath and looked down. She gulped as she acknowledged the height. She didn't remember it being this high. It was going to hurt.

Could she reach the bottom in one go, or would she bang a few times on different rocks along the way?

'Oh, for goodness' sake, really!' Mikie exclaimed, scrunching his eyes closed with the awfulness of what she was seeing and thinking.

Since the Pandemic, life was precious, and it frustrated him the amount of mental health issues preventing people from realising this. Especially teenagers who were raised unloved and as orphans. To see someone from a wealthy home this disturbed wasn't nice at all. Mikie had been forced to deal with grown-up problems from a very young age. He still struggled to come to terms with things he saw and couldn't unsee.

'People are so messed up,' he muttered.

He crept slowly towards her, not needing to try and hide now she was focused on the drop. She was terrified, adrenaline coursing through her body as she contemplated what she must do. Mikie was not appreciating being able to read her mind and see what she was seeing. The sheer thought of what she would experience on the way down was unimaginable. How could people do it? He knew deep down that she didn't really want to but felt she had nowhere else to turn.

'Stop, take a step back, you don't have to do this,' Mikie said, trying to push his thoughts into her mind.

Kate frowned and tilted her head in confusion to the side, trying to understand where that idea had come from. That wasn't what she wanted to hear. That wasn't what she was thinking. She shook the idea off and took one more step towards the edge.

'I won't let them hurt me anymore,' she whispered to no one in particular.

THE CHILDREN OF PISCES

The fear engulfed her, making her gulp a dry and difficult swallow that wouldn't quite work its way down her throat. How she wished she had a bottle of water right now. She hadn't thought of a dry throat. Well, she wouldn't feel much for longer. But as she willed herself to jump off the top of the cliff, her legs refused to follow and fear gripped her from top to bottom.

'Come on, surely you can do this! Do you really have to fail at everything!' she heard herself saying, but it was her mother's voice in her head and not hers. Kate was actually an exceptionally smart student, but her mother couldn't see that. She tried to will herself to jump again and this time her body listened.

'No!' Mikie pushed his will towards Kate.

She paused, confused.

'End it,' her mind instructed, and she leaned towards the edge again.

'Stop and come away from the edge,' Mikie forced into her mind.

Kate fought the idea Mikie was pushing into her head and tried to stubbornly stick with her initial thought of going over the edge of the cliff. They battled for a while until Kate leaned forward. She screamed, a gargled, strangled sound, as Mikie changed her mind and left her in conflict as to what to do. But it was too late. She was over the edge and gravity began to take effect, her body leaning forward in slow motion.

'Nooooooo,' Mikie shouted, racing towards her as she went over the edge of the cliff.

He forced his mind onto hers as he ran, making her turn her body so she was facing the cliff and falling backwards now, forcing her arm to reach out and grab the side of the cliff edge. Kate blinked in shock, not sure how she ended up facing the cliff and trying to grab on. She let go, wanting to fall, but her hands quickly grabbed the edge of the cliff again, clinging on for dear life. Kate frowned; she didn't want this, she didn't want to cling on – did she? No, she wanted to fall, to end the pain and suffering, but every time she tried to let go, as she dangled over the edge, her hands just grabbed back onto the edge or the grass. Suddenly, from out of nowhere, a young kid arrived, peeked over the edge of the cliff and grabbed one of her wrists.

'Hold on, will you,' he said impatiently.

'Leave me alone!' she shouted.

'Ahhh, can't do that, sorry. I am too invested in you now and know too much. I can't just walk away. Sorry.' Mikie sighed and started to heave her up.

Kate started fighting him, so, rolling his eyes again with impatience, Mikie forced his mind onto hers and made her do exactly what he wanted her to do and work with him to get herself back up. They both fell back, exhausted, onto the grass, away from the edge. They both breathed heavily.

'Who are you?' Kate asked, turning to look at him.

'No one special,' Mikie replied, giving her his cutest smile.

'I don't believe that,' she said.

'Trust me, I am no one,' Mikie said with a sigh. He must remain anonymous. 'But you are a strong and beautiful woman. Don't let them break you. Fight. You are stronger than this.'

Kate blushed. He was too young to be saying such a thing to her but there was something beyond wisdom with this boy. He was special. That much was clear. And he thought she was far better than she felt she was, and that was just nice to hear for once in her life.

'You think I'm strong?' she muttered. 'After what I just tried to do?'

'Yes,' he replied. 'You felt you had nowhere to turn, but I am telling you that's not the way it is. Your dad loves you.'

'My dad has gone back to Africa! He doesn't care about me.' Kate couldn't help the anger that came from her. She felt abandoned by him, left with her spiteful mother and narcissistic stepfather.

'That's not true,' Mikie said, sitting up and encouraging her to do the same.

They sat side by side. Kate's mind wasn't the only one he had read today.

'Your mum told you that, but he is in London training for the next match. He never left. She has used her skills as a lawyer to get a restraining order on him and prevent him from seeing you, but he has been trying to fight her in court. He hasn't given up. All you need to do is go to your dad and tell him the truth and he will get custody of you. You are now old enough to speak in court and they have to listen to you.' Mikie smiled at her reassuringly.

Kate stared at him for a long time. 'How could you possibly know that?'

Mikie chewed on his bottom lip and jumped up. Held out a hand to help pull her up too. 'Come on, let's walk.'

They walked in silence for a while before Kate asked, 'So, are you going to tell me how you could know that?'

'I am not. Sorry. You just have to take my word for it.'

Kate stared at him and was about to say something when she felt she shouldn't. She tried to talk again but if seemed like a thought in her mind was fighting her and telling her not to. Something forcing her to be quiet.

'Seriously, be safe, go and find your dad. Tell him what has been happening. He's a good man. He's a good football player too. I can't wait for the next game,' he said, laughing. 'But I am late and have to go.'

And with that, Mikie ran off. Kate was left staring after him. She was just about to think she had no idea where her dad lived when a thought popped into her mind with a house number and street. She had no idea how she could know this but headed towards the bus stop all the same and somehow knew what bus to take and what direction to go in. As if someone was directing her and making her follow the strange unknown thoughts.

'Oh, whatever,' she said with a sigh. It was, after all, better than going back to her mother.

FOUR

BRUNSWICK SAFARI PARK

Tammy was out of bed before Jude's cockerel had finished cock-a-doodle-do-ing. She quickly looked out of her window, squealed with delight at finding it was not a dream after all, and then hurriedly brushed her teeth.

'Hmm, what shall I wear?' she mused as she looked in her new wardrobe. She decided on some beige shorts and a green T-shirt with a matching jumper that she wrapped around her waist. She raced down the stairs to find Ed already in the kitchen, drinking coffee. She could see Jude through the window out in the garden, making strange shapes with her arms.

'What's Jude doing?' she asked, pulling a face.

'It's called tai chi,' Ed said with a smile. 'It's a series of movements, a lot like martial arts, yet slower. It helps Jude relax.'

'It looks really good. I've never seen anyone move like that before.'

'Well, perhaps you can try it one day and see if you like it.' Ed said.

Jude came to a standing position, closed a fist into the palm of one hand and bowed. She then turned to the house and joined them in the kitchen.

'I hope the animals didn't keep you awake,' Jude said. 'They can be really noisy sometimes.'

'No, they didn't. I don't mind them,' Tammy told her. 'I enjoy listening to them. I can't wait to see them all.'

'Well, Ed will take you down to the safari park when you finish breakfast. He's incredibly good at doing tours so I know you'll have fun. Mind you don't drive too fast, Ed.'

'I won't, dear.' Ed mischievously winked at Tammy.

'Can I take breakfast with me and eat it on the way, please?' Tammy asked hopefully.

'You really are keen to get going, aren't you?' Ed said cheerily as Jude poured her a glass of orange juice. 'Well, the sooner we get there, the more time we'll have before the visitors arrive and we'll have the animals all to ourselves. Let's get going then.' He pushed his chair back and stretched. Fudge, who had been sitting patiently up until now, began wagging her tail excitedly. It was time to go.

'You're the tallest person I have ever seen,' Tammy said, taking a sip of her juice.

'It's all Jude's good food,' he said with a grin.

'Now, you two, don't get carried away and forget dinner – six o'clock or else!' Jude warned.

Ed pecked her on the cheek and headed out of the kitchen. Tammy grabbed a couple of pieces of buttered toast and went after him. Fudge was close at their heels.

It was a beautiful drive into the safari park. They passed through forests of magnificent trees and fields brimming with gorgeous flowers of all colours. Many of the animals were quite close to Brunswick House, which was why they seemed so loud last night. They went past animal-shaped bushes and statues. One in particular caught her eye.

'What's that?' she asked Ed.

'I'll take you over and show you,' he said, turning the Jeep.

The statue was almost as tall as Ed, and Tammy could just about make out the words written beneath as they pulled alongside it.

Sampson – The Finest Siberian Tiger at Brunswick Safari Park

Died March 2054

'Oh, what a shame,' Tammy sighed, 'I would have liked to meet him.'

'He was a very fierce and powerful beast. I've never met one like him. That's why I had a statue made in his honour.'

'Why did he die?'

'He was shot.'

'Shot – in a safari park?' Tammy gasped.

'No, not in the Park. You see, I don't believe animals should be in captivity when it can be avoided. However, it's sometimes the only way we can educate people and increase endangered numbers in the wild. This was proved beyond a shadow of a doubt when Pisces hit. Do you remember much about that from your studies at school?'

'A little. I think it was just being contained when I was born,' Tammy answered.

'It was a terrible virus that came from the ocean, so they said. It wiped out two-thirds of our planet, affecting animals and humans alike – the most horrible virus known to mankind, because normally a viral outbreak will only affect certain species.'

'Like bird flu?' Tammy asked.

'Yes, like bird flu. That was around for years before it was able to infect anything other than birds, and even that didn't have such a big impact. However, Pisces, well, that became airborne in days and it evolved at a terrifying rate, using anything and everything it could as a host.' Ed shivered at the memory.

'At least you saved all the animals.'

'Well, not quite all. I did my best. There were many cases of extinction, that's for certain.' He sighed.

'How did they stay safe here if it was airborne?'

'That's a secret that I shall save for another day.' Ed smiled, tapping his nose knowingly. 'As I was saying, a safari park can be a good thing even though it is preferable for all animals to be free. It keeps endangered populations safe and gives people the chance to see animals from all over the world. However, Sampson, for example, was an endangered species and born wild. He had been injured in a fight, most likely another tiger, and needed medical help. He wouldn't have survived alone in the wild for much longer without intervention. We decided to bring him to this safari park as a last resort and because we had a female we could breed him with. We planned to set his young free,' Ed said as he started up the Jeep and continued with their tour.

'Your safari park is so big the animals have a lot of freedom.'

'Yes, we are lucky to be able to provide them with enough space. Anyway, Sampson was about two years old when he arrived, normally far too old for a wild cat to be suddenly put in an enclosure, and yet under the circumstances, we didn't have a whole lot of choice. In no time at all, we realised he would never adapt to park life. He was miserable. We decided to set him free again in Siberia and within a month he had been shot by a hunter. Park life had softened him a little and made him less scared of men than he should have been. He was a prime example of how wrong a safari park can be. I felt so bad about his death that I had this statue made to remind me of how careful to be in the future.'

'So that's why you had the statue erected, because you felt guilty?'

'Exactly, I just admired him so much – it was such a terrible mistake. He was a magnificent creature and such a rare breed.' Ed sighed. 'At least I have managed to breed and set free a few of his kind since.'

Tammy watched Ed's face closely as he seemed lost in his memories. She'd never seen an adult so distressed – all she'd known before had been bossy and hard, and never had she been shown a tender side. Not knowing what to say, she stayed quiet. As they got closer to the safari park, the noises of the animals grew louder. Tammy looked at the other animal statues as they passed and wondered what stories they told. Finally, Ed bought the Jeep to a stop.

'Here we are.' He turned to her, grinning like a Cheshire cat.

'I still can't see anything,' said Tammy, trying to see past the brick wall and trees blocking her view.

'Be patient, this is my secret parking place.'

Tammy almost flew out of the Jeep. Fudge was ahead of her, full of the excitement and sheer joy of being out in the fresh air, as dogs often are.

'We're behind the bird house,' he said. 'Just a little walk and we'll be right by the monkeys.'

Sure enough, in less than five minutes, they were in front of the monkey section. Tammy's mouth dropped open as she saw the monkeys so close.

'These are spider monkeys,' Ed said, pointing at small black and white monkeys. 'And over here are the orang-utans and gorillas, which are a larger breed of monkeys known as the apes.'

As she stared, one of the apes winked at her and gave a big smile. She smiled back.

'They look just like us,' she said, getting closer to the gorilla enclosure.

'Yes, they do, hence Darwin's theory of evolution,' Ed said.

'We evolved from apes or monkeys, Darwin said. Am I right?' asked Tammy.

'Yes, well remembered.'

'I remember everything I was taught about animals. I don't remember much else from school, though.' She shrugged and smiled.

'I was the same when I was your age. Sometimes I see similarities in all animals, not just with monkeys and apes, and I think we are all related. Follow me.'

As soon as Tammy saw where they were heading, she forgot about Ed and ran towards the lions. She grabbed the fence that surrounded their enclosure and watched them lying in the sun. Ed didn't hurry to catch up with Tammy; he was still watching the strange way the monkeys were behaving. They were once again unusually quiet and had followed Ed and Tammy along the path, at least as far as their enclosures allowed. It was uncharacteristic to say the least and reminded Ed of that first day he had seen Tammy. He couldn't understand it. It wasn't even just one. It was all of them; the spider monkeys, chimpanzees, gorillas, all acting strange. Deep down, he was pleased, since this reassured him about his suspicions when he first met Tammy – she must be the one Sarah had meant.

'They're fantastic,' she exclaimed. 'Lieutenant Cole kept me so close to her last time and as I was right at the back, I could barely see anything. I just want to get closer.'

Ed laughed. 'I don't think that's a wise thing to do, Tammy. There wouldn't be much of you left if you did. You won't be able to see everything here in just a day.'

Tammy didn't hear Ed.

'Tigers!' she cried, and ran towards their pen. As she did, two of the lions got up and charged towards the end of their pen, almost as if trying to keep up with her.

That's ridiculous, Ed thought, and followed her.

After seeing the tigers, Ed took Tammy to see the elephants. There was always a guaranteed admiration for elephants. He had seen many kids come to the safari park and no matter how naughty or spoilt some of them were, he could always rely on the elephants to ground them. They really were incredible animals. Their size demanded immediate respect from all other animals.

'Wonderful, aren't they?' he said. 'You never get used to their size and each time you see them is as tremendous as the first.'

Tammy agreed with a slight nod then looked down at the floor to see Minnie staring up at her.

'Minnie, you look so small next to them,' she exclaimed, and picked her up with a kiss.

'Well, she hasn't forgotten you. You have her well trained,' Ed said.

Just then, one of the larger elephants raised its trunk and made a loud trumpeting sound. One by one, the other elephants joined in. Ed frowned in puzzlement. 'It's unusual for them to behave like that,' he said.

'They're just saying hello to me,' Tammy told him.

'Oh, sure.' Ed laughed, thinking she was joking.

'Are those tusks?' Tammy asked.

'Yes. They're actually large teeth. They start growing when the elephant is about two years old and continue to grow for the rest of its life,' he told her.

'What do they do with them?'

'In the wild, elephants sometimes have to go days without water. They can smell water underground, so they use their tusks to dig for the water and also to strip the bark off trees to eat.'

'They can really smell water from beneath the ground?' Tammy was impressed.

'Oh yes. If you look at an elephant, you can tell whether it's left or right-tusked – just like a person is left or right-handed. Look at that one there.'

Ed pointed to one of the elephants.

'The left tusk is more worn down,' Tammy observed.

'Which means it is left-handed, well, left-tusked,' Ed said.

'There is so much to learn. A teacher once told me that elephants were the dumbest animals she had ever known.'

'Well, I would say elephants were not that teacher's area of expertise.' Ed chuckled. 'Elephants never forget. What's more, in the wild, they can end up walking forty-five miles a day in search of food. It's funny that they walk on their tiptoes too.'

'No!'

'Yes, their weight is distributed on the tip of each toe. They can run like that too.' Ed laughed. He enjoyed talking to Tammy; her enthusiasm for animals equalled his own.

'That one is different, isn't it?' she asked, pointing to one of the elephants.

It was smaller than the other elephants, especially its trunk.

'That's an Asian elephant. The others are African. The African elephants are much larger and have stronger trunks, great for knocking down trees. Elephants are used to help with tree felling, as they can carry four tons, or even more, of tree trunks on their tusks – and that's uphill.'

Tammy left Minnie with the elephants. Then they went on to see the rhinoceroses. They had the same dry grey skin that the elephants had, only the rhinoceroses' hides looked much tougher.

'Is the tusk on a rhino's head the same as an elephant's?' she asked.

'No, their horn is not a tooth. It doesn't continue to grow like the tusk on an elephant, and is used purely as a weapon. Their skin is almost as strong as metal armour. It takes a lot to scare a rhino. Even lions keep their distance. If you look, you can see that those two rhinos are different,' he said, pointing.

'I can't see how they're different with all that mud on them,' Tammy said, squinting.

'It is difficult. The mud hides it. He's actually a black rhino, while the other is a white rhino. Even without the mud, it's hard to be sure. It's easier to tell them apart by their eating habits. White rhinos eat on low ground – on grass – while black rhinos feed higher – on prickly bushes.'

'What are all those birds doing on their backs?' Tammy asked.

'Rhinos get a lot of bugs on their skin,' Ed explained. 'The bugs on a rhino are a great feast for birds, and as the rhino gets bothered by the bugs, he doesn't mind the birds sitting on his back and eating them. The only other way of getting rid of the bugs is to go in water, and rhinos prefer mud, as it keeps their skin in good condition.'

'They look very strong,' Tammy said.

'They have to be. It's a tough life out there in the wild.'

Then she met the giraffes, who apparently only slept for three hours a day. Then the zebras, bears, camels and the park's most famous and shyest attraction, the panda – as well as the various farm animals like goats and pigs. The animals were following them as far as their enclosures would allow them to. It was impossible to ignore, no matter how hard Ed tried.

'You would think the animals had come to see you as opposed to the other way around. How about we look at the reptiles and the exotic birds and then sea life after lunch?' Ed said.

'What about the panthers?' she asked.

She had fallen in love with a picture of a panther a long time ago. Knowing this, Lieutenant Cole hadn't let her see them during their visit. There was something about the animal's silky black fur, which contrasted so strongly with the bright yellow eyes, that caught her attention more than any other cat.

'We only have one panther. I guess I can take you there before lunch,' he said with a smile.

When Tammy set eyes on the panther, she was speechless; he was the most beautiful creature she had ever seen. His fur was pitch-black and his eyes as bright as fire – just as she remembered. The eyes contrasted magnificently with the darkness of his coat. As she looked into his eyes, sadness washed over her. She could feel how unhappy the panther was, so desperately lonely. It made her long to climb into the enclosure and give him a huge hug.

'He doesn't have a name,' Ed told her. 'We never could think of an appropriate one for him. You can name him if you like.'

'Jet,' she said, without even thinking about it. 'He should be called Jet.'

Ed raised his eyebrows in surprise.

'If that's what you think he should be called, then so be it. Jet it is.'

'He will like that.'

'Do you know what type of cat he is?' Ed asked.

'He's a panther,' Tammy murmured sadly.

'Actually, he's a jaguar. A black panther isn't a type of cat. It is a common name given to any large cat that is black in colour,' Ed told her.

'How can a panther not be a type of cat? It is the only black cat there is.'

'Most of the large cats can have black fur. The black is caused by melanistic colouration – this is an increased amount of black or nearly black pigmentation in the fur.

If you see any black cat, it is because it has this melanistic colouration,' Ed explained.

'Melanistic?'

'The word is derived from *melanin*, which is found in fur and skin and causes the change in colour. If you look closely, you can see the markings of the jaguar through the black. Look where the sunlight shines on his coat.' Ed pointed to Jet's coat, showing the almost spot-like markings in the fur.

'Oh, I see.' Tammy gasped excitedly.

'So, when you see a black panther, you are most likely looking at a leopard or a jaguar. It's easy to get the two mixed up, as their markings are so similar. Jaguars have a much more stocky and muscular body with a shorter tail. It is possible to see this coloration in larger lions, tigers, cougars and even other species of wild cat,' Ed told her.

'A black lion? Well, Jet does look a lot stronger than the other cats,' Tammy said.

'Unlike the other cats, the jaguar has no other rivals out in the wild. No other predator can compete with it. It has particularly powerful jaws and often kills its prey by piercing the skull with one swift bite,' Ed said.

'Wow!'

A man walked towards them. He was wearing dirty green overalls. He had long blond hair pulled back into a ponytail and walked with slow and lazy strides.

'Hello, Ed,' he called.

'Dave, I'd like you to meet Tammy,' Ed said.

'Hello, Tammy,' Dave said with a big smile. 'We've been looking forward to having another young face about the place.'

'Tammy, this is Dave, and he looks after all the animals in the pachyderm section. That's the animals with thick skin, such as the elephants and rhinos.'

'Hello,' Tammy said with a smile.

'We've not had anyone young live on this island for years, so you're like a breath of fresh air to all us oldies. Of course, Ed's nephew visits during school holidays – have you met Jax yet?'

'No, not yet.'

'Of course, it'll be the summer holidays when he next comes, right, Ed? You'll like him, nice kid.'

'You're right, they'll brighten this place up; that's for sure. So how are things in the pachyderm section?' Ed asked.

'Going quite well. Nutt has been taking up all of the vet's time lately, getting better by the day.'

'Nutt?' Tammy asked.

'That's the baby elephant,' Dave said. 'He was born a few weeks ago, really sick and very small. He was born much sooner than he should have been but he's hanging in there.'

'I see,' Tammy nodded, 'I'd love to meet him.'

'You will soon enough. Where is the vet now? I want to talk to him,' Ed said.

'At the hospital with Nutt.'

'I'm going over to see him. Do you want to join me?'

'I'll wait here for you,' Tammy said. 'I'd like to spend some more time with Jet.'

'Okay. Don't get too close to the enclosure, he's not used to people. I won't be too long. Come, girl,' Ed said, and Fudge obediently followed.

'Bye, Tammy. See you around,' said Dave as he and Ed walked away.

'Bye,' Tammy replied absentmindedly.

She was looking at Jet. Jet was still looking at her. He wanted some company for a while. Nobody noticed the faint green glow around Tammy's pendant.

FIVE

TESTING BOUNDARIES

Ed was soon out of sight and didn't see Tammy climb the tall fence surrounding Jet's enclosure. She dropped down the other side and landed next to him. The panther nudged her in the stomach. Tammy laughed. Then he jumped up, putting his front paws on her shoulders. Tammy could hardly keep her balance and finally, still laughing, she fell to the floor. She rubbed his head and back and then got up and let him chase her for a while.

Exhausted, she let Jet push her to the ground once more. Jet was on top of her, playfully nipping her arms and legs, when Ed returned.

'You just want to play,' she chuckled, trying to push him off, but he was heavy. 'You're a big baby.'

'Oh no,' Ed gasped, trembling as he mistook the play for fighting. 'Dave! DAVE!' he shouted.

Dave came running and froze as he saw Tammy in the enclosure.

'Get the key to the enclosure, Dave,' Ed shouted.

'Tammy!' he yelled.

Tammy managed to push Jet off her and sat up.

'I wasn't doing anything bad,' she said as Ed approached the door.

Jet sat calmly next to her, Tammy's arm draped casually across his back. Neither Ed nor Dave moved. They couldn't believe what they were seeing.

'Tammy, walk slowly towards the enclosure door,' Ed told her. 'Dave—'

'Don't worry, he won't hurt me,' Tammy interrupted.

'He doesn't look angry,' Dave whispered to Ed.

Ed ignored him. 'Tammy, it's dangerous in there. I want you out!'

Tammy put her hand on Jet's head and stroked him.

'I'm sorry, Jet,' she said. 'I have to go. I'll play with you again as soon as I can.'

Jet leaned over and licked her on the cheek. She kissed the top of his head and then went to the enclosure door as Dave opened it for her.

Ed was dumbstruck. He knew what he had just seen and yet still couldn't believe it. A fully grown jaguar acting as friendly and playfully as a dog – it was impossible. The cat was not used to human contact; it should have torn her apart.

Tammy was looking at Ed with a puzzled frown.

'I don't understand, he only wanted to play. He's lonely,' she said. 'Aren't I allowed to play with the animals?'

'They are dangerous – usually. I can't believe he didn't hurt you. It doesn't make sense.'

'I don't understand either,' she said. 'Why would an animal hurt me? Why do you think an animal would hurt me?'

'Because they aren't like us, they're wild. They don't understand us,' Ed said, exasperated and still stunned by what he had seen.

'They understand me,' Tammy said.

'We'll talk about this later, after lunch.' Ed took a deep breath.

Dave rubbed his forehead thoughtfully and looked back and forth between Tammy and Jet.

*

Jude had prepared a packed lunch and while it was delicious, neither Tammy nor Ed did much more than pick at it. Tammy kept glancing at Ed from under her lashes; neither of them knew what to say or do next.

'I don't know what to say except I'm sorry, Ed. I didn't mean to upset you,' Tammy said, although still unsure as to what she had done wrong.

'It's not your fault, Tammy,' Ed sighed, 'I was so sure that the jaguar would hurt you.'

'Jet,' she said.

'Yes – Jet. I know that under normal circumstances, I would have every right to be angry and concerned at such careless behaviour, and yet somehow I think I am being unreasonable.'

They were silent for a while.

'Tammy, there's something I don't understand.' He paused, looking down at his hands, trying to think what it was he wanted to ask. 'You are very confident with animals, in a way that I think is unique to you. I noticed the way the monkeys were when you were around them. In fact, all the animals react in an unusual manner towards you. At first, I thought it was my imagination. Now, well, I think you might have some sort of connection with animals. Do you understand what I'm saying?'

'I think so, something happens to me when I'm around all these animals and I can't explain it. Can I show you?'

All she wanted to do was spend time with the animals, play with them and talk with them. With animals, she felt normal, which was not the case when she was around people. If Ed understood that, he wouldn't be angry with her when she played with the animals. She had to show him that it was all right.

'How will you show me?' he asked. 'I don't want you jumping in with the lions to prove it!'

'The animals that are locked up. I can show you with them first. What about the reptiles? You keep them in glass enclosures, don't you?'

'Yes. In vivariums.'

'Okay. Let's go to the reptile house. I'll show you that even the most venomous of snakes will be my friend while they're safely behind glass.' Tammy got up excitedly. 'You know what, Ed?'

'What?' he said, getting up hesitantly and somewhat nervous.

'Maybe it is something only I can do. Maybe that's what makes me strange.'

'Different, not strange,' Ed said with a smile.

Ed watched Tammy run towards the Jeep. She was excited and happy. He was puzzled by what she had said – she seemed very mature for her age and this went beyond his expectations. He had already suspected that she had a real gift with animals and was now excited that she was about to show him something quite extraordinary.

The darkness and warmth of the reptile house took Tammy by surprise. The hot, moist air made it difficult to breathe and she couldn't help but cover her mouth with her hand until she had got used to it. Ed patiently waited in silence as Tammy took in her surroundings.

They were surrounded by various man-made jungle themes, separated by large walls of glass and brick. Snakes were coiled in small pools of water and around branches. Lizards stood motionless on rocks and branches as they basked under hot artificial lights. Turtles chewed continuously, while various small and bizarre-looking frogs hung upside down from surrounding leaves. There were some exceptionally large snakes with bodies as wide as a football. As Tammy walked past, they all watched her with their strange reptilian eyes.

One snake in particular caught her eye. It was approximately five metres in length, black in colour and was eagerly pushing itself up against the glass panel, trying to reach her. Tammy walked over to it.

'What's this?' she asked.

'That is a black king cobra. One of the most venomous snakes there is,' Ed told her. 'So dangerous that his vivarium is labelled *hot* so that when the snake experts go to open the door, either to feed, clean or extract some venom, they are reminded by a big red label that this snake can really do some harm.'

'Surely it wouldn't harm the people that feed it?'

'Not intentionally. A snake will bite for two reasons: if it feels threatened or is hungry. Venomous snakes are most dangerous to us when they want food. We try to make sure they have food available before they get too hungry. Most of our snakes are raised here from birth so don't feel too threatened by people. They recognise a person's smell and know it isn't food.'

'Has this one ever bitten anyone?'

'Oh yes, he's got a couple of trained and very experienced men already. He's fast. When a snake bites in fear, he just wants to get you out of his way. When he's hungry, there's no escape. He's out for a kill. The first time he bit someone was as an act of defence. He only struck once. The second time, he wanted food and bit more vigorously. It wasn't that he wanted to bite the hand that fed him; he was just going for the first thing that came his way. The man who opened the door that time, Ben, was bitten three times…'

'He didn't—'

'No, thank goodness. He almost died. You'll meet him later – a good man. His experience with handling snakes was the only reason he got away from the cobra in time to administer antivenom.'

'Does their venom take long to kill you?' Tammy put her face closer to the glass separating her and the snake.

'It varies with different snakes. It can all be over in a matter of minutes. Your heart, brain and lungs stop working one by one. It feels as if you are suffocating. Breathing gets harder and harder until finally it becomes impossible to draw breath. That's why I try to tell you that not all animals are safe and cute.' He laughed nervously.

Tammy moved her hand around in a circle and smiled as the snake's head followed her movements. Ed watched as the snake pushed itself up even closer against the glass. He could almost sense its desire to reach out to Tammy. He wondered if it was just his imagination again. Ed placed his hand next to hers. The snake immediately recoiled, the sides of its neck opening up in readiness to attack. It hissed as it swayed back and forth in warning. He had never known this snake to even notice anyone being by the glass, let alone react as it had, not while the glass door was closed.

Ed frowned and moved his hand away. The snake settled down once more, its head close to Tammy's hand. It was just playing a game with Ed, and Tammy had to hide the smile that crept across her face. She gave Ed a questioning look, wanting so desperately to hold the snake.

'No,' he said. 'Absolutely not, you are not touching that cobra. It would be completely irresponsible of me to allow that and Jude would kill me.'

The wounded look on Tammy's face drew a sympathetic smile from Ed. He could understand her innocence in wanting to love all animals as if they were safe to approach. They walked on through the reptile house. Ed watched Tammy briefly play with several other snakes through the protective glass. He saw how the poisonous frogs hopped up and down excitedly as she passed. The reptiles all acted the same way. She had more control over them than the snake charmers he had seen on his travels. He was aware that some charmers drugged their snakes and it was as though Tammy had the same effect on them – they were hypnotised by her.

At the back of the reptile house rested a small family of crocodiles. Tammy studied each one as she drew closer. There were two adults and two babies in the large glass room and they were very still. The female lay basking in the heat at the side of a shallow pool of water, her jaws wide open, drinking in the heat. The male was partially submerged in the pool, his small eyes peering up at Tammy. The babies lay beside the female. Tammy looked into the eyes of the two adults. She looked back and forth, trying to find some connection. There was no response. They were eerily statue-like. She found it hard to believe they were alive.

'Can I go in there?' she asked, already knowing what Ed's response would be.

'Definitely not, they seem as antisocial with you as they are with me. Those jaws can do a lot of damage in a very short time.'

'I must know how they see me,' she pleaded.

Ed shook his head.

Suddenly the crocodiles began to move.

The male slowly climbed out of the pool. Meanwhile, the female had slipped into the pool, swum to the side of the male and got out before him. Tammy knelt down and placed both hands flat on the glass. The crocodiles were close enough for the tips of their jaws to touch the glass. They seemed curious about Tammy.

Ed felt the sweat run from his forehead down his cheek. He wiped it away uneasily. The crocodiles were awfully close to her now, their large jaws would be touching her hand if not for the glass that separated them. Both crocodiles were still once more. Tammy stared into their eyes, mesmerised by their cold intensity.

Ed had to keep his distance; he couldn't help himself. He had always been petrified of crocodiles and alligators despite the glass barrier that separated him from them.

They had always seemed so cold-blooded and merciless to him. The way they looked at Tammy only reinforced that belief. The crocodiles didn't seem to respond to Tammy in the same way the other animals did.

She couldn't understand why they weren't connecting with her like the others. They were obviously curious and confused. Tammy felt no connection with them whatsoever. Nonetheless, she felt sure that once she touched them, they would understand her. At the same time, some instinct told her to be wary. Curious as to why she was experiencing these conflicting feelings, Tammy knew that she would have to get closer to the crocodiles. Just not yet. Ed was too worried to allow her to go in now, so she would have to wait until another opportunity presented itself. Absentmindedly, she took hold of her pendant, not realising the heat she felt in her chest was due to the red glow emanating from it.

*

Jude watched them drive up to the house. Her smile slowly faded as she saw the look on her husband's face. She knew him well enough to know he was worried about something. She hurried to greet them in the hallway.

'How was your first day?' she asked cautiously.

'Great,' Tammy said.

'Strange,' Ed told her, 'VERY strange. It's all right, everything is okay,' he added, noticing her concern.

Jude relaxed and ushered them into the living room. She went into the kitchen and brought out some orange squash and chocolate bourbons. Fudge settled at Tammy's feet.

'Looks like you've lost your companion,' Jude said smilingly, upon seeing Fudge.

'Tell me about it. So much for loyalty. She follows Tammy around now instead of me,' Ed moaned, lightheartedly.

Tammy shrugged. Fudge got up and went over to Ed. She placed her head in his lap, whined as he petted her and then settled on the floor at his side. Her eyes remained on Tammy.

Jude smiled. 'Tell me what happened today.' She took a seat next to Tammy and took hold of her hand.

Ed explained the day's events to Jude, who listened patiently and with an open mind. He told her how he had noticed from the very start that all the animals seemed to act oddly around Tammy, from the monkeys to the elephants. He described how Tammy had played with the black panther. How she had mesmerised the black king cobra and how the crocodiles had reacted strangely. Upon hearing about the crocodiles, Jude released a long-held breath.

'Well,' she said, swallowing hard, 'I didn't expect to hear anything like that! Ed, I know you told me you had your suspicions from the first moment you met Tammy, and I know and trust your gut instinct better than my own. It has never let us down. But…' She paused. 'What do you make of it, dear? Is it just a strange day or does Tammy have some special connection with the animals?'

Ed already knew the answer to that.

'I think there's no doubt about it, although I'm a little worried about the crocodiles. I don't think we should jump to conclusions and we still need to be very responsible around all animals. I don't want Tammy getting ideas without us safely checking things first. What do you think, Tammy?' Ed asked.

Tammy walked towards the window and looked outside, her back to Ed and Jude, as she decided what to say. 'It's hard to explain. I always thought it was normal to connect with animals like I do,' she said eventually. 'I never told anyone before, as I thought everyone could do it. I could always understand animals I found around the orphan school. Squirrels, mice, even insects. But it's different here. I feel different.'

'How do you feel different?' he asked.

Tammy shrugged. 'I guess I feel almost stronger. Stronger inside. When I see the animals, I feel a big bubble of energy in my stomach. I thought it was just excitement at first. But now...'

Ed nodded, understanding. Jude looked confused.

Ed took a deep breath. 'Tammy, I believe you are a very smart girl with a special way with animals. Since you've been here, from the moment you arrived in this house, you've been growing that talent. The animals are feeding you. Maybe even the scent of the animals increases the power of your gift. I think even you are starting to realise things about yourself that you didn't know before.' Ed leaned back in his chair and was quiet for a moment. 'A few years ago, a woman named Sarah appeared from nowhere and helped me make this island virus-safe. We didn't know about the virus outbreak at the time until she came along. We were lucky to have her. She fancied herself as a prophet and I believed her. Sarah told me how one day an orphan would come to visit, and that orphan would have a very special way with animals. It would be my destiny to help that child to use their power to help animals all over the world,' Ed said, smiling as he looked at Tammy.

'Sarah was right about everything she told us,' Jude said, nodding excitedly.

'I think we could use this talent or power – whatever it may be – to really do some good. What do you think, Jude?' Ed asked, looking at her.

'I think we should give it some time,' she said. 'Give Tammy some sort of a job to keep her occupied for now. She won't be starting school until autumn, so we have plenty of time. Then it's up to both of you to watch and learn from each other. Tammy, don't do anything too hasty on your own. Always have an expert with you – okay?'

Tammy nodded.

'That should eliminate any risks until we find out how safe you are with the more dangerous animals. Ed, you must keep a close eye on Tammy and note how all of the animals react with her. We need to establish any behavioural patterns.'

Ed nodded his agreement.

'Basically, it's a matter of watching and learning at the moment,' Jude said.

'What work can I do at the safari park? Can I look after the cats?' Tammy asked hopefully.

Ed couldn't resist a smile at Tammy's eagerness to work with the cats.

'Not yet, Tammy. I think I'll put you on cleaning duty to start off with.' He raised his hand as Tammy pulled a face and started to protest. 'Everyone has to start at the bottom. Everyone. That includes you. I've mucked out a good few pens in my time, I'll have you know.'

'And he still does occasionally,' Jude added.

Tammy lowered her head, sticking out her lower lip.

'You couldn't travel to and from school from this island and I don't want to send you away to school, as we'll never get to know you. Moreover, it may be dangerous. Goodness knows what sort of trouble you'd get into, so we'll have a teacher come here during the week. As it's almost the summer holidays, you have a while to settle in first. Would you like that?'

'That sounds great,' Tammy said happily.

'I'll teach you all I know about the animals and what I don't know, I'll get the keepers to teach you. The more you learn about them, the greater your power will be. Knowledge is power. It's easy to learn something that you're interested in, isn't it?' he said.

'Yes. I'm looking forward to it.'

'I could tell you about the help we offer to animals outside the safari park – all the charities we deal with. While Ed teaches you about the animals, here and in the wild, I can show you where they come from. You could learn a little geography. It would be good if you knew about the lands where these animals are originally from. For instance, I think you'd love Africa. We sponsor a safari team over there. Maybe one day you could even visit Africa. What do you think?' Jude asked excitedly.

'I would love to learn about Africa and the other place where Sampson came from. Siberia, wasn't it?'

'Yes,' Ed said.

'I think we should all get ready for dinner,' Jude suggested.

'Good idea. I'll discuss some of your duties with you during dinner, Tammy. How about starting tomorrow?' Ed asked.

'Sounds good,' Tammy responded.

She had her back to the window now and neither saw nor heard what was behind her. Fudge did. She sensed it. It was Fudge's behaviour that drew Tammy's attention. Slowly, Fudge stood up, walked over to Tammy and barked. A *seeker* hovered outside the window, buzzing as it stared at Tammy. Her pendant began to turn red and heat up, but Tammy didn't notice it – too much was happening at once. The *seeker* acknowledged the dog as a threat and buzzed out of sight. Tammy spun around and saw nothing. She opened the window and stuck her head outside.

'What is it?' Ed asked.

'I don't know,' Tammy answered.

Fudge barked even more furiously now. The *seeker* was hiding behind a bush, not far from the window, and saw its opportunity as Tammy looked outside. She turned her head side to side, knowing that something was there but unsure what it was. Fudge wasn't sure either, but her instincts knew it was danger. She grabbed Tammy's shorts and tried to pull her back into the room.

'Get off!' Tammy said trying not to laugh as she pulled her shorts out of Fudge's mouth. 'How am I supposed to see what you're barking at while you're doing that?'

As she said it, it dawned on Tammy that this was precisely why Fudge was pulling her – she didn't want her to see. The message finally got through to Tammy. But it was too late. The *seeker* ceased its opportunity and lunged forward, in front of the window, and right beside Tammy. The side of Tammy's face was right in front of it as it buzzed towards her. One more second and it would be able to see her whole face.

Desperate, Fudge let go of Tammy and flung herself out of the window. The *seeker* had no time to move out of the way. Fudge grabbed the *seeker* in her jaws and ran away from the house.

'Fudge!' Ed shouted after her, leaning out of the window. 'What on earth has gotten into her?'

'She's after something,' Tammy said, frowning.

As Fudge disappeared from view and ran into the trees, the *seeker* buzzed angrily in her mouth. It turned and stuck a small needle into her tongue. Fudge yelped and let the *seeker* go. It stopped to look at her before flying away. Fudge stumbled before she fell to the floor.

*

Dinner consisted of vegetarian toad in the hole with peas, mash and the best gravy Tammy had ever experienced, followed by rhubarb crumble and custard. Jude was a good cook and Tammy was only used to having puddings on special occasions. While Ed and Jude were among the few who could afford to eat meat, they rarely did, and also respected that Tammy was a vegetarian. While they ate, Ed explained some of Tammy's duties. She was to help in the pachyderm section, looking after the elephants. She would be responsible for keeping their pens and grounds clean and washing them. The job appealed more to Tammy once she realised that it wasn't just about cleaning. She would be giving the animals a clean environment to live in. She could wash the elephants and get to see and look after the new baby, Nutt.

She felt that Ed and Jude had trust in her to give her the job. The way they treated her was wholly different to how she had been treated in the past. Since being at the safari park, she had felt a rising power within her, as Ed suggested. It made her confident and gave her the feeling that she could do almost anything she wanted to do.

Fudge had been missing for hours and Ed had failed to find her. They were worried but just before they went to bed she turned up. She was drowsy, as if she had been drugged, but couldn't explain to Tammy what had happened. Tammy watched Ed check Fudge over then get her some food and water. She knew that Fudge had saved her from something bad, but what? Tammy swallowed nervously as she wondered what had been outside that window.

S I X

MIKIE FORCES A CONFESSION

Once Mikie had met someone, he was then able to tap into their mind from quite a distance and "check in" on them as he liked to put it. Stephen said it was being nosy and invading their space but Mikie couldn't agree. How could anyone know what it was like to be able to read people and control them and just expect you to put that aside and ignore it every day? It was impossible. No one could understand. Sometimes Mikie could read random faraway thoughts, but it was hard to know who they were from and was chaotic and didn't make sense, and yet he knew that this gift and curse could be so much more powerful than it was if only he could learn how to wield it. If there were a few "accidents" along the way there wasn't much he could do about it. He tried his hardest to help people but sometimes he was tempted to do the opposite. Dishing out punishment to those who deserved it was tempting for Mikie, and Stephen grew increasingly concerned about this unhealthy appetite.

Like this morning, Mikie had been lying in bed checking in on Kate to ensure she had found her father safely. She had. However, her mother had received an angry phone call from her ex-husband, letting her know that Kate was with him, and now the mother had called the police. The police, who knew Kate's mum well, being one of the few lawyers in the area, were in the progress of removing Kate from her father's house and intended to return her to the mother and stepfather. This was not good. Mikie could feel the anger in the mother and Jared, the stepfather. Kate was going to get it when the police got her home. She was in danger. Mikie could not ignore that. He was annoyed that he couldn't stop Kate's dad from calling her mum, but he had never met him and couldn't connect with a stranger that far away. Not yet. He could only seem to do that with his siblings now and then but without control. It was random.

Mikie got up reluctantly, threw a T-shirt and jeans on and headed downstairs, where Stephen was already in his white karate karategi and doing his early-morning practice.

'You not joining me?' Stephen asked, taking in the jeans and lack of karategi.

'Not today, didn't sleep well, walking it off,' Mikie said, and dashed out of the door before Stephen had chance to fire further questions at him.

Stephen knew something was up; Mikie could tell by his thoughts. He knew Mikie far too well and it was as if he could also read minds sometimes.

'Stop reading my mind!' Stephen yelled as Mikie slammed the door shut.

'Freaky!' Mikie muttered, unable to stop the smile. How did he know?

Kate's family lived the other side of the park. It took Mikie half an hour to get there. He could read Kate and knew that she was now in the police car and her father was screaming that they had no right putting his daughter in further danger. The police wouldn't listen to him. He was a black British African football player with a slightly blemished record of aggression, which his ex-wife had used to her advantage when getting a restraining order and optimising the amount of child maintenance. One was a bar fight aged nineteen, in which he was actually protecting a woman from her violent, drunken boyfriend, and the other was grievous body harm towards a stranger in a bar, who now just so happened to be married to his witch of a wife. She was a lawyer and she was smart. She had played him well. And now he could do nothing as his daughter was forced into a police car against her will.

Mikie read all this from Kate and could feel her pain as she saw her dad's eyes well up with tears. She now knew, since he had spent the evening telling her and showing her his attempts in court to get her, how much he loved her. She felt trapped and terrified of what awaited her at her mother's house and trembled in the police car as it sped along the road.

'Please don't take me back,' she said.

'Your mum is a well-known lawyer with a hard reputation, so we know she isn't all soft and affectionate, but you shouldn't run away to a violent father all the same,' one cop replied.

'Judgy and wrong,' she spat back, crossing her arms sulkily but deciding not to say anything else. What was the point? No one would listen and everyone thought the sun shone out of her mother's rear end. She was a world-class actress for sure. Adults were an endangered species and children were considered privileged to have a parent still alive. Kate did not feel the same way.

Mikie needed to be closer to Kate's mum and Jared. Not necessarily as close as he was but he did want to see what happened. He hid behind a tree trunk. Stephen would be furious if he ever found out, but Mikie couldn't help it. He wanted to and fully intended to teach this pair a lesson and more than anything else, protect Kate. He saw something special in her. Plus, she was just too pretty for him to ignore. He just couldn't stay out of this family matter. Domestic abuse was something Mikie couldn't bear. He had seen far too much of it as he watched people torture each other mentally or physically because they were unhappy inside or couldn't control their emotions. It was the worst part about being able to read people – seeing what skeletons were in their closet. It was often not pretty. Something he had been forced to see and deal with all his childhood and it had forced him to grow up fast.

Mikie had about ten minutes before the police car arrived with Kate. He couldn't resist a slight smile as he made his choice as to how he was going to handle this.

'I'm going to whip her into shape this time!' Jared shouted, pacing the lounge in the large house, clenching and unclenching his fists.

They had a huge house. Where the cries of a young girl couldn't be heard by anyone.

'Calm down, Jared. We need to smile sweetly and act like the relieved parents when she gets here,' Kate's mum soothed. 'You can't show any anger in front of the police or it will ruin everything.'

'I can't swallow this anger down, woman!' he bellowed.

'Well, you'll have to! You shouldn't go gambling everything we have away then, should you? If you can't play the game, leave and don't come back. I am sick of covering your bills. It's financially crippling me. I cannot earn quickly enough with you. We wouldn't need her and her dad's money if it weren't for you!'

'Oh, shut up!' Jared glowered but he took a deep breath and tried to calm down. He couldn't lose this woman. She was his gravy train and he knew it. Plus, she let him have all the child maintenance that was meant for Kate.

Mikie focused on Jared's mind. It was horrible to read, unpleasant and dark; he had an awful background and had done some horrible things. He was going to pay for that. Mikie tried to push past all the darkness and rubbish and access his primary motor cortex in the frontal lobe of his brain. This is where movement is controlled. The role of the primary motor cortex is to generate neural impulses that control the execution of movement. Signals from the primary motor cortex activate muscles on the opposite side of the body, so that the left hemisphere of the brain controls the right side of the body, and the right hemisphere controls the left side of the body. Mikie had got this wrong a couple of times. Every part of the body is represented in the primary motor cortex, and these representations are arranged and linked very specifically. For example, the hand is linked to the arm and the foot to the leg, and so on. The amount of brain matter that is devoted to any particular body part represents the amount of control that the primary motor cortex has over that particular part. This gets very complicated and Mikie had tried many times to explain to Stephen just how complex his power really was.

No one could understand how smart Mikie was. Other regions of the cortex are also involved in motor function and hence movement. These are the secondary motor cortices. These regions include the posterior parietal cortex, the premotor cortex and the supplementary motor area. Each has a different function and Mikie needed to learn and understand how they work. His science teachers in the past had become very concerned with a six-year-old asking about such things. Things they didn't even know how to pronounce. It had ended badly and was one of the reasons why Stephen would not allow Mikie to attend school anymore.

He also needed to read other people, in this case, Kate's mum, in order to see what Jared was doing or how far away from her he was standing. Often, the individual wasn't aware of certain things. Small things. And the small details had to be right. The posterior parietal cortex transforms visual information into motor commands, like determining how to steer the arm to a glass of water based on where the glass is located in space. This was where Mikie might need someone else's point of view as to where that glass stood. Or, in this case, how to land a punch from one person to another and ensure the distance was calculated correctly. The posterior parietal areas send this information on to the premotor cortex and the supplementary motor area. The premotor cortex lies just in front of the primary motor cortex. It is involved in the sensory guidance of movement and controls the more proximal (closer to the body) muscles and trunk muscles of the body. This was where Mikie needed to focus.

Jared turned towards Kate's mum, raised his arm and started to clench his fist, ready to punch. Kate's mum opened her eyes in shock – he had never raised a hand to her in the past. Jared looked equally as shocked and tried to pull his arm back, but his mind wouldn't listen to him. He seemed shocked as time froze and they just stood staring at his arm that seemed to have a life of its own.

'Don't you even dare!' Kate's mum warned.

'I don't want to!' Jared whimpered but his fist came forward, in slow motion, to the astonishment of both of them, and gently landed on the side of her face.

'Oh, that was pathetic!' Mikie muttered, annoyed with his lack of control. He was better than this.

Kate's mum frowned and looked at Jared. It was a weak and ridiculous punch. What was he doing? He looked stressed and was sweating but again his hand came up.

She touched her cheek where the weak punch had landed. 'What was that?'

'I don't know – I didn't mean to – my arm, it just…'

As Jared tried to explain that his arm suddenly seemed to have a mind of its own, he landed a harder blow to her jawline and sent her falling backwards to the floor. Kate's mum glared at him, furious, eyes wide and shocked. As the anger surged through her, she got up and smacked him hard in the face, her large ring cutting his lip and making it bleed, and drops fell onto his white T-shirt. Jared's hand came up again and landed a perfect punch directly to her right eye. That would be a black eye in no time. She again fell to the floor. Her face was already starting to bruise by the time the cop rang the doorbell, and Jared was trying to help her up with a look of mortification on his face. He had punched his gravy train and was going to get it now.

A silent and stunned red-headed woman opened the door to the policeman standing with Kate and swallowed hard as she tried to force a painful and fake smile. Kate stared at her mum's face in surprise. Jared had never hit her mum before. This was new. He must be furious.

'Good morning, Officer. Oh, Kate, how lovely to have you home. How are you today?' she said with effort.

'Ma'am, are you all right?' the policeman asked.

'Yes... no...' She glanced at her daughter then the policeman. 'My husband beats me – he has just hit me repeatedly and he is very violent to me all the time,' Kate's mum blurted out and gasped in shock as the words left her lips. She covered her mouth with her hands and tried to shut herself up.

'Oh well, I shall report this and take him into custody right now. I am well versed in domestic abuse, don't you worry, my dear. I am here to help you,' the policeman said, quickly escorting Kate back into the police car, not knowing what he was going to do with her yet but not willing to let her wander around a home with a violent stepfather in it. He indicated to the other cop in the car to watch Kate then headed back to the door.

'And I lied about her dad – he isn't violent – he is loving and kind and would never ever harm me or Kate. Take her back to him while we sort this out. He is a wonderful father.' She again looked shocked and horrified at what had come out of her mouth and covered it with both hands this time, trying to stop herself from talking.

Jared came up behind her, eyes incredulous, lip still bleeding, blood on his white T-shirt as he watched Kate being put back in the car and his wife covering her mouth with both hands.

'Why would you say all that?' he asked.

'Why did you hit me?' she replied.

'I don't know, I tried not to.'

'And that's exactly my answer too!' she retorted.

They stared at each other, mouths agape. The policeman took in the state of both of them. Making the judgement that this was at least one heck of a wasted vaccine for sure. More likely two, but lawyers were hard to find.

'Sir, I am going to have to ask you to leave the house immediately, please,' he told Jared.

'No way!' Jared shouted. Then, reluctantly, he added, 'I have done many bad things, Officer. I want to tell you everything. I beat up Kate. I have beaten up a few women in the past. And it was me who robbed the petrol station three years ago. I also set Kate's dad up in the pub – he had no choice but to hit me – we planned it all, you see.'

'Jared!' Kate's mum screamed desperately.

'I don't know why…' Jared said, astonishment all over his face as he looked at her helplessly and raised the palms of his hands in a plea for help.

'I think it's best if you come with me, sir,' the policeman said, waving to his colleague by the car to come over and help him.

'No, that's not necessary,' Jared said. 'I don't know why I said all that. All I know is…' Jared blinked and took a deep breath before continuing. 'All I know is that I have a whole lot more I need to tell you. You'll need to get your notepad and pen out.'

'I sure will, mate,' the policeman replied. 'Confession is good for the soul. Sometimes it just feels right getting it all out of the system, doesn't it?'

The other policeman came and stood by them.

'What do you want me to do?' he asked his colleague.

'Call for another car to take the young lady back to her father and keep an eye on her while I take this gentleman's statement before he has a change of heart,' the officer said with a smirk.

Jared blinked, in shock, at Kate's mum, wanting to ask her to help him but finding the words stuck in his throat. Kate's mum slid down the door to her knees, mouth wide in shock, as she listened to Jared spill all his dirty past to the police.

'Oh, and you'll want to know about the drugs stolen from the police station. I needed a lawyer to help me get in there and take them. Funnily enough, that's how we met...'

Mikie punched the air and shouted, 'Yessss!' with excitement. 'Damn, I'm good.'

Kate would be safe now. She sat in the police car staring in shock at what she had just seen, and couldn't help but smile that she would soon be with her dad again, never having to worry about being punched or kicked or whipped with Jared's leather belt. She was free. Kate smiled. Her first smile in the last three years.

SEVEN

JET

Tammy went to bed early, exhausted from the day's events. Once in bed, however, she couldn't sleep. For the first time in her life, she was excited at the thought of learning as much as she could. In the quiet of the night, Tammy could hear the animals in the safari park. It sounded as if they were calling out to her. As she lay listening, she could hear the low growling noise of one of the large cats. She concentrated on that noise, blocking out all others from her mind. The longer she listened, the surer she became that it was Jet. Yes, it was definitely Jet. He was lonely and unhappy because he knew Tammy was close and yet she wasn't with him, and it was such a long time since he had had company. Tammy heard his pleas and felt guilty. Why had she not spent more time with Jet during the day?

Tammy knew she had to go and see Jet now. She couldn't possibly sleep with him calling out to her like this. Yet how would she get there? It would take her ages to get there by foot and she didn't know how to drive the Jeep yet. Even if she tried, it would wake Ed and Jude, who wouldn't let her go.

Then, she had an idea. She could hear one of the zebras calling out loudly. Could one of the zebras come and fetch her? As the thought entered her head, the zebra made another noise. It seemed to be telling her that it would. As the sound of the zebra grew closer, Tammy frowned. Could it be possible? There was the sound again, closer still. She could hear the zebra breathing hard. It was galloping fast and getting nearer by the minute. Tammy threw back her covers and raced to the window. She pulled the curtain aside and looked out. It would have been dark if the moon wasn't shining so brightly, allowing her to see a fair distance. Still unable to see the zebra, she listened to her as she got closer. Tammy wasn't sure how she knew the zebra was a female; she just knew.

Just then, she saw something moving across the fields. It rapidly became clear that it was the zebra galloping towards the house. She grabbed a jumper from her wardrobe, pulled it over her pyjamas, then opened her bedroom window as quietly as she could and climbed down the drainpipe she had spotted earlier in the day. Tammy pulled herself up onto the zebra's rough back, clutching at the tufts of mane, and let it take her galloping back to the safari park. Opening the gate to the zebras' pen, she let her back in. Jet was pacing back and forth when Tammy arrived, a slim shadow in the darkness of the night. Tammy smiled as she sensed how happy he was to see her. He continued pacing impatiently until Tammy climbed over the fence and was beside him.

'Hello, Jet,' she said, taking hold of his head as he gently nudged her in greeting. Jet started to push her over and over, forcing Tammy backwards. 'Stop it,' she chuckled, turning her back on him and running away. Jet joined in the game of chase. Tammy ran as fast as she could. Jet deliberately held back his speed to make the game last longer. His run was languid, almost lazy-looking. Tammy panted fast and hard as she ran faster and faster, trying to give Jet a good chase. He picked up speed and started to gain on her. She avoided him for a few minutes longer by zigzagging out of his reach. She was just about to run behind one of the barrels when Jet caught up with her. He pounced on her, knocking her to the floor.

Tammy laughed, out of breath, as Jet pinned her down and licked her face. She tried to avoid the wet tongue by turning her head from side to side. Then, Jet jumped up and moved away from Tammy, indicating that it was her turn to chase him. Tammy, still out of breath, began the chase. He still kept his speed down and even stopped, waiting for Tammy to get closer, before starting to run away again – tormenting her with the obvious fact that he was much faster than she could ever be. The game continued until Tammy had to stop to catch her breath. She started after Jet again, determined to get him this time. Realising that Tammy couldn't go on much longer, Jet let her catch him.

They came to a rest by some tyres, both breathing hard and tired by the play. Tammy lay on her back with Jet next to her, licking her face. She was staring up at the sky as she stroked Jet's long black back. She didn't recall ever being so happy and content. Tammy remembered the way she had seen the children at school play with each other and decided that this was much better. Who cared about skipping? Who cared about playing ball? When she had tried joining in, Lieutenant Cole had stopped the game, so no one wanted Tammy to play with them.

Suddenly she felt a warm sensation on her throat and looked down to see her pendant was glowing green. It felt warm too and she hesitantly touched it. She held it in front of her eyes and admired the colour. It had become a beautiful rich green colour, glowing magnificently in the starlight. She pressed the warm pendant back to her throat, snuggled into Jet and fell asleep.

*

'Tammy! Tammy!' Ed shouted desperately as he and Jude searched the house and then the grounds for her. They had been searching for half an hour now and there was still no sign of Tammy. They were outside the front of the house when Ed noticed the hoof marks on the grass.

'Jude, look at this,' he said, waving for Jude to join him.

She ran over to him. 'Where did they come from?'

'I don't know, let's follow them.'

They got into the Jeep and followed the trail to the zebras' pen. A quick count revealed none of them to be missing.

'The hoof marks were definitely made by one of the zebras and yet I don't know how it could have got out,' Ed said.

'Do you think Tammy had anything to do with it?' asked Jude.

'I know she did. I can tell by how deep the hoof marks are that the zebra was carrying something.'

'Tammy?'

'Who else!' Ed said.

Neither of them noticed the *seeker* hovering in the bushes, comparing their images.

*

The safari park had been open almost an hour when they heard a commotion coming from the panther's pen.

'Jet!' Ed shouted, sprinting towards the enclosure.

He pushed himself to the front of the crowd. Sure enough, there was Tammy lying in the enclosure with Jet cuddled up close to her, as if guarding his prey. Was there any blood? Was she still breathing?

A couple of women in the crowd were crying. One started to scream hysterically, assuming the worst.

'It's all right, everybody.' Ed turned to the crowd. 'The girl works here and has a very close relationship with the panther. There's no reason to panic. She must have fallen asleep. If you wouldn't mind just moving back a little and keeping quiet, as we wouldn't want to spook the panther while she's in there now, would we?'

He might have been talking to a brick wall; no one moved. Arms stretched wide, as if herding cattle, he stepped forward. The people at the front dropped back a pace to avoid being trodden on by this large man, and so did the others in turn. Meanwhile, Jude was trying to wake Tammy by calling her name. Jet, having been fully awake for a while, looked in no hurry to move. Jude was terrified. What if her calling enraged the panther? Tammy was completely at his mercy.

'She hasn't stirred,' Jude told Ed when he came alongside her. 'I'm getting nowhere – what if I went in myself?'

'Don't even think about it. His whole attitude will change as soon as you go near him. Remember what I told you about the cobra? They're only safe with Tammy,' Ed told her.

Jet started to lick Tammy's face. She stirred a little. Jet continued to lick until Tammy awoke. When she realised where she was, she sat up, rubbing her eyes and squinting in the bright sunlight.

'Hello, Tammy,' Jude said.

Tammy looked up and went red with embarrassment as she saw the gathered crowd. Now Jet was nudging her to her feet, easing her towards the door. Her arm around his neck, she headed towards Ed and Jude. Would they be furious with her? She deserved it, she supposed, sneaking off in the night – she'd meant to sneak back before dawn. Could they really be smiling? Yes, they were smiling.

'I'll open the door for you,' Ed said, as he started to make his way to the back of the pen.

Jet accompanied Tammy to the door, making no effort to stop her or to follow himself. Even those at the back of the crowd could hear the rumble of his purring, as if a domestic cat had just got larger. Tammy gave him a huge hug and kiss then left the pen.

'I couldn't let the crowd see you climb the fence in case it put any ideas into their heads,' Ed told her.

'So, you aren't angry with me?'

'I was at first, until I saw you fast asleep next to Jet. You had a smile on your face, even in your sleep.'

'Hello, sleepyhead,' said Jude, joining them behind the pen. 'We'd better wait in here until the crowd disperses a little.' She gave Tammy a hug.

'I thought you'd both be angry with me.' Tammy smiled, squeezing Jude's hand.

'It's hard to be angry with someone who seems so happy,' Jude said with a smile. 'Besides, I think both Ed and I realise that you need a friend. We understand that you've never really had a friend and if Jet fills that gap then so be it. Why you couldn't have just fallen in love with the Labradors, though, is beyond me. I can only assume that isn't your style.'

Tammy looked at Ed, who nodded his agreement.

'Can I sleep here every night then?' asked Tammy.

'Oh no, that's not a good idea at all. It's not healthy. You are a young girl and you couldn't possibly sleep in the safari park!' Ed said.

Tammy lowered her head, disappointed.

'Do you think you could make the panther not hurt anyone else? I mean…' Jude began.

'Jude!' exclaimed Ed.

'Listen to me, Ed – I'm just wondering if Tammy could somehow tame Jet enough so he can spend the night at the house, that's all.'

'I know Jet would understand,' said Tammy. 'He would be good, honestly. He's so lonely he wouldn't risk hurting anyone because then he'd have to sleep here. I know he would be friendly around people if I told him to be.'

'I'll think about it,' Ed replied with a heavy sigh.

*

Tammy showered and dressed then went downstairs to have breakfast. Ed and Jude were already at the table, waiting for her.

'I'm sorry I fell asleep. I had meant to get back before morning,' Tammy said, before sitting down.

'Just sit and eat, you must be starving,' said Jude.

Tammy helped herself to egg and soldiers, suddenly realising how hungry she was.

'So already you're trying to sneak out of the house at night,' Ed said. 'I know you didn't tell us because you thought we'd say no, but we might have said yes.'

'You wouldn't have let me go,' Tammy said.

'You're probably right, I would have objected to it. However, things are different now. Although you're only twelve, I've decided that I'm not going to tell you what you can and cannot do. You aren't like most kids your age, so next time you feel you have to do something that I would object to, tell me anyway. I need to know everything you do and where you are at all times. We're a team, aren't we?'

'Yes, we are,' Tammy replied.

'Good. Then let's start acting like one. I don't fully understand this situation with you and the animals. However, we have to understand it together. Anything you think or do, I want to know about immediately. We all have to work together on this.' Ed smiled reassuringly.

'I know, that's only fair, I'm sorry. I need you both to help me, yet sometimes I get distracted by the animals and forget about everything but them,' Tammy explained.

'That's understandable, we'll work on it. I presume you're ready to start your chores after breakfast?'

'Absolutely!' Tammy smiled. She hurried through the rest of her breakfast, eager to begin the first day of her job. It was already late and she had a lot to see and do.

EIGHT

THE ELEPHANTS

'Your main concern will be the elephants,' Ed told her on the way to the pachyderm section. 'They're not always easy to handle. We have eight elephants in all. Two Asian – well, three including Nutt – and five African. Elephants can be extremely dangerous. I have three keepers who work with the elephants. Dave is the head keeper – you met him yesterday – and the other two are part-time volunteers. We have been through several volunteers, because if the elephants don't take to you then you can't work with them – they make it impossible. Here's Dave now,' said Ed, pointing.

They stopped by the elephant pen.

'Good morning,' he said.

'Morning, Dave. How's Nutt?' Tammy asked.

'Better, he's going to be all right. He was just born a little weak, that's all. It's not uncommon when elephants are kept in captivity.'

'Dave, I'm going to leave Tammy with you. I want you to train her as a keeper in this section. For the time being, keep her with the elephants and rhinos. I don't want her to get confused.'

'No problem, Ed. One small thing, what if the elephants don't want to work with her?'

'Oh, they will, Dave, they will,' said Ed. 'I'll come and see how you're doing at the end of the day, Tammy. Okay?'

'Sure. See you later, and thanks, Ed.'

Ed returned Tammy's smile and left her with Dave.

'Well, Tammy, do you know how the safari park is laid out yet?' Tammy shook her head. 'Come with me then and I'll get you a map,' he said.

Tammy followed Dave towards a nearby building.

'Welcome to the pachyderm house – the centre for all the thick-skinned animals at the safari park and my humble home. It's a bit messy,' he said, smiling, as he looked through one pile of paper after another. 'I'm not particularly good at paperwork. I'm more of a hands-on person.'

Tammy looked around the room. There wasn't much in it except for piles of paper and a closet at the back labelled *Feed*, which is where she saw Minnie sitting and watching her. She had put on some weight and looked happy. Tammy smiled at her.

'Here it is,' said Dave, holding up a piece of paper. 'Now, this is the layout of the park. This is the entrance, this is where you live and this is where we are.' Dave explained where all the various animals were housed.

She suddenly realised just how big the safari park actually was; there was still so much she hadn't seen. 'It's so big!' she exclaimed.

'I know. We really do have one of the best parks in the world, considering the variety of animals and the space allocated to each of them,' said Dave.

'I haven't seen any of the attractions yet, Dave. Can I see them?' asked Tammy.

'On your own time, dear,' he smiled, 'right, now, you have a job to do. When you're on my time, you work.'

'Okay,' Tammy said with a laugh.

'This cupboard is where the feed is kept. We've already given the elephants their breakfast today. They have a mixture of different grains and I'll show you how to mix that up tomorrow. I'll find you in the black panther's enclosure, will I?' he said laughingly.

Tammy blushed and lowered her head in embarrassment.

'Actually, they're thinking of bringing Jet up to the house tonight so he can sleep there,' she told him.

'Really? Well, I'm not going to say anything, as I'm not sure what is going on here. Ed told me not to ask questions and to just keep notes.' Dave smiled. 'Anyway, our elephants eat about 30 kilograms of hay, 10 kilograms of carrots and 5 to 10 kilograms of bread a day. The diet may vary slightly, which you'll notice when you see what is here,' he said laughingly.

'Will I always find what I need in here?' Tammy asked.

'Yes. We have porters that bring the food around to each area. All you have to do is let them in to refill the feed bins. Here's your key. Don't let anyone else get access to it. There have been incidents where people have got into the animals' food supply and poisoned it.'

'That's awful – why would someone do that?'

'Some people hate safari parks and think the animals are better off dead than in captivity despite what we have done as a result of Pisces,' Dave said.

'How awful! Did it happen here?' Tammy asked.

'No, in another safari park. We have exceptionally good security here. You can hand the key back to me at the end of each day if you don't want the responsibility.'

'I'll guard it with my life,' she said, clutching the key tightly to her chest.

'Good. These are the scales to weigh the food. Above it is a list of who gets what, in case you forget,' he said, pointing to the large scales behind Tammy. 'In the back here are all the vitamins that need to be mixed into the food. There is the table of information to remind you.' He pointed to a chart on the wall above the vitamins.

'Why are some marked in red?' Tammy asked.

'Those are the most essential ones for the animal to have. You can see here, under *Elephants*, that the most important ones are vitamins A and D, the minerals, salt and calcium and the most important of the trace elements, selenium.'

'So, I mix those and the ones marked in black into the food each time I feed them?'

'Just in their breakfast. They only get vitamins and minerals once a day,' Dave told her.

'What do they do in the wild? They can't get vitamins then, can they?'

'Not like this, each elephant can eat up to 300 kilograms a day in the wild so gets much more nutrition. If they ate that much in captivity, they would become very overweight.'

'I see. It's very complicated, isn't it?'

'Yes, but the more you do it, the easier it gets. Now, Tammy, it's important to keep their water trough filled and clean. It's a constant job. Depending upon the heat, an elephant can drink 100 to 300 litres of water a day.'

'That sounds like a lot,' she said.

'It is. You'll realise how much when you've done it a few times. Before we go out and meet the elephants, you must know a few things about them. You'll learn as you go along mainly. Just always be aware of how dangerous they can be. It doesn't matter how well trained you are with elephants. If they don't like you, they won't let you near them. I almost hired a man who had worked for over ten years with elephants, but ours didn't like him,' Dave said.

'What did the man do wrong?'

'Nothing. It's a gut reaction. Humphry, the largest male African we have, is the leader. He took an instant dislike to the man and turned the rest against him too. That's why I asked Ed what I should do if they don't take to you. I guess you know something that I don't, eh?' he said with a laugh.

'Let's go and meet the elephants,' she said.

The elephants sensed Dave and Tammy were coming before they were in sight. They watched eagerly as Dave held the gate open for Tammy. Before the gate was closed, the elephants started to run towards them. For a split second, Dave thought they were charging, until he recognised the almost dizzy look of joy in their eyes as they neared Tammy. A deep rumbling noise began – it was coming from Humphry. It got louder as all of the elephants joined in. Dave was stunned. He knew this was the way an elephant expressed joy. However, for all of them to do it at the same time was unusual. Also, Humphry had never reacted this way to a human before. It was very strange.

'I think they have taken to you in a big way,' he said, watching Tammy tenderly caress each elephant.

'They are glad to see me. They've been expecting me,' Tammy said.

'Expecting you?' Dave didn't understand.

'Yes. I saw them yesterday and they wanted me to get closer. I said I would next time and here I am. This is an Asian one?' Tammy pointed to one of the smaller elephants.

'Yes. Sidney is twenty-nine years old. Humphry is twenty-six. The oldest one is the African female you're stroking now, Katie, she's thirty-two. The rest are females aged between twelve and twenty-four years old. They aren't all fully grown. They usually reach full size between the ages of twenty and twenty-five.'

'How long do they live?'

'In the wild, they live until they're about sixty. Then they usually die of starvation. Elephants gradually wear each set of their teeth away and replace them up to six times. When their sixth sets are worn down, they can't eat anymore,' he explained.

'What about in captivity?' asked Tammy, as she rested her forehead on Humphrey's trunk.

'They should live longer than that due to softer food. Unfortunately, they develop stomach problems or problems with their pads – feet. Even just having to adjust to a new environment in a safari park can lead to life-threatening problems.'

Dave continued to tell Tammy all he knew about elephants. He introduced her properly to each in turn and told her a little about each one. There was Sidney, the Asian male and then there was Humphry, Molly and Polly (twins, which wasn't common among elephants), Katie and Gem.

'The other female Asian is Suzie. She's the one who just had the little bull. That's what we call male elephants. The females are called cows,' Dave said.

'Is Nutt still at the hospital?' asked Tammy.

'Yes, under observation. Hopefully, Nutt and his mother will be back within a couple of weeks. Now I have something for you to do that will keep you very busy for a while.'

'That sounds like a threat,' Tammy said, laughing.

'It is. The hose is next to their watering trough. You use it to refill the troughs and to wash the elephants down. The soap we use is in the pachyderm house, under the sink. The brushes you'll need are next to it. They all need a wash and I suggest you use the overalls hanging up by the sink – you'll need them! Can I leave you to it?' asked Dave.

'Yep. I can manage that,' said Tammy, as she skipped away towards the pachyderm house.

'One more thing, Tammy,' Dave shouted after her.

She turned to look at him.

'Don't forget to wash behind their ears. If you need me, I'll be around section one somewhere, and don't answer any questions the visitors ask you or let anyone but me into the pen. Okay?'

'No problem,' she said with a chuckle, and skipped off enthusiastically.

Dave liked Tammy; it was hard not to and he was glad he had her help. The other two keepers were usually volunteers forced upon him by a school for work experience; they didn't care much about the quality of their work, preferring only to play with the elephants, and hardly ever showed up. He had a feeling that Tammy was different.

Tammy was already soaking wet after washing just one elephant. The safari park's visitors gathered around the pen to watch the spectacular performance in front of them. It was as if they were watching an elephant's birthday party.

The elephants were making a lot of noise, squirting water with their trunks and jumping back and forth. Tammy was screaming with delight as she got wetter and wetter. Humphry squirted her in the face with a trunkful of water. Tammy held her hose high and squirted him back. Then, Humphry picked Tammy up with his trunk and held her high in the air so she couldn't get him again. He carried her over to the water trough as she screamed to be released. He finally let go, dropping her into the trough.

The crowd howled with delight as Tammy sat up and clambered out. Humphry pushed her back in with his head. The crowd roared again. Three times Tammy tried to get out and each time Humphry pushed her back.

'This means war!' she said with a laugh.

She grabbed the hose and began soaking the nearest elephant, Polly. Then she grabbed the soap and brush and started scrubbing her down. When Polly was finished, it was Katie's turn, and so on until they were all clean. Throughout it all, the elephants not being washed kept attacking Tammy with trunks full of water. She found it exhausting as she tried to wash the elephants while avoiding well-aimed squirts.

When she was finished, Tammy emptied the trough and filled it up with clean water. As the water rose, she could see her own reflection and noticed her pendant was again glowing green. It seemed brighter than before. Then she turned the hose off and put it back on its post. The elephants were still playing. Tammy dropped onto the soaking wet ground, exhausted yet happy. She lay watching the elephants. What fun animals they could be, so big and yet so gentle. They treated Tammy as if she were one of them. Just then, Humphry came over and blew a trunkful of water all over her. He had been saving it until she was least expecting it. He then lifted a large ball of soapsuds from the floor and dumped them over her head.

'Humphry!' she screamed. She stayed sitting, not yet having the energy to get up.

The crowd began to disperse. Tammy didn't notice Ed, Jude, Dave and a few other of the safari park's employees smiling and shaking their heads as they walked off with the crowd. She was also completely unaware of the small *seeker* hovering about the elephant section trying to compare her soap-sodden features to that of a picture it carried of her mother, Sarah. The *seeker* had been covering the whole of the island over the last few days.

Lacking the technical capability to dismiss the soapsuds or wait until they had been wiped away, the *seeker* simply dismissed Tammy and reported that no one on the island remotely resembled Sarah in any way. However, at precisely this moment, Tammy did notice that her pendant suddenly felt very hot – painfully hot – and was glowing bright red. She bit her lip, puzzled.

It was getting late in the afternoon and Tammy had to tidy up. She stood up, stretched and walked over to the elephants. She shook the soap away from her face and pushed her wet hair behind her ears.

'I have to go now,' she said as she petted and kissed them all goodbye. 'I'll see you again soon. I'll be in the pachyderm house if you need me,' she said laughingly.

'So how is everything?' Dave asked when he walked into the pachyderm house.

'Good, I think,' said Tammy. 'It took me all afternoon to wash the elephants, though. Is that too long?'

'Not at all. It's an all-day job. They're more time-consuming than most of the other animals. Well, that's all you can do for today. I'll give you plenty more to do in the morning. You are going to show up for their breakfast tomorrow, aren't you?' he asked jokingly.

'Yes, I am. Do you know where Ed is?'

'Yeah, he told me to tell you to meet him at Jet's enclosure.' Dave smiled warmly at Tammy. He could sense how special she was. She had to be if the elephants took to her so quickly and if Ed was about to allow a panther into Brunswick House. In an ordinary world, events such as these would surprise him, but life on this island had never been ordinary.

'I should go then. See you in the morning, Dave,' she shouted over her shoulder as she ran out of the door.

'I'll see you tonight first. I've been invited to have dinner with you.'

'Great. See you then,' she said, running off.

Dave watched her running towards Jet's enclosure and smiled. He wasn't sure what it was about Tammy, yet everyone at the safari park seemed to be in higher spirits since she had been here. Both the people and the animals seemed happier. It was obvious she could connect with the animals, but to affect the entire atmosphere on the island in such a way was remarkable. Could this young girl and the positive energy she radiated really be having such an effect?

NINE

MIKIE TAKES ON BULLIES

Mikie leaned against the tree watching the school he used to go to as the kids laughed and talked on their way out. The bell had gone five minutes ago. He often came to watch this part and torture himself over the lonely life he led without any interaction with other kids. He missed school. He loved being around other kids, their minds mostly nicer than adults, and learning and playing games at breaktime. Stephen had removed him when he was nine years of age. Mikie's power had been hard to control and impossible to hide. He had accidentally read people or made them do things, and was starting to make himself look suspicious. The intensely intelligent questions had been the biggest problem. When his Uncle Stephen had been called in to talk about sending Mikie to a more advanced school that might train him for NASA, things changed, and that was when things had turned sour.

'Discreet, Mikie, I said discreet!' Stephen had raged on the way home.

'I can't help it,' Mikie had said, in a sulk.

'That's exactly why I need to remove you from school and homeschool you. You can control other people and make them do things, but you can't keep your own mouth shut for a few hours? I mean, you just can't go telling your teachers they got the maths wrong then march up there and put the right equations up on the board that a kid in university would only just about grasp! Not a nine-year-old! You just can't resist showing off, can you?'

'It's not my fault most people aren't very smart.'

That comment had sealed his fate. That along with the fact that he had made a teacher scratch her bottom vigorously in front of the entire class, pick her nose and smear bogies on the chalkboard, and fart while wearing a giant grin and declaring that no one could beat that one, could they? All in front of a school inspector assessing her class at the time. Yes, that had not helped either. It had been an act of revenge, true, and she had surely deserved it, according to Mikie, for accusing him of cheating. That hurt Mikie's pride big time. Cheating – him! He wanted people to know how smart he was. He was sick of playing the quiet little weird boy in the background. Just because he could accurately draw, label and describe things with his photographic memory as if he had an open book right by him, didn't mean he could be unfairly accused of cheating. And how could a nine-year-old boy know they would sack her for being inappropriate in class anyway? How was he to know that? All he saw was how he made an entire class laugh hysterically. That was his work and his contribution to the class. And his revenge.

Stephen had hit the roof and, as always, fixed it. The young teacher, Miss Willow, was only working at the school to save money for university. Adults were not that great in number, so university lecturers were few and far between, making university very much a privilege for the rich. Some teenagers worked several years to save the funds for university and make something more of themselves. Miss Willow was one such young woman, desperately wanting to study Marine Biology and unable to afford the cost of the course. Stephen explained that a chemical had been used on her to make her do such things and it wasn't her fault at all. He was deeply sorry that his child had found this substance and thought it funny to affect her, and she mustn't be upset about it. If she would just sign this non-disclosure document, he could cover the entire cost of her education...

She had signed and accepted Stephen's story. Stephen lectured Mikie for a whole month about how that could have hurt her mental health as a vulnerable young woman and ruined her career. What if she had been a mother supporting her family? Mikie had felt bad but was still angry she had accused him unfairly and without evidence of cheating. Apparently, that didn't matter to Stephen. It mattered to Mikie. It mattered a lot. He missed school. Homeschooling was boring. He was too young to have to understand everyone else's mental health issues – his own were hard enough – and even adults didn't understand. It felt unfair. And yet there was a peaceful side to being homeschooled. No more chaos with all the thoughts of teachers and children drifting into his mind and polluting his energy. Only Stephen. And his mind was boring and read so often that there was never anything new to digest. So, to bridge the gap, Mikie occasionally stopped by the school at the end of the day and watched the kids he couldn't join lead a normal everyday existence he could never know. Billy No-Mates. That was how he felt.

A group of older teenagers, about sixteen years old, caught Mikie's attention with their devious and troublesome thoughts. They were out to get someone. Piqued with curiosity, Mikie read them and watched them, learning what their intentions were and towards whom. Dan came out of the school. A boy Mikie remembered from his own class, the same age as him, twelve, and one of the few boys who talked with him at the time. Dan was also smart. Nowhere near as clever as Mikie but smart enough to enjoy Mikie's conversation and not feel lost or threatened by it. He liked Dan. He missed him even. And Dan was going to get it.

Adam was captain of the rugby team and had the height and muscles to show for it. He loomed over all the other kids in school with his muscles and jet-black hair. People were terrified of him. It was Rick who led them all, having slightly more brains than the others. He had brown hair, was average height and build, relatively good-looking according to the girls but not as popular as Adam. Rick just used Adam as his thug. Simon was a skinny, tall, weak, blond kid that hardly ever spoke. Introvert was putting it mildly. He was sneaky and caused trouble in the background, normally making Rick and Adam act upon what he himself had started. Then finally there was Kyle. A slightly podgy, mousy brown, short kid who rarely ever had a thought of his own and just needed someone to follow and to be told what to do. His mind really was one of the emptiest Mikie had ever reluctantly explored.

This gang of Neanderthals, standing smugly with their snidey grins and plotting their cruelty, were going to get

Dan and teach him a lesson. Laughing and jeering with each other on the things they were going to do to him, like turn him into a human pretzel. It had been brewing for a while. Dan was scared and alert as he nervously came out of school, and you could see his face and shoulders sag as he realised the gang was waiting for him still. He had avoided them twice. This was third time unlucky. Mikie could read Dan's mind as he accepted something really bad was about to happen and skulked off on his way home. The gang of four smiled and followed. The four lads were bullies. Rick, Kyle, Simon and Adam had been friends throughout school and were not very bright. To hide this fact, they acted hard and uninterested in school academy and used intimidation tactics to avoid being bullied themselves. *Bully others before you get bullied back* was their motto.

'Hmm, not this time,' Mikie muttered.

He could hear his uncle's voice in his head warning him to be hidden, stay in the background, don't show yourself up, don't get involved. But this was his old friend Dan. The only kid who would talk to him at the end. The only one. He couldn't simply abandon him to this fate all alone. He was outnumbered and going to get a beating, and there was no way Mikie could just stand by and let it happen. It was also clear that Dan's previous loyalty to him had caused him to have no friends at all once Mikie had left. There was no one for Dan. That was Mikie's fault and it was time to make amends.

Ducking around trees, bushes or pretending to be looking at something with his back turned to them was how Mikie followed them without them realising it. Every time someone turned to look, Mikie hid. He knew when they were going to look before they did. If there was nowhere to hide, then Mikie controlled their minds and stopped the lads from turning to look back. Dan had to cross most of the park to get home and that was a long stretch of green. There was a small dark alleyway leading from the park to the back of his house. If he tried to go the other way there was an abandoned factory, no longer used, along the street that the gang would just drag him into. Dan knew it was this building or the alleyway where he would get it. It really didn't matter which way he took. Both directions had the perfect place for him to have the stuffing kicked out of him and no one would hear a sound. Mikie could read Dan's thoughts as he decided which route might be the least painful solution.

Mikie preferred the alleyway. It was closed in small and narrow so he could control them all better. His heart pounded with excitement at what he knew was going to happen. This would be the ultimate challenge to him. Could he control so many all at the same time? It was going to be pretty cool finding out; that much was for sure. Adam was particularly big – far bigger than the others – and stood almost at a ginormous six foot. But he wasn't as hard as he looked and none of them had any martial arts training like Mikie had. They were just meat and muscle. No class. No style. No ninja. Mikie smiled. This was a wonderful opportunity to test his abilities.

Dan chose to walk the front way to his house, past the abandoned factory, so was taken by surprise when his body turned at the last moment and did the opposite and went towards the back alleyway. It was unexpected and strange, but Dan just kept putting one foot in front of the other.

What did it matter? This was going to hurt regardless of where it happened. Dan's heart sank with a heavy thud into his gut as he turned into the alleyway. Kyle, Adam, Simon and Rick chuckled menacingly as they turned in after him.

Mikie wasn't far behind them but none of them had spotted him yet. Halfway down the alleyway, Mikie made Dan stop, turn and face the gang. He dropped his bag and stood in the *Daichi* position, which is a basic karate stance. Dan looked confused, clueless as to what his body was doing and legs trembling at the fact that he was now facing the four large teenagers heading closer to him, instead of walking as quickly as possible to his home. Then he spotted Mikie behind the gang. Recognition slowly sinking in past his fear as he tried to place how he recognised him, slowly remembering him as his old friend from before.

'Hey, Dan, I was just walking by and thought I recognised you! How the devil are you?' Mikie sang loudly and happily, wearing the biggest smile on his face.

Kyle, Simon, Adam and Rick swung around in surprise and took Mikie and his small frame in. Dan frowned, confused, trying to figure out what was happening.

'Get lost, rug rat, before we do you in,' Rick shouted.

'You and whose army?' Mikie asked cheerily.

Rick laughed, Adam sneered and the other two stepped towards Mikie. Dan was rooted to the spot, still in a karate stance mode, temporarily forgotten. Mikie focused on Simon, skinny and smaller-framed than Adam but still tall for his age. He went into Simon's mind, located the primary motor cortex, and made him raise his hand and slap Adam's face four times in a row. Left, right, backhanded, and then left again. It was hard to see who looked the most shocked

– Simon or Adam. Mikie laughed, he couldn't help himself, as he saw the red rise in Adam's cheeks and anger flare his nostrils. Simon's Adam's apple bobbed nervously up and down. Just as Adam punched him really hard in the face and sent him to the floor. Gobsmacked, Rick turned to look at Adam.

'Just get him for now!' Rick yelled, pointing to Mikie. 'And Kyle, you get that weasel over there.'

Dan hadn't moved as Kyle walked towards him. Mikie went into Dan's mind, ready for action, as Adam moved towards him ready to attack. Just as Adam went to grab Mikie, Dan lifted his arm and landed a fast and perfect punch right on Kyle's nose. Kyle immediately covered his nose with both hands and stared at Dan in surprise.

'You broke my nose!' he squealed as blood ran through his fingers.

Then Dan raised his left leg off the floor, without any idea how or why he was doing it, toes pointed down and the other knee bent for a perfect balance then flicked his leg out and landed a perfect kick straight to the groin area. Kyle grimaced, held his groin in agony and slowly shrunk into a ball of groaning agony on the floor.

'Now that's called a *Kin-geri*, mate.' Mikie winked at Dan. 'You should remember that one. Very easy self-defence move.'

Dan couldn't speak. He looked between Mikie and his strange cheery attitude and Kyle moaning in a pile on the floor.

Meanwhile, Adam had grabbed Mikie by the collar and was raising his hand about to punch him in the face but Mikie was too fast for him. He spun around, at a speed that surprised Adam, avoided the punch and put a little distance between them and then, with expert precision, jumped into the air. Both feet left the ground, taking him higher than Adam as everyone watched in shock; he bent one knee back before lunging it forward into a perfect flying front kick. His foot hit Adam full in the chest, winding him and sending him flying backwards onto the cold, hard floor.

'Yahhhhh,' Mikie shouted as he kicked out then landed in a perfect stance, knowing how cool he had looked. 'And that little baby is one of my personal favourites called the *Mae Tobi Geri*,' Mikie said.

Then he jumped into the air again and flew towards Adam, whose eyes opened so wide in shock at this small lunatic of a boy flying towards him that his eyeballs almost popped out. Mikie landed on Adam's stomach, winding him even more before landing a couple of punches in his face and pulling his trousers down and jumper over his head, then tying his arms behind his back so he couldn't move. Mikie stood up and faced Rick and Simon, both now standing gaping at him.

'Who the hell are you?' Rick asked, scared now.

'I'm your worst nightmare,' Mike said, and ran towards Rick.

Simon and Rick both turned and ran as fast as they could. Mikie flew into the air and landed a hard, painful kick in the centre of Rick's back, sending him flying forward and skidding along the floor. He lost skin on his chin and hands and was winded, unable to speak or stand for a moment. Mikie approached him and dragged him to his feet.

'Stand up, you coward. I can't even tell you to pick on someone your own size because you can't even stand and face me. You're only brave when there are four of you against one younger lad. You make me sick. Today is your day of reckoning, mate!'

Mikie forced him to stand and face him then showered him with several punches before throwing him into the wall at the other end of the alleyway, where he landed with a thud, groaning and whining. At the same time, Mikie had taken control of Dan and made him kick out a leg and trip Simon up as he tried to run past him. Simon then scrambled to his feet, ready to get up and run again. Dan walked up to him, grabbed him by the shoulder, helped him up and turned him to face him. The shock and fear in Simon's face gave Dan a courage he hadn't felt before. He pulled his fist back, scrunched up his nose and punched Simon firmly in the face.

'I'll let you do that one,' Mikie said quietly, smiling to himself, not controlling Dan but letting him find his own strength and courage. They would never mess with Dan again.

They stood for a while catching their breath and smiling as the four teenagers moaned and groaned in agony. Then Mikie walked up to Dan, placed his arm around his shoulders and said, 'Come on, I'll walk you home.'

As they left the alleyway, Dan turned to Mikie and looked at him in wonder. 'I'm not sure what happened back there but I'm super glad you were with me.'

'Like I said, I just saw you, was about to come and say hello when I realised these goofs were following you. You did great, good for you. I didn't realise you were quite the fighter.'

'Neither did I,' Dan smiled broadly, 'but then you always had a way of making things appear strange.'

Dan took a deep breath. It wasn't worth asking any questions. Mikie never answered them. 'I can't wait to tell everyone at school about this.'

'That will be a good moment. Don't mention me, Take all the credit for yourself – you deserve it. Because of me you have no friends, so see this as a thank you. Take the credit. You did whip them into shape after all, and they won't ever talk about it to anyone. Admit they were all beaten up by one or two twelve-year-olds? They won't bring it up ever. If you don't mention me, you'll soon get friends back. Don't let me spoil that for you again.'

Mikie knew Dan would be the most popular kid in his year from now on, like his popular older sister, and the thought made him feel a bit less guilty.

'It shouldn't be that way,' Dan said.

'I know.'

'Are you coming back to school?'

'No. Never.'

'That's a shame.'

'Yeah.'

They stood awkwardly for a moment outside Dan's house and then Mikie took a deep breath and smacked him playfully on the shoulder.

'Well, look after yourself, Dan, and enjoy the moment tomorrow,' he said, then turned and walked briskly away from the only friend he had ever known.

TEN

SIROCCO

Ed was scratching his chin thoughtfully as Tammy approached. He hoped he wasn't going to regret this.

'Hi, Ed,' Tammy called, slightly out of breath.

'Hi. How was your first day?' he asked.

'Great! And very wet,' she said with a laugh.

'Well, we should get back to the house for supper. Are you sure you can make Jet understand?'

'Don't worry, I've told you already. I wouldn't be so positive otherwise. I want to be with him on my own first. Then I'll bring him out and see if he's okay with you. If it goes well, we know he'll be all right with everyone else,' Tammy declared.

Ed shook his head and looked down at the floor. He wished he had Tammy's confidence. 'What if he isn't all right with me?'

'He won't hurt you, I promise.'

'Let's just get it over with then,' he said reluctantly.

Tammy was about to climb the fence when Ed suggested that she use the door this time. She laughed and agreed. It was funny how she felt more comfortable climbing the fence. She wasn't sure why; perhaps it was the rebel in her. Jet greeted her in his usual manner. He pushed his head into her stomach, nudging her backwards. She laughed.

Ed watched with amused interest as Tammy and Jet played push and shove with one another. It really was a delightful sight. He watched Tammy kneel down and start talking in Jet's ear. She spoke to him as she would a person, yet not as timidly. Jet seemed to be listening. Ed wondered why it was Jet could understand Tammy and no one else. She seemed to use nothing more than a normal person would: just words and touch.

Maybe it was just a case of wanting to listen, he thought to himself.

Tammy started to walk out, with Jet close behind her.

'I was thinking perhaps a lead of some sort,' Ed said, rather nervously.

'Oh no, you couldn't do that,' Tammy shook her head, 'Jet isn't used to wearing a lead, plus he wants to be out of an enclosure, out of captivity. A lead is just another form of captivity to him.'

'Oh.' Ed was disappointed – and a little scared. He still lacked Tammy's trust in Jet.

'Do you really think anyone would be able to control him on a lead against his will, Ed?' Tammy smiled.

'I guess it was a silly idea,' he said with a sigh.

Jet stayed close to Tammy's side. He had a very languid, elegant walk. He was cautious at first, as if seeing everything around him for the first time – nothing looked the same from outside the enclosure. Jet would have been scared and very anxious were it not for the fact that Tammy was right beside him.

'Stroke his head,' Tammy suggested.

Ed slowly and hesitantly reached his hand out, palm facing upwards, and petted Jet under his chin. It was a wise move considering Jet wasn't used to being petted by anyone other than Tammy. If Ed had reached out quickly, lowering his hand to Jet's head, Jet might have mistaken it as a form of attack. Jet allowed Ed to pet him. He made no effort to be friendly with Ed and yet he wasn't unfriendly either. He was still, tolerating Ed for the benefit of Tammy but not wishing to be friends. Jet didn't like humans much and wasn't about to start now. Tammy was not exactly human. She was as much a wild beast as Jet was. She just hid it better. Ed wasn't keen on the idea of trying to get too friendly either. All he was worried about was Jet attacking him or someone else.

'I have to admit,' Ed said, 'this brings back old memories of Sampson.'

'Sampson let you pet him?' Tammy asked.

'Not really. He was sedated when he was brought here, to calm him down. He was too tired to attack me, so I sat and stroked him until the drug started to wear off. It really is a wonderful sensation to stroke such a strong and wild animal as if he were your best friend. It seemed safe but when he started to wake up, I can tell you, I moved faster than the speed of light out of his pen!' Ed took his hand off Jet's head.

'This is different, it will be safe,' said Tammy.

'Let's go and give it a try then. Tonight is just a trial, Jet. Don't let Tammy down,' Ed said, feeling a little more comfortable.

Tammy and Ed drove in the Jeep while Jet followed on foot. Fudge seemed completely at ease with having Jet around and watched calmly from the back seat. Jet preferred the exercise. He was running around in circles, relishing his freedom and enjoying the newfound space.

'I feel bad that he will never be allowed to be free and wild,' Ed told Tammy.

'He's happy here – safe. Why didn't you just set every animal free?' Tammy asked.

'Because of another pandemic, for one thing. I know it was a biological attack, not a natural disaster, and it's not over yet. I can't tell you how I know or say anything else yet, but the bottom line is I worry about another virus wiping out the rare species we have left. Some of them are endangered in the wild for many other reasons too. It's not always safe for them out there and if we don't try to look after the rare ones, they'll become extinct. We must try to preserve their species, as we have lost too much already. Also, we want to show people who can't travel what animals are like, so they respect them, in the hope of discouraging them from wanting to hurt animals,' he said with a sigh.

'I know saving them from Pisces was a miracle, but it seems strange that they should still be endangered now. Why?'

'Lots of reasons really and they're all to do with people. They're hunted, their vast lands are destroyed by development – many reasons that have existed since before Pisces. I thought that such a virus outbreak would wake people up, that they would learn to appreciate all God's creatures. Still some people just didn't value this at all and their ignorance and selfishness continued. A safari park is educational and benefits the young mostly. It gives us a chance to help them see how wonderful these animals are and how wrong it is to endanger them. I believe that without such an opportunity many children would grow up to be adults who represent danger to wildlife. A lot of your generation still haven't seen any of these animals and if I can ensure that all the children of today grow up to respect animals then I can make a difference.'

'What do you mean?' Tammy asked.

'There are two types of people, Tammy. Fundamentally, the good and the bad. The rest of us just fall somewhere in the middle but always end up more at one end than the other. What I cannot bear are the ones who hurt animals. Zoos and safari parks and petting parks were old-fashioned ways by which we got young children to empathise with and love animals, so they grow up into adults who care about and love animals instead of those who dish out cruelty. Now too many grow up hardly ever seeing a dog or a cat, let alone other animals. It makes people forget that animals have feelings too. We have increased cruelty across the globe. Trophy hunting for ivory or tiger skins, for example, has never been fully prevented, but it is more dangerous now since numbers are even lower. The trouble is when something becomes illegal, it becomes more wanted.'

'That's terrible.' Tammy was thoughtful for a minute as she watched Jet race behind a bunch of trees then back to the Jeep. 'Isn't there more we can do?'

Ed smiled at her. 'That's where I'm hoping your talent with animals can come in very handy. I think you could help a great deal with animals.'

As the Jeep stopped outside the front of the house, Jude and the rest of the Labradors raced down to greet them. 'Where's Jet?' she asked.

Tammy walked to Jude's side and pointed to some trees to their right. Just then, Jet used his last burst of energy and darted out from behind the trees. He ran so fast that Ed and Jude held their breath in fear of an attack. Ed pushed Tammy and Jude behind him, to protect them. Tammy put a reassuring hand on Ed's arm, as Jet got closer. They relaxed. Jet slowed down and circled around them, before coming to a stop at Tammy's side. He was breathing hard, not used to this much exercise.

'I knew you could do it,' Jude said, as she grabbed Tammy and gave her the biggest hug she could.

Tammy laughed.

'Can I?' Jude asked, indicating that she wanted to pet Jet.

'Sure,' Tammy said, nodding her head.

Jet allowed Jude to pet him. He understood that they meant no harm. Jude smiled at Tammy and then noticed her pendant.

'It's glowing green!' she exclaimed.

'What is?' Ed asked.

'Tammy's pendant.' Jude pointed.

'Is this what you mentioned to me last night?' Ed asked Jude.

'Yes.'

'How very strange,' he mused as he turned it over and over in his hand. 'It's quite warm, isn't it?'

'Yes,' Tammy replied. 'It goes green a lot and feels warm. Earlier, it went bright red and felt so hot that I almost had to take it off.'

'Is it always either warm or hot?' Ed asked.

'No, normally I don't notice if it feels hot or cold. It's just normal. Then warmer when green and hot when red.'

'Hmm, how very strange. I'll have to look this up in the library and see what I can find out. In the meantime, try to pay attention to it and let me know anything else you see.' Looking at Jude, Ed said, 'Did *it* arrive?'

'Oh, yes *it* did,' said Jude, straightening up. '*It's* in the barn.'

'What?' asked Tammy.

'Your surprise.' Ed smiled mischievously.

Jude followed as Ed led Tammy to the barn. Tired, Jet walked slowly behind.

'You know I said I was going to get you your own small Jeep, more like a golf cart really, so you could go to the safari park by yourself?' Ed said.

'Yes?' Tammy was excited.

'Well, after what happened with the zebra, I decided not to,' he said with a smile.

'Oh,' Tammy said with disappointment.

'I got you this instead,' he said, pointing into the barn.

It was dark inside and Tammy could see nothing. Ed indicated that she go in. Tammy noticed a familiar smell as she walked into the barn, similar to that of the zebra. However, it was not a zebra that greeted Tammy's startled eyes. It was a very large horse. His coat was a shiny chestnut colour with a bright white stripe running down to his pink nose. His mane was a darker shade of brown, which matched his long, swishing tail.

Tammy gasped. 'He's gigantic!'

'The best purebred I could find you and yes, enormous. He's sixteen and a half hands and is still growing. He'll be seventeen hands,' Ed said proudly. 'He's almost five years old, just about the right age to start riding him properly. A friend of mine owed me a favour, a BIG favour. He is bred from the best Arabian bloodlines but be careful, stallions like this are known to be hot-blooded. Combine that with their agility, speed and spirit and you have a dangerous animal on your hands – not for everyone. However, my instinct told me this would be perfect for you.'

Tammy didn't answer. She couldn't. A tear of happiness rolled down her cheek and her throat seemed very tight. She put her arms around the horse and rested her head on his chest.

'Do you like him?' asked Jude.

Tammy still couldn't speak.

'It's love at first sight,' Jude whispered to Ed.

Ed nodded; the kind of smile on his face was the sort only a satisfied parent knows when a gift has been so gratefully received.

'This is the best thing that's ever happened to me,' Tammy said, as more tears of joy fell down her face.

'I had a feeling you would like a horse more than a Jeep. I hope I was right. Do you like him?' Ed asked.

'I love him. He's perfect,' Tammy said shakily.

'Then climb up on his back. What are you waiting for? I'll teach you to ride. For now, have a walk about on him,' Ed said.

Tammy pulled herself up onto the horse's bare back. The horse took a few steps and Tammy smiled. She leaned forward, whispered into the horse's ear then galloped at high speed through the field, with Jet following closely behind her.

'Well, so much for lessons. I hope she doesn't go too far,' said Jude.

'I don't think the horse or Jet will let anything happen to our little girl,' Ed reassured Jude.

'I hope you're right.'

'I know I am; my instinct says so. Tammy needs animals around her. I can see her changing by the hour. Jet adores her and the horse will too. I've always believed animals make the best friends a person can have,' Ed said, as he put his arm around Jude and they walked towards the house.

Dave arrived before Tammy was back from her horse ride. He, Ed and Jude watched as Tammy came charging towards the house astride the flying horse, Jet racing at their side. It was a marvellous sight. Tammy had taken to the horse easily, as Ed suspected. She was a natural rider. The look on her face as she came to a halt alongside them was one of pure pleasure, something that Tammy had not known much of during her short life.

'I'm sorry I took so long. You weren't waiting for me, were you?' she asked, throwing her legs over the side of Sirocco and dismounting.

'Don't worry, we're glad to see you enjoying yourself,' Jude said happily.

'I'll take the horse in while you shower,' Ed said, taking hold of the reins.

'No, it's all right, I'll do it. I won't be long. Thanks for the ride, Sirocco,' she said, kissing the horse in gratitude.

'Sirocco?' asked Dave in puzzlement.

'That's his name,' said Tammy.

'What made you choose Sirocco?' Dave asked.

'One of the teachers at school was born in Italy and told me all about the Sirocco wind. It's an extremely hot wind that blows from the north coast of Africa over the Mediterranean and parts of South Europe, especially Italy. It is immensely powerful and can cause a lot of damage. When the Sirocco wind passes by you, it moves your entire world. Sirocco's speed and strength as he ran reminded me of the story. Everything we passed felt him move through like a forceful storm. I'd forgotten all about the Sirocco wind until today. So that makes it a very appropriate name, doesn't it?'

Tammy skipped off to the barn with Sirocco, leaving an amused Dave staring after her. When she returned, they went into the house together for dinner.

*

'More pudding, anyone?'

'Oh no, I'm full, thank you, Jude. That was delicious,' Dave said.

'Yes, it was, especially the apple pie. I love apple pie,' added Tammy.

Jude cleared away the plates while Ed, Dave and Tammy carried on talking.

'I'm impressed with Jet's behaviour,' Dave said.

Jet had hardly moved from Tammy's side all evening. He was exhausted from the day's exercise and lay happy in the knowledge that Tammy was near.

'He has been good,' she said, stroking his head.

Jet purred in response.

'You ought to take her to Africa, Ed,' Dave said, after consideration.

'I've been thinking about it,' he replied. 'It is a good idea, just not yet. Tammy hasn't even had time to settle in at Brunswick and we're still not sure of what she can do.'

'Talking of Africa,' Jude said, returning from the kitchen, 'come into the library so I can show Tammy where it is on the map.'

Tammy listened intently, fascinated, as Jude showed her Africa and told her a little about it.

'Africa is the second largest continent on the planet. Earth is only one third land, and Africa is twenty-two percent of this,' Jude told her. 'A quarter of Africa is desert – the Sahara Desert.'

'Where does Jet come from?' Tammy asked.

'Jet is actually from the Amazon Basin, South America.' Jude pointed to the map.

'The Florida panther, which lives not far from Jet's natural home, is extremely endangered,' Ed added. 'There are only about fifty left in the wild. That's why we have Jet here. We were hoping to breed him with another female – it didn't work out.'

'Poor Jet,' Tammy said.

They all looked at Jet, who was lying on his back with all four paws in the air and his tongue hanging out the side of his mouth as he slept. They laughed.

'He doesn't seem to mind right now,' chuckled Dave.

'So, would you like to go to Africa, Tammy?' Jude asked.

'Very much. What was it you said about a safari team?'

'We sponsor a team to observe the wildlife in the parks. They watch all sorts of animals, though my main concern is with the cats. I'm eager to learn more about the leopard, cheetah and lion, who are all on the endangered species list at the moment,' Jude said.

'We always focus on the list and helping the populations in most danger there,' Ed explained.

'So, what could I do to help?' asked Tammy.

'That's just it, we still don't know. That's why we should wait a while. Illegal hunting is still a problem,' Jude said.

'If it's illegal and people obviously know they are endangering various species, why do people still do it?' Tammy asked.

'Selfishly, for the money or the sport,' Dave said bitterly. 'It works in their favour for the species to be endangered, as it drives the prices up.'

'On a lighter note, Tammy, it would also be a beautiful thing to experience. I adore driving around Africa in a Jeep and watching all the animals in their natural habitat,' Ed told her.

'And if an animal is injured, we have our own hospital that helps bring them back to health. It's really a wonderful experience to set an animal free,' Jude added, with a gleam in her eye. 'I'll never forget the day I set that cheetah free. Remember that, Ed? His leg had been caught in a trap and was injured quite badly so it took a while to heal. Once the little fellow was better, we took him out in a secure cage, back to his homeland. I stood on top of the small cage and opened it up. At any time, the cheetah could have turned and attacked me. That was the risk I took when opening the box. I wanted to be the one to do it. The cheetah took a while and then ran like crazy. I don't think he even saw me, but it was still frightening. I was so relieved when it was over. Yet as I watched him run away, remembering how he hadn't even been able to walk when we found him, I felt so happy.'

'She cried,' Ed said lovingly. 'It was a very emotional experience, to feel frightened by the animal and at the same time happy for it to be free.'

'Words can't explain it, dear. I hope you get the chance to experience that someday, Tammy,' Jude said with a smile.

Tammy made Jude tell her all about the experiences she had in Africa. Though exhausted, she struggled to stay awake to hear as much as possible. She finally fell asleep and Ed carried her up to bed. Jet jumped on the bed alongside her. Ed and Jude smiled as the two slept peacefully together.

*

They joined Dave in the library.

'So, what do you think of our dear Tammy, Dave?' Jude asked as she sat down next to the fireplace.

'Nothing short of a miracle, Jude. I was just thinking how the animals seem to be much happier here lately, and I think it's to do with Tammy.'

'I've noticed that too,' she said.

'What about you, Ed? You've been awfully quiet,' Dave asked.

'I'm contemplating taking another big risk tomorrow,' Ed said thoughtfully.

'Oh?' Dave enquired.

'I'm going to test Tammy to her full ability. What work did you have planned for her tomorrow, Dave?'

'I want her to watch the elephants in the morning and then start on the rhinos. I think she can handle it,' Dave answered.

'I agree. However, don't start her on the rhinos yet. Take her to see the little bull, Nutt, in the afternoon. Then she'll have met all the elephants. Then have her meet Ben and me at the reptile house at three o'clock.'

'Ed, what are you thinking?' Jude asked.

'I want Ben and Tammy to work together with the snakes.'

'Are you sure that's safe?' Dave asked, a little startled.

'No. However, I'm willing to risk it if Tammy is, and I know she is. I need to know how far she can charm these animals. I would rather find out here, at the safari park, than out in the wild,' Ed said.

'I see your point. I'll arrange it,' Dave said.

'Do that,' said Ed.

He was nervous, knowing that tomorrow was going to be yet another remarkable day.

*

Tammy tossed and turned in her bed, her restlessness forcing Jet to get off and lay down on the floor instead. She was sweating, mumbling, trying to work out what was happening. She could see a boy and she recognised him. She knew it was a dream and yet there was something different about this dream. This was similar to ones she had experienced in the past. The kind of dream that feels real. The boy, about her age, looked a little like her, same colour eyes and hair. He was calling her name over and over again. His arms were reaching out to her. It scared her. She didn't know why but as his arms reached out to touch her, she felt scared and was trying to get away.

Then she awoke. Breathing heavily, she looked around the room and then at Jet. He was watching her calmly. The dream was over. She smiled and patted Jet's head. The sun was barely up and she thought about a morning ride with Sirocco before going to the safari park. Sirocco was so strong that it took Tammy's breath away, galloping at a speed and with a power that thrilled her. It made her feel so alive. Sometimes she would ride with her face resting on his neck, feeling his strength with every stride. She adored Sirocco. Like her, he was young and yielded a power he had not yet mastered. She smiled, got dressed and told Jet to follow her.

Ed watched them from his bedroom window. 'Look at this,' he told Jude.

She joined Ed at the window and they watched Tammy and Sirocco gallop towards the house. It was an incredible sight.

'She's a brilliant rider,' Ed admitted. 'She rides as if she was born on a horse.'

Jude placed her hand on Ed's shoulder.

'You love her very much, don't you?' she asked.

He nodded and returned her smile. 'Yes, she's an incredible girl. There is something else too, as if she is a kindred spirit or something, like I felt with Sarah too.'

'I do know what you mean and I think getting her that horse was the best idea you've ever had,' Jude told him.

*

Later, Tammy rode Sirocco alongside the Jeep, with Jet keeping pace behind them, down to the safari park. The morning went quickly. It was Tammy's first breakfast with the elephants. She had started with mixing their breakfast with the various vitamins and minerals Dave had shown her. The elephants were not as playful as they were when taking their showers; breakfast just wasn't as much fun.

'I was thinking that we could go to the animal hospital and see Nutt. First, we have to clean up here. Is that okay with you?' Dave asked.

'Definitely,' Tammy said with a smile.

It took a while to clean up the pachyderm house, mostly because of all the paperwork. Then they ate lunch. By two o'clock, they were at the animal hospital. Nutt was an adorable little creature. Thanks to Dr Crane's efforts, he was now so strong it was hard to imagine he had almost died for being too weak and small.

Suzie, the mother, wouldn't let Dave near her baby; she wouldn't let anyone except the vet near him. Until Tammy came along. Within five minutes, Tammy and Nutt were playing.

'Well, this is a surprise! You must be Tammy?' Dr Crane asked as he approached the pen. He walked lazily, as if he had no interest in anything and was in no hurry. His balding mousy brown hair lay flat and lifeless on his shiny head. His face was serious and stern, looking as if he hadn't smiled for many years, just blank – no laughter or frown lines. Despite this, he had a warmness about him and made you feel comfortable in his presence.

'Yes. You must be the vet, Dr Crane?'

'I am indeed. Everyone calls me Crane. Pleased to meet you,' he said, shaking her hand. 'I see Suzy and Nutt have taken a liking to you already. I'm surprised.'

'You'll be even more surprised to learn that Ed has allowed Tammy to take the black panther up to the house.' Dave winked knowingly.

Crane raised his eyebrows.

'Only at night-time,' Tammy explained.

'Tammy and the panther have become very close friends,' Dave said, in a tone that said *I know something you don't know.*

'In the house?' Crane said. 'I can't believe that.'

'When you see it, you'll believe it,' Dave said smugly.

Just then, a small grey-haired woman came running up. Her face was flushed and she looked worried.

'Crane! Oh, Crane! You must help me. The rhino woke up before I had chance to move him from the operating theatre,' she said, gasping breathlessly.

Tammy and Dave followed Crane as he ran after his assistant towards the operating theatre. As they got nearer, they heard a loud banging – it was the rhino charging at the door to the operating theatre.

'I don't believe this,' Crane yelled. 'How come he woke up? I gave him a shot that should have put him out cold for hours. Jenny, get me a syringe.'

They were watching the confused rhino from behind a glass wall several inches thick. While Crane and Jenny were getting a syringe prepared, Tammy got up close to the glass and looked in at the rhino. It wasn't too long before the creature sensed Tammy's presence. Once the rhino saw Tammy, he started to calm down and move towards her. The rhino was scared. He had just had an operation to remove a lump in his side and had woken up confused and bewildered. Tammy could tell that her presence made him feel secure – she told him nothing could happen to him while she was around. In no time at all, he had calmed down.

Tammy moved away from the window and went to the door. Crane went to stop her; Dave held him back.

'Watch,' was all he said.

Although he felt uneasy, Crane let Tammy go.

Tammy placed a reassuring hand on the rhino's back.

'It'll be all right. We'll have you back home in no time,' she said.

Crane cautiously slipped into the theatre.

'I'm just going to give him this injection. It should put him back to sleep until we get him back to his pen,' he said.

'Don't drug him. I'll take him back to his pen. Nothing will happen,' Tammy assured him.

'And how do you propose to do that?' Crane asked.

'I'll walk him back,' she said.

'No way!'

'He'll be all right, honestly.'

'Tammy, this is a safari park. There are visitors out there. If they see a rhino coming towards them, they'll run. It'll cause a panic,' he said abruptly.

Tammy looked down at the floor, upset at Crane's response.

'I know, let Tammy walk the rhino to the hospital Jeep and then she can ride with him to his pen. That way, you're both happy,' Dave suggested.

So, Tammy found herself riding in the back of the covered Jeep with a rhino. After unloading him, she watched in satisfaction as he rejoined his mate.

'I don't believe it,' Crane said as Tammy joined him and Dave by the gate of the pen.

'I told you so,' Dave said, smiling.

'How did you do that?' Crane asked.

Tammy looked at Dave and smiled.

'Animals seem to like me,' she said.

'Well, that was something I haven't seen before. By the way, I'm Crane's assistant, Jenny,' said the grey-haired woman by way of introduction.

'Hi,' Tammy said, shaking her hand. 'Are you a veterinary nurse?'

'They call me the nurse but I'm not yet qualified so I'm still an assistant. You were really incredible with that rhino,' she said.

'You should see her with the elephants, and the panther for that matter,' Dave said, laughing.

'Where have you been hiding her?' Crane asked as he placed his arm around Tammy's shoulder. 'We could have done with her last month when the gorilla refused to have his infected gums treated. Gave me a black eye! That was one black eye I could have done without. Hard to operate on anyone when one eye is swollen shut!'

'I only got here a couple of days ago,' Tammy explained.

'If you want some more excitement, you could come to the reptile house with us,' Dave said.

'Are we going there now?' Tammy asked. It was the first she had heard about it.

'Yes, we are. We're meeting Ed and Ben there.'

'What are you going there for?' asked Jenny.

'That would be telling. You'd better come and see.' Dave chuckled mischievously.

ELEVEN

A DEADLY RISK

Ed was standing outside the reptile house with a hesitant smile on his lips. Tammy chuckled at his anxiety. She wasn't worried at all and felt that everything would be all right. She had felt it all along and only now could she be confident about it.

'What's all this?' Ed asked, as he surveyed the crowd behind Tammy.

'Crane and Jenny had a little help off Tammy at the hospital and wanted to witness more of her gift,' Dave explained.

'I see,' said Ed, not sounding pleased. He didn't want everyone to know about Tammy yet.

'Where's Ben?' asked Tammy.

'Inside. Let's go in and join him, shall we?' Ed said, as they followed him in.

Ben struck Tammy as a strange sort of person. He was short and skinny. Yet he had a large, square face and thick, curly black hair. His head seemed too big for his body and Tammy couldn't help staring a little longer than she should have. Ben noticed and yet said nothing – he was used to it.

His body had always been out of proportion and he knew that was why he had liked snakes since he was a boy: they also looked odd. In addition, his small body enabled him to be extremely quick in moving out of their way when necessary.

Ben didn't normally like people and by the same token most people were wary of him. He was different and only the Brunswicks had ever made him feel comfortable. They understood his love of reptiles and appreciated him for it. There was something about Tammy that made him feel comfortable in much the same way.

They were in the supply room, where all the antivenom and food was stored. Only the backs of the snakes' vivariums were visible from here, each covered with a wooden door. Some of the doors had *HOT* marked on them in big red letters. She remembered Ed telling her about that – those were the venomous ones. Now she knew why they were labelled, since you couldn't actually see the snakes from here.

There were also some snakes in vivariums that she could see. These weren't on show for the safari park visitors. 'Why are these here?' she asked.

'For various reasons. Some are new and would be too nervous if put out on display straight away. We give them some time to settle in here first,' Ben explained.

'Which ones are new?' she asked.

Ben pointed out two of the snakes.

'This one here has something wrong with her. I'm not sure what yet. Crane won't deal with the reptiles at his hospital.' Ben gave Crane a condescending look.

'You're not scared of them, are you?' Tammy asked him.

'Not at all, I just don't like them,' Crane replied hastily, and looked away, trying to hide his embarrassment.

'Are you one of those rare people who appreciate reptiles for what they are?' Ben asked.

'What do you mean?'

'Well, I think reptiles are greatly misunderstood. People don't like them because they are not furry or cute to look at. I see something different in you; you treat all animals equally,' he said.

'You can tell that just from looking at me?' Tammy asked, surprised.

'It's not hard,' Ben said, laughing. 'There is usually a look of fear, disgust or confusion on most people's faces when they look at something like a snake. You don't have any of those expressions.'

'I don't understand why I should see them differently,' she replied. She liked Ben; he was upfront and blunt and she liked that about him.

'You're very perceptive, Ben. I want you to help Tammy get to know the snakes,' Ed said. Until now, he had kept Ben in the dark about the reason she was here.

'It'd be my pleasure.' Ben smiled; he liked talking about snakes.

'Well, not in the usual way,' Ed said, anticipating what Ben was thinking. 'She wants to hold them – all of them.'

'It's not that simple,' Ben replied, a little confused. He knew Ed well enough to know he understood the dangers of the snakes and that he would never ask Ben to let a young girl hold one of them.

'Ben, Tammy has a way with animals. She seems to have a connection with them, even the most dangerous. We have the black panther sleeping at our house at night because he's become so attached to her – you'd think he was a normal house kitten to see him now.'

Ben looked at Tammy in surprise, who avoided his stare and then turned back to Ed. 'So, what exactly do you want me to do?' Ben asked.

'Basically, get ready to administer some antivenom if the snakes don't react the way I expect them to,' Ed said.

'There's a specific way of picking them up, a particular way to approach them, she needs to learn—'

'I'll be fine,' Tammy said.

'I just want you on hand to get the snake away and do what's necessary if anything goes wrong,' Ed told Ben.

Ben nodded. He knew better than to ask Ed if he knew what he was doing – Ed always knew what he was doing. Furthermore, Crane, his assistant, Jenny, and Dave all seemed impatient with Ben for needing an explanation. They all seemed convinced that nothing would go amiss and wanted to get on with it.

'Just show me the king cobra's door and you'll see,' Tammy said.

'Okay. Just a minute,' Ben said.

It was obvious that Ben wasn't happy with the situation. He went to a fridge and brought out two large syringes with a yellow serum in them.

'The antivenom,' Ben said, and then pointed to one of the doors labelled *HOT*.

Tammy slowly opened the door Ben had pointed to. As soon as she did, the cobra uncoiled himself and swayed from side to side. The sides of his neck opened up, making his head look spoon-shaped. He was ready to attack.

Everyone held their breath as the snake swayed back and forth at Tammy. Ben stepped forward, ready to grab the snake. Suddenly the snake relaxed. He slithered closer to the door as Tammy held out her hand. The now thin black head poked out of the door and the snake surveyed everyone in the room with an intelligence he hadn't shown before. Then he looked back at Tammy. She touched the snake's head. The snake pushed his head closer into her hand before moving up her arm and around her neck, so that his long body was now hanging over her shoulders. With his tail draping down her arm and his head around her shoulder, the snake turned to look directly into Tammy's face. As Tammy stroked the snake, he lowered his head, content to be held. She turned around and smiled at everyone. They were all tense and motionless.

'You can relax now,' she said.

Ed let out a long sigh that he had been holding a while. Dave smiled and nodded to Crane.

'You see,' he chuckled, as his point was proven.

Crane nodded, completely amazed.

'This is fantastic,' Ben said excitedly, his concerns forgotten.

He looked so thrilled they all thought he was going to start bouncing up and down. 'What about the others?'

'I could hold them all,' Tammy said, confidently, and turned to the next door labelled *HOT*.

Within half an hour, Ben, Dave, Crane, Jenny and Ed were pressed up against the wall, as far away from Tammy as they could get. They were looking on as Tammy sat on the floor with sixteen highly venomous snakes moving around her. None of the snakes moved too far away from Tammy's side, which didn't stop the other occupants of the room from being worried. They were no longer concerned about Tammy; it was what the snakes would do to them if they got too close that made them all worry. Ed remembered the way the cobra had reacted to him through the glass and knew it was only Tammy they wouldn't hurt. There were just too many snakes about the room for it to be safe. Ed noticed how green Tammy's pendant had become.

'Maybe you should start putting them back now,' Ed said, as calmly as he could.

'Yes, Tammy. There's too many out,' Dave added.

'I'll put them back on one condition,' Tammy said with a smile.

'What's that?' Ed frowned.

'I want to go into the crocodile quarters.'

'I don't know.' Ed hesitated.

'If she can hold that many snakes, I don't see the problem,' Ben said.

'The crocodiles acted differently to her, though,' Ed said.

'That's why I have to see them,' Tammy explained. 'Besides, I'm not putting the snakes back until you say yes.'

They all looked at Ed and he knew he had little choice in the matter.

'Oh, all right then,' he said reluctantly.

'Can I keep her with me, Ed? She'd be a great help with the snakes,' Ben said, after all the snakes had been put away.

'No, she's my helper with the elephants and I've never had such a good assistant. I'm not about to lose her,' Dave said.

'Stop it, you lot,' Ed said with a smile.

'Tammy, before we go to the crocodiles, can you take a look at this sick snake and see if you can tell what's wrong with her?' Ben asked.

'Of course,' she said, going over to where Ben stood.

'What are the symptoms?' Crane asked.

'She won't eat, her skin is pale, and she hardly moves at all.' Ben sighed.

'It sounds more like she's sulking about something,' Crane said with a sniff, promptly receiving a dirty look from Ben.

Tammy was holding the snake and stroking her, feeling her body and looking into her eyes. She turned and looked at Ben.

'Well?' he said.

'She's had a very long journey,' Tammy said sadly.

'What do you mean?' he asked.

'She came from a dry area. A lot of sand, dry bushes and hardly any water.'

'Are you sure? I was told she had been bred in captivity,' Ben said.

Tammy shook her head.

'It's been illegally imported,' Ed said. 'Who did you get it off, Ben?'

'A guy I know. I know where he is,' Ben said angrily. 'So, is she going to die, Tammy?'

'No, not now, she'll bounce back. Also, the vivarium is too humid for her. It needs to be drier. She isn't used to all this moistness.'

'Where is this type of snake's native home?' Dave asked.

'Australia. They are usually used to a bit more humidity if captive bred. I'll set up a dry vivarium to resemble the Australian bush. She'll feel more at home there.'

'That's a good idea,' Tammy said. She was still stroking the snake, who now appeared more contented.

'Find the man you got her from, Ben. I want an explanation and I want the police involved, understood?' Ed said.

'It goes without saying, Ed. I want him caught more than you do. Snakes are a lot more sensitive than people give them credit for. A slight change of environment completely unsettles them, and this is cruelty,' Ben agreed.

'Let me know if you need my assistance,' Ed said.

'I will.'

'She's travelled far and been treated roughly. She has several small fractures along her skeleton. They're not too bad and are healing by themselves now. I've made her feel safe and if you give her a home similar to what she's used to, she'll get better soon. Let's feed her now, she's hungry,' Tammy said.

'So why wouldn't she eat before?' Ben asked.

'She didn't have the heart to, now she wants to live.'

Everyone exchanged looks and then looked at Tammy as she took a dead mouse from Ben's fridge and dangled it over the snake. Crane looked away as the snake leapt into the air, grabbed her food and wrapped herself around it. The snake dislocated her jaw to swallow her dinner.

'She has a gift,' Ben said, nudging Crane, who still looked disgusted.

They all nodded in agreement.

*

Everybody went with Tammy to the crocodile quarters. They all lined up alongside the glass partition and looked in.

No one wanted to miss a thing. Tammy left them standing there and went around to the back, entering through the staff door. None of the crocodiles moved as Tammy opened the door.

'These don't seem to show the same respect to Tammy as the other animals,' Ed commented.

'Crocodiles come across that way. They are generally loners, who survive by themselves. If she gets close to snakes, she can get close to anything, I think,' Dave said reassuringly.

'I'm not so sure, crocs don't act like any other species,' Ben replied.

Tammy walked to the side of the pool and knelt down. She held out her hand and waited. It was even hotter inside the crocodiles' enclosure than it was in the reptile house. The air, hot and clammy, made it hard for her to breathe. However, she hid her discomfort from the others – she didn't want them to see how uncomfortable she felt now that she was close to the crocodiles. She had been worried about the crocodiles from the start. She could not read or understand them like she could the other animals she had met. They seemed to have a barrier that she couldn't break through.

'Why don't you talk to me?' she asked. Still they didn't move. She looked into their stone-like eyes and saw no sign of life. They could have been statues for all she knew.

Tammy's legs were starting to ache, so she shifted position. For a brief moment, she thought she saw a glimmer of understanding in the female's eyes. Then, the male started to slowly move and headed towards Tammy. He came to a stop when he was very close alongside her. Suddenly the female made a fast turn and darted to Tammy's other side. The movement was so quick it almost made Tammy jump back – she managed to stay still. A tremor of fear ran through her body as she realised they were not friendly.

The pendant around Tammy's neck felt suddenly hot and, looking down, Tammy noticed it was glowing red. Both crocodiles were now awfully close. The tips of their large jaws were within reach of Tammy's hand. Tammy didn't move her hand, though she did not intend putting it any closer either. She knew they would snap. She had looked into their eyes and seen something evil. It wasn't hate, just a natural instinct to destroy. The crocodiles were cold and calculating killers. They saw Tammy as nothing more than another meal.

'I don't like this,' Ed said. He knew something wasn't right and he was heading towards the back door when Tammy looked up.

'Ed,' Dave shouted.

Ed stopped and looked across at Tammy. She had a tear in her eye and silently mouthed the words *stay there* to him. He stayed where he was and they all watched as one of the crocodiles opened its large jaws and launched itself at Tammy.

Tammy saw the glint in the female's eyes as she leapt forward, taking Tammy's arm between her large, strong jaws. Tammy stopped a cry of pain escaping from her mouth as she felt the jaw snap shut, determined not to let the crocodiles know she was scared and maintaining eye contact. Then the male pushed himself up and forward, grabbing Tammy's other arm. Tammy knew what was coming next. The pain in her arms was intense and she could feel the crocodiles' teeth – readying themselves to pull and tear her apart.

Ed gulped. 'Why did I let her do this?'

'Crocodiles don't think about tearing someone apart, they just do it,' Ben said, in a surprisingly calmer tone. 'However, they're thinking about it. A crocodile wouldn't hold a person like that. They bite and yank whatever they've got straight off. Look, they've paused.'

'Don't do it,' Tammy said, as she looked from one to the other. She saw something in their eyes; it was only slight, but it was there. Some type of communication was getting through. This gave Tammy some hope. They were wondering about her. Their instinct told them to tear at her arms, yet something stronger was preventing them from doing it. Feeling more confident, yet still scared, Tammy leaned closer to their eyes.

'I said don't do it!' she told them.

Still they didn't loosen their hold on her. Tammy tried pulling her arm out of the female's mouth and felt the jaws tighten. However, the death-like intensity in their eyes had subsided a little and Tammy sensed their confusion.

Tammy dropped her head closer still, until her chin rested on the crocodile's jaw and their eyes were level. It was an uncomfortable position because the male still had a tight hold on her other arm. Then, Tammy realised what was happening: their instinct told them to hurt her – her willpower prevented them from doing it.

'That's how I do it,' Tammy whispered to herself. She stared at the female, willing her to let go of her arm. It seemed a long time that their gazes were locked, and then the female suddenly released her grip.

Tammy let her arm fall to her side. It was bleeding and hurt. Ignoring the pain, she turned her attention to the male and did the same to him and he too let go. The crocodiles didn't back away. They were not scared of Tammy and did not respect her like the other animals did. They now knew that they couldn't hurt her. Looking down at her pendant, she now saw it had changed to white and felt as cold as ice.

'Crocodiles just don't need friends,' Tammy muttered. 'They don't need anyone.' She knew where she stood with them and she knew how to deal with it. Tammy was surprised by her discovery and couldn't wait to tell Ed.

*

They had all nearly cried with relief when they saw the crocodiles let go of Tammy's arms.

'Thank God!' Ed exclaimed.

'Yes, thank God,' Dave said shakily.

Tammy came back to them, her arms hanging loosely at her side, still bleeding.

'Are you okay?' Crane asked, as he investigated the damage.

'Yes,' she said, 'I think so.'

'That must have been frightening,' Ben said. 'I felt useless just watching.'

Tammy nodded and smiled.

'Let's find somewhere to sit and I'll bandage your arms up. As far as I can see, it doesn't look serious, just small scratches where the teeth have pierced the skin. You're so lucky,' Crane said.

'That's not luck,' Dave said, arms folded.

'I'll get your medical bag.'

'Thanks, Jenny.'

*

They were seated in the room where the snake antivenom was held. Crane was busy attending to Tammy's wounds.

'I thought you were a goner there,' Ed said, as he brushed her hair back off her face.

Tammy smiled at his affection. She realised how much Ed loved her.

'I don't understand what happened, Tammy. Tell me about it,' Ben asked.

'Not now, Ben. It must have been very traumatic for Tammy,' Ed said.

'It's all right. I'm fine, honestly. Besides, you ought to know what happened.'

Dave passed Tammy a cup of sweet tea that she gingerly sipped as she told them about how the crocodiles had reacted.

'They don't need or want me. Other animals need me, hear me and tell me their thoughts – they want me to be by their side. It makes them feel safe and secure, as if they have a protective friend in me. To some animals, like the mammals, there is an automatic connection. There is not much of a difference between them and us.'

'The reptiles are different?' Ben asked.

'Yes, snakes are charmed by me as if I'm putting them under a spell of some sort – I make them feel relaxed and at peace.'

'The crocodiles have no connection with you, so they don't need a friend, eh?' said Crane, as he finished bandaging her arms and stood up.

'They don't need anyone and they aren't scared of anything. All they know what to do is kill to survive, and they saw me as another meal. When they went to attack, they couldn't, and it confused them. They went for my arms without even thinking about it. When it came to tearing them off, they stopped. The reason is because I wouldn't let them. I understand what it is I do to them. With animals like the crocodiles, I have to force my will upon them. I can feel their instinctive nature and I influence it to my own advantage. I make them feel my instinct, if you like.' Tammy paused to take a sip of tea.

'Do you mean you made them not hurt you?' Ed asked.

'Yes. Imagine you're in a shop and you see something you want, like a toy. You want this toy so badly that you're tempted to just take it, without having the money for it. There's a voice in your head that tells you it's wrong, that you shouldn't do it. Whether you listen to the voice or not depends upon what is strongest. The urge to take the toy or the voice that tells you not to. That's how it was with the crocodiles. Their instinct told them to attack me, but my will became their conscience. I was the voice inside their head telling them that they shouldn't do it. I didn't realise it at first, and that's why they got as far as they did. I had to be stronger than their instinct and make them feel that what they thought was right was actually wrong. Once they understood, they backed off. They now know that they can't hurt me because it feels wrong to hurt me. They're not sure why, which unsettles them, so they don't want me around. I go against all that they know, you see.'

'You changed their instinctive behaviour?' Ben asked.

'No. I added to it,' Tammy said.

'So that's why they don't want you around, you confuse them. They've gone against their instinct by not hurting you, which complicates matters for them.' Ben smiled in understanding.

'Incredible,' Dave said.

'What I really want to know is whether there are any animals that are a big threat to you, Tammy?' Ed asked.

'Not really. I'll just have to be on my guard with animals like the crocodiles,' she said.

'You have to consider that crocodiles have been around for millions of years, surviving as they are with little need to evolve in any way. Maybe you have to be a pure killer and not need anyone else to survive for that long,' Ben said.

'Yes, and I do respect them,' Tammy said. 'I just wish they'd respect me.'

'This is fantastic, do you realise what we could do with your talent?' Ben said excitedly.

'We won't jump to conclusions yet,' Ed said. 'I want to get Tammy to Africa and see how much help she can be with wild animals. We must keep this secret among ourselves, as who knows what the world at large might do if they found out about this. I know I can trust each and every one of you.'

'I can go to Africa with you?' Tammy squealed excitedly.

'Yes, when I think you are ready,' Ed said with a nod of the head.

'You can't take her away. This place will feel odd without her, even though she hasn't been here long. It's as if you've always been a part of this place, Tammy. I'll even miss you myself, it won't be just the animals,' Dave said.

Tammy smiled sweetly.

'Well, she won't be in Africa for a long time yet and it'll only be a short trip away. Let's call it a day, we have a lot to tell Jude,' Ed said.

Ben stayed behind to lock up and make sure the animals were all right before he left. He stopped an extra-long time to look at the crocodiles, remembering the way they had held Tammy in their jaws. It sent a shiver down his spine and he shook his head in disbelief.

'What a girl,' he said, and turned away.

TWELVE

MIKIE DISHES OUT
EMBARRASSMENT

Mikie was at the school gates again, discreetly watching the kids leave school, as he did now and then. He had only been once since the fight he and Dan had finished with the older teenagers and for the second time in a row he was happy to see Dan walking out of school with a group of kids around him and no longer on his own. The gang stood quiet and a little bit dubious watching him and still trying to figure out how a thin little twelve-year-old had knocked the stuffing out of them with just one friend. None of them could really remember. Dan was happy. Popular. Mikie was pleased despite the sense of loss he felt inside. He would do anything to have even just one friend.

Dan caught his older sister smiling at Adam, one of the bullies, as she walked past him and the gang slowly and deliberately. He didn't yet fancy girls and found his flirtatious sister a huge embarrassment, but all the older lads fancied her. What upset him even more was her now flirting with Adam. Dan couldn't bear it if she started dating the rugby captain that had once been his bully. Imagine that. Dan would sooner die. Mikie watched as Dan glared at his sister.

Just then, Adam stepped forward and fell into stride with Claire, Dan's older sister. Her eyes lit up. All the girls fancied Adam. They would be the most handsome and popular couple in the school if they got together. She could almost feel everyone watching her with jealousy as he walked next to her awkwardly and shyly, wondering how to ask her out on a date. Dan glared as they walked away from the school, across the park, far too close together for his liking. Mikie smiled and, after telling himself to leave it three times in a row, found he couldn't resist, and went after them.

'So, I've seen you come and watch the rugby a lot with your friends,' Adam said nervously.

'Yeah, we like rugby,' she said, smiling.

'Right.'

'Do you like rugby?' Claire could have hit herself for such a stupid question, but it was out there now and there was nothing she could do about it.

'Yeah.'

'Nice.'

They walked in an awkward silence. After a painful age and far too many attempts to speak, Adam finally found his tongue.

'So, I wondered if you were free. For a date like…'

'Yeah.'

'Cool. Erm, I was going to get you a bunch of flowers, but I didn't know if girls really like that sort of thing,' Adam mumbled, flushing awkwardly, his cheeks glowing bright red.

'Yeah, we do. We girls like things like that.' Claire smiled. 'If you don't have money to buy any you can always pick some. It's the thought that counts. and I love freshly picked ones.'

Mikie saw his opportunity as he carefully followed them. Sniggering to himself as he invaded Adam's mind. All he could think about was what a shame no one else would ever witness such a special moment. Mikie took control of Adam and tried not to make a noise laughing as Claire gaped in disgust at what she saw next. Adam stuck his index finger far up his left nostril and began digging about deeply for the biggest bogie he could find. Not much there. He removed his finger, wiped it on the sleeve of Claire's cardigan, much to her open-mouthed chagrin, and then tried the other nostril. After a fair bit of digging around, he pulled out a nice, big, juicy green bogie and promptly examined it. Smiling proudly, he then stuck his index finger out to her.

'Here you go, I picked this for you. How's that for fresh pickings?' As the words came out of Adam's mouth, he felt all the blood drain from his face in sheer embarrassment and wondered what on earth he was thinking and doing.

'Oh my God!' Claire gasped with disgust and took a step backwards as he tried to wipe it on her cardigan again. 'That is so gross. What is wrong with you?'

'What, that not big enough?' Adam said, wiping it on his trouser leg, where it remained large and intrusive and a big focal point for Claire. Then, as mortified as he was, he couldn't stop himself from adding, 'Well, I would also like to buy you a bottle of perfume. Do you like perfume?'

'I do…' she said, but more hesitantly now.

'Well, smell this and tell me if you would like this bottled.'

With which Adam turned around, bent over and aimed his rear end in her direction, letting off the most disgusting loud and lengthy fart Claire had heard in the longest time. She was so mortified and disgusted that she couldn't speak. She just clamped her jaws shut and marched away as fast as her legs could carry her.

'Claire, wait!' Adam yelled, turning to face her with a look of shock and horror all over his face.

Claire didn't see it. She barely glanced back as she shouted over her shoulder, 'You are a horrible pig, Adam Stanley, a pig, I tell you!'

Mikie dropped to his knees laughing hysterically and trying not to get noticed. His cheeks ached with the constant smiling and his belly was killing him as he held it, laughing and rolling on the grass. It was the funniest thing he had ever done. If only he had been able to share that with Dan and let him see what he had done. Oh, to have such a wonderful moment and no one to share it with. And then someone spoke to him.

'I owe you one,' Dan said, smiling broadly.

Mikie, startled, stood up and looked at Dan. He hadn't seen him coming. He had been too focused on embarrassing Adam.

'Where did you come from?' Mikie gasped.

'I saw you follow them, so I followed you. I knew you could make things happen, I just knew it.' Dan was still smiling. 'That was flipping awesome!'

'It was, wasn't it?' Mikie said with a smile.

'Yeah, look at his face, he's mortified!' Dan laughed.

'You mustn't tell anyone,' Mikie said, looking serious and worried now, thinking what Uncle Stephen would say if he ever found out.

'I never talk about you, Mikie,' Dan said seriously. 'You're my friend and I will never tell people what you can do. I didn't before and I won't now.'

Mikie nodded. He knew Dan was reliable and trustworthy.

'Thanks, Dan.'

'Oh no, thank you. That was priceless. That was absolutely amazing to see.'

'It was pretty good, wasn't it?' Mikie nodded, proud that he could share this with someone for once. What harm could it do after all?

'Yes, it was. Come with me, let's catch up over an ice cream and have a laugh at Adam's expense,' Dan said, and they headed across the park. 'I have really missed you, Mikie.'

'Well, being the only friend I ever had, I missed you too,' Mikie replied.

'Everyone is so boring compared to you,' Dan said. And he meant it.

What harm can having a secret friend do? Mikie thought as they walked together laughing and completely unaware of the small metal insect buzzing about behind them trying to get a look at their faces and analyse the data. Mikie had pulled out his baseball cap and shoved it over his head as far as it would go, just in case Stephen spotted him with Dan, not wanting to be recognised or caught out. But the seeker had captured his name, part of his face and Dan's whole face. That might be all that was needed.

THIRTEEN

JAX

Time passed quickly for Tammy. There were so many animals and hours of fun to be had that she struggled to fit in everything she wanted to do. In no time at all, it was the first weekend of the summer holidays and the arrival of the Brunswicks' nephew, Jax, was upon them. He was a couple of years older than Tammy. Despite reassurances from Ed and Jude, Tammy was anxious about the visit. She had made only one friend at the orphan school and was worried what would happen if Jax disliked her. She was used to being unpopular.

Ed set off with Fudge to meet Jax at the hovercraft landing stage and bring him back to the house, which was almost Jax's second home. Ed privately believed it was Jax's first home, apart from his boarding school, since his parents were often away working. Jax adored the island; the Brunswicks adored Jax. Fudge would replay all he saw to Tammy as if she were there. She smiled and winked at Fudge as he left.

'Hello, Uncle Ed,' Jax said, hugging his uncle then stroking Fudge.

'Oh, look at you, taller and more grown up every time.' Ed laughed and pulled Jax into a tight hug. 'How's that sister of mine?'

'She sends her love, as always, and thanks you for having me. Mum and Dad are exhibiting some huge European art tour this summer so won't even have time to come here for a week. It's just us – again!'

'Just the way I like it.' Ed laughed, pulling Jax closer to his side. His sister was the most selfish woman he had ever known, and it broke his heart how she treated Jax – as if he was always an annoying obstacle in her way. She hardly ever saw the boy; sent him away to boarding school most of the year and the safari park in the holidays. Ed and Jude couldn't understand it, not being able to have children themselves, so they showered him with their love to compensate. 'Let's get in the Jeep and you can tell me all about uni,' Ed said.

Jax was an advanced student and had been put forward by four years. He was already studying to be a vet even though he should have still been in school. Ed had been the same as a boy, as had his sister. Their whole family history boasted many famed academics.

'Uni is okay, I suppose. Some things I don't like and others are fun. My grades are good.' Jax smiled up at Ed.

'Still stuck with the vet thing, eh?'

'Always.'

'You're still young and could always change your mind.'

'Isn't that what you've been telling me since I was six, Uncle Ed?'

'No doubt I'll be saying the same thing in another six years' time. You will make a good vet. I just expected you to want to be running this island, and you won't be able to do that and be a full-time vet.'

'I just need to be a vet. That's all I know right now. Your island is in safe hands with you for a very long time yet. My heart lies with helping animals. I care less for humans.'

'I suppose I can try to live a while longer then,' Ed grinned, 'if you promise to stop calling me Uncle. It makes me feel too old now you're growing up.'

'Stop it!' Jax nudged him in the ribs, making Ed flinch and rub the area. 'You're getting softer, old man, better cut back on all that good food Aunt Jude keeps making you.' They laughed.

'So, Jax, are you looking forward to meeting Tammy?' Ed asked, glancing at him sideways.

'Yes, I can't wait.'

'Are you nervous?'

'No, should I be?'

'Of course not, but she is a little nervous about meeting you. I guess she hasn't had much opportunity to meet people outside of the orphan school. Be gentle with her, won't you? Give her time if she needs it.'

'She won't need time with me, she'll adore me, just like you and Aunt Jude adore me. I am an adorable person, you know.'

'I know, but...'

'I'll be careful.'

'Thanks, Jax, I appreciate it.' Ed half smiled. Jax's confidence in being adorable was an act and he knew it. The boy had felt unloved and rejected by his own parents. It broke Ed's heart. Fudge was still watching them like a hawk and sharing everything with Tammy, who was listening intently and trying not to think how handsome she thought Jax was.

'So, what is this about Tammy having a special connection with animals?'

'Oh, you'll have to wait and see that for yourself,' Ed teased.

'Where is she? I can't wait to meet her.'

'She's at the house doing tai chi with Jude.'

'Really? Tai chi? She'll fit in great with us then.'

'Oh yes, she is quite into it now – Jude has converted her,' said Ed with a laugh. Jude had been practising tai chi for as long as he could remember. It was something they often did together and with Jax on his visits. Ed couldn't help but smile that his family was getting bigger.

*

'Tammy, pull your hips in a little more and you can sink a little lower into them,' Jude said. 'That's better, now move into *single whip*. Ignore the chickens. You must learn to be at one with your chi and put the animals out of your mind.' Jude had been trying to encourage some form of control in Tammy for the last few weeks. The chickens hovered around them, interested in Tammy, communicating on some level.

'I know tai chi builds strength in mind and body but I'm not sure I'm getting this chi thing.'

'It's energy, a force that exists all around us and not visible to the naked eye,' Jude said, continuing with the languid movements. 'An immensely powerful energy. Think of *Star Wars* – the force – it's real and the same thing but not as dramatic as in the movies.'

'Yeah, I like that,' Tammy said, giggling. 'I feel it and just wish I knew how to use it. Make people give me things all the time.'

'Ha! I like it. Jedi mind games – lovely. I'm sure if you combine your powers with what you're learning with the tai chi, you'll find something special. It is special to me even without your powers,' Jude said, chuckling.

'Well, I like the energy more because it's easier for me. I get lost on all these different tai chi moves. When I feel the energy it's as if I can feel and see everything. I feel connected to everything around me. If there is so much energy and power, why doesn't everyone tune into it?'

'It isn't easy to do so. It takes a lot of practice and time. You are naturally gifted. I've told you that already and you're picking it up much easier than most other people would. I think your age works well for you – it's easier to learn when you're younger. Yet look at how hard you find it switching off from the attention of the animals. You cannot turn off your mind when you wish to. Now, move into *white crane spreads its wings.*'

Tammy moved her one leg to balance on tiptoe and then raised one hand up in the air in the required movement, matching Jude perfectly. It really was helping her to clear her mind and find inner calm.

'I just think this will be particularly good for you,' Jude said with a smile. 'If you have the patience to do this, it will be a way to escape the animals if you need to think. Now move into *white snake sticks out its tongue* and then into *pat foot to subdue tiger.* That's good.'

Jet basked in the early-morning sunshine, watching them, stretched out on the lawn. Suddenly he heard a noise and his head jerked towards the trees. There was something about the noise that unnerved him and he sat up. This drew Tammy's attention. She watched him. He knew something was there.

'Tammy, you must concentrate,' Jude said sternly.

Tammy didn't hear her, a frown forming on her forehead as she tried to see what Jet was seeing. Whatever it was, it was too small and quick for Tammy to focus on, but she knew Jet had seen it. A creepy small buzzing creature that Tammy didn't realise was a *seeker*. Looking down, Tammy felt and saw the red heat burning from her pendant and had to lift it off her chest. She peered into the trees, wondering what Jet was so worried about. Then he pounced.

Tammy gasped in shock as Jet raced towards her and pounced on her. With an almighty splash, she went flying backwards into the pond. Jet stayed on top of her, both of their bodies sinking below the water. Tammy looked into his eyes as they sank and realised that he was somehow saving her life by hiding her from whatever that thing was. It scared her. How could she not see it too? How did it move so fast?

The *seeker* buzzed around the pool, comparing Jude's image to that of the hologram held in its memory bank. It saw nothing that resembled the image. Ignoring the splash from the pool, having no interest in such trivialities, the *seeker* continued on its search and left the pond. Jude didn't see it. She was staring at the pond.

Tammy surfaced, barely out of breath, and helped Jet from the pond.

'Are you all right?' Jude asked, helping her.

'Yes, Jet isn't, though. He doesn't like water.'

'Of course he doesn't! What happened? Why would he do that?'

'He saw something, and it meant danger to me – he was saving my life.'

'What did he see?'

'I don't know, some sort of buzzing thing, my pendant went hot and red,' she said, looking down at it now. It was the plain blue colour – neutral. 'It was red before he pushed me in the water to hide me from whatever was out there.'

Jet tried to shake himself dry, in obvious distress, not liking the wetness on him.

'I'd best go and dry him off, he isn't happy,' Tammy explained, and took Jet back to the house. She didn't like the look on Jude's face and when she looked back over her shoulder, Jude was still watching her, the look of concern growing.

*

'Jax, look,' Ed pointed to the pond where Jude and Tammy were. As he spoke, he realised the look on Jude's face and frowned at the way Tammy and Jet were walking back to the house. Then, it dawned on him that they were soaking wet. He frowned and put his foot down on the accelerator.

Jax stared for the first time at Tammy, and the beautiful panther loyally at her side, glad to be able to get a good look at this new addition to the family while she was unaware of him. She was pretty, that was for sure, in a very natural way. She looked older than she should. It took all of Jax's strength to appear cool and uninterested as they parked up next to the house. He was slightly upset that Tammy didn't notice him or turn to look in his direction as she disappeared into the house, but there was clearly something on her mind.

In the time it took for Jax and Ed to walk round to the pond, Tammy had gone.

'Where is she?' Ed asked.

'I'll explain later. We didn't see you coming. Come here, darling,' Jude said as she grabbed Jax and hugged him tightly.

*

Tammy stood on the front porch of Brunswick House, as she did often now, and whistled. Jet was alongside her, almost dry and anxiously waiting to go for a run. Within seconds of whistling, Sirocco came galloping around to the front of the house from the barn. Tammy smiled and stroked his head.

'You're getting faster,' she told him.

Sirocco neighed in response. Without a saddle or reins, Tammy climbed onto Sirocco's bare back and they cantered off across the field, Jet and all the dogs close at their side. She remained unaware that Jax had arrived and was watching her.

Jet leapt into the air and overtook Tammy and Sirocco as they sped across the fields. Tammy laughed loudly as she watched him go. 'Faster, Sirocco,' she said. 'We can't let him beat us.'

Tammy laughed when she saw Jet and the dogs slow down and come to a stop. Jet was a little faster than Sirocco on a short sprint, whereas Sirocco could keep his speed constant for an exceptionally long time. They had races like this on every ride they took. Jet won the short races and Sirocco won the rest. The dogs just enjoyed the exercise but were no match for either Jet or Sirocco. Their rides were exhilarating and Tammy believed that nothing else in life could ever feel as good as riding with her favourite companions.

After her ride, Tammy brushed and cleaned Sirocco before going back into the house to change. It was getting late and she had to get to the safari park to do some work with the elephants and still hadn't met Jax. She was nervous and secretly trying to avoid him. Jet and the dogs stayed out in the field with Sirocco, all catching their breath. Tammy saw how Sirocco gleamed; he was getting fitter and more muscular by the day.

Tammy understood the way Jet, the dogs and Sirocco felt about her, and loved them back dearly; she would do anything for them. She accepted it as the way true friends felt about each other. They loved each other so much they would fight to the death in order to save their friend. It made Tammy feel good to know she had such friends. Everything about her life made her feel good lately.

*

Except meeting Jax. She was overcome with shyness and she spent most of the introduction staring at her feet. On occasion, she stared at his feet instead. Brunch was awkward. Jax seemed to feel equally shy and stared at Tammy throughout most of the meal, thinking she wasn't noticing, since her eyes never left her shoes, his shoes, or her plate.

Ed tried desperately to keep the conversation going. Jude was frowning and looked out of sorts. Tammy assumed this was either because of the awkwardness between her and Jax or what had happened at the pond.

Tammy was frustrated that she couldn't talk with Jax, but then she had never spoken to another boy in her life. They were kept separate at camp, and even girls didn't talk to her beyond Sukie. She knew it was also Lieutenant Cole's treatment over the years and it had shattered her confidence with other kids. However, that hadn't stopped her making friends with Sukie. It was something about the way Jax looked at her. It made the words stick in her throat and her palms go sweaty.

'Nutt is going to be put in with the other elephants for the first time today,' Ed said.

'That's the baby elephant, isn't it?' Jax asked, taking his eyes off Tammy for the first time in ages.

'Yes. He's a lot stronger now and his mother can do the rest. Crane has done a wonderful job. It will be nice to see Nutt with the rest of the elephants. Jude is coming to join us,' Ed said with a smile.

'Well, you know I do have a lot to do about the house most of the time, but I adore the elephants. I couldn't possibly miss seeing little Nutt go back to his rightful place,' Jude said.

Tammy noticed Jude was distracted and worried about something; it was clear to all of them. Something was bothering Jude, but what? Tammy was about to ask but Jude could almost see the way Tammy and Jax were exchanging glances and wanted to avoid questions right now.

'Why don't you two go and get in the Jeep? We'll be

there shortly. I just want a quick word with Ed in private,' Jude said hurriedly. 'Go on now.'

Tammy felt uncomfortable, knowing this was about her, and gave Fudge a quick glance. Fudge was sitting in the corner of the kitchen, keeping the other Labradors back, and nodded her understanding. Tammy followed Jax outside. No one had seen the exchange between her and Fudge.

'Something is wrong,' Jude stated, quietly so no one could hear. Except Fudge. No one noticed Fudge walk quietly over to Jude's feet and lie down, listening intently. Everything Fudge heard, Tammy heard as she walked away.

'Did something happen during tai chi?' Ed asked.

'Yes. Jet saw something and jumped on Tammy, pushing her into the pond and hiding her from whatever was stalking us. We don't know what it was. I never imagined a cat would hold someone, especially itself, under water like that! But that isn't the worst of it.'

'What is it?'

'I meditated earlier, just for a moment, just to collect my thoughts. I saw something. I saw...' Jude looked away from Ed, suddenly feeling uncomfortable.

He took her hands in his and lowered his voice. 'It's okay, you can tell me anything. You know that.'

'It sounds crazy.'

'A lot of our conversations lately have sounded crazy.' Ed smiled reassuringly.

'I saw Sarah...'

'While meditating?'

'Yes, but she seemed so real. She gave me a message.'

'Jude, calm down and tell me what she said.'

Jude was shaking a little and her voice trembled. 'She looked terrible, Ed, really bad. There was blood on her hands and face, she was wet, and she looked like she had been to hell and back. She stood at the side of my bed and called to me. When I opened my eyes, I saw her. It scared me to death. You know me, I don't have dreams or visions or whatever you call them. These sorts of things don't happen to me. It felt too real.'

'Breathe slowly and take your time telling me,' Ed said calmly.

'Sarah walked closer to my bed and sat down next to me. I was frozen with fear, I couldn't move. She said Tammy was in danger here and we must get her away from the island for a while. We had to hurry and do it now – there was no time. I know it has something to do with whatever was stalking us by the pond earlier – perhaps it is just my imagination.' Jude sighed.

'Perhaps. One thing I know is that I always listen to my instincts. If something – whether it is Sarah or your imagination – is strong enough to tell you something like this, then I would listen to it.'

'Do you really think it could be Sarah?'

'No, just your mind making connections maybe and finding a way to understand them. I don't know but I think you should listen to the message.'

'Then you must take her to Africa now, Ed, so it doesn't look too obvious. I don't want to frighten her.'

'Yes, I could say we decided that now was probably the best time because Jax can stay and keep you company.'

'Exactly.'

'Okay. They're waiting for us. We can still go to the park and tell them our plan on the way.'

'Thank you – for believing me.' Jude stood on tiptoe and kissed him on the cheek. Fudge watched them leave and joined Tammy at the Jeep.

Ed, Jude and Jax rode slowly in the Jeep, Tammy upon Sirocco alongside and Jet strolling at the back. Tammy didn't let on that she knew what had occurred. She wouldn't allow herself to think about her mother, Sarah – if it really was her mother – visiting Jude instead of her own daughter. It couldn't have been her mother; Tammy was certain. But somehow someone had managed to get this message across to Jude in a way that she would listen to it. Tammy was sure it was her father.

'He has the laziest walk I've ever seen,' Jax said, looking at Jet.

Tammy, her thoughts returning to the present, smiled at Jet. He always took his time walking. It was only when he ran that you could appreciate his speed.

'I just love the way in which cats move,' Ed said. 'They have such grace.'

'That they do,' Jude said, laughing, 'though I consider Jet to be a bit of a snob at times. He's rather particular with his choice of company. Nobody but Tammy is good enough for him.'

'Are we going to visit Kruger this summer?' Jax asked. 'Since we didn't go last year?'

Tammy watched the exchange of looks that went between Ed and Jude and felt her throat tighten. She was a little scared about the conversation she had overheard and yet she was also excited about finally being able to see Africa.

'Well, funny you should ask that. Jude and I were just talking about it and we were thinking of taking Tammy now. It's a good time to go. We could disappear for a little while, just the two of us, and then Jude wouldn't be all alone here – she'd have you, Jax. It's sooner than I intended but an opportunity arose…'

'I'm more confident with animals and want to continue growing my experience with them. Ed is going to take me around some of his favourite places,' Tammy answered, sounding more upbeat than she felt. 'I've heard so much about it from Jude and Ed, I'm so excited.'

'So, you're just taking Tammy?' Jax asked sulkily.

Ed turned to Jax. 'Look, I know you'd rather come to Africa too. I've discussed it with Jude and it really is better if just Tammy and I go. I'm just really sorry we couldn't all go together.'

'Once they have been over there together and we have more time to plan, then we'll all go together,' Jude added. 'If the three of you went and left me behind, I'd be gutted.'

'Then I hope we all go soon, or I'll be even more gutted,' Jax said sulkily. Jude touched his hand lovingly.

When Suzie and Nutt were put back in their pen, there was a lot of noise from the other elephants. They were all excited at having them back. One by one, the elephants approached the little bull and took a good look at him. The male Asian elephant, Sidney, looked at his son with pride. The little bull was awestruck with all the attention he was receiving. Suzie was a little overprotective at first and didn't want the other females around her son, but she eventually relaxed. They all watched with smiles on their faces as the elephants were finally reunited. Jude loved watching the reaction of the little bull as all the other elephants paid him lots of attention.

'I think he's going to fit in rather well,' she said with a smile.

'I think you're right,' Tammy agreed.

'Well, you have some work to do,' Ed told Tammy. 'Just because Jax has arrived, don't think you can be neglecting your chores.'

'I wouldn't dream of it,' she said, laughing.

'We'll have a walk around and meet you back at the house for lunch, okay?' Jude said.

'Of course, see you later, Jax,' she said, and skipped away towards the elephants' food pen where Dave awaited her.

*

They waited until lunch was almost cold and there was still no sign of Tammy.

'Well, Sirocco went to fetch her ages ago.' Ed stroked his chin.

'You don't think anything has happened to her, do you?' Jude frowned.

'It isn't the first time she's lost track of time, is it? I thought with Jax here, though…' Ed sighed.

'Yes, that isn't to be rude to you, Jax, so don't take it that way. She just gets carried away. That's one of the reasons I'm hoping tai chi and meditation will help her to be more in control of her emotions. She needs to be able to switch off from the animals' needs and show a little more control over the effect they have on her,' Jude said.

'Well, I'll go and look for her then,' Jax said.

'That's a good idea. If you hear a commotion, head towards the noise and you'll find her,' Ed said with a smile.

'Failing that, look for the horse. Don't be too long, you must need a rest after your long journey,' Jude said.

'I won't be long and I'm not tired. I slept a lot on the way,' said Jax. Kissing his aunt on the cheek, he headed for the door.

*

Jax had been given a golf cart to get to and from the safari park while he was on the island. Ed had taught him to drive it years ago. He had covered most of the safari park and still hadn't seen any sign of Tammy or the horse. He passed Dave, who suggested he try by the tigers, having been told that Tammy was spending quite a bit of time by the big cats. As he neared their area, he heard a horse neigh in the distance. It was only a soft neigh; it was enough for Jax to change direction and follow the sound. Before long, he saw Sirocco standing next to the sea lions' pool. He couldn't help noticing how magnificent Sirocco was – typical of his uncle to get the best. Jax got out of the Jeep and looked around. Sirocco neighed again and looked at Jax suspiciously. There was no sign of Tammy.

He moved closer to the sea lions' enclosure and looked into the pool. Jax's mouth dropped open as he saw Tammy swimming alongside one of the sea lions. She was so engrossed in playing with the sea lion that she never noticed him. He watched as Tammy went under the water and swam as if she were one of them, before coming back up again for air, then going back under. Jax didn't know how long he stood there, fascinated by what he saw. It was when Sirocco approached him that he came back to his senses and realised where he was.

Jax felt a little scared as Sirocco looked at him. He was a large horse, much taller than Jax. For a moment, he thought the horse was going to attack him, until Sirocco backed away. He saw Jax as no threat to Tammy.

Sensing something was bothering Sirocco, Tammy surfaced and approached the side of the pool. Jax looked away from Sirocco and saw Tammy looking at him. He smiled. He had a nice smile, Tammy thought. It reminded her of Ed. His eyes were the same sparkling ice-blue as Ed, although his hair was far from white, being dark brown and curly in a cute and messy kind of way.

'Hello,' she said with a smile. 'I'm late, aren't I?'

'Yes, you are.' He smiled back. 'I didn't expect to find you in here, though.'

'It's very nice in here.' Tammy blushed, feeling a little embarrassed in just her T-shirt and pants, which she was now thankful was so long and covered the tops of her legs. 'It smells a bit, though.'

'Yes, it does. By the way, this is a beautiful horse.'

'He is beautiful, isn't he? He seems to get more beautiful every day. His name is Sirocco, as in the sirocco wind,' she said.

'Yes, I've heard of that. That's a really good name for a horse like him. I admire you. I don't think I'd have the bottle to ride a horse like him on my own,' Jax said. 'I helped Ed pick him for you. It was me who suggested a horse.'

Tammy smiled. 'Thank you – I have never been so happy. Want to join me for a swim before we go? They're really good fun to swim with.'

'Will they mind? I know some places do things like swimming with dolphins and seals. I didn't think these were trained to be friendly, and they're much bigger than seals, so is it safe?' They were a little large for Jax's liking.

'They'll like it. They enjoy company. It will take a few minutes before they feel comfortable with you. They won't harm you, not while I'm here.' Tammy smiled encouragingly.

Jax took his jeans and T-shirt off, leaving just his shorts on, and climbed over the plastic barrier into the pool. He stepped in slowly so as not to scare the sea lions. Tammy took his hand and started swimming around with him. One of the sea lions swam up to him and Tammy placed Jax's hand on the sea lion's back. The sea lion swam under the water, pulling Jax along with him.

Jax was holding on to one sea lion and Tammy was holding on to the other. They smiled at each other under the water. Jax had never experienced such a wonderful feeling as he felt now. He felt special being here and swimming alongside a sea lion. More than special. He had swum with a dolphin once before, and yet it hadn't felt as natural as this. Although he had been awestruck when with the dolphin, this was better; now he felt as if he was as free and natural as a person could be.

Tammy swam to the side of the pool and picked up the red ball the sea lions liked to play with. She threw it to Jax and watched as he and the sea lions played catch. Jax threw the ball and one of the sea lions jumped up and headed it back to him. The second time he threw the ball, the sea lion headbutted it to Tammy. She laughed and joined in the game.

They went under the water again and this time Jax was gasping for air.

'How can you hold your breath so long?' he asked breathlessly.

'I practise holding my breath and breathing very slowly when I'm doing meditation and tai chi. I've been sneaking in here and practising when Ed isn't looking. Sirocco lets me know if any visitors come by. They're all having picnics on the other side of the safari park at this time. It's normally about three thirty that they come here to watch the sea lions being fed. Fun, isn't it?' Tammy smiled.

'It's brilliant.' Jax laughed and dived back under the water.

*

It was getting extremely late and Jude had started to worry about Tammy and Jax.

'Well, that's both of them late. I hope they're all right,' she said.

'I've told you not to worry. They both know this safari park like the back of their hands. Jax would have let us know if anything was wrong. I bet Tammy's just showing him something with the animals. You know Jax couldn't wait to see what she was like. Besides, it's good for them to have time together and build up a friendship,' Ed said. He had a lot of faith in them both.

'I know, I know. I just remember what age they are, that's all, and what happened earlier. I know they are more mature than kids their own age. That doesn't make them any older as far as I'm concerned. They're still very young and need to be looked after,' Jude replied.

'You're right. I'm trying not to forget that. I've always treated Jax like a man, and Tammy is just extraordinary. I'll try to remember their ages, I promise.'

'Especially in Africa. What was that?' Jude went to the window. 'I heard a noise.'

'It's probably them coming back,' Ed said.

They both looked through the window and saw Jax heading towards the house on the back of Sirocco with Tammy. Jet was running ahead of them towards the house.

'You see, nothing to worry about,' Ed said. They went to the front porch to wait.

'They're wet!' Jude said, hands on hips, shaking her head back and forth.

'Hi,' Jax said with a wave.

They dismounted Sirocco and Tammy sent him to the barn as usual.

'Why are you wet?' Jude asked.

'We were swimming with the sea lions,' Tammy said.

'It was absolutely fantastic,' Jax said.

Ed looked at the way Jax was looking at Tammy as he spoke. The awkwardness had disappeared between them and they obviously liked each other. He was relieved.

'You'd better get washed, you absolutely stink,' Ed said laughingly.

'And you'll catch a cold – fancy swimming with sea lions, whatever next!' Jude rolled her eyes in mock annoyance and ushered them into the house.

'You two go and get cleaned up then come down to eat. You must be starving now,' Jude said.

'I am,' Tammy said.

'Me too,' said Jax.

Tammy had never enjoyed food so much in her life until she'd moved in with the Brunswicks. Jude had prepared a marvellous stew with dumplings and homemade bread rolls.

It took all the strength Tammy had not to keep snatching more bread rolls and to politely ensure everyone had helped themselves to the same amount as she had before taking the last one. The butterflies she felt with Jax being around helped prevent her from acting like a savage.

'It was even better than the dolphins at the marine park last year,' Jax said as he ate. 'I actually felt as if I belonged with the sea lions.'

'Tammy makes it seem that way, doesn't she? She becomes one of them when she's with them. She had me feeling the same way when we sat in with the monkeys last week. I really felt as if I was one of the monkeys. I even started picking lice out of one of the monkey's fur,' Ed said.

'Did they pick the lice from you too?' Jax teased. They all laughed.

'What are you going to do with Sirocco and Jet while you're in Africa?' Jax asked.

'What do you mean? They'll be with us, of course,' Tammy said, as if it was obvious.

'There is no way I am taking them with us,' Ed said.

'What? Why? I can't go to Africa then,' Tammy said. 'We couldn't be apart for that long.'

Tammy looked sadly at Ed. He looked away, only to find Jude and Jax giving him the same sad looks.

'It's not that easy to transport large animals,' Ed retorted, feeling awkward under the stares. 'There are quarantine regulations to follow, the huge cost it would mean, not to mention that it wouldn't be nice for either of the animals to travel such a distance.'

'I will only leave them here if you force me to,' she told Ed.

'Ed?' Jude whispered. He looked at her. 'You know you have to take them, don't you?'

'All right, all right, if you make all the arrangements,' he told Jude.

'You are exaggerating how hard it is, Ed. I'm happy to do everything,' Jude said with a smile.

'Thank you.' Tammy smiled and ran around the table to kiss Jude in gratitude, knowing just how much effort she was making for her.

'She has you wrapped around her little finger,' Jax said sulkily, wishing he could go with them.

'I think she has,' Ed agreed.

'Is it putting you to too much trouble?' Tammy asked.

'Not really,' Jude replied. 'Ed actually has an open passport for animal transportation. Don't forget all the animals around the world now actually came from this island, so Ed doesn't have to do quarantine above and beyond what he always does here on this island anyway. In a matter of hours, we would have all the tests done that used to take months before Pisces. We'll only need to test them upon their return, as we know there is nothing bad living on this island. They'll be a little uncomfortable for a few hours during travel, but that can't be helped.'

'They'll understand, thank you.' Tammy smiled.

*

Tammy had finished cleaning out the elephants' pen and was about to call it a day when she saw Jax heading towards her. He had spent the morning with Ed and Crane at the animal hospital.

'Hi, Tammy.'

'Hi, Jax. Did Crane help you with all your questions?'

'Yes, and more, he's a good vet. It's just a shame that he refuses to treat reptiles,' Jax said with a sigh.

'I thought Ben looked after the reptiles when they became ill,' Tammy said.

'He does if he can. He isn't trained to, though. If he can't cure them, he has to call a vet to the island, which happens more than you'd think. I think it's silly to pay for a vet to come in when we already have a vet here.'

'You don't like him, do you?' Tammy said.

'I like him enough,' Jax sighed, 'I just think he's too choosy considering his position here. My attitude is that if you're a vet, you help all animals, even if you're not too keen on some of them.'

'Maybe he has good reason not to like reptiles. Maybe he was hurt once,' Tammy suggested. She agreed with Jax, but something told her there was more to Crane's dislike of reptiles than they knew.

'Possibly.' Jax didn't sound convinced. 'Anyway, I have a favour to ask.'

'What sort of favour?'

'I have always wanted to stroke a tiger. Ever since I heard about Ed stroking Sampson, I knew I had to do the same, only I want the tiger to be wide awake. Do you think you could help me?'

Tammy considered it for a moment then smiled. 'I think I can,' she said.

'I'll never forget it,' Jax said, smiling. 'I've always adored them in the same way you are drawn to panthers. It would mean so much to me and I'll pay you back. Someday, somehow, I'll pay you back. I promise.'

'I guess we'll see the female tiger,' Tammy suggested. She had spent a lot of time with her and felt she would be the most receptive to Jax.

'Actually, I'd like to see the big male,' Jax said.

'Okay then,' she said. 'I'll have to go in on my own first and see how he is.'

Jax nodded.

Almost all the safari park visitors had left now, which meant it was all right to play with the animals. Ed had warned her not to let any of the visitors see her. It could put ideas into their heads or attract media attention, which Ed didn't want. They headed towards one of the tigers' enclosures. There were six tigers altogether. Tammy smiled at Jax. She could see how excited he was. Jax watched as the big male strolled to Tammy's side as she entered, and watched her speak softly in his ear. Jax felt a touch of envy at how the animals felt towards Tammy. He wished they felt the same way towards him as they did her. Tammy waved to Jax to come and join her. He suddenly felt nervous as he approached Tammy and the tiger.

'Move slowly,' she said quietly. 'He won't hurt you.'

Jax reached out his hand and touched the tiger's head. The tiger seemed content to let Jax touch him. Feeling more comfortable, Jax moved closer and ran his hands all over the tiger, feeling its large, strong body. The tiger was growling softly. If he had been a smaller cat, it would have been a purr. This purr sounded louder and deeper, more like a growl.

'Beautiful!' he whispered under his breath.

Tammy smiled as she watched Jax. The admiration in his eyes made her happy. She could tell he loved animals with all his heart and his regard for the cats almost matched her own.

*

Jax had a bounce in his walk as they left the tigers' pen. Tammy couldn't help laughing.

'What are you laughing at?' he said, smiling.

'I'm waiting for you to start dancing at any moment,' she said, still laughing.

'Then I'll dance,' he said, and spun around in a circle. He grabbed hold of Tammy and spun her around with him. They both laughed.

'Do you think he'll ever let me in there on my own?' Jax asked.

'Yes, he should be all right with you now but just take it slowly. Jude told me a story about a keeper who had built up such a good friendship with the tigers that he went in there all the time.'

'And they never hurt him?'

'Well, that's the problem. One day, for no apparent reason, one of the tigers attacked and killed him. This was about five years after he'd first gone in on his own,' Tammy said softly.

'That's awful. I don't understand why animals do things like that.'

'It all depends on their mood. I reckon that the tiger had become frustrated with his enclosure. He must have been getting angrier and angrier by the day until finally he lost his temper altogether. Or perhaps he was ill.'

'You'd think that a keeper would have thought something was wrong if he spent so much time with them,' Jax said.

'That's what I thought. Jude said that people get too confident with the animals and stop noticing anything unusual in their habits,' Tammy told him. 'Ed likes me to play with the animals because I can sense their moods and let him know if there are any big problems before anyone else can tell.'

Jax looked at Tammy with raised eyebrows.

'How come you know so much about animals?'

'I don't know. I just do. In fact, I understand them better than I understand you, really. I can only go by what you, or other people, say, whereas animals tell me things, and I can also sense them.'

'You are so incredible.' The words slipped out before he realised it, and he blushed.

'Do you really think so?' she said, looking down at her shoes again.

'Of course I do.' He smiled and put his arm around her shoulder.

'Ed and Jude have taught me a lot since I've been here. They want me to know all about animals. They said the more I know, the stronger my power will be.'

'That's for sure,' Jax agreed.

They heard Sirocco coming towards them and Tammy turned around to hug him. 'I guess this means it's time to go,' Tammy said.

'Does he always know where you are?' Jax asked.

'Yes. He calls to me on his way here and I tell him.' Tammy climbed up onto Sirocco. 'Want a ride?'

'Sure,' Jax said, and climbed up behind her.

They went to Jet's enclosure and Tammy leaned over to open his door without getting off Sirocco. Jet strolled out of his enclosure and followed them home.

*

'Uncle Ed, I stroked the big tiger,' Jax shouted as he came running through the front door.

'You did?' Ed asked.

'I've wanted to do that for years,' he said with a smile.

'Well, Tammy, you have a friend for life now,' Ed smiled, 'Jax will never forget this.'

'It wasn't a problem.' Tammy was stroking Jet's head as he sat patiently beside her.

'Come on, you lot, get cleaned up for dinner. We're having vegan soya mince burritos and salad tonight and I'd like it hot. Not warm, not cold. Hot! Dinner time is getting later and later in this house and I won't be having it!' Jude scolded.

'Then Tammy and I shall leave after dinner and go to Africa,' Ed added.

'That soon?' Jax said, sighing.

'Yes, I'm afraid so,' Ed replied.

'We've only just met,' Jax grumbled as they headed upstairs to wash.

Tammy couldn't help feeling excited, despite knowing she would miss the island. She longed to see Africa after all she had heard. Jude laughed as Jet and Fudge raced past Jax, nearly knocking him over as they went.

'Whoa!' said Jax, catching his balance.

'We win,' Tammy said with a laugh, pushing her way past Jax too.

Jax watched her run up the stairs.

Tammy was smiling as she showered. She liked Jax. Everyone here at the safari park was nice. She even liked getting told off for being late for dinner. Every little thing was perfect here. Tammy felt that nothing bad could ever happen to her at Brunswick Safari Park.

*

Jude was nervous. She hoped there was enough time to get Tammy away from the island. Ed was too wise to patronise her. He knew something wasn't right too. His instinct told him to trust in his wife, as he always did. He kept himself busy packing and preparing to leave as Jude paced anxiously in their bedroom. She watched him, kissing his cheek now and then, not really wanting him to leave. Fudge returned to Ed's side but didn't settle. She went to the window, looked outside and whined.

'Something's bothering her,' Ed said.

'Something's bothering me too!' Jude retorted.

'I know. You'll wear a hole in the floor if you're not careful.'

Fudge sat alert, looking out of the window, whining then barking at something outside. Ed and Jude took turns in looking outside but neither of them saw anything. Fudge could see them: the *seekers*, four of them. They gathered together in a group, as if conspiring, before splitting up in separate directions. Fudge barked and ran upstairs to Tammy. She must keep her away from the window.

FOURTEEN

AFRICA – KRUGER NATIONAL PARK

It was time to leave. The excitement felt like a knot of rope pulling tighter and tighter in Tammy's stomach. This was the real thing; this was seeing nature first-hand. The excitement mingled with fear; Fudge knew something was outside and was doing everything in her power to protect Tammy and keep her away from the windows. Tammy didn't need to understand what it was; she avoided the windows, even more desperate to get to Africa. Somehow, she had lost that safe feeling. She couldn't help but keep looking over her shoulder as they loaded up the Jeep.

'Be careful while you're out there and try not to get into too much trouble,' Jude said.

'We'll be careful, darling, don't you worry. I just wish we could all go together,' Ed said, taking Jude into his arms.

'I know, I want to, but I have too much to do here and it'll be better for Tammy if you work closely with her on your own.'

'I'll miss you,' Tammy told Jude, hugging her.

'I want to hear all about what you get up to when you come back. I bet you'll have loads of fun,' Jax said, a little gloomily.

'I will, and keep an eye on your tiger. If you notice any mood swings, don't go in,' Tammy replied.

'I'll be all right and so will the animals,' Jax said with a smile.

'You'd best get a move on then or you'll miss the hoverplane at this rate.' Jude tapped her watch.

'You're right,' Ed replied, and kissed her on the cheek.

They waved goodbye and left for the hovercraft. They would travel from the island to Southampton, where they would take a taxi to Heathrow Airport in London. They expected to get there for midnight.

*

'Planes are not what they used to be, but then I guess you haven't been on any before, have you?' Ed asked, as the taxi pulled up at the airport.

'No, I have never flown. To be honest, I don't know anyone who has. I remember in history that people used to travel on them all the time, just like we do now with the hovercraft,' Tammy explained.

'Yes, aeroplanes used to be fuelled by oil and petrol and were terrible for the environment. Pisces saw an end to that era, though. With more modern technology, such as the New Age internet and hoverplane, international travel changed forever. The hovercraft was developed and could reach immense speed while still being comfortable, making it the most efficient mode of transport.'

'Efficient in what way?'

'By using natural resources to fuel them, such as water and air. It's faster than the traditional aeroplane so it became the obvious solution. Of course, the hovercraft I use is of a lower specification – the long-distance hovercrafts can really build up some speed.'

'So why aren't we taking the faster hovercraft?' asked Tammy.

'Because Africa is just that much further away that it wouldn't be as economical. The HP, that's the hoverplane, is even more economical than the hovercraft on such a long journey. That is how it is calculated so, by law, you have to take the most environmentally friendly route. In this instance, it's the HP. The government restricts unnecessary travel whenever possible to protect our planet, but tourism is still accepted as a good thing – just in proportion. There's the airport.' Ed pointed ahead.

Tammy saw a relatively small building, almost see-through, since it was made of glass and plastic. The HPs were shaped like large white duck eggs and sat upon something resembling a clear plastic slide.

'We had a rather unpleasant problem with plastic waste in the past as well,' Ed continued. 'Plastic caused all sorts of environmental issues. No one knew what to do with it and all the greatest scientists and inventors were competing to find a solution. Basically, the HPs won. All the plastic, which takes centuries to decompose, was collectively used to create a road that connected all main areas of land via the oceans. Then, using a similar technology to that of the hovercraft, the HP was designed to hover above these plastic roads on a cushion of air.'

'Like slides,' Tammy observed.

'Yes, not quite slippery enough and certainly not steep enough for my idea of a slide.'

'That's a steep one there.' Tammy pointed to the one they were approaching.

'They are steep at the beginning, like a roller coaster, it's a slow crawl up, they are mechanically pulled and then you go down the steep slope. This helps the air build up between the plastic road and the bottom of the HP and then the road evens out and away you go. Makes your stomach feel a little odd at first, then it's smooth until the very end.'

'I'm very lucky to get the chance to travel in this way, aren't I?' asked Tammy.

'Yes, there isn't much need to travel frequently nowadays, so it's expensive and the HPs don't run too often. Spaces are hard to find and cost a fortune for most people. I, however, travel to Africa frequently, so I bought the airport,' Ed said, laughing.

'Why am I not surprised?' Tammy smiled.

'That is our HP. You see the underneath and how thin it is? It's designed to be very aerodynamic and because of the thin exterior, it cannot hover over water, like the hovercraft, nor can it move in the air without a vast amount of fuel. It needs a smooth surface to work with, which is where the plastic came in perfectly. Two problems solved in one go. The other reason it needs the plastic beneath it is in case it breaks down for any reason – rare – yet always possible. The HP would sink, unlike the hovercraft, so at least it has the plastic road to rest on until help arrives.'

Tammy walked Sirocco and Jet into a sectioned area of the hoverplane, explaining to them that it would be a long journey. They understood and quietly climbed on board.

The flight went well – once her stomach had settled after the initial launch. Tammy was surprised when she saw the refreshments and light meal. They were in such small packages.

'These are cute,' she told Ed. He smiled back at her, nodding.

They tasted surprisingly good. She chose a vegetable lasagne with spinach and ricotta, which came with a miniature side salad and a chocolate brownie not much bigger than a plum. It didn't taste anywhere near as good as Jude's food, yet it was fun to eat and somehow managed to fill her up. They were given miniature cans of orange juice that Tammy intended to save as a souvenir, until the thirst became too much and she drank it down in two gulps.

*

Tammy managed to get a short nap in, despite her excitement. Her dreams were filled with animals and Ed noticed, as she slept, how her pendant gradually started to glow an even brighter green the closer they got. He let her sleep until they arrived.

'We shouldn't suffer from the effects of HP lag too much,' he said, stepping off the HP.

'What's HP lag? Is it what I'm feeling now?' she asked, feeling surprisingly sluggish.

'I doubt it. HP lag is tiredness brought on by travelling long distances through different time zones, but Africa is not far and only three hours ahead of England. You just haven't had much sleep, we left late, but you'll probably feel groggier later. It'll go quickly.'

'What time is it?' Tammy asked, yawning and stretching.

'Just past seven in the morning. The flight was barely six hours and that was with stopping via Johannesburg.'

'Johannesburg?'

'You slept through that, but I didn't wake you because it was dark and there was nothing to see. You probably wouldn't have gone back to sleep. Johannesburg is a large airport, further south. We dropped off most of the passengers before we flew here.'

'So where are we now?'

'In a small airport, at Sabi Sabi, a small game reserve in Kruger National Park.'

The landing was smooth, which surprised Tammy, and there were only a handful of passengers left on the flight. They disembarked in a matter of minutes. Ed waited for everyone to get out of sight before he let Jet and Sirocco off the plane. It would have looked strange to the other passengers. They were fine once they'd stretched their legs.

They took a safari Jeep from the airport. Tammy smiled as she looked around the large open country they were driving through. Jet sat beside Ed and Tammy rode Sirocco alongside. The driver seemed uncomfortable with Jet being in the Jeep and kept looking at him from the corner of his eye.

'Mavuso, don't worry, he is a pet,' Ed told the driver in Mavuso's native Zulu language.

Mavuso didn't look convinced. It made Tammy smile as she thought how odd it must appear to the man. They saw a black-breasted snake eagle hovering above until it dived, caught a snake and carried it back into the air.

'That is an amazing bird,' Ed told her. 'He catches the

snake, kills it and eats it while he's still flying. It's also the only eagle that hovers for such long periods of time.'

'He really does all that in the air?' Tammy gasped.

Ed nodded. The black-breasted snake eagle circled them as he consumed the snake in no time at all and then flew and landed on Tammy's shoulder. Ed gasped as the eagle and Tammy looked at each other. The eagle travelled on Tammy's shoulder for a while before flying away and going back to hunting. Mavuso looked stressed.

'Very elegant,' Tammy said.

Ed didn't know what to say so just nodded. They saw a green sandpiper, a redshank and a group of African jacanas. The jacanas were almost all black with a little white and chased one another while calling out a loud noise that sounded like *kyowrrr*.

The people they drove past, walking in the roads or sitting outside small huts in their villages, amazed Tammy. The local population had insisted, over the years, on maintaining their ancient and traditional way of living. Little had changed. The streets were full of stalls offering hundreds of different items for sale, from hot nuts covered in a strange sticky red coating to tribal garments and beautiful multi-coloured satin scarves. They received a few strange glances as people acknowledged Jet brazenly sitting in the Jeep. Mavuso returned their looks nervously as he grudgingly drove on.

'Kruger National Park is the largest safari park in South Africa, covering 20,000 square kilometres, and is home to a great variety of birds and reptiles plus 147 mammal species. This is a great opportunity to see the *Big Five:* the lion, leopard, elephant, rhino and buffalo. We should also get a good look at the cheetah, zebra, giraffe and several species of baboon, hippo and warthog.'

'Am I supposed to remember all this?' Tammy said with a smile.

As they went deeper into the park, Tammy caught a glimpse of a lioness hiding behind some bushes. When Tammy smiled at her, the lioness ran away, leaving Tammy puzzled. Tammy rode Sirocco ahead of the Jeep and, at this point, realised the difference between a free animal and a caged one. The lioness had been careful not to let anyone other than Tammy see her. An animal kept in captivity, even for the shortest time, would lose the talent for being able to avoid being seen. Tammy remembered the story of Sampson, the Siberian tiger, and now understood how captivity had made him an easy target.

Mavuso turned to Ed and muttered something in Zulu. Ed raised his hand calmly and spoke to him. Tammy looked over her shoulder, watching. Mavuso certainly didn't like being their driver but she didn't know what they were talking about. Mavuso turned, annoyed, back to the wheel. Tammy frowned at Ed.

'He isn't happy with you on the horse. He thinks it puts you at risk of an attack from the wildlife. Normally, he'd be right,' Ed explained, shrugging.

It was about two miles later that Tammy again saw the lioness, now with the rest of her pride, walking across the field towards the Jeep. They walked slowly with long, graceful strides, only occasionally breaking into a brief run to keep up. 'Are they welcoming you into their territory?' Ed smiled cheerily as he watched the way they greeted Tammy.

'I'm not sure.' There were four lionesses, including the

one Tammy had first seen in the bushes, and one lion. It didn't take long before Tammy began to get the feeling that something was wrong.

'Stop the Jeep,' she shouted.

Mavuso started arguing, again in Zulu, adamant that he wouldn't stop when so many lions were nearby.

'Please, make him stop,' Tammy pleaded.

Ed saw the panic on Tammy's face and wondered what was wrong. He leaned over to Mavuso and placed a reassuring hand on his shoulder, telling him it would be all right to stop. Mavuso wasn't convinced and reluctantly followed Ed's command. Tammy walked towards the front of the Jeep. Then stopped and waited. The lionesses stayed where they were as the lion approached Tammy. Mavuso started to reach for his gun. Ed stopped him. As the lion got awfully close to the Jeep, Mavuso panicked and started arguing again. Tammy couldn't understand him and wished she could speak Zulu like Ed. She made a silent vow that she would learn.

'Calm down,' Ed said forcefully, shaking his shoulder roughly, forcing Mavuso to look at him and not the lion.

The lion was right next to Tammy. She knelt down and placed her hand on the thick mane. They stared into each other's eyes as the lion tried to tell Tammy what was wrong. She suddenly understood and nodded.

'Ed, I have to go with them,' she said.

'Go where?' Ed asked.

'There's no time, just get your radio and follow me. I'll explain later,' she said.

Ed grabbed the radio and started to reach for his gun.

'Don't bring the gun, it'll intimidate the lions,' Tammy said.

'It'll intimidate me not having one!' Ed replied.

At Tammy's pleading expression, Ed reluctantly left the gun behind. He jumped out of the Jeep and followed Tammy, the lions, Jet and Sirocco into the bush. They hadn't gone far when Ed heard the Jeep driving away at speed. Mavuso had obviously had enough and was too scared to wait around.

'Oh, that's just great,' he moaned.

'We're quite safe,' Tammy assured Ed.

'I don't doubt it for a minute, I'm just wondering how long we're going to be stuck out here.'

The lions led them a long way from the road, deep into the park. Ed was becoming tired from walking in the heat and although he kept asking Tammy what was wrong, she hadn't answered. She was busy following the lions and had a deep frown of concentration on her brow.

'Are you actually talking with the lions now?' he asked.

'Yes.'

Suddenly Tammy and the lions broke into a run and headed towards a large tree. Ed looked at the tree and at first couldn't see anything. Then he saw a lioness lying under it, motionless. Tammy crouched over the lioness, stroking her head and feeling her stomach, which was red with blood.

'She's been shot and lost a lot of blood,' said Ed.

'If she dies, her cubs will die,' Tammy replied.

'Cubs?' Ed was puzzled; he hadn't seen any cubs.

He looked around at the five lions standing anxiously around them. He saw no lion cubs anywhere.

'Over there,' Tammy said, pointing behind the tree.

Ed saw the heads of three little cubs peering out from behind a bush. They were just visible, hiding in fear after the shock of seeing their wounded mother. His heart sank in sympathy as he looked at them.

'Is there anything you can do?' Tammy asked.

Ed bent down and nervously touched the wounded lioness, looking at the other lions in case they attacked. They paid no attention to him.

'The injury is too serious for us to do anything. She'll need proper care. I'm no good at this sort of thing. It doesn't look good. I wish Crane was here,' Ed said.

'Can you call for help on the radio?' Tammy asked.

'Yes, that I can do. Clever of you to remind me to bring it, especially since the driver ran away,' he said, and clicked the radio on. Ed spoke to one of the park rangers and informed him of the situation. He told them where he was and that their hired driver had abandoned them.

'Just hurry and bring medical supplies,' he said, and switched off the radio.

'They're sending a new driver who is also a vet. You'll have to keep a hand over the wound until he gets here, to stop as much bleeding as you can.'

'Okay, Ed.'

Tammy was still stroking the wounded lioness as the three cubs, sensing some safety in Tammy's presence, started to move closer to their mother. They whimpered as they huddled around their mother and Tammy, trying to understand what was going on.

'It's all right,' Tammy whispered. 'It'll be all right, you'll see.'

The other lions gathered closer to Tammy, and Ed backed off, not wanting to get in their way. They all paced around, restless with worry for the wounded lioness and eager for Tammy to do something. She kept her hand over the lioness's wound and talked constantly, telling the lioness and her cubs that everything would be all right if they could just hold on a while longer. As she softly spoke to the lioness, she practised her Energy control and tried to spread a white healing light throughout the wound. The bleeding started to stop and it was helping.

The ranger's Jeep eventually came into sight and the lions looked worried as it approached.

'Don't be scared,' Tammy whispered to them.

They still backed away as the Jeep pulled up. A tall, thin African stepped out of the Jeep.

'I followed the coordinates taken from the radio signal and…' He stopped as he saw the lions, the black panther and the horse.

'Please don't be alarmed, it's all right,' Ed assured him.

The man looked at Ed, hesitated for a moment and then looked at the lions and Jet suspiciously.

'Really, it's all right,' Ed repeated, and moved towards Tammy.

The man cautiously followed.

'It looks pretty bad, eh?' the man said.

'Yes,' Ed replied.

'Can you help her?' Tammy asked.

The man examined the lioness and shook his head.

'If I don't do something straight away, she will die. She has lost a lot of blood. There is no time to get her to the hospital, so I'll have to work here.'

'What are her chances?' Tammy asked.

'Not good,' he said, taking some medical supplies from his bag. 'She is very weak and there is not as good a chance of recovery if she's not at hospital. I have more equipment there. Who will help me?'

'Tammy, you go ahead. I don't really have the stomach for it,' Ed admitted reluctantly.

'No problem, just tell me what I can do,' Tammy said.

The man gave the lioness an anaesthetic to numb any pain. Then he told Tammy what to pass him from his equipment as he started to gently cut the bullet out of the lion's stomach. Once the bullet was out, he calmly cleaned the wound before sewing it up. Tammy and Ed watched in amazement as the man worked.

'Bandages, please,' he asked. Tammy passed them to him.

He bandaged up the wound then sat back and wiped his forehead, breathing with a sigh of relief.

'She is holding on pretty good, considering,' he said. 'I'm surprised she's still alive, to be honest.'

The cubs snuggled close to Tammy and their mother as they waited for the lioness to wake up from the anaesthetic. Tammy didn't stop stroking the lioness or her cubs. She placed her hands over the lioness and felt the healing energy moving through her body into the lioness, who was instantly soothed, and the pain lifted.

'She is lucky,' the man said. 'I think she is going to make it. Her breathing seems steady enough.'

'I hope so,' Tammy said.

'She was lucky this bullet didn't kill her,' he said as he examined it. 'Whoever fired this knew what he was doing. The only reason it didn't kill her straight away was because she was fast. She ran quite a distance to get here after she was shot, judging by the amount of blood she's lost.'

'She did run a long way and every step hurt her immensely. The only reason she managed to get here was because of her cubs. They gave her the strength and the reason to run,' Tammy said.

The man looked at Tammy curiously and wondered how she knew. 'You are a special person, eh?' he asked.

Tammy looked down at the lioness to avoid his stare. She didn't know what to say. Ed had told her he didn't want people to know about her ability. The man looked around at the rest of the lions seated quietly around them, then at the horse and panther. He had been preoccupied with the lioness and forgotten the other animals until now.

'Yes, you are a special person. You are the animals' friend, aren't you?' he asked.

Tammy looked into his eyes and nodded.

'No wonder you didn't want anyone to come with you,' he said, looking up at Ed.

'Most people wouldn't understand,' Ed explained.

'You are right about that,' the man agreed. 'I can be your driver for the rest of the safari if you like.'

'That would be really nice. I'm Ed Brunswick, call me Ed. This is Tammy.'

'I know who you are. My name is Watanas,' he said, shaking hands with Ed and then Tammy.

'You must be new here, I haven't met you before,' Ed said.

'I only started here last month. I used to work at Hwang National Park.'

The lioness began to stir and they all became focused on her again. She was still drowsy from the drug and tried to sit up.

'Shush,' Tammy whispered tenderly, stroking her head.

The lioness lay back down and gave her cubs a couple of weak licks as they excitedly climbed over her.

'Don't climb on her stomach,' Tammy told the cubs.

One of the other lionesses took it upon herself to stand over the mother and push the cubs away every time they went near their mother's stomach.

'I think she'll be all right. We'll just have to keep an eye on her,' Watanas said.

'Then maybe we should set up camp here for the night?' Ed suggested.

'That would be great.' Tammy smiled at Ed.

'I have food and milk in the Jeep for the lioness and her cubs. You can give it to her if you like.' Watanas said.

'Thank you, I'd like that,' Tammy said with a smile.

*

They ended up camping with the lions for five days before they felt the lioness was well enough to be left alone with the rest of the pride. She had recovered almost completely and although she was still weak, she was moving around and caring for her cubs again. They were very attached to the lions and this had been a special time in their lives. Tammy felt a little sad when she thought about Jax, and wished he was here to share this – he would have loved it. It surprised her to suddenly think about him, and she realised just how much she liked him.

They said their goodbyes to the lions and continued with the rest of their safari. Tammy rode Sirocco alongside the Jeep. Watanas drove with Ed next to him and Jet in the back.

'Have we tamed the lions?' Watanas asked.

'That's a good question, I was wondering that myself. I'm not actually sure,' Ed said, frowning.

'Don't worry. They understand the situation. They

probably wouldn't even be nice to you two if they met you face to face again.' Tammy smiled sweetly.

The idea saddened Ed and Watanas. They felt as if there had been a special connection between them and the lions too. It reminded Ed that Tammy had a way of making you feel like that, even though it would always be a unique connection between her and the animals alone.

'It's for the best,' was all he said.

They hadn't gone very far when Tammy pulled Sirocco to a sudden stop. Watanas saw that she had a serious look on her face as he pulled the Jeep up alongside her.

'What's the matter?' Watanas asked.

'I've just had a really funny feeling,' Tammy said. 'I think the lions are still in danger.'

'Why?' Ed asked.

'I just thought that as the lioness was shot by a hunter, and she escaped, then wouldn't he still be wanting to hunt a lion?' She looked at Ed and Watanas questioningly.

'That's a very good point,' Watanas said. 'The hunter still hasn't got what he came for, so he'll still be looking.'

Ed nodded as he realised Tammy was right. 'I can't believe I never thought of it before. It's so obvious!' he said, angry with himself.

'I just had a weird feeling come over me. I think the hunter is close to the lions now. The lions can sense him, and I picked up their fear, I think,' Tammy said.

'Turn around, Watanas. It looks as if we get to see our lions again,' Ed said.

'I'll go ahead on Sirocco, I can go faster than you,' Tammy said, and was heading back to the lions before she'd finished speaking.

FIFTEEN

TO BECOME THE HUNTED

The lions ran out and joined Jet, running alongside Sirocco to where they had camped the previous night. They came to a stop by the tree. The hunter was near, extremely near. Tammy couldn't sense him, but the lions could, and she felt him through them. They were reluctant to move on because the lioness was still too weak to travel far and wouldn't make it.

'It's okay, I'm here now,' Tammy said.

She dismounted Sirocco, left him out of sight in the bushes and joined the lions. They felt safe now Tammy was here.

*

Sirocco could see the hunter through the bushes, and through his eyes, Tammy could see what was happening. The hunter heard the lions before he saw them. 'Got you,' he said as he wiped his nose on his sleeve. He slowly crept through the grass being as quiet as he could until he caught sight of a lioness standing in the open field.

'Stupid, stupid thing!' he muttered. 'Unusual for you to be so out in the open, you must sense that I'm here. Still, whether easy or hard, a kill is a kill.'

He crouched behind a bush and aimed his gun. His finger was on the trigger, ready to pull, when he saw something move next to the lioness. He opened his other eye and saw the lion. Sirocco watched him smile as he aimed at the lion.

'A little closer,' he murmured.

*

The lions had become agitated again and started to move about restlessly. Tammy felt the heat and looked down to see the pendant blazing bright red. The lions had a good sixth sense and knew they were in great danger.

'Oh, where are Ed and Watanas?' she moaned.

Not knowing what to do, yet knowing she was running out of time, Tammy started to call the lions to her.

'Come on, gather around the tree. Get close now, as close as you can,' she said, and the lions obeyed.

*

Sirocco watched the hunter lower his gun in anger as the lion moved out of shot. He had to quietly move around the bush to get a better aim. His smile disappeared as he saw the whole pride of lions – and Tammy standing in the middle of them.

'What…?' he uttered before falling silent. He didn't know what to do.

*

Tammy had all the lions pacing anxiously around her as she wondered what to do next. Just then, the hunter stepped out from behind a bush, aiming a rifle at the lions.

'Don't move, just don't move,' he said, as he slowly inched further out of the bush.

'Don't shoot!' Tammy shouted.

'It's all right, little girl. I won't let them hurt you,' he said.

Tammy could see his finger shake on the trigger as she realised that he thought she was in danger. The lions turned towards the hunter and started to growl as they paced side to side.

'Just start moving towards me real slow. I'll shoot the first one that goes for you,' he said.

Tammy silently spoke to the lions and told them what to do. She began to move slowly forward while the lions moved behind her, one by one. The hunter frowned, unable to believe what he was seeing. As the girl moved closer towards him, the lions were lining up, in single file, behind her.

'Wait. What's going on here?' the hunter asked, astounded.

'What do you mean?' Tammy asked innocently. All the lions were directly behind her now. The hunter couldn't shoot any of them without hitting her.

The hunter took a step to his left to try and get a better aim at the lions. Tammy took a step to her right and the lions followed, continuing to be protected by Tammy's body.

He stared in disbelief at the girl. 'What did you do that for?' he asked.

Tammy just shrugged and smiled as she saw Jet and Sirocco sneaking up behind him. Sensing something was wrong, the hunter lowered the gun and turned to look at what was happening behind him. He didn't have chance to raise his gun as the panther jumped at him and seized the arm holding the gun in his jaws. He screamed in pain as the panther bit harder. Then he saw an enormous horse rise up on its hind legs and throw two strong front legs in his direction. The hunter tried to avoid the hooves despite the panther biting into his arm and weighing him down. He saw the two large hooves heading directly for his face and closed his eyes in fear. He felt an almighty pulse of pain then fell to the floor, forgetting all about the panther on his arm.

*

The hunter groaned and went to put his hand to his jaw; moving his arm caused him to grimace even more. He remembered then the panther's attack. He used his other arm instead and felt his jaw. The pain was excruciating and he wondered if his jaw was broken. He slowly opened his eyes, wondering for a moment if he was dead. If his jaw hadn't hurt so much, he would have screamed at what he saw.

The young girl stood over him with a look of pure hatred on her face. Next to her was the panther, which still had his blood around his mouth, and the girl's arm was resting upon his head. Standing behind her was the chestnut purebred – the largest horse he had ever seen. Circled all around him was the pride of lions. He was scared – he could sense their desire to attack him. What scared him the most was the way the girl looked down at him with those animal-like green eyes with golden sparkles. As he tried to speak, darkness passed over him as he fell unconscious again.

*

Ed and Watanas couldn't believe their eyes as they drove towards the group of animals gathered with Tammy around what looked like the corpse of a man.

'Will he make it?' Watanas asked as he stepped out of the Jeep.

'I don't know. You'd better stay back until I get the lions away. They're really out to kill someone,' Tammy warned.

Ed glanced at Tammy and didn't like the way she was looking at the man on the ground. He had very rarely seen that look on a person's face, and to see it on one so young worried him. He noticed her pendant was solid white and seemed to be glowing much brighter than usual. A cold chill ran down his back.

Tammy didn't say anything to the animals, at least not as far as Watanas could tell. Yet they started moving away from the man on the ground. Tammy climbed up on Sirocco's back and set off at a fast gallop across the field. Jet and the lions followed at a run, with the wounded lioness and her cubs walking behind. Ed watched in amazement as Tammy rode away without saying a word to him.

'He's still alive,' Watanas shouted. 'We should get him to a hospital.'

Ed nodded blankly, still looking where Tammy had been only seconds before.

'I could do with some help.' Watanas said.

'Sorry,' Ed said, and went over to help Watanas load the man into the back of the Jeep.

'Should we wait here for her?' Watanas asked, meaning Tammy.

Ed shook his head. 'She won't be back for a while,' he said.

They drove back to the hospital with the wounded man in the back.

'How do you think she did it?' Watanas asked.

'I can't even begin to guess,' Ed said with a sigh.

'She is some special person,' Watanas said, unable to stop the smile forming on his lips.

*

Ed was standing outside the hospital staring out at the park and wondering where Tammy could be. Surely, she would know to come here? It had been dark for over two hours now and she still hadn't shown up. Ed wasn't worried that she was in danger; he knew nobody could be as safe as Tammy in a place like this. Plus, she was with Sirocco and Jet.

'She'll be back when she's ready,' Watanas said, as he joined Ed outside the hospital.

'How is he?' Ed asked.

'Scared stiff, barely conscious. One of the cats mauled his arm pretty badly and the horse made a mess of his jaw. He can't speak and will have to eat liquids through a straw for a very long time. He'll live.' Watanas smiled happily.

'How can you be so happy?' Ed asked.

'Because he never expected anything like that to happen today, did he? Imagine how embarrassed a hunter would be to know he's been beaten by a little girl.' Watanas burst out laughing.

Ed thought about it for a while. A macho hunter beaten by a girl? He had to admit it was funny, and Ed laughed too.

*

It was late when Tammy eventually showed up at the hospital. Ed ran to meet her as he saw her arrive, riding Sirocco towards him.

'Tammy, I was so worried about you. Are you all right?' he asked, helping her down from the horse.

'I'm fine,' she said meekly. Her eyes were red and puffy from hours of crying.

'You're exhausted,' Ed said, helping her into the hospital. 'You've been crying. You shouldn't be upset, Tammy.'

'What you did today was a wonderful thing,' Watanas said.

Tammy tried to smile.

'You need to rest, we can sleep here in the hospital tonight,' Ed said softly.

'Sirocco,' Tammy whispered.

'I'll take care of him,' Ed said. 'I'll feed him and brush him down. He must be exhausted too.'

Tammy nodded, too tired to talk. Watanas had put a large T-shirt on the bed for her. Ed waited outside until she had put it on. It went past her knees.

'I'm in bed now,' Tammy said, pulling the covers over her. Ed came and sat next to her, taking her hand in his.

'Sirocco will be fine for the night. I found a good stable for him,' Ed said.

'Thanks,' she replied.

'Sleep tight, little angel,' Ed whispered as he kissed her on the forehead.

'Night,' she whispered back, and fell asleep instantly.

Jet jumped up onto the bed and lay down next to Tammy. Ed stroked him on the head and smiled down at the two of them. 'Thanks for looking after her, Jet,' Ed whispered. For a moment, he thought Jet nodded at him. Ed returned the nod, unsure whether he was imagining it, and pulled the door shut as he left the room.

*

Tammy slept until late the next day. Ed knew she needed the rest so wouldn't let her be disturbed. When she finally woke up, Ed had prepared her a hearty meal. She ate the omelette and toast greedily and downed her orange juice in one go.

'I knew you'd be hungry,' Ed said, laughing.

Tammy smiled. She told them what had happened the previous day, frowning when she got to the part about the man becoming conscious again.

'It's nothing to be ashamed of. It's perfectly natural to feel hate towards a man like that,' Ed said reassuringly.

'It's wrong. I really wanted to let the lions have him,' Tammy confessed. 'I felt the same anger and hate that the lions did. If anything, I felt it more than them.'

'Don't punish yourself for the way you felt, Tammy, especially since your feelings are influenced by the animals.

The most important thing is that you didn't let the lions have him. That's what counts. You did the right thing,' Ed told her.

'There is another problem too,' Tammy said.

Ed raised his eyebrows and waited for her to tell him.

'He wasn't the main hunter,' she said.

'What? Wasn't he the one who shot the lioness?' Ed asked.

'No. He wasn't the one. There is a leader and he was one of three men who was with the leader,' Tammy said.

'How do you know this?' Ed asked.

'The lions are very smart,' Tammy smiled, 'a lot smarter than you'd like to think.'

'I think we should go on a hunting trip of our own,' Watanas said.

'That sounds like a good idea to me but let's not involve anyone else. I trust you to keep Tammy a secret,' Ed told him.

'Of course, I'll get the Jeep organised then.' Watanas smiled excitedly.

'Are you up to it?' Ed asked Tammy.

'The sooner, the better,' Tammy said with a nod. 'I don't want any animals hurt.'

'Then we'll leave now,' Ed said.

'I'll ask a couple of birds to help us find out where they are,' Tammy said.

'Can you do that?'

'Of course I can.'

'This is going to be easy,' Ed said.

'I hope so,' said Tammy, not feeling so sure.

*

Tammy met them at the Jeep with a bird resting on her arm that she was busy whispering to. The bird was known as a bateleur, a distinctive bulky-looking black eagle with a creamy-white back and scarlet face and legs. Once Tammy had told the bird what she wanted her to do, she raised her arm and watched her fly away. As the bateleur flew into the sky, she made a loud *schaaaaaaaw* sound. Tammy also had the black-breasted snake eagle hovering above them as extra ground cover and protection.

'Ready?' Ed called to Tammy.

She nodded, jumped on Sirocco and fell in alongside the Jeep.

They followed the birds for hours, watching them circle around the wide-open land of the park. The birds searched continuously, only stopping in a tree every so often to regain some strength. Tammy had considered using a whole flock of birds, thinking that they would cover the ground more quickly. However, it would look too suspicious to the hunters to have a whole flock of birds flying around. Ed didn't want the hunters to know they were coming. He suspected that the hunters would already be on their guard after the disappearance of the one they had caught. The leader couldn't know he was in hospital so would probably think he'd been arrested. They might even be worried he had told the rangers where to find the rest of his group.

It had just started to get dark when the black-breasted snake eagle circled the Jeep a couple of times before landing on Tammy's shoulder. Then the bateleur did the same thing, this time landing on Tammy's outstretched arm. The bateleur made a soft *kau-kau-kau-ko-aaagh* sound a couple of times as Tammy spoke to her. Then Tammy nodded her understanding.

'They're just over there,' she told Ed and Watanas as she pointed to their left. 'About a mile, as the crow, or rather eagle, flies.'

Both birds flew into the air again, circled the Jeep twice then flew away and left them to it.

'All right, we should think about the best way of handling this,' Ed said.

'How many are there? Still one leader and two others?' Watanas asked.

'Yes,' Tammy answered.

'Three altogether? Will we be able to handle them?' Watanas pulled a face.

'They're loading their guns and are about to start a group hunt,' Tammy said.

'Of course, this is the best time to find game. The animals are most active at dawn and dusk,' Watanas said.

'We must think of something to do and act fast,' Ed said.

Ed and Tammy agreed, and they all stayed quiet as they tried to think of a plan to stop the hunters once and for all.

'I have an idea,' Tammy said.

Ed and Watanas listened carefully as she told them what she planned to do.

*

Tammy and Jet hid in the bushes, watching the hunters get ready. There were three of them, as expected.

'George, you are the biggest fool there ever was,' said one of the hunters to the young man. Tammy could tell he was the leader. The young boy, George, didn't want to be with him. Tammy knew this from what the animals had told her. George had dropped the box of bullets and was hurriedly picking them up off the ground. He blushed with embarrassment as the leader scolded him.

'Just one week left,' George murmured as the leader walked away. He had counted every day of this hunting trip, eager for it to end.

'Why did we have to have this boy come with us?' moaned the other hunter.

'I know his father and did it as a favour. If I'd known how much trouble he was going to be, I'd never have let him come, but his father wanted me to turn him into *a man!* Would you believe it! Asking the impossible, I say,' the leader said.

'Useless,' the hunter said with a snort, looking at George.

'Come on, we can't afford to lose any more time,' the leader said, and started off ahead of the others.

As the hunter walked past George, he stepped on some of the bullets and pushed them further into the dirt with the end of his shoe.

'You are a useless young idiot,' he told George.

'At least I'm not an old man with nothing in life except the clothes I wear,' George said defiantly, and pushed the old man's foot away.

'I've just been unlucky, that's all,' said the hunter. 'At least I have the brains to hunt. Good brains are what make a hunter, you know. You'll never be a hunter.'

'I don't want to be a hunter, and having the brains to hunt isn't something I'd be too proud of. Just remember this, when you come unstuck, which you will someday, ask yourself one question: what good are brains to hunt with when you don't have the speed to run away? I'm young and fast and should anything go wrong while we're hunting, don't expect me to hang around to help you,' George said with a smile.

'Will you girls stop it and catch up,' the leader yelled at them.

'I know that you deliberately miss on purpose. You could easily have shot that lioness the other day and I know you chose not to, and you ruined my shot too! You are a coward, whatever you say!' The hunter gave George one last dirty look before joining the leader.

George picked the rest of the bullets up off the floor and sluggishly followed. Tammy and Jet quietly crawled after them.

'Quiet.' The leader mouthed the word as George approached.

They were kneeling behind a bush, looking through their binoculars. George came up beside them and knelt down too.

'What is it?' George asked.

'Over there.' The leader handed his binoculars to George and pointed.

George looked and saw a herd of elephants walking past some trees.

'How far away are they?' he asked.

'Five hundred yards or so,' the leader answered.

'They're making a lot of noise,' the hunter said.

'Yes, they are.' The leader frowned. 'If I didn't know better, I'd think they were deliberately trying to get our attention.'

They moved closer to the herd, keeping their heads low. They were not too far away when the leader signalled for them to split up. He sent the hunter to his right and George stayed behind. They had all started to crawl on their stomachs when George saw something out of the corner of his eye in the bushes. He was about to call the leader then decided against it. He would only yell at him for making a noise. George looked into the bushes where he'd seen something move.

The bushes were swaying as something moved through them. George aimed his rifle at the swaying bushes, waiting for whatever it was to come out. Then a black panther stuck his head out from behind the bush and looked straight at George. George was stunned and lay frozen on the floor. The panther was really close to him. He didn't want to shoot him; he didn't have the heart to hurt an animal.

He stared at the panther for a long time when Tammy appeared at his side. George stared at her, not realising that his mouth had dropped wide open. The girl placed a finger over her lips, telling George to be quiet. She looked to see where the other men were and then waved to George, indicating that he should come to her. George looked at the hunters, who were far ahead of him now. Without much thought, George crawled quietly towards Tammy and Jet.

'Stay here, be quiet and you'll be all right,' she whispered.

He nodded. He didn't understand what was going on and yet he knew it would be trouble. He knew a trap when he saw one, no matter how odd it seemed, and this was definitely a trap. The elephants had been a lot noisier than they should have been and here was a young girl standing next to a panther. That in itself should worry any person who saw it.

'I may not have the brains to be a hunter, but at least I have the brains to know trouble,' Tammy heard George mutter as she and Jet moved away.

*

The hunters were still crawling towards the elephants. The lion, watching them from the bushes, kept Tammy informed on their progress. They reached a point where they could get a good shot. The leader waved his hand to indicate they should stop. He looked behind him to see where George was. When he saw no sign of him, he looked at the other hunter, who smiled.

'Ran away,' he mouthed.

The leader wasn't so sure. He shrugged his shoulders, then checked his rifle and took aim. He had a smile on his face as he aimed the rifle between the eyes of the largest elephant he could see. He always fired the first shot before the others were allowed to shoot. His finger was just about to pull the trigger when he had a funny feeling that something was behind him. Looking over his shoulder, he saw the lion. Shocked, he started to roll away so that he could take aim at the lion.

'Don't move,' Ed shouted.

The leader stared in disbelief at the man emerging from a nearby bush holding a gun aimed right at him. He didn't move. As he looked around, he noticed that aside from this man there were three lions around him. The first lion he had noticed standing to his left, a lioness at his feet and another lioness to his right. He looked for the other hunter and saw that he too was in the same situation. Three lions had surrounded him and Watanas stood nearby with a gun.

Tammy walked out of the bushes with Jet at her side. Slightly behind her came Sirocco. The leader looked on in amazement. 'What's going on?' he asked in total confusion.

'You are under arrest for illegal hunting,' Watanas shouted.

'Now just a minute,' he said, and started to get up.

The lion at his left growled and took a step forward. The leader froze and decided to forget about getting up after all. At that point, a puzzled-looking George came out from the bushes.

'You!' the hunter hissed.

George just shook his head and smiled.

*

Ed and Watanas handcuffed the two men and loaded them into the Jeep. Tammy stood watching with all the animals around her. The animals watched too as the hunters were made to get in the Jeep. None of the hunters could speak. They were too surprised and too shocked to fully understand what had happened.

Tammy said goodbye to the lions and climbed onto Sirocco's back. She rode beside the Jeep and Jet rode in the back with the hunters. The hunters stared wide-eyed at him, wondering whether he was going to attack or not. They headed back to the rangers' station at the entrance of the park.

'Is this your idea of a circus?' the leader eventually asked, sarcastically. He had realised that the panther wasn't going to attack him and suspected that they had used trained lions to scare him. Tammy looked at him then continued to look straight ahead.

'I assure you this is no circus,' Ed said.

'The animals look tame to me,' the hunter said. 'Especially this panther.'

'I wouldn't put that to the test if I were you. Your colleague learnt the hard way. He'll be eating through a straw for months,' Watanas said.

The leader frowned and looked at Tammy as she rode Sirocco. She didn't look at him. She didn't want to talk to him. She didn't like him. She didn't like the mean sparkle he had in his eyes or the rough, grating laugh he had.

When they reached the station, the two men were locked up without being given any further explanation as to why the lions and panther hadn't attacked them. In view of his age, George was allowed to go free. He wasn't more than sixteen and obviously wasn't really a hunter. They were sitting on a wooden bench outside the building being used to hold the prisoners. It was a warm night and Ed wanted to talk to George.

'My dad made me come. I didn't want to. He's not the sort of man you argue with,' he told them.

'That was your dad?' Ed asked, referring to the leader.

'No, he is a friend of my dad's,' he said.

George looked at Tammy, who had been silent all the way back from the park.

'Why did you call me into the bushes and not just have me caught like the others?' he asked.

'Because I knew what you were like,' she said.

'What do you mean?'

'You weren't a hunter and you didn't like being there,' she said.

'How did you know?' George was confused.

'Out here, I have many eyes,' Tammy said. 'I know you had a couple of opportunities to shoot a lioness and deliberately didn't take them.'

Jet had been sitting at Tammy's feet the whole time they were outside. He purred as Tammy stroked his head. Feeling a little left out, Sirocco approached the bench and pushed his head against Tammy's cheek. Tammy smiled, closed her eyes and rested her head against Sirocco's. George knew she wasn't going to talk to him anymore, and he didn't expect her to. She didn't seem too keen on people; she seemed to like the company of animals more.

'What are you going to do now?' Ed asked.

George shrugged. 'I don't know. I dare not face my dad after this. The hunters think I set them up, my dad will too.'

Ed looked at Watanas questioningly and Watanas nodded.

'We need field rangers here. Fancy being on the right side for a change?' Ed said.

George smiled.

SIXTEEN

MIKIE NEEDS CASH

'Mikie, head down to the shop and grab some more almond milk, eggs and bread, will you?' Stephen asked as he raced into the room, brushing his wavy brown hair back for his date. 'She might want to stay for breakfast, you never know!'

'Oh sick! Do I have to? I need to meditate and clear my head, there is too much noise today,' Mikie replied sulkily.

'Then go now and meditate after, or you'll only get more noise going to the shops and passing all those people. Why so much noise anyway? Where were you earlier?'

'Just in the park. Walking dis-creeeeeeet-leeey about.' Mikie sarcastically emphasised and dragged out the word *discreetly*.

'Right,' Stephen said, looking him suspiciously up and down. 'Just go, will you? Get something to munch on for yourself tonight while I'm out, and don't be lurking around when I get back with her. This one is a bombshell. Body like...' Stephen tried to shape a woman's hourglass figure for him.

'I really don't need to hear it,' Mikie said, putting up his hand to stop the words, and grabbing his jacket as he headed towards the door.

'Put it on account,' Stephen shouted after him as he left.

Mikie sighed and headed into town. It was a twenty-minute walk and the weather was nice. Too nice. That meant lots of people about and too many thoughts floating through the atmosphere, and after the earlier shenanigans at the school with Dan and Adam, which were worth every migraine he could get, the pounding was starting to get too much now. When it got like this, Mikie became moody and all he could do was lie down in bed and meditate. When he was able to get into a trance-like state, he could often see his siblings, especially Tammy. She was more like him in looks and character. He felt more connected with her somehow. He had flashes of images and memories in his dreams and got the impression that Tammy and he had similar abilities when it came to manipulating the earth's energy field. Bio-magnetic energy manipulation. Still people refused to believe or see it, but even in ancient and old-fashioned movies like *Star Wars*, the force was acknowledged and known about. Too many people struggled to connect with it but not Mikie and Tammy. It was very much a part of them.

'The force is strong in my family,' he said with a chuckle.

Lost in thought and minding his own business, Mikie was surprised when someone banged hard into him while passing on the pavement. The pain shot through his shoulder and woke him from his thoughts.

'Hey, watch where you're going,' he yelled.

An older middle-aged gentleman, clearly rich according to his clothes and egotistical attitude of self-importance

Mikie could read, turned, looked down his nose at Mikie and promptly ignored him without so much as an apology. From what he glimpsed in the man's mind, he was a very selfish and greedy, powerful man who ran a large bank and abused his employees. In fact, this year he had claimed no one was to have a bonus due to poor performance and profit, despite landing himself and his very much younger secretary-cum-mistress a six-figured bonus each. Such glimpses angered Mikie and kicked off his righteousness.

'So rude and self-absorbed,' Mikie muttered, and reluctantly carried on walking to the shop, stung by the rudeness and pride, causing him to seethe at the lack of respect. He stopped in his tracks, wanting to turn around and go after the man.

'No, keep walking, to the shop. Go,' he told himself.

Mikie started walking and tried hard to forget about the man.

He passed a homeless man, very old, frail and shaky, sitting on the road, and a glimpse into his mind showed him that the rich guy who had bumped rudely into Mikie had also rudely passed this homeless man earlier, kicked his almost empty can of coins over, and told him to get off his bum and get a job and earn his own money. This added fuel to the fire already simmering to boiling point in Mikie's gut.

'Spare some change, boy, can you, please?' he asked, shaking his little can towards Mikie.

Mikie sighed. He hadn't got a penny. Stephen never used cash. He was rich and well known and did everything on account. Mikie didn't even get pocket money like other kids because he just had to call and order whatever he wanted, and people got it for him and invoiced Stephen directly.

'No, sorry, I don't.' The old man's face broke Mikie's heart. He looked miserable. 'But I'll be back in a moment with some.'

Mikie turned on his heels and went after the rich man. To hell with it. Who would ever know? The homeless man looked sad and had no expectation of ever seeing Mikie again, and this haunted Mikie. It didn't take long to catch up with the man who had bumped into him. Mikie watched him, read him and when he was sure no one was watching and everything was okay, he probed his mind. The man, Eric, he was called, stopped in his tracks and stood motionless for a moment. Then, he turned and crossed the road and walked a few doors up to the machine outside the bank where he could withdraw money. He took out a credit card and withdrew the maximum amount of cash he could on that card. He placed the wad of money in his left pocket. Then he took out a further two cards and did the same.

Mikie then made him cross the street again and walk past him, taking out the wad of notes and handing them to Mikie.

'Here lad, take these. I don't need them anymore,' he said gloomily, handing the cash to Mikie.

'Why, thank you, Eric. That is very decent of you, I have to say,' Mikie said, and tried to take the money.

Eric wouldn't release his grip and there was a moment's pause as his conflicted will fought the mind's logic and Eric wouldn't release the notes. Mikie tried to take them. Of course, eventually, Mikie overcame the conflict and Eric released the money.

'You deserve it,' Eric said, looking confused and angry at the same time.

'I certainly think I do, and thank you again, Eric. You have a lovely day now, won't you,' with which Mikie turned and headed back towards the homeless man.

Mikie smiled as he approached and saw the surprise on the homeless man's face. Not as surprised and lost as Eric's face had been as he still, ten minutes later, stood lost and confused in the middle of the street. It would take him a while to process that, Mikie thought, as he took a small bundle of cash for himself and left it in his pocket, then gave the massive bundle of what remained to the homeless man.

'Here you go, told you I'd be back,' Mikie said as he handed over the money. 'You go get some food and book a nice room in a hotel and have a hot bath and take care of yourself.'

'Thank you, oh my, why… thank you, boy,' the man mumbled, not quite believing what his eyes told him.

Mikie smiled. Revenge was something Mikie had to confess he liked. It worried Stephen immensely and Mikie knew why, since this side of him had caused much trouble in the past. It wasn't a very nice thing to do. It was really bad. He should feel guilty. But it felt so very good.

SEVENTEEN

CROCODILE RIVER

Considering the amount of days they had spent at Kruger Park, they had hardly seen anything. The time had passed quickly, and they had been preoccupied with the lions and hunters. Ed decided that now it was time to finally complete the safari.

'That's if nothing else crops up,' he said, laughing.

Tammy and Watanas laughed with him. They packed their Jeep and set off once again to view the rest of Kruger National Park. They travelled and camped for five days, viewing whatever game they could find. They saw the lions again and the herd of elephants they had used to lure the hunters into their trap. They saw one cheetah as it hunted and caught an antelope. It had been an amazing sight. Tammy felt sad for the antelope, despite the knowledge that the cheetah couldn't survive without it. However, the scene made her realise something about herself that she hadn't thought of before.

'I have never eaten meat, even on the rare occasion it has been in front of me, as if I always knew how wrong it was. I would never even try it to see if I liked it,' she declared, watching the antelope get ripped apart.

'I may well be a vegetarian myself one day but we adults find it hard to let go of what we considered special once upon a time. And now it is a rare privilege, making it even more special to us and hence making us want it more. I am a victim of this myself, I have to admit,' Ed said with a shrug.

'I don't know how you can do it. I could never eat meat; I don't need to and so I won't. Jax is the same.'

'Fair enough,' Ed said with a chuckle. 'Come on, we're almost there.'

*

'Here it is,' Ed said, a couple of hours later.

'Crocodile River, Mpumalanga,' Watanas said, dropping them off. He had agreed to drive the Jeep, taking Sirocco and Jet with him, while Ed took Tammy along the river on a rather old-fashioned boat. They were to meet up at the end of the day. It was soon obvious why the river was called *Crocodile River.* The water didn't look very clean and was full to the brim with crocodiles.

They weren't the only ones on the boat. Also travelling was a man, his wife and their three children aged one, three and five, who were all visiting from India. Two, obviously rich, male students from Hawaii who were presently travelling the world, a husband and wife from France and a woman from Florida with her four-year-old boy. And the two male crew members were also on board.

Tammy thoroughly enjoyed the first hour of the cruise. Everyone on the boat held onto the rails and watched the numerous hippos and crocodiles both in the water and on the side of the riverbank. They all laughed as a hippo popped up out of the water and opened his large mouth, showing a few stumpy teeth. Tammy smiled as she saw the eyes and ears of another hippo as he hid almost completely under the water. The crocodiles swam lazily, almost as if they were floating logs.

It really was a wonderful experience. The sudden outbursts of laughter from the children made the adults smile and Tammy felt an instant of awkwardness as she wondered whether she was an adult or a child. She didn't feel as if she was either, somewhere in between. It was one of those moments when Tammy felt she didn't fit in anywhere. It was while she was pondering on this thought that the peacefulness of the cruise abruptly ended and was replaced by a sudden surge of fear.

The Indian boy decided it would be fun to climb over the rails of the boat and hold on from the opposite side, partly to show off to his younger brother. His parents didn't notice what he was doing until he had actually done it.

'Oh my goodness!' the boy's mother screamed, and raced towards her son.

The scream made the boy panic, and he let go of the rails. His parents watched in horror as he fell into the water.

Several crocodiles heard the splash as the boy hit the water, and swam from the riverbank towards the boat. Everyone on the boat froze with fear. They didn't know what they could possibly do to save him. The sides of the boat were too high for them to be able to reach over and pull him out. The crew were too scared to jump into the water and so were the other passengers on the boat.

'Do something! Help him!' the boy's mother screamed hysterically.

They couldn't see the crocodiles anymore. They had disappeared under the water, heading towards the boy, who was barely able to swim and kept going under. The boy's father, thinking he could do nothing else, started to climb over the side of the boat, about to dive in next to his son. He was scared. He paused when he saw something out of the corner of his eye, followed by a loud splash. Tammy had jumped into the water and was swimming towards the boy.

'Wait with us,' Ed told the man, placing a reassuring arm around his shoulder and pulling him back onto the boat. 'There's little you can do. She can help – she isn't just a young girl.'

The father didn't want to leave it up to the girl; he naturally wanted to go in and save his own son. Ed's grasp became tighter, forcing the man back onto the boat.

*

Tammy reached the scared boy and took hold of him by his waist. 'I'm going to help you,' she told him. 'I need you to help me to help you.'

The boy grabbed hold of Tammy. He was scared and confused, and she saw he was also brave.

'I need you to take a deep breath because we're going to go under water,' she said. The boy nodded. He was too scared to speak and although he didn't understand why, he was willing to do anything this girl told him to do. Anything to get out of the water and away from the crocodiles.

They took a deep breath and Tammy pulled the two of them under the water. They sank further and further until they were almost touching the bottom. Tammy had decided it was better to face the crocodiles down here, where she could make eye contact with them and see them coming. While they were on the surface, the crocodiles would only see her body, not her face. Then, they would undoubtedly attack her.

She held the boy close to her and looked around through the dirty water. Her pendant glowed bright red and then bright white, lighting up the water and helping her see more clearly. There were so many crocodiles. They were very close to them now. Tammy was shocked at how many there were. She could count over thirty. She couldn't think about being scared; she was too busy trying to decide what to do. How she was going to get herself and the boy out of the water alive.

*

The boy's parents and the rest of the passengers gasped in fear as Tammy and the boy disappeared under water. They couldn't see them now and feared the crocodiles had already attacked. Ed's heart sank as he feared he would never see Tammy again. The water began to move in strange circles; dozens of whirlpools began to form. The people watching from the boat mistook this for the crocodiles' movements.

Ed frowned, knowing that crocodiles didn't create such whirlpools.

*

Tammy watched the crocodiles getting closer and closer. She concentrated very hard to make them stay away. She felt the water move around her and the boy, swirling in circles, helping her to stay away from the crocodiles and easing her towards the riverbank. The water was helping her. Tammy didn't know how but she was grateful for it.

'Don't come closer! Don't come any closer!' she said, over and over in her head, trying to make the crocodiles hear her.

One crocodile came right up to them. The blurred discoloured water made their cold statue-like faces appear even more eerie. The boy hugged Tammy close when he saw the crocodile open his jaws and glide towards his face. His jaws slowly opened, as if it were easy feeding here in the river and this boy was nothing but an appetiser. The boy's eyes bulged in terror at the large white teeth coming towards him. His heart pounded and echoed in his tiny chest. He needed air and couldn't hold his breath for much longer. He needed to scream. Now.

Tammy, sensing the boy's distress, willed the crocodile away with all her might. The boy's fear brought out a protective streak in her she didn't know she had, and she wasn't scared at all. She looked right at the crocodile and silently willed him to turn and leave just as he got almost close enough to bite. Suddenly, at the very last minute, the crocodile snapped his jaw shut, turned and swam away. Tammy started to swim backwards, pulling the boy with her and making the water move in whirlpools, creating a gap of air between them and the water, allowing herself and the boy to gasp a few breaths of air.

'You can take a breath,' she whispered to the boy.

He looked puzzled but took a breath anyway and then another. It was hard work controlling the crocodiles and the water and the air bubble, and she couldn't hold it for long, but enough to help the boy for now. If she had to, Tammy could have held her breath this entire time. She had practised well enough and her lungs worked more like those of the seals at the park than a human's. She was still heading towards the riverbank. They couldn't afford to surface. Tammy knew that the crocodiles wouldn't hear her if they couldn't see her eyes. To surface now would be suicide.

The crocodiles were still all around them. Most stayed slightly away; some kept trying to get closer. Every time one came too close, Tammy willed them away. They were confused and agitated, which made it especially dangerous for Tammy. They were nearing the bank now; the boy started to struggle. He needed air and couldn't hold his breath any longer. Tammy had been practising holding her breath for a long time when swimming with the sea lions. She was glad of this now. She let the boy swim to the surface to catch his breath. The whirlpools in the water helped to keep the crocodiles clear of the boy as he gasped for air. Tammy stayed under water next to him, willing the crocodiles away.

*

'Over there!' Ed shouted, and pointed to the boy as he surfaced.

Everyone looked. Ed scanned the surface for Tammy. His heart sank when he saw no sign of her. The boy disappeared under water again, leaving his parents more scared than ever.

*

Tammy pulled the boy back under the water and started swimming backwards, faster and faster. The bank was still quite a way away and the crocodiles were becoming ever more frustrated.

It is wrong to hurt us, Tammy silently told them. *You must leave us alone.*

The crocodiles started to understand. They were keeping their distance more now. Eventually, they realised that they had to stay away. They no longer tried to attack, because they knew it was useless. They couldn't hurt these people. They didn't know why, and it confused them, yet they obeyed. Tammy had a feeling something was approaching her from behind. She turned around and saw a hippo. He looked angry and confused. The hippo had sensed the confusion in the crocodiles. He was angry at having someone on his territory causing all this confusion. Tammy looked at the hippo and told him to go away. The hippo hesitated, and then continued towards Tammy. She told him to go away again and concentrated all her will on the hippo. He stared at her but let them pass.

Tammy pulled the boy towards the bank. Not far now. Tammy hugged the boy closer to her and smiled. He had done well with holding his breath; it wasn't easy when you were scared. He had trusted Tammy and done what she told him to do. The crocodiles paid no attention to Tammy and the boy now. Some stayed in the water and some got out, ready to bask in the sun for a while longer. Tammy and the boy swam to the surface and held onto the sides of the bank. They breathed heavily, trying to catch their breath. Tammy helped the boy until he was sitting on the bank, and then joined him.

*

Ed breathed a sigh of relief as he saw Tammy. It had only been a matter of minutes since the boy had fallen into the water and yet, to everyone involved, it had felt like hours. Tammy waved at the boat and smiled with relief when she saw it turn and head towards her.

Ed and the boy's father jumped off the boat and joined the pair on the bank. The boy's father grabbed hold of his son, kissing his face and checking him for any injuries. Ed put his arm around Tammy and whispered, 'Well done.' They were all overjoyed to see them both alive. They got back on the boat and the boy was quickly reunited with his mother. She cried as she held her son.

'I thought I'd lost him,' his father told Tammy, unable to hold back his tears. 'I don't know how you managed to do it. I thank you with all my heart.'

Tammy choked up, biting her lip to stop the trembling. A lump rose in her throat, rendering her unable to speak, as the tension of the past few minutes started to weigh upon her.

'That was very brave of you,' Ed told her.

'The boy was brave,' Tammy said. 'He was so brave. What is your name?'

'His name is Sanish,' his mother said.

Sanish was in shock and couldn't speak. One of the crew members brought blankets to wrap around them.

'You are a crazy girl,' he said, as he handed Tammy a blanket.

'How did you manage to get to the bank with all those crocodiles there?' Sanish's father asked.

Tammy was too tired to explain and didn't want to tell him how she willed the crocodiles away. He wouldn't understand.

'I don't know. I guess I was just lucky,' was all she said.

'You must be tired. Sit down,' Ed told her.

'I think maybe we've had enough excitement for one day,' said one of the crew members.

'Let's head back early,' the other crewman agreed.

They were all shaken up from the experience, especially Sanish. He would have to go to hospital because he was clearly suffering from shock. Tammy sat next to Ed, resting her head on his shoulder as she stared at the river. She was exhausted and shaken. It had been too close an encounter for her liking. She closed her eyes and pretended she was back at the safari park, swimming with Jax, feeling his warm smile and that warm glow she felt when she was around him. She felt safe there.

*

Tammy was glad to see Sirocco and Jet waiting for her when they returned from the cruise. Sanish was still in shock. He managed to give Tammy a kiss on her cheek and say goodbye before he was taken to hospital.

'We can never thank you enough for what you did,' his father told Tammy.

Tammy smiled as he kissed her on the cheek. Sanish's mother was too upset to speak. Instead, she grabbed Tammy and gave her a tight squeeze before walking away with her family.

Ed smiled with pride at Tammy, who was walking over to Sirocco and Jet. She embraced them both and then climbed onto Sirocco's back. She rode Sirocco alongside the Jeep, occasionally disappearing for a short canter.

*

Their time in Africa was over, Ed decided that evening, and they should return to Vivacity Island the following day. They made their goodbyes quickly and Tammy felt heartbroken at having to leave. They would spend one last night with Watanas at the rangers' camp.

'We'll be coming back regularly,' Ed reassured her.

'I don't want to go. There is so much I haven't seen yet.'

'You'll see it all eventually,' Ed said softly, his words offering her little consolation.

As they boarded the HP, Tammy could hear the animals crying out to her. She stared out of the window and watched Africa disappear – a tear rolled down her cheek, followed by another, then another. Ed took hold of Tammy's hand and gave it a gentle squeeze; he understood how she felt. He couldn't help wondering if one day Tammy would return to Africa for good.

EIGHTEEN

DR CRANE'S SECRET

Jax and Jude received a rushed summary of Tammy and Ed's adventures when they met them at the hovercraft. Despite feeling groggy from the long time she had spent travelling, Tammy wanted to go straight to the safari park. The animals expected it; she had been gone a very long time and they had all missed her immensely. She rode Sirocco – he needed the exercise after the long flight and his legs hurt. Jet also needed a run, so they sped towards the elephants, where Dave would be waiting to test for infections.

Tammy was happy to find that nothing had changed at the safari park. The animals were happy, and the visitors kept coming. Humphry did a couple of turns in excitement as he felt Tammy getting nearer. The rest of the elephants followed suit. Dave watched the elephants and knew what was going on. He knew his elephants well and understood how they felt towards Tammy. Sure enough, only minutes later, Dave saw the reason for the elephants acting so excitedly.

'Just how did I know you were coming?' he said with a laugh as Sirocco came to a stop next to him.

Tammy smiled and dismounted Sirocco.

'Hello, Dave. Have you missed me?' she said with a smile.

'You know I have. Though not as much as they have,' he said, pointing at the elephants. 'Go and say hello to them while I run some quarantine safety checks on Jet and Sirocco. We have to keep on top of our procedures.'

'All right then, they'll be good for you.' She stroked Sirocco and Jet, letting them know what was about to happen. Then she smiled warmly at Humphry and the other elephants as she headed towards them.

'I thought about you every single day,' she told them, and entered their pen.

Dave smiled as he took blood samples and watched the elephants and Tammy greet each other. They were loud and playful and in higher spirits than they had been since Tammy had left. The excitement and happiness were so strong that Dave felt a warm feeling flood through him. He suddenly felt like joining them and having some fun himself. He placed the blood samples into a small hand-held computer, and loaded a program to run the analysis.

Just then, Humphry looked directly at Dave. Dave sighed unhappily; Humphry wouldn't want him around while Tammy was there. He loved the elephants deeply and felt upset that they couldn't love him as much as they loved Tammy. Dave suddenly felt like an intruder at their party and slowly turned away. Humphry made a noise and stepped forward. Dave turned to look at him. They stared at each other.

'Where are you going, Dave?' Tammy asked. 'Humphry wants you to come and join us.'

Dave's spirits lifted and he smiled brightly. He knew Humphry wanted him there now. It wasn't just Tammy asking him; it was Humphry too. Dave almost ran into the pen and stood in front of the big bull.

'So, you do love me after all, you big softy,' he said with a smile.

Humphry nudged Dave with his trunk, nearly knocking him over. Tammy laughed. 'He's just very proud,' she said.

'Stubborn, more like.' Dave laughed.

Nutt suddenly appeared and squirted Dave with a trunkful of water. Humphrey's eyes lit up with glee and Dave stood shocked and wet.

'You sly devil,' he said, grinning.

Tammy explained how the elephants in Africa had helped them catch some hunters. Dave was impressed. The elephants raised their trunks with pride and Tammy smiled. They were all happily playing together when Jax arrived. He smiled as he saw how wet Dave was.

'I didn't think you would ever be part of a water fight,' Jax said.

'I didn't have much choice,' Dave replied.

'They look glad to see you home, Tammy.'

'They are. Dave's looked after them well, though,' Tammy said with a smile.

'Anyone would think it was the first time I'd ever looked after them,' Dave moaned.

'Are the results ready yet?' Tammy asked.

Dave took the small computer out of his pocket and pushed a couple of buttons.

'It finished five minutes ago and they're all clear,' he said with a smile.

'So, they can move about the island as normal?'

'Yes, they've brought nothing back and are in the clear. Many years ago, it would take a number of months to be sure of an animal's health, which made travelling with animals very expensive for us and stressful for them. Much easier nowadays.'

'Well, thanks, Dave. We're going to head off around the safari park and say hi to everyone now,' Tammy said.

'See you later then, bye.'

'Bye,' both Tammy and Jax responded.

A quick trip around the safari park showed the animals to be in good spirits, except Jax's tiger – he had been acting strangely, Jax told her. Tammy promised she would look at the tiger the following morning. For now, she had to get back to the house and sleep. Exhausted, she fell into bed, breathing a heavy sigh as she looked up at the flamingos on her ceiling. As much as she missed Africa, it felt good to be back in her own room. She smiled softly as she realised that it did feel like her own room after all, and she fell fast asleep.

*

It took a while for Tammy to settle back into being at the safari park. Her dreams were full of what had happened in Africa and she wondered what the animals were up to. She wanted to know if the lioness and her cubs were all right and if the hunters were still under lock and key. She wondered if Watanas and George were doing anything exciting while on patrol. She even wondered how the crocodiles were doing; were they still a little confused? There was so much she wanted to know about all the animals over there. She was sure she would go insane thinking about it at times.

Ed and Jude were busy trying to catch up with problems that had arisen while Ed had been away, and Jax helped, while Tammy visited all the animals at the park. She visited the tiger who was in pain, and it had been getting worse by the day. Tammy wished she had come before but time had held her back. She waited for all the safari park visitors to leave, then told the tiger to follow her.

She walked to the hospital with the tiger close behind. Crane was filling out a few forms when she walked in. He looked up and frowned when he saw the tiger with her.

'What's wrong with him?' he asked.

'I'm not sure. He has pains in his stomach. They've been getting worse,' she said as she stroked his head.

'How long has he had these pains?' Crane asked.

'Quite a while,' Tammy said.

Crane stood up and approached the tiger.

'He won't hurt me I take it?' He smiled sheepishly.

Tammy shook her head.

Crane proceeded to examine the tiger. He checked his mouth and ears and felt his stomach.

'I can't see anything wrong.' He frowned, rubbing his chin.

'I know it's serious,' Tammy said.

'I'll have to do an X-ray and run further tests. Get him onto the table so I can put him to sleep.'

*

Crane released a long sigh and shook his head as he looked at the X-rays.

'What is it?' Tammy asked.

'Cancer,' he told her.

'Will he live?' she asked.

'I think so. The cancer has started to eat away at his stomach. I'm quite sure we've caught it just in time. I'll have to operate as soon as I can get him ready. It's a good job you noticed,' he told her.

'Actually, Jax was the first to notice something was wrong,' Tammy told him.

'Jax? Hmm.' Crane didn't look too pleased.

'You don't like Jax very much, do you?' she asked.

'I think he has too much to say for a young boy.'

'What is it you have against snakes?' Tammy decided to ask.

She regretted asking the moment she said it. Crane's face went stiff as he looked at her. 'It just so happens I have a very good reason for avoiding snakes,' he said shortly.

'So, tell me,' Tammy pushed.

'I went through medical school with the same friend I went through high school with. I loved her very much. We both graduated as vets from university at the same time. She was going to be my wife, you see,' he said, looking at Tammy. 'We worked together. Everyone knew us as a team. We were always together. Then one day we received a call from a man who said he'd been bitten by his pet snake. He somehow managed to call us before passing out. As he fell, he knocked over several of the vivariums he owned. There were snakes all over the place. We didn't realise until we got there that there were so many venomous snakes loose in his house. Sally was standing beside me when I noticed all the upturned vivariums. I was about to tell her to get out when she started to scream.

'She was trapped in a corner with snakes all around her. They started to bite, one after the other. I tried to help her. I got bitten a couple of times myself. I watched as she fell to the floor. The snakes didn't stop attacking, even after she was dead. I couldn't move. I had started to have difficulty breathing due to being bitten myself. It felt like a long time that I stood there not caring about the fact that I had been bitten. I didn't want to live without her.'

Crane looked down at the floor in an attempt to hold back the tears. Tammy was silent.

'The man who originally called us must have called someone else too, because a man arrived and got me outside. He gave me antivenom and saved my life. At the time, I hated him for it. I wanted to die with Sally – I didn't want to go on without her. Do you understand?'

Tammy nodded. Her throat was too tight to say anything.

'It's hard to lose someone you love so much,' he said as he wiped his eyes. 'Now every time I see a snake, I hate it with a vengeance. The reason I don't have them in this hospital is because I know I wouldn't be able to resist killing them. Can you understand what it is like to feel such hatred?'

Tammy thought about how she had felt the day they caught the hunter.

'Yes, I understand,' she said weakly. 'It's something we must overcome.'

'Perhaps it is time to try,' Crane reflected.

Tammy smiled and nodded.

NINETEEN

MIKIE AND STEPHEN

Sirocco paced anxiously up and down his stable and snorted. Something was not right. His neigh awoke Jet, who lay resting on the end of Tammy's bed. As Jet looked around, he saw a hazy white mist creeping up from beneath the bed. He growled at the mist. It rose steadily, forming around Tammy's sleeping body, and there was nothing he could do about it. Jet watched as Tammy tossed and turned in the mist, sweat dripping from her forehead. She kicked so restlessly that she knocked Jet off the bed. He paced the room, his unease growing, as he watched Tammy disappear within the mist. Not knowing what else to do, Jet ran from the room.

Tammy didn't notice; she was too caught up in her dream. She had somehow arrived at a large mansion in Surrey, a bright red brick building with extensive grounds and stables. She knew it was a dream, and that she wasn't really there, but it was also real. She heard a sound, coming from the side of the house, and followed the noise. There stood a man and a boy. They were doing karate. She knew them.

The man was an entrepreneur and had been ever since he made his millions as a computer whizz-kid when he was only sixteen. His parents had been killed in a car crash, and it was only upon reading his father's will that this man, Stephen, learnt of his half-sister, Sarah. Since this was merely a strange dream, Tammy was not surprised that she knew this. The boy looked similar to Stephen and identical to Tammy, except for his closely shaved head of hair.

'Mikie,' Tammy whispered. 'My brother.'

Tammy somehow knew, probably through talks with Mikie during meditation or sleep, that Stephen and Sarah were brother and sister, but this was a fact not commonly known, as they were not from the same mother. But they got on really well.

As she watched Stephen and Mikie fight, enjoying pushing each other to their martial arts limits, she realised this was her twin brother. Twelve years ago, her twin, Mikie, had been left with his uncle. Stephen told everyone that Mikie was his son, and that the mother had abandoned them. This was in accordance with the letter Sarah had left with him in order to protect the boy. Tammy frowned, wondering how Mikie had conveyed all of this information in the few moments they had linked up. She walked closer to them.

They were in the garden doing their early-evening karate practice. They did this every day. Stephen was a black belt in karate and had taught Mikie since he was able to walk. Tammy could tell that Mikie was already better than Stephen had ever been. They bowed to each other, their practice completed, and retired to the house to see what their cook had prepared for dinner. Tammy, apparently unnoticed, followed.

'Hmm, it smells good,' Stephen said as they approached the dining room.

'Stephen, can we talk about school?' Mikie asked.

Stephen was too busy lifting the lids of the steaming food left in the centre of the dining table. 'Chicken,' he said, rubbing his hands together happily. 'Good, I'm starving, and stop calling me Stephen.'

'What am I supposed to call you then? We both know you're not my dad.' It was not said harshly, just simply a matter of fact.

Tammy watched them, fascinated by how real this dream seemed. It was unlike any other she had experienced.

'Is it that hard? People get adopted and still call their adoptive parents Mum and Dad, you know. I don't know why it has to be such a big deal with you. It's embarrassing telling people you are going through a *phase* and insist on calling me by my first name. Isn't it enough that everyone thinks I'm a bad person for not being able to find the woman who ran off on me, hmm? That my son doesn't respect me either?'

'You know it's not about respect.'

'Of course I do, but I'm not talking about me, am I? Can you just please try to understand the importance of my reputation, because I am not having an easy time of it getting girlfriends lately, you know, and God help me should I ever expect to settle down and marry.'

'You don't have trouble getting girls, and settle down – you? Ha! Pigs will fly first.' Mikie roared with laughter.

Tammy couldn't help but smile at them; they had a good relationship, more like two friends than an adult and his son – or nephew.

'Stop it.' Stephen laughed, throwing a napkin across the table into Mikie's face, where it was caught and returned with speed and accuracy.

'Oh no, you really are thinking about settling down.' Mikie stopped laughing and looked seriously at Stephen.

'I've told you not to pry into my thoughts,' Stephen scolded. 'I like my privacy and I know you don't have to read my mind just because you can.'

'It was an accident,' Mikie replied. 'It just happened.'

'I know. I trust you and I know you don't poke around in my head unless you have to.'

'It isn't a nice place to be.' Mikie laughed again.

'That's it.' Stephen jumped up from the table and chased Mikie around the room. 'Get here, you little…'

Stephen caught up with Mikie and they faced each other, still laughing. Mikie made the first move and they fell into a friendly karate fight. They laughed and joked as they avoided each other's punches and kicks.

'You're getting faster by the day,' Stephen said.

'You're getting slower,' Mikie replied cheekily.

'I'm holding back.'

'It's all the wine you drink.'

'I'll ground you if you keep up the attitude.'

'As if I go anywhere.'

Stephen rubbed the top of Mikie's head affectionately and they returned to the dinner table once more.

'Now about school…' Mikie started.

'I was well aware of your earlier question and chose not to answer then. That by no means gives you the leeway to raise it at the table.'

'I want to go to school,' Mikie moaned.

'And do what exactly? Read everyone's minds? Find out secrets about the teachers? I told you to prove to me that you could do it without causing a problem and you screwed up.' Stephen skewered a large piece of chicken on his fork, which he then waved at Mikie to underline his point.

'That's not fair.' Mikie banged his fist onto the table.

'Yes, my lad, it certainly is. You have seen off every teacher that I have hired for you. Perhaps you're too clever for your own good. I sent you to summer camp and that was your opportunity to prove it – what did you do? Hmm, tell me what you did with that opportunity.'

Mikie hung his head in disappointment. Tammy grew curious as to what had happened and at the same time felt sorry for Mikie. She understood his feeling of isolation. He was so similar to her. She started to wonder if she was making up this twin brother of hers to make her feel better and less lonely. How real was what she was seeing? Despite knowing she was in her own bed, Tammy couldn't shake the feeling that this dream was actually real.

'What did you do?' Stephen pressed.

'That teacher was stealing, we had to do something.'

'What did you do?' Stephen repeated.

'I blew it,' Mikie whispered.

'So why are we having this conversation again?'

'I want to be around kids.'

'I understand that, I really do, but no. You know you can't – you're different, Mikie. You know that.'

Mikie could read people's minds and he did it easily. Along with a letter, Sarah had left her son a pendant that looked very similar to Tammy's, which also matched a birthmark, the same as hers, on his arm. Tammy walked closer and looked at it. The mark on his arm was identical to hers.

Mikie placed his finger through a space in the overlapping circles, pulling the pendant free of its clasp and visualised what he wanted. He could turn the pendant into any weapon of his choice. One day a sword, perhaps a bow, maybe even a tin opener. Tammy watched as it became a knife and he used it to cut into his chicken.

'Can you use the normal cutlery on the table,' Stephen said with a sigh.

'It's not sharp enough. This chicken is tough, they've cooked it too quickly again,' Mikie moaned.

'Normal cutlery will do the job,' Stephen insisted.

Mikie sighed and reluctantly replaced the pendant around his neck. Taking up the normal knife from the table, he emphasised how blunt it was in cutting into his chicken. Stephen pretended to ignore him and carried on with his meal. Tammy could see that Mikie was frustrated.

'I never understood why your mother would leave you with that thing,' Stephen said.

'Why?' Mikie asked.

'It's dangerous, that's why.'

'I've never once hurt myself with it.'

'I know. That never ceases to amaze me, but you always were very lucky.'

Tammy wondered where the letter from her mother for Mikie was. *Where is it?* she asked silently, and somehow the answer come to her, most likely from Mikie's mind. She walked over to a small cupboard in the corner of the room and removed the letter from inside an empty but beautiful Chinese vase. It was the letter, and she immediately recognised the handwriting – it was the same as that on hers. A letter from their mother. Tammy pulled the letter out, opened it and read the contents.

Dear Stephen

I am sorry to do this to you and trust me when I say I had no choice. Please take good care of my son, Mikie. It is essential that our relationship remains a secret. No one knows I am your half-sister except Lei. This ensures no one knows he is my child. Stay away from Lei and don't let her know. Use whatever story fits best but remain secret about our shared father. Mikie's life will depend upon this more than you'll ever know. Teach him to fight. Don't be merciful – he will need to defend himself.

Time will show you the answers and you will come to know the meaning of all this. Please tell him how much I love him and will forever regret not being able to be there throughout his life. Tell him he is special and will know immense popularity – he will always know the truth and who is trustworthy. He will always instinctively know good from bad, which will guide him forward.

I am not well and do not have much time left. On his thirteenth birthday, his father will find him. Until then, I know you will guide and protect him throughout all his endeavours.

All my love
Sarah.

Tammy blinked and returned the letter back where she had found it.

With a sigh, Stephen continued. 'I know it's cool to be popular and I know you think you can trust people—'

'Mum said that I would always know who to trust,' Mikie interrupted.

Tammy stared at him, wanting to reach out and touch him, make him aware that she was there. Her hand almost touched his shoulder but then she pulled it back, nervous as to what would happen if she dared to touch him. They both remained oblivious to her presence.

'I know she did and you always do trust the right people – somehow! It doesn't mean you can go around telling your friends all about it. It will only draw attention to you in the long run. It's one thing you reading my mind and knowing the truth about your mum and I; it is quite another telling your friends what your teachers do after school. So far, you've been lucky but it's just not appropriate, Mikie, and until you learn the difference then it is not up for debate, understood?'

'I'm not a child!' Mikie replied sulkily. 'And it was funny.'

'But that's the problem here, Mikie, you are – in fact – most definitely a child! Technically. I know you're special, but you are still very young. And no, it really wasn't funny,' Stephen replied sternly. 'Do you have any idea of the humiliation you caused that man, all for a bit of fun with your friends? Until you can learn more responsibility, you're under lock and key.'

'I know. I am blatantly aware of that. I have lived in a prison for the last two years.'

'So, what about your dreams, are you still seeing those other kids in them?'

Tammy became more alert at the mention of dreams and took a seat next to Mikie, eagerly watching for his response.

'Yes, I am. I'm sure they are the same age as me. I can't see them clearly or get their names, although I am getting closer.' Mikie sighed.

'In what way?'

'I can often feel them, as if they are here, but never see their faces,' Mikie said.

'Do you always feel them in your sleep?' Stephen asked.

'Yes. Sometimes I can see what they are seeing, as if I am looking through their eyes, but I never quite seem to see their faces.'

Tammy licked her lips, nervously, and leaned closer to Mikie. She reached out, slowly touching his arm. 'Can you feel me here now?' she asked.

Mikie jumped and pulled his arm away.

'What's the matter?' Stephen asked, frowning.

'Nothing, just a strange feeling that someone is here now,' Mikie said, rubbing his arm absentmindedly, where Tammy had touched him.

Tammy stared at him, mouth agape, as she realised this was a lot more real than she had imagined.

'Never mind. It will make sense with time, it always does,' Stephen said.

'Yes, I guess,' Mikie mumbled, still touching the place Tammy had touched. 'I have a headache. I'm not hungry anymore, I'm going to lie down.'

Stephen nodded as Mikie left the table. Tammy followed.

*

Mikie sat on his bed, crossed his legs, closed his eyes and rubbed his forehead. Something with his migraines felt different tonight and he wanted to do more than meditate. He wanted to find his sister. He felt she was near for some reason, but the throbbing migraine distracted him. Tammy watched as he relaxed and tried to meditate, breathing deeply, and doing 6-3 breaths, and she sat opposite him doing the same thing. A mist began to encircle them. It began like a heatwave, distorting the air around them, making the air appear blurry. Then, the mist settled in and the air around them became strange. Tammy touched the bottom of his bed. It felt real, just as touching his arm had. Just as touching and opening the letter had. Mikie's breathing began to slow down as he slipped into a deep meditation. Images began to appear within the mist around them. Tammy gasped as she watched.

They were surrounded by a forest, a very dark forest. Only the smallest amount of light came through.

'Mikie, Mikie,' a girl's voice called out from behind the trees.

'Who are you?' Mikie frowned in his sleep as he asked the question.

'I am your sister, Mikie – I am Mina. Are you coming to find me?'

'My sister?' Mikie whispered.

Tammy could see the shadow of a girl as she moved from behind a tree and took a step closer towards Mikie's bed. Tammy swallowed nervously. The girl also seemed unaware of Tammy's presence.

'Mikie, if this isn't a dream, come and find me,' Mina said. 'I am alone.'

'Where are you?' Mikie asked.

'Near,' she whispered.

Just then, she came out of the trees and for a brief moment Tammy saw her. She was pale and thin, with rosy cheeks, her hair a dazzling dark golden blonde colour and long, all the way down to her waist. It made Tammy think of Rapunzel. She was pretty and delicate-looking with very dark brown eyes, so dark they could be mistaken for black in the right light. Tammy knew that this was her sister, Mina. She had dreamed of her many times before. She looked different to Tammy and Mikie but there was no doubt in Tammy's mind that this was their sister – exactly the same age too – triplets? Then, Mina stepped back behind a tree and disappeared.

'Where are you?' Mikie asked. There was no response; Mina had gone.

Tammy watched Mikie toss and turn some more; his eyes remained closed at all times.

'Mikie…' Another voice came from another tree behind him. This time, it was a boy.

'Who are you?' Mikie asked.

'I'm your brother,' said a big smiling face, as it appeared right in front of Mikie.

Mikie couldn't see him but Tammy could. Her mouth fell open as she stared at him. He too had golden blond hair and dark eyes, just like Mina's. They were like two sets of twins, Tammy and Mikie, and Mina and Diego. Tammy staggered back a step, overwhelmed by what she was learning.

'Brother?' Mikie whispered.

'I'm Diego. Is this really happening?' Diego suddenly looked right at Tammy and frowned. Tammy gasped as she realised he could see her. 'If this is real then stay away from me, stop trying to contact me. I want to be left alone.'

'Why?' Tammy asked.

'Just stay away from me!' Diego shouted at her and disappeared behind one of the trees.

'Who else is there?' Mikie asked.

Tammy stepped forward and took a seat beside him, on the bed. 'Tammy.'

'Tammy?' Mikie smiled. 'I thought I had lost you, I hadn't heard from you in months.'

'What do you mean? How can that be?' Tammy asked.

'I used to see you all the time, at the orphan school, but then you went away and disappeared. I always felt the closest to you until then. Where have you been? You feel so close to me now, as if you are right by me.'

'I am right by you in a way – I see you clearly. I am here. I have been a while. It doesn't make sense, but it is more than a dream. It must be the energy; I am connecting with it more powerfully every day in different ways now and it's fascinating.'

'You feel the energy too?' Mikie asked excitedly. 'I knew it.'

'Yes. It travels through me and is everywhere and in everything. Like a phone – you can't see it, but you can be connected to someone across the other side of the world through this invisible force.'

'Exactly! I think this is how my telepathy works – it's like waves of electricity in the air connecting my mind to that of others.'

Tammy gently touched his hand, feeling his skin and realising this was really her brother. Mikie returned the touch. His fingers closed around her hand, and she heard him gasp. He sat bolt upright in bed, gulped and slowly opened his eyes. The mist was all around him and it took a moment for his eyes to focus. Then, Tammy slowly came into sight and he saw her. Tammy smiled at him.

'You're here?' He gasped.

'Yes, I have been all evening. I watched you have dinner with your uncle.'

'Our uncle,' he said. 'We look so alike.'

'Yes, but you don't have much hair,' Tammy said.

'I do a lot of martial arts and it gets in the way. I have it shaved really close. We have the same colour hair and eyes.'

'Mina and Diego look alike too,' Tammy told him.

'Really?'

'Yes, it's strange how we look like two separate pairs of twins.'

'Quadruplets.'

'Yes, but how?' Tammy asked.

'I don't know, I just don't know.' Mikie sighed. 'I have just always seen you all or rather seen things through your eyes. I didn't know we were quads or that we looked alike. You were always the strongest to me. I'd see you looking down at your shoes, like you always do, or I'd see you holding a mouse – Minnie. I remember Minnie.'

'You do?'

'Yes, and Lieutenant Gremlin – she was horrible to you. We tried to find an orphan school run by a Lieutenant Gremlin once but couldn't.'

'That wasn't her real name,' Tammy said.

'Yes, that's what Stephen said.'

'Then I lost you, you were gone one day.'

'That must have been when the Brunswicks took me. They adopted me. I have been living on Vivacity Island ever since.'

'Is it nice there? You sound happy.'

'Oh yes, they're lovely people. They knew Sarah. Oh, she must be…'

'Yes, our mother. They knew her?'

'Yes, they are the ones who repopulated the earth with animals after Pisces,' Tammy said.

'Brunswick Safari Park, of course!' Mikie gasped. 'Mum must have had a good reason for splitting us all up.'

'Do you think so? Then how come we are able to talk like this now and not before?'

'My powers are weaker the further apart we are. The orphan school was nearer than where you are now and that's why I stopped being able to find you in my sleep. However, something about you has changed, Tammy. Your power is stronger than I have ever known.'

'My power?'

'Yes. We each have special abilities. You can read the minds of animals, can't you,' Mikie asked, 'like I do with people?'

'Yes, I guess I can,' Tammy said.

'This mind-reading power lets me seek you out when I sleep or meditate, and your connection with nature, the animals and energy has now made this link stronger. Now you aren't in a concrete camp, you are getting more powerful. The bond between us is strong. I can feel it. Be aware of your pendant, Tammy. It will help you and it has powers only you can wield. You and I are the only two with pendants and I see yours change colour sometimes. You must learn what else it can do.'

'What does yours do?'

'Mine becomes a weapon when I want it to. Yours glows red when you are in danger. Be careful, Tammy, they are looking for us.'

'Who are?'

'I don't know who they are. They are the reason Mum split us up and hid us, I'm certain of it. They used to come into my dreams and find me before I learnt to block them. They're dangerous and would kill our father if they could. I think that's why he hasn't come yet, so we have to be careful. I know they have been looking for us since we were born. They give me nightmares sometimes. They really are scary,' Mikie told her.

'I'm scared too,' Tammy said.

'I know, but Mum did leave us with good people.'

'I don't think an orphan school is good,' Tammy replied.

'She planned on the Brunswicks having you somehow, I'm sure she did.'

Tammy remembered the conversation with Ed. 'Yes, she is the reason he saved all the animals and she was the one who told him to look out for a special child who he would find from orphan school visits. Ed then offered free visits to all orphans waiting to find me. So, she was my mother and knew I would end up here after all.'

'Yes, when the time was right. There you go.' Mikie smiled. 'She did a good job making sure each of us was in a safe place where they wouldn't find us. I guess her connection with the Brunswicks made it unsafe to leave you there from the start.'

'What about our uncle, though?'

'No one knows that Stephen and Sarah are brother and sister.'

'What about waiting until we are thirteen? Like in the letter?'

'I think as long as we are careful, there is no reason why we shouldn't find each other before Father finds us. Besides, I want to meet you.'

'Mikie, how do you know all this?'

'Because Stephen has helped me understand everything about Pisces, about our mother and about my powers. You have not been encouraged to discover yours until now. Use the energy and be at one with it. Our pendants are not mere gifts.'

'What do you know about Diego and Mina?'

'Diego can harness electricity but he can't control it yet, and Mina is a shape-shifter – not changing into animals but changing her physical form to blend into an object like a tree or a wall, and she can manipulate objects, like bending buildings, metal or walking through walls. She is quite the tomboy.'

'She didn't look like a tomboy when I saw her earlier. She looked like Rapunzel with her long, flowing hair,' Tammy said.

'She always ties her hair back or wears it under a hat of some sort. The woman she lives with is always telling her off for hiding her pretty looks, and tries to get her to dress more like a girl,' Mikie explained.

'Who is this woman?'

'I don't know her name or anything. All I know is that she is an MI6 agent. Diego is with a dodgy dealer. The police are after him for some reason. He runs underground operations that always somehow manage to do good for most people even if they are illegal. Because of his connections he has been able to cover up and hide Diego's power – and mistakes!'

'We must get together and find them,' Tammy said.

'I'll speak with Stephen and we'll arrange to come to you. I've always wanted an excuse to visit the park.'

'Perfect, I'll make sure Ed and Jude are expecting your call. Diego didn't seem to want to be found. He saw me too, you know,' Tammy said.

'He did? Maybe he is more powerful than we realise. He never seems to want to be found. He always seems nervous or scared of something. Perhaps it's his power, as it is so strong and quite out of his control. He almost caused a nuclear incident once.'

'Well, I think we should look for them anyway.'

'I think you're right, Tammy, and I can tell that our combined energy is stronger than when we are alone. We should be able to do it. I can't wait to meet you,' Mikie said.

'I can't believe I have a brother!'

'Two! Oh, and a sister. There is just one thing I think you should be aware of.' Mikie sighed and looked down at their hands.

'What is it?' Tammy asked.

Mikie looked her straight in the eyes and took a deep breath. 'It's things our uncle and I have spoken about in the past regarding the things Mother got up to. How did she and the others who helped her know the virus was coming before anyone else did, and how did she learn all the things nobody could possibly know at the time? Why did she run away and hide us all and what gave us the special powers? Was it the virus? Who or what is our father?'

'What are you saying, Mikie?'

'I'm saying that there are things we need to think about before we go looking for Mina and Diego. I'll tell you more when we meet, and I can sit next to you properly. Right now, I believe we are all in great danger and I do not think we have time to wait for our father to arrive. This is why I have been trying to find you all more lately.'

Their eyes met and they held each other's gaze for a long time. Tammy saw the fear in Mikie's eyes, and it made her shiver.

'My nightmares are getting worse; I see a war is coming. In fact, I think it has been here for many years already. We just haven't been part of it yet.'

'A war?' Tammy gasped.

'Yes, a terrible war. That is why our father is coming back to get us. It isn't safe for him to do so yet and whoever is looking for us is at war with our father.'

'What do they want with us? To kill us?'

'I get the feeling it is a fate worse than death awaiting us, Tammy, if this enemy finds us before Father. I don't think we can afford to wait any longer.'

Tammy licked her lips nervously and went to speak, when she found no words would come out.

'Tammy?' Mikie whispered.

She saw him whisper the words but was unable to respond. He started to fade away from sight and the mist swirled around her. Fear gripped her heart as she felt something wrenching her away from her brother. Hands closed around her chest, tightly, making it hard for her to breathe. She couldn't speak or utter a sound. She tried to scream but found there was no air left in her lungs to make the sound. Everything around her went black.

TWENTY

THE PENDANT

'Tammy, wake up! Come on, Tammy, listen to me,' Jax shouted, shaking her shoulders roughly.

Tammy opened her eyes and saw Jax staring down at her. He looked worried. He stopped shaking her and closed his eyes, breathing a sigh of relief as he saw she was awake.

'You scared the living daylights out of me!' he exclaimed.

'Wh...' Tammy tried to talk but her mouth was too dry.

Jax ran into the bathroom, poured her a glass of water and helped her sip it. She gulped down the water, relieving her enormous thirst, and looked around her. She was in her bed at home, where she had gone to sleep. Mikie was no longer visible. Jet sat, nervously, alongside her bed, watching her. She petted his head.

'Tammy, what happened?'

She frowned, trying to focus her thoughts and remember.

'Jet was so scared he ran into my room and dragged me out of bed!' Jax continued. 'When I got here, there was this strange mist all around your bed and you were sitting up talking to someone who I couldn't see. Then you passed out and I thought you were dead! What on earth happened, Tammy?'

She smiled. A soft, gentle smile that told him everything was all right. She finished her water.

'Oh, Jax, I have so much to tell you!' she said. 'Wake Ed and Jude and I'll meet you all in the kitchen. I'm a quadruplet!

'A what?' Jax gasped.

Tammy jumped out of bed, almost knocking Jet over, and took some clothes out of her wardrobe. She flung them onto the bed and skipped to the bathroom to take a shower. 'A quadruplet, Jax, and you're about to meet my brother.'

Jax sighed as he looked at Jet. The door slammed shut and he heard Tammy turn the shower on. Jet stood up and followed Jax out of the room.

*

'Are you sure it wasn't just a dream?' Jude asked as she poured herself some more tea.

'Yes, I'm positive,' Tammy said.

'It couldn't have been a dream, the mist was too real,' Jax added.

'But you didn't *see* who she was talking to?' Jude asked.

'No, but there was someone there, I could tell,' Jax said. 'I could feel his presence and it spooked me out.'

'Mikie can read people's minds and speak to them even at a distance,' Tammy continued.

'And Mikie is your brother?' Ed replied, scratching his chin.

'Yes and Sarah was my mother. I'd like you to read this.' Tammy handed Ed the letter from her mother. 'I'm sorry I never mentioned this before, but I didn't want you to change your minds about adopting me.'

She watched Ed read it and, sighing, he handed it to Jude to read. 'I should have known. Perhaps deep down I did,' Ed said thoughtfully. 'I cannot believe I didn't notice the resemblance before – even just your eyes.'

'So, you think it's true?' Jude asked, handing the letter to Jax.

'There's no doubt in my mind,' Ed said.

Tammy breathed a sigh of relief; she knew she could count on Ed and Jude.

'Were you very lonely at the orphan school?' Jax asked, finishing the letter and handing it back to Tammy. She tucked it away in her pocket.

'A little, yes. Lieutenant Gremlin didn't like me much and that made making friends difficult. Anyone who became my friend went into her bad books, you see.' Tammy looked down at her untouched cornflakes. 'It's been wonderful since I've been here, and when Mum said that the feeling of loneliness wouldn't last, she was right.'

'Yes, your mother was a very clever woman, quite amazing actually,' Ed said.

'Tell me about her,' Tammy begged. 'Tell me everything you know.'

'Yes, you should know. It was three months before the start of the Pisces outbreak when Sarah first came to visit me. She found me by what seemed like an accident at first, at the safari park. Later, of course, I realised she had planned the whole meeting. We talked for a while and since she was so intriguing, I found myself telling her everything.'

'Your mother had a way with people,' said Jude. 'She made you feel very comfortable and you told her things you wouldn't tell your own friends.'

'I invited Sarah to stay with us and she did, for two months. I think it was almost straight away that she told us her real reason for being here,' Ed went on.

'It was the third day,' Jude confirmed. 'I remember that because it felt quite natural for her to be so open and honest. That night, I remember asking you if you thought it strange that she had told us so much, having only known us three days. Do you remember that, Ed?'

'Yes, I do now,' he replied. 'At the time, she said she was a sort of prophet and was working with an organisation to protect all the different species on our planet. She explained that this organisation was the very same one that had prevented extinctions throughout the ages whenever they could. As you can imagine, I was over the moon. She had inside information that would be invaluable to the work I was trying to do.

'She told us that there was going to be a worldwide catastrophe that would wipe out most of the species on the planet. She didn't mention at this time any threat to humans, and she didn't tell us about the virus outbreak. I assumed she meant pollution, some sort of natural disaster or perhaps a nuclear war. She wouldn't tell us anything else about the organisation and explained that she only knew that I had been chosen to help the animals.'

'You were chosen to be the modern-day Noah?' Jax asked excitedly.

'Yes, in a way. For the two months Sarah was with us, we were in a race against time to home at least two of every species on the planet. This included animals, trees, flowers, insects, sealife, and so on – the list was endless. I could never have done it without Sar... your mother. She made it seem so easy. I do not know how she or the organisation she represented did it; we had ships full of everything turning up daily in the last month.'

'Why have you never told me any of this?' Jax asked.

'It was not something to talk about,' Ed replied.

'It was a very crazy time,' said Jude. 'We had to expand the island dramatically, as most of it wasn't set up as a sanctuary at the time.'

'How?' Tammy and Jax asked at the same time, smiling at each other as they both revelled in the story.

'Well, it was complicated, that's for sure. We had to address so many problems and increase the number of animals we had,' Jude said.

'The most complicated solution was within the ocean itself. I asked your mother once what we were to do if any pollution came to our island. I was concerned about contamination. If it was a worldwide problem, then what would save my island from the fate befalling the rest of the planet? She told me that would be taken care of. She said we were to build up our own supply of water on the island and not to use any water from elsewhere for two years. Well, that is a lot of water I had to store. So, the organisation came and built huge storage tanks, in the ocean near the island, to keep it in.' Ed used his arms to emphasise the size of the tanks.

'We were not allowed to see or work with anyone from the organisation – only Sarah,' Jude said. 'They would only work at night and wore black suits, like ninjas, so that we couldn't identify them.'

'Why hide themselves?' Tammy asked.

'That's what I was just wondering,' Jax added.

'We often wondered that ourselves, but Sarah wouldn't give us a reason. She just said that was the way it was.' Jude sighed. 'We knew they were aliens. We were hoping Sarah would trust us and share that with us, but we never pushed it. We trusted her – and them – completely. We had no reason not to – they were doing lots of good.'

Ed continued. 'These storage tanks helped to make us very self-sufficient. The organisation also sectioned off areas of the ocean around the island and installed large glass panels to create large aquaria within the ocean itself. These were isolated glass tanks for us to farm fish for the seals, sea lions, penguins and other animals that needed fish in their diet. You cannot even begin to imagine the cost, or the work, involved in that.'

'The manual cost and the financial cost,' Jude added.

'Exactly! Well, the aquaria were designed in such a way that once built, no water could get in and none could get out, making the island completely isolated. It was like having our own private ocean. Of course, we were given very strict instructions on how to use and maintain all this equipment. I asked your mother whether that meant it would be something from the ocean that would devastate the planet, since that seemed to be what we were preparing for. She told me that initially yes, that was where it would start and then it would spread everywhere, even into the air we breathe. Of course, I then asked how we could help the animals survive that, and what she told me I couldn't at first believe.' Ed paused, taking a long, slow breath.

'What was it?' Tammy asked in barely a whisper.

'The organisation had been working on the ocean floor to build a massive dome, a little like the aquarium. Only this dome would act as a shield, and it would cover the entire island – like a huge bubble. Of course, I just couldn't believe it. We didn't have the technology to do such a thing. When it was ready, she showed me how to activate and deactivate the shield. It was incredible. You could barely see the shield as it came up through the water and over the island. It barely made a noise. Yet, sure enough, it enclosed the island and we were completely isolated. There was an entrance for the hovercraft to come and go, and nobody, not even the staff on the island, could tell it was there. I couldn't believe how much was done and no one knew about it.' Ed paused to have a sip of his cold tea.

'Noah's Ark.' Jax shook his head in disbelief. 'Only here on this island. I can't believe you've never mentioned any of this to me before.'

'Once, I tried to ask how Sarah could do all this, how the organisation had such resources at its disposal; she wouldn't tell me. She just laughed and said some secrets should not be shared until the time was right. She apologised for holding back information, said it was for our own good, and we accepted that.'

'Because you trusted her,' Tammy said.

'Yes. I wondered why we didn't build another boat – like Noah,' said Jude. 'Sarah explained that the floods had lasted a very short time back then and that this catastrophe would last much longer.'

Ed nodded in agreement and replied. 'She couldn't say how long, maybe a year, maybe more. The island was now completely self-contained and safe. Then she left us. We insisted all our staff bring their closest friends and family to the island for the summer, without telling them why. We already had our own fruit and vegetable farm and we just expanded it to cater for the additional numbers we had. Jude increased the number of chickens we had, and we had enough water to last us two years, if we were careful.'

'My pet chickens are just for eggs,' Jude explained. 'I never eat anything I name – too emotional. I have another bunch of chickens away from the house, and they aren't pets. Baby chicks feed the owls and the hawks. Like Ed said, we were, and still are, completely self-contained.'

'Not long after Sarah left, things started to happen,' Ed continued. 'News of a virus outbreak spread across the world. It started in America, Britain, China and Russia at the same time – apparently caused by a build-up of man-made pollution that affected the fish. That is why they named the virus Pisces, the symbol of the fish. Chaos broke out across the world and by now, we had activated the shield. We just closed the door to the hovercraft – nothing came in, nothing went out. We had no contact with the outside world except for television, phones and radio. In every country, quarantine zones called safe camps were set up for everyone to go to in an attempt to contain the virus.'

Jude took up the story. 'It became airborne in a matter of months. Hundreds of thousands died. The virus killed in a matter of days. There was no cure and although they did manage to create a vaccine, there was not enough to go around quickly enough. Only about ten percent of the human race could be vaccinated and that didn't even cover VIPs. Meanwhile, governments around the world panicked and began to take drastic measures to protect those that remained uninfected. Billions died from the virus or were exterminated in an attempt to contain it. Your mother, along with the organisation, had a different plan. I do not know the details, as I never saw your mother after the day she left here. I knew it had to be her from the reports we heard. Somehow she managed to save millions – protecting them both from the virus and the containment measures employed by their own governments. The people had to be kept safe and vaccinated before the government could be trusted not to overreact and destroy them as a potential risk,' she explained.

'So, your mother and this organisation saved the human race. She gave us the ability to save the animals while she concentrated on the people. Without her and this secret organisation, the planet would have been wiped clean.' Ed squeezed Tammy's cold hand reassuringly.

'You have a cool mum,' Jax said kindly.

Tammy smiled at him. 'So, what happened with me and my brothers and sister?'

'I don't know. I can guess,' Ed said. 'Sarah told me the catastrophe would only be the beginning – that a great war was brewing. At first, I thought the government's reaction to Pisces was the war. Then, I thought maybe it would be a world war over the cause of the outbreak. Nothing I have seen has come close to resembling the great war she described to me, which leads me to think it is still to come.'

'Mikie said something about a war coming,' Tammy told Ed.

'Did he say why or when?' Jude asked.

'No, not that I can remember,' Tammy answered.

'I do not know what the war will be fought over, or who it will be between, and yet I believe Sarah's prophecy hasn't yet been fulfilled,' Ed said with a sigh.

'She told you to trust in your instincts,' Jude told him.

'Yes, she did. Sarah was a big believer in the Brunswick instinct,' Ed smiled proudly, 'and my instinct tells me this war is coming. I suspect that is why your mother had to go into hiding before you were born and then hide you all to protect you from someone, or something.'

'Mikie also said someone was after us. Who?' Tammy asked.

'I bet they knew that you were a quad. That's why your mum had to separate you all,' Jax suggested.

'Yes, you'd be easier to find together, since quadruplets are so rare,' Jude agreed.

'But who?' Tammy insisted.

'We don't know. There are a couple of strange things that bother me,' Ed said with a sigh. 'First, there are the special powers that you and your siblings have. I do not know if it is something the virus did to you while your mother was pregnant or…'

'What?' Jax asked excitedly.

Ed let out a long breath and looked at Jude, who shrugged. He was hesitant to voice his thoughts aloud. 'Well, I trusted your mother with all my heart. I knew she was a good person and meant well. However, all the things she made happen we just couldn't have done alone with the technology that currently exists today, let alone back then. The organisation did things at such a speed and so easily that it seemed rather, well, out of this world really.'

'Aliens?' Jax gasped. Tammy turned very pale and remained speechless.

'Yes, in a nutshell, I guess that is what I am suggesting. Why not? They may have been a superior race or just had advanced technology. Either way, they were helping us,' Ed said.

'Tammy is an alien?' Jax asked, fascinated by the idea.

Tammy didn't know what to say and felt the sick rising in her chest. She licked her lips and gulped.

'Only half alien, possibly,' Jude comforted. 'Sarah was very much one of us.'

'I am not the sort of person to readily believe in other planets and life beyond the stars,' Ed said. 'I much prefer to think we are all there is. That's just the way I like it. However, I must confess that with everything I have seen over the years I cannot believe we didn't have some superior help. I saw certain things that couldn't be explained in any other way.'

'Let's not forget that the organisation could just be an incredibly powerful group of people,' Jude said. 'We have discussed conspiracies for generations. Perhaps the organisation is really in charge and the government is just a front. Who really knows?'

'Other planet life forms is only one ideology, so let us not focus too much on that until we know for sure. I could be completely wrong. We will probably have to wait until you are thirteen, when your real father comes and finds you,' Ed said.

'I think Mikie knows the truth,' Tammy whispered, still feeling sick.

'Then he'll tell us when he gets here,' Jax said.

'What if my father *is* an alien?' Tammy reluctantly asked.

'I think that is a possibility you should bear in mind, Tammy. Just remember that he will be a good person, alien or not. Otherwise, your mother wouldn't let him find you, would she?' Jude said soothingly.

Tammy nodded.

'This is so cool,' Jax said with a smile.

'You think so?' Tammy asked, surprised. His positive enthusiasm cheered her up. It was nice he didn't seem to care whether she was half alien or not. The relief she felt surprised her and she blushed.

'Of course, it's awesome. Can we see the shield?'

'No, I don't like to draw attention to it.'

'You said it was quiet.' Jax insisted.

'True, to us anyhow. However, you never know who is watching, and Tammy does not need to attract any attention right now,' Ed replied.

Jax pouted.

'I did some research on your pendant and I found a number of rocks and crystals that have special qualities. However, nothing along the lines of your pendant – nothing else changes colour and resembles it in any way,' Jude explained.

'We do not think your pendant is of this earth,' Ed added.

'Oh.' Tammy held her pendant and looked at it. 'So, this is alien too? Perhaps from my father?'

'It's certainly a possibility. I suggest we spend the rest of today looking at your pendant, Tammy. We should experiment when it changes colour and what happens.

You can practise making things happen with it, like your brother suggested,' Ed said.

'Not until Tammy and I have done some tai chi,' Jude said. 'The poor girl is a little shocked, Ed, and it will help her find some peace and balance after receiving all this information. Try to imagine what it must be like hearing all this for the first time. It has taken us years to be able to get our heads around it, Ed.'

'Of course. I'm sorry, Tammy. I thought it was best to tell you what I knew,' Ed apologised.

'It's okay, I think deep down I knew the truth. I just... Well...' She sighed.

'Come, let us recharge our energy.' Jude smiled, stood up and held out her hand to Tammy.

Tammy returned the smile and went with Jude. Jet remained with Ed and Jax, as silently requested by Tammy.

'Uncle Ed, why have you never mentioned any of this before?' Jax asked once Tammy was out of earshot. He never considered that she could hear him through her communication with Jet.

'There was never any reason to. Jax, I know I can trust you and this must all remain secret. I also need you to do me a big favour.'

'Of course, just tell me what.'

'I need you to help Tammy and be a really good friend to her. Being the same age will help. She needs comfort and support right now – you must not treat her differently.'

'How can I not? She is different – she is awesome. I understand what you're trying to say and I really like her, so I'll be the best friend she has ever had,' Jax said with a smile.

'Thank you, Jax. I know you will.' Ed smiled back.

Tammy smiled widely as she followed Jude out into the garden. She kept repeating the words in her head, *I really like her...*

*

Later that same day, Ed, Jax and Tammy headed towards the safari park. As usual, Tammy rode Sirocco beside the Jeep.

'The pendant is glowing green,' Jax noted.

'It always does when I am near Sirocco or Jet,' Tammy said.

'Right,' said Ed. 'So, in its natural state, the pendant is blue. When Tammy is around animals and feeling happy, the pendant is green. When did it go red?'

'I was with the crocodiles. Oh, and once when I was with the elephants,' Tammy replied.

'Then let us start with the elephants,' Ed said.

The elephants greeted them in their normal cheerful fashion and Tammy said hello to them all. The pendant glowed green.

'Were you ever in any doubt as to their behaviour towards you when it turned red before?' Ed asked.

'Not at all. We were laughing and having fun,' Tammy replied.

'Tell me exactly what you were doing,' he asked, puzzled.

'I was washing them, laughing, and having a lot of fun. People were watching and I was covered in soap and water. Then the pendant started to feel hot on my chest and that's when I looked down to see it was red. I didn't notice anything else.'

'Yes, I remember that day.' Ed stroked his chin thoughtfully. 'I was in the crowd of people watching you. I wonder if there was someone in the crowd who posed a danger to you.'

'Then they would know where I am,' Tammy said.

'I don't think so. Otherwise, we would have surely seen them again. It has never gone red apart from those two occasions?'

'No, not that I remember.'

'Okay, then let's go and see the crocodiles – happy to do your thing again?'

'Oh yes, I know just what to do now. There won't be a problem,' Tammy said.

'Well, I'll get Ben in with you just to be safe,' Ed said.

*

Ben used a hoop on the end of a long pole to hold one of the crocodiles in place and then attached another hoop around his jaws. The pendant turned white and felt cold.

'I don't like this much,' Ben said. 'It makes me feel uneasy.'

Tammy smiled as they left the crocodiles.

'No red, only white now,' she told Ed. 'It was ice-cold too.'

'I will, for the time being, assume that is because the danger has gone now that you know how to control them. However, they remained cold towards you. I can't think of any other reason.'

'That sounds right to me,' Tammy said. 'Perhaps the snakes?'

*

They spent the day visiting all the animals in the safari park. Some snakes turned the pendant white, while others turned it green. In all cases, it was never red. All other animals in the safari park turned it green. It was consistent.

'Mikie said he could turn his pendant into a sword or another type of weapon,' Tammy said. 'Perhaps I should try that.'

'Let's go back to the house and do that then. You never know who we might bump into out here,' Ed suggested.

*

Ed and Jax watched from a distance as Jude helped Tammy channel her energy and be at one with her chi. They were practising breathing techniques and mental control. 'Now, close your eyes, hold the pendant and picture what you want it to be,' Jude suggested.

Tammy closed her eyes and tried to imagine a sword. She felt the pendant changing in temperature and Jude watched as it flickered through all the different colours of the rainbow. Nothing happened. Tammy tried again; still nothing happened.

'Perhaps we should try a different approach,' Jude suggested. 'Walk slowly around the pond and breathe deeply. Think about the air on your arms, the grass under your feet, and try to feel what the pendant is telling you.'

Ed pulled a face at Jude, indicating that he thought she was a little crazy. Jude impatiently waved him away. Tammy did as she suggested. She could feel every breath of air she inhaled and exhaled. She had removed her shoes and socks and could feel the grass between her toes – it felt soft and warm. She came to a standstill and focused on her feet. They were getting hotter. The warmth of the sun was beating down on her bare skin and the chi energy was making her hands and feet feel hotter and hotter. She imagined she could see water, cool water, and she wanted to feel it splash on her toes, taking away the heat.

Jude watched in astonishment as the water in the pond started to stir. It was like a small whirlpool, the size of an apple at first, and then it began to grow. It shot a fountain of water high up into the air and straight at Tammy. Tammy gasped and opened her eyes. She was soaked. The pond was still, and she looked around her, not sure where the water had come from. She looked at Jude, who had covered her open mouth with her hand.

'Where did that come from?' Tammy asked.

'From the pond! Tell me what you were thinking. Tell me now before you forget,' Jude whispered.

'My feet were getting hot and I wanted to cool them down,' Tammy explained.

'Do it again,' Jude said. 'Imagine the water cooling you down.'

Tammy smiled mischievously and closed her eyes. The water started to swirl once more, and the whirlpool grew larger this time. A large spray of water shot up into the air and drenched Jude. Tammy opened her eyes and laughed loudly. Ed and Jax tried hard to stifle their laughs.

'That's just what I pictured,' she gloated.

'Well, thank you very much!' Jude exclaimed, squeezing

the water from her hair and clothes. 'Now, see if you can make the water move in different ways.'

Tammy suddenly remembered the little boy and the crocodiles in Africa. The water had helped them, the whirlpools, which she must have created without realising it. She concentrated on the water and moved her hands as though she was conducting an orchestra. Slowly at first, and then more rapidly, the water began to move about and jump up in the air. She created a display of waterfalls and a series of interlocking wave patterns. It soon started to feel easy and natural. When she had finished, she turned to Jude, who was laughing and clapping along with Ed and Jax.

'Do it again,' Jax yelled.

She did, and each time she got better at it. After a time, she started to feel tired and looked at Jude.

'It's exhausting,' she explained.

'Take a break,' Jude smiled, 'I'll get us all something to drink and then we can try something else.'

Jude returned with some squash, which everyone gulped down. Tammy licked her lips and tried again to make a weapon. Nothing happened.

'It's definitely not going to turn into a weapon like your brother's, is it?' Jude mused.

'I guess not,' Tammy said.

Jude looked around the garden for something else to try. 'Since you can move water, try that,' she said, pointing to the passion fruit plant climbing up the side of the house.

It was all leaves; no flowers or fruit yet showing. Tammy focused on the climbing plant, and a feeling of warmth washed over her. The plant started to shake and twitch. Buds burst forth and turned into pretty blue and white flowers. These in turn became orange passion fruits and the whole plant grew further up the house, a year of growth accomplished in the blink of an eye. It was breathtakingly beautiful. The pendant glowed greener and brighter than ever before and Tammy began to understand.

'Awesome!' Jax exclaimed when Tammy had finished. 'Do something else.'

There was a large weeping willow hanging over the pond that caught Tammy's attention. She focused on it. The tree began to shake a little and then it swayed back and forth. The branches stretched out and grew longer and had almost reached Tammy when they suddenly stopped.

'I'm too tired now,' Tammy said.

'Come and sit down,' Ed said. As he spoke, she tumbled. He caught her just before she hit the ground.

'Tammy!' Jude gasped.

'It's all right. She's just exhausted,' Ed said, carrying her inside the house, Jude and Jax following close behind.

TWENTY-ONE

A FAMILY GATHERING

It was Sunday and Mikie was due to arrive any moment. Jude and Tammy were practising tai chi, finding it hard to concentrate. Jax and Ed had gone down to the port to meet the hovercraft. Jude finished their tai chi forms earlier than usual and, unable to wait any longer, Tammy decided to take Sirocco down to the port and meet Mikie sooner.

She arrived just in time to see a boy her age stepping from the hovercraft and being welcomed by Ed. He looked just like in her dream and she again marvelled at his closely shaved head. Her heart raced with excitement as they drew nearer. Mikie saw her first and before anyone else; he smiled.

'You must be Stephen.' Ed said, as they shook hands.

'Yes, and you must be Ed Brunswick. It's really good to meet you,' Stephen replied.

They heard the horse and turned to face Tammy as she dismounted.

'Tammy.' Mikie was already by her side; they hugged as if they had known each other forever.

'So, this is Tammy? You look so much like your mother,' Stephen said warmly, moving towards her.

'Hello, Uncle Stephen,' she said with a smile.

'Ah, come here.' He laughed and hugged her.

Mikie felt Jax's cold stare and the slight touch of jealousy behind it. They watched each other. Mikie understood.

'Hi, Jax,' Mikie said.

'Oh yes, Mikie, Uncle Stephen, meet Jax. He's my best friend,' Tammy said excitedly.

Jax muttered a quiet hello and blushed at the compliment. When he looked up, he could see Mikie was still staring at him.

'*So, you like my sister,*' Mikie said, though no one apart from Jax heard it.

'Don't read my mind!' Jax shouted.

'Mikie! Don't be rude. Give people their privacy,' Stephen scolded.

'Of course, Uncle. Sorry, Jax, it's a bad habit,' Mikie apologised. 'I hope we can be friends as well.'

Jax smiled and awkwardly took the hand he was offered, not being used to shaking hands with anyone at his age. He breathed a sigh of relief as he realised Mikie didn't mean any harm, and decided he liked him.

'Come, let me take you up to the house so you can meet my wife,' Ed said, ushering them into the Jeep.

'Mikie, why don't you go with Tammy on Sirocco?' Jax offered generously. It was normally his place to ride with Tammy and he didn't give up the post lightly.

'It's nice of you to offer but I wouldn't like to take your place,' Mikie answered.

'No need,' said Tammy, just as a zebra appeared through the trees.

'I can't ride,' Mikie said, shocked, preferring to hold on to Tammy than go on alone.

'Oh yes, you can and you will,' Tammy said, laughing.

He didn't know how he did it but Mikie managed to get on the zebra's back. Jax jumped up behind Tammy and they galloped away. Mikie bounced unsteadily, clinging to the zebra's mane so tightly his knuckles were white.

'Well, what a sight,' said Stephen. 'Not every day you see that.'

'Oh, you have no idea.' Ed rolled his eyes.

'I'm sure I don't,' Stephen said with a laugh.

They were travelling quickly across the fields and even when carrying two passengers, Sirocco easily outran the zebra. Mikie gripped the zebra's mane and bobbed about without any of the elegance that Tammy showed. He scanned Tammy's mind and watched her movements for tips on how to ride, picking up barely enough to keep him upright. She did it automatically, naturally, without thinking about it. He admired Sirocco and marvelled at how Jet followed happily alongside.

'You have mastered the animals well,' Mikie told Tammy, though he uttered no words.

'It just happens,' she replied aloud.

'What?' Jax asked.

'Nothing,' said Tammy.

'You don't need to speak out loud, I'll hear you,' Mikie told her.

'Can you read my mind?' she asked.

'Of course,' he said with a smile.

'I even know you are smiling.' She laughed.

'What are you laughing at?' Jax asked.

'Why can't Jax hear you too?' Tammy asked, not answering Jax.

'Because I wasn't letting him. I'm getting really good at controlling minds and choosing who can or cannot hear me. I want to practise a bit now – it isn't often I get the chance to do so openly.'

'I know what you mean. We have to be careful, don't we?'

'Yes, we can't afford to be found by those Mother hid us from.'

'Do you know much about them?'

'No.'

'Ed thinks they might be aliens.'

'I think he is right.'

'Do you think we are half alien?'

'Yes, I think so, but I think we are something else too. Part human, part alien and part something else.'

'Pisces?'

'Yes. A war is coming, you know. I see it in my dreams. I think I can pick up on what they are planning sometimes. At least I used to be able to and then the dreams stopped.'

'Ed said a war was coming too. Why do you think your dreams stopped?'

'I think they knew I was reading them and blocked me somehow.'

'Do you think they can read you?'

'I think they try but I learnt how to block them quite easily. It seemed the most natural thing in the world for me to stop them from entering my mind.'

'Yes, I know what you mean. It comes naturally sometimes, doesn't it? Effortlessly, like I find it with animals.'

'*Yes, that's right. Did you get anywhere with your pendant?*'

'*Yes, shall I show you?*'

'*Go ahead.*'

'*Look to your left,*' she told him. He looked towards a small area of newly planted trees. They were less than a metre high and one of them had begun to move, shooting upwards at great speed until, in a few short seconds, it was fully grown. The branches opened up and spread wide, with fruit hanging below. Sirocco and the zebra followed Tammy's instructions to turn around, and slowly came to a stop under the tree.

'*Jude's new apple trees,*' Tammy said with a smile. Sirocco and the zebra reached up and helped themselves to an apple. Tammy, Mikie and Jax did likewise.

'Wow! They taste great,' said Mikie, licking his lips.

'I feel really boring next to you pair,' Jax moaned. 'But if it means sharing the fruits of your labour then I can hardly moan.'

They all laughed. They were almost at the house and enjoyed a leisurely walk the rest of the way. Jude, Ed and Stephen were waiting by the front.

'What distracted you this time?' Ed asked.

'We stopped for apples,' Jax said, smiling.

Mikie silently told Stephen what had happened. He looked at Tammy with raised eyebrows.

'I'll show you what I can do with water,' Tammy said. She took them to the pond and demonstrated how she could make water dance.

'Beautiful. I thought Mina was the one who could manipulate things.' Stephen looked at Mikie.

'Yes, hard things like stone and metal. Water and nature are Tammy's area, I guess,' said Mikie. 'Can you manipulate solid objects, Tammy?'

She thought for a moment and looked at a small rockery next to the pond then shook her head. 'No.'

'Look,' Jax shouted. He pointed at a large frog that had jumped out of the pond and was leaping desperately, as far as his legs would carry him, as a grass snake mercilessly chased him.

'Oh my,' Jude exclaimed. 'I didn't know frogs could go that fast.'

'I have never given it much thought, myself. Look how fast the snake is going,' Ed said, laughing.

'You can't interfere,' Mikie told Tammy, reading her thoughts.

'I don't want the frog to get eaten.'

'Everything needs to eat,' he replied. 'Perhaps the snake is starving.'

'Well, I certainly don't want to see it, so I'm happy for Tammy to help the frog. Snakes take ages swallowing those things and we'd have to sit here and watch it,' Stephen said.

'You let nature be in Africa,' Ed reminded her. 'Everyone must eat to survive.'

Reluctantly, Tammy didn't interfere and was secretly relieved when the frog, after giving the snake a merry chase around the pond, dived back in. The snake was close behind it.

'Well, at least we can now hope the frog escapes completely, and even if he doesn't, I don't have to watch it,' Stephen said with relief.

Tammy frowned, still uncertain as to where she stood with loving all animals and yet knowing a lot of them were just part of a food chain.

'Strange, isn't it?' Mikie said.

Tammy nodded.

'Tell me about Mina and Diego,' Jude said. 'Come and sit here, have some squash and sandwiches.' She indicated to the table on the patio.

'I have only seen glimpses of them,' Mikie began.

'Mikie, should we be telling them this?' Stephen silently asked.

'Yes, they are good people and we can trust them as much as we trust each other,' Mikie replied.

'Okay,' Stephen said, nodding.

Ed and Jude looked puzzled, as they suspected something had just been communicated that they couldn't hear. It made them feel uneasy.

'Please excuse us,' Stephen apologised. 'It's a bad habit; we are used to being very secretive.'

'I understand.' Ed smiled reassuringly.

'Now, Mikie, tell me about your brother and sister then,' Jude asked.

'Well, I don't see them often. Diego is often the hardest to get to because he is a little out of control. He has very strong powers, that are difficult to wield, and he can harness electricity. He makes it dance like you do with water, and he can do the same with fire, and even generate storms out of thin air.'

'Nice,' Jax said, through a mouthful of sandwich.

'It might be if he could control it – his mind is all over the place from what I've seen. However, just as I see him, he disappears again. I think he has done some bad things; I don't know what. It's just what I think or pick up on sometimes. I don't think he has done bad things intentionally. It's just that he can't control his power. Mina – Mina is very much into martial arts, like me, and she's a gymnastic and skateboarding whizz. She works with chi energy on a physical level, as we all do, but Tammy and I also use it on a mind level. Well, I guess we all use the energy in one way or another, only Diego doesn't realise it yet. Mina can walk through walls. I'm not too sure how her powers work in other ways. She is a good fighter, I know that much, and can manipulate solid objects.'

'How does she do that?' Jax asked.

'Well, I remember a dream once – bear in mind I didn't know this was my sister at the time – and she was trying to hide from a group of people chasing her. I didn't see much, except Mina standing by a wall, and somehow the wall moved and changed and it was as if it closed around her. Anyway, when the people ran past her, all that could be seen was the wall. Then, Mina just leaned forward, stepped out of the wall and went in the other direction. There is something about both Mina and Diego that concerns me, though.'

'What is it?' Tammy asked.

'I don't really know. I guess it's just, well... trouble.'

'Mikie, you're all only twelve years old and that is a difficult age at the best of times, and you also have to understand your wonderful gifts,' Jude said. 'Both you and Tammy seem to have a mature sense of doing the right thing. Perhaps Mina and Diego do not find it as easy as you to make the right choices.'

'That's a very good point, Jude. You both have such good hearts and a great sense of duty. Is it realistic to think all four of you have the same character?' Stephen added.

'I haven't considered that. Mina fights all the time, for real. I only fight in training with Stephen. I guess I could equally have gone out to see what I could do with strangers...'

'That's so cool, so you do martial arts as well then?' Jax asked.

'Oh yes,' Mikie said with a smile. 'I love it.'

'You'll have to show me.'

'I will,' Mikie promised.

'Well, we have enough to think about, I reckon. I've been dying to ask if it's safe to stroke him?' Stephen asked Tammy, pointing to Jet, who was sitting quietly by her side.

'Of course,' Tammy answered.

Stephen slowly approached Jet and carefully placed a hand on his head then stroked downwards. Jet was silky smooth and watched him with large, intimidating yellow eyes.

'How does it work? Do you tame them, or will they become wild again once you are gone?' he asked.

'I talk to them as I would to you. If I told Jet to never hurt another human being again and then set him free in the wild, he would obey. We should do that one day, Ed, set Jet free, that is. To avoid anything like what happened with Sampson, I'd also explain how he had to avoid humans. He knows the difference. Without me around, he might tolerate you stroking him, or he might not. It's Jet's choice really, he's starting to like people more and more. Even so, I don't think he would ever let a stranger, or someone I hadn't said was all right, come near him,' Tammy explained.

'Who is Sampson?' Stephen returned to his chair, brushing the large amount of cat hair from him.

'Come and take a walk with me and I'll tell you all about it,' Ed invited. 'I'll tell you some of the things Tammy has shown me since she has been here, and you can tell me all about Mikie.'

'Why don't we all go to the safari park and have a look around instead? You can talk on the way in the Jeep. I bet Mikie is desperate to look around,' Jude suggested.

'You read my mind!' Mikie said, laughing.

'Fancy a swim with the sea lions?' Jax asked.

'Can we really?' Mikie stood up, excited.

'Oh, please make sure you take some swimwear with you this time,' Jude muttered.

'We will, we will. Come on, Mikie.' Jax jumped up and ran into the house, with Mikie and Tammy following. They returned moments later wearing swimwear and carrying towels. Ed laughed and put his arm around Stephen as they headed towards the Jeep.

'Wait,' said Jude.

They stopped and looked at Jude.

'What is it?' asked Ed.

'The birthmarks. They both have exactly the same marks – look.'

'He's always had that,' Stephen said.

'So have I,' Tammy said.

Ed examined the marks and frowned. 'Hard to tell how it was made,' he stated.

'I assumed it was a birthmark. What do you think, Ed?' asked Stephen.

'It could be, but it's a very weird birthmark to have –

too specific. I can't imagine Sarah branding them at birth, though.'

'When our father arrives, I'll ask him for you,' Mikie said with a grin.

*

Tammy and Jude were washing up after dinner when they heard a commotion coming from the living room. Ed, Jax, Mikie and Stephen were all talking loudly and angrily.

'I wonder what's up with them.' Jude frowned.

Tammy dried her hands and followed Jude into the living room. They were watching something on the television that had annoyed them. The television was a small computerised device, the size of an apple, affixed to the wall. It reflected holographic images within the room, giving people and characters an eerie sense of being there with them. It was rarely on, since there was always so much to do around the island. A three-dimensional hologram of a man stood in the living room, facing them, as if he was actually there.

'What is it?' Jude asked.

'Look at this! It's lunacy, that's what it is,' Ed said angrily.

Tammy froze as she saw what they were watching. The man was talking them through a graphic documentary about whale hunting. They watched several minke and humpback whales brutally harpooned by Japanese whalers. Being 3-D, the images were horribly real as they all blinked in the devastating scenes before them. Tammy couldn't speak as she heard the cries of the whales and saw the sea turn red with blood. The whales splashed and fought to get away, hopelessly, as they were hauled aboard the waiting boats. Later, back in port, the whalers posed proudly next to their catch as onlookers took photographs.

'It should be illegal,' Jax said angrily.

'Isn't it illegal?' Tammy gasped. 'But animals are rare!'

'No, not illegal everywhere, there are still some places in Japan that reserve the right to hunt. It is their tradition and their food source. It is something we have been fighting for decades. We're still working on it,' Ed said.

Ed turned and looked at Tammy. She had gone very pale and tears ran down her cheeks.

'You shouldn't be watching this,' Ed said, turning the television off. 'It's too upsetting.'

'It has to be stopped,' Tammy said quietly.

'It has been part of their culture for many centuries, Tammy. You cannot change the culture of a nation overnight.'

She felt sick. Upon seeing her face, Ed stood up and helped her into his chair. Jude fetched a glass of water and watched her slowly sip it.

'Are you feeling better?' Jude asked.

'No,' Tammy said, shaking her head.

Jet was sitting by the fire. He stood up and walked over to Tammy, placing his chin on her lap. Tammy stroked his head.

'I should have realised how upsetting this would be for you to watch,' Ed said.

'I felt their pain,' Tammy whispered. 'It's been happening a lot more lately. I seem to feel the animals' pain a lot more deeply now.'

'Is your connection with the animals still getting stronger?' Ed asked.

'Yes, with pain, it can feel as if I am the one hurting,' Tammy said with a sigh.

'Tammy,' said Mikie, taking her hand.

'We won't let you watch anything like that again,' Ed said.

'Come on, Tammy. I'll take you up to bed. You'll feel better after a good night's sleep,' Jude said.

TWENTY-TWO

A CLEVER PLAN IN JAPAN

Tammy couldn't sleep. She tossed and turned until midnight then gave up on sleeping completely. She sat up in bed, wondering where Jet had gone – she'd kicked him off the bed with her restlessness and he lay on the floor. He sat up, attentive.

'I have to go, Jet,' she whispered.

'*I thought you'd say that,*' Mikie said.

'Mikie, you're awake?'

'*Yes, and I knew you were too. I knew what you were thinking before you did.*'

'Will you help me?'

'*Of course.*'

'*I have no idea how to get there. Ed and Jude will never let me go alone and I don't have a clue how to get onto HPs.*'

'*Not a problem. We'll ask Jax.*'

'He knows how to get us on a HP?'

'*Even better. I'll bring him with us. Meet us at the pond.*'

*

'What took you so long?' Tammy asked impatiently as Mikie and Jax walked towards her.

'Picking up a few supplies,' Mikie said, indicating the rucksack on his back.

'I have everything we need,' she said, showing him a small bag.

'Perfect. So how do we do this?'

'Ed has a secret he shared with me. It will get us to Japan,' Jax said, with a gleam in his eye that made Tammy smile.

'Tell me more,' she said.

'I'll show you. You are lucky that I just so happen to be a bit of a computer whizz and I can honestly hack just about anything,' Jax said with a wink.

Tammy smiled. Jax was full of surprises.

Sirocco just about managed to carry all three of them to the edge of the island where there was a small hidden harbour. Tammy hadn't seen this before. There were a few boats, nothing capable of getting them to Japan.

'This way,' Jax said.

He led them to a small sailing boat and Tammy was just about to complain that it wouldn't do the job when she saw something else in the water hidden behind it. 'What is that?'

'That is what will get us to Japan before morning,' Jax said smugly, folding his arms over his chest.

'It looks small.'

'It is small, barely big enough for us of all to fit in. It's actually a two-man submersible, but it can move with the speed of light.'

'Absolutely fantastic!' Tammy exclaimed, grabbing Jax and kissing his cheek. He blushed.

'How did you know, Mikie?'

Mikie raised his eyebrows.

'Silly question,' Jax said.

Smiling, Jax opened the top and let Mikie and Tammy climb into the sub. 'As you can tell, it's almost invisible, being grey and white, like a shark – light at the bottom and dark at the top – it's hard to see. It can't be detected by radar or satellite or anything else in existence. It uses only water to move; like a squid, it uses precise jet propulsion to move under the water.'

Inside was small and cosy. Two seats, a large window showing the ocean and a few control panels. It looked quite plain and simple. The interior was pale blue and grey inside.

'Ed shared this with you?'

'Yes. It was our secret. This is his little toy that only he and Jude knew about – until he told me, that is. Nothing else exists like this. I guess your mum helped him convert it into such a nippy underwater sub.'

'How does it work?'

'Well, it's supposed to be a basic sub, with complex modifications that you probably wouldn't understand, even if I tried to explain. To be honest, I don't think Ed really knows. It just moves really fast and that's all we need to know. I have been in trouble twice with the police for hacking, I just can't help myself, so I used to sneak in here and play with it and figure it out. Now Ed asks me to help him a lot and shows me things most people can't imagine exist, because I am the only one who can maintain them.'

'Wow, I like you more by the minute,' Mikie said, laughing.

'Wait until you see this baby in action.' Jax laughed.

'Then let's go, it won't be long before they miss us. I've left a note on the kitchen table anyway,' Mikie said. 'I have enough food for a couple of days; we should be back the day after tomorrow.'

'What else is in that rucksack then? It's huge,' Tammy asked.

'Jax's medical bag,' Mikie said with a sigh.

'Well, Crane's actually. I borrowed it. I figured we might run into some injuries along the way. Better to be safe than sorry,' Jax said, firing up the engines.

'Good thinking,' Tammy said. 'You think you can fix them in the ocean?'

'Only one way to find out, isn't there? Here we go,' said Jax, excitedly. 'You two will have to squeeze into the one seat, I'll drive from here.'

The sub lurched forward. Mikie fell into the seat and caught Tammy before she hit the floor. Mikie and Tammy exchanged looks as Jax took them forward, jerkily, away from the island.

*

Six hours later, they had made it to the North Pacific Ocean.

'Okay, you know what I want to do,' Tammy said. 'Let's action this and get out of here quickly.'

'Come on, then,' Mikie said. Jax surfaced with the sub, far away from land and ships, and turned the engines off.

'No one must recognise me,' Tammy said.

'They won't,' Jax said, joining her and Mikie.

It was a warm and sunny day, with a large number of gulls flying about and making a lot of noise. Tammy smiled as she watched them. It felt good to be out at sea. The slow rocking felt relaxing and comforting.

'Where will we find them?' Jax asked.

'They'll find us,' she replied.

'Are you sure about this, Tammy? Will you be safe enough?' asked Mikie.

'I'll be safe enough,' Tammy said reassuringly.

Tammy leaned over the side of the sub and closed her eyes. She concentrated very hard as she tried to sense where the whales were. She felt nothing. She kept her eyes closed and concentrated on the sound of the wind and the movement of the water. Connecting with the energy around her, she awakened every sense in her body. Then she felt something. It was only faint – someone was calling out to her. An animal knew that she was near and that she was looking for the whales. She saw nothing at first, and then something caught her eye. It was a shadow in the water, close to the sub.

Suddenly a dolphin leapt out of the water and flipped over in the air. They watched as the dolphin appeared to look at them before falling back into the water. Then, they watched another dolphin do the same, followed by another. Now there was a whole school of dolphins around them, excitedly showing off their acrobatic skills. The dolphins were jumping so close to the sub it would have been almost intimidating to anyone but Tammy. Tammy listened to the dolphins as they performed their display. She nodded, understanding what they were saying. She told them of her plan to stop the whale hunters and they began singing with excitement.

'What's the matter with them?' Mikie asked.

'They're excited and they're going to help us,' Tammy said.

'What are they going to do?' Jax asked.

'They are going to take me to the whales. There is a whaling boat about twenty miles from here, they say. It's heading straight towards a school of whales. If I don't get there soon, I won't be able to help them, so I'm going with the dolphins,' Tammy said.

'Why can't I take you? This sub goes fast,' asked Jax.

'You can for a little while, but this sub has to be out of sight for the plan to work,' Tammy said.

'Okay, we'll follow them and you can change on the way,' Mikie said.

They followed the dolphins underwater as far as they dared risk without being seen. They both kept their backs to Tammy as she changed into her dress – a pure white dress, almost bridal-looking. They were shocked when she came out of the small cabin. Her hair was long and flowing and the white dress swayed as she moved.

'You really do look like an angel!' Jax remarked. Mikie smiled at him and laughed as he blushed. Tammy didn't notice.

'That's the idea. Now I just need the finishing touch.' She smiled happily at Jax's response.

Mikie rummaged through her rucksack and pulled out some paints. He carefully painted small gold stars along Tammy's forehead and around her wrists. The paint was designed to stay on, even in salt water, and it sparkled when the sun shone on it. He took a tiara from the rucksack and placed it in her hair, fixing it so that it wouldn't come off in the water.

'Perfect,' he said, standing back and looking at her.

Tammy smiled. 'You have to wait here so I can find you,' she told Jax.

Jax nodded, surfaced with the sub, opened the hatch and watched as Tammy dived into the sea. She took hold of a dolphin's fin and waved as it pulled her away from the boat.

'I hope nothing happens to her,' Jax said, as he watched Tammy and the dolphins disappear.

'She'll be fine,' Mikie reassured him. *'Be really careful, Tammy,'* he told her.

'I will,' she replied.

*

Tammy didn't hold on to the same dolphin all the way. She kept changing so that they wouldn't become too tired. The dolphins came to a stop and waited. Tammy listened. She could hear the whales – they were close and the whalers had already begun the attack.

Suddenly a large sperm whale appeared at Tammy's side. Although its size surprised her – it must have been over fifty feet long – she knew this was small for a sperm whale, as the males could reach up to sixty feet in length. Every second counted now. If she was going to save the whales, she had to act quickly. Tammy climbed onto the whale's back and held on tightly as he swam away.

She could now hold her breath for far longer than any human could. It was hard riding on the whale's back and she almost fell off several times. The whale was large and powerful, moving at an incredible speed through the water and while used to diving deep, for Tammy's sake, it kept close to the surface. Tammy could see the boat in the distance. She heard the cries of the whales and the loud shouts of triumph from the whalers. A cold feeling of terror pulled at Tammy's heart as she experienced the fear felt by the whales.

One of the whalers was laughing with a friend when he saw something coming towards them. His smile froze on his lips as he stared in disbelief at Tammy and the whale. He blinked a couple of times, thinking he was seeing things. The girl was still there. He rubbed his eyes then shaded them from the sun. He still saw the girl. He pointed at the girl riding up to them on the back of a whale. He was too stunned to speak. He couldn't believe what he was seeing and just stood, speechless, pointing.

One of the other men on board turned to look at what he was pointing at. He screamed and shouted to the rest of the crew to look too. They all watched in disbelief as the young girl, all in white, sat high upon a whale's back and came straight at them. Tammy's face was cold and hostile. Two of the whales were severely hurt by harpoons and were bleeding into the water. They swam over to Tammy and stayed close by her side. One by one, the rest of the school joined her too.

The men were still staring open-mouthed as the whale and Tammy reached their boat. She came close enough that they could all hear her. 'I have been sent to give you a warning,' she said.

The men looked at each other in amazement. They wanted to make sure they weren't the only ones seeing and hearing this.

'I am the protector of the whales,' she said loudly, in the Japanese Mikie had looked up for her. 'If you try to harm these whales again, a curse will be put upon you and your families for three generations to come.'

The men looked scared. They looked around frantically, to see if there was a boat in sight. They were totally alone with this girl in white. There was no way she should be out here alone like this.

'She is an angel from the sea,' one man whispered.

'She has come to punish us,' said another.

Tammy hid a smile as she heard this. One of them stepped forward. He was the captain of the boat. He placed his hands on his hips and looked boldly at Tammy. 'Who are you? How did you get out here?' he shouted.

'I am a messenger. This is your last chance to save yourselves. I give you a small example of things that can happen if you hurt the whales again,' Tammy replied.

She told three of the whales what to do. She raised her arms into the air and looked up at the sky. The three whales rammed into the side of the boat simultaneously, unseen by the men on board. The force of the blow made the boat rock violently. The men screamed and grabbed on to something to stop them from falling over. The captain remained silent. He, too, was scared. This sort of thing just didn't happen.

Tammy closed her eyes and concentrated on the water. A whirlpool started to form alongside the boat, and those on board watched, horrified, as it grew bigger and bigger. The boat started to spin slowly at first, then faster and faster. The men screamed and held on to anything solid they could find, petrified of falling overboard. Eventually, the spinning slowed down and stopped – the sea calm once more.

'That is nothing compared to what could happen to you,' Tammy warned loudly.

The captain looked at Tammy then at his men. He ordered them to turn the boat around and head back for shore. Tammy told the whale to slowly sink under the water, making it look as though she had disappeared. They stayed under water until the boat was long out of sight.

Tammy headed back to the sub with the injured whales.

*

'Thank goodness you're all right. You've been gone a long time,' Jax said, as Tammy pulled up alongside the sub, still on top of a whale.

'It was a long way,' Tammy replied. 'It worked, I scared them off. I think your medical bag will come in handy after all; two of the whales are hurt badly. Can you help them?'

Jax looked at the blood the whales were losing.

'It looks bad,' said Jax, opening up the rucksack. He began pulling out medical supplies. Some looked quite unusual to Tammy. 'I can't swim and work at the same time,' he told her.

Tammy smiled at him. With great difficulty, Jax sat on top of a whale with his medical supplies next to him. He removed a broken harpoon from his side and tended to the wound. When he was finished, he climbed onto the next injured whale. Tammy swam next to them, applying the healing energy to her best ability to each whale. When Jax had finished, he was satisfied that there would be no fatalities today. It was the first time he had ever helped a wounded animal all by himself and he was proud of the results.

'I don't think even Crane could have done a better job, especially while sitting on the back of a whale. It's not the most convenient of places to work,' said Tammy.

'You did a marvellous job,' Mikie said, patting him on the shoulder. 'How did you know what to do? I wouldn't even know where to start.'

'I am very serious about wanting to be a vet. I watch Crane all the time; he hates it when I stare. I've helped him treat seals and sea lions loads of times,' Jax explained.

'Well, you should be extremely proud of yourself,' Tammy said.

'I must admit I was scared stiff to get in the water with them at first. I can't believe how big they are!' Jax said, as he stared at the whales.

'There are bigger whales than these,' Tammy said.

'How do you know?' asked Jax.

'I can sense them and hear them when I am in the water. The sperm whales have the largest brain compared to all other animals. It weighs twenty pounds, compared to a human's brain only weighing three.' Tammy smiled at Jax's surprise.

'Or one in your case,' Mikie teased. Jax punched him in the arm.

*

They went on to locate more whalers. That day, they came across ten boats in all and each time Tammy performed in the same way. Each boat turned around and headed back to shore. Jax was able to save several more injured whales and the trip was a lot more successful than they had hoped. They decided to take a look around on land and see what was happening. As they reached the harbour, they saw the chaos. They hid the sub carefully between the ships.

'Here, put this on, no one will recognise you,' Jax said, giving her a change of clothes. Tammy dressed up as a boy to ensure no one would recognise her and hid her hair in a beanie. Jax and Mikie put beanies on also. They grinned proudly at each other as they walked along the harbour, listening to the confused chatter among the whalers.

As Mikie walked, he took the opportunity to practise some of his mind-reading abilities. He moved around the crowds, enforcing the strength of the stories that were being told, putting thoughts into people's minds.

'What are you doing?' Jax asked.

'Playing with people's minds,' Mikie said.

'Like Jedi mind tricks? Oh, no one would ever believe this!' Jax laughed.

When he had finished, even people who hadn't been on the boats believed they had been there and that the stories had to be true. The local news channels had picked up on the story too and there were several cameramen capturing the events. Mikie didn't pay them any attention.

*

Stephen was sitting with Ed and Jude, who were aghast as they sat watching the late-night news. There was uproar in Japan – everyone was suddenly refusing to hunt any whales. The whalers were all in agreement that they had seen the same vision of an "angel". The angel had threatened them with a curse if they should try hunting whales again and consequently, they were too scared to return to work.

'She was all in white and she sparkled,' one man said to the camera.

'She was sitting on top of the whale, right out there in the middle of the ocean,' said another.

'She had a glowing light all around her,' said yet another man.

'If she wasn't an angel then you tell me how she got out into the middle of nowhere and why the ocean moved to her command.'

The news ended with a final sign-off from the reporter. 'Normally, in incidents such as this, there are a lot of conflicting stories,' he said. 'One thing that makes this so different is that every story is the same. Almost 300 men claim to have seen a young girl dressed in white, riding on a whale. She spoke to them, made the ocean move and made their boat shake. She warned them to stop what they were doing. The problem now is that whalers all over the world are afraid to hunt. Even those who never saw the angel are scared to go out onto the water. They all believe it is a message. This may be good news for animal lovers but it's having a devastating financial effect on Japan and science all around the world.'

Jude looked at Ed, who smiled and shook his head in amazement.

'Now we know where they went,' Jude said with a sigh.

'They'd better bring my sub back in one piece, that's all I know,' Ed said. He rewound the news and watched it again. Then again. Each time, Ed's features grew more serious.

'What's the matter?' Jude asked.

'I think I saw Mikie, yes, there,' said Ed, pausing the report and pointing to a young boy in the crowd.

'Oh yes, there he is, how exciting.' Jude clapped her hands.

'It's dangerous,' Ed said.

'Why?' asked Jude and then she realised. 'Oh no!'

'Precisely. If the wrong people see this, it won't take long for them to realise what he is doing.' Ed covered his eyes with both hands.

'What, exactly, is he doing?'

'Mind games,' said Stephen, huffing.

'Don't ask,' Ed said.

'Did you see any of the others?' Jude asked.

'No, that is why I kept rewinding it.'

'Careless! I'd have thought better of Mikie,' Stephen said.

'Let's face it; what they did was a very good thing. Think how many whales they have saved because those whalers won't go back out in their boats,' Jude said, trying to see the positive side.

'Yes, and what about Mikie being caught on camera? What if the others were as well?'

Jude let out a long breath and placed a reassuring arm around Ed's shoulders. 'Did you really expect this to all be easy, Ed? If a war is coming, do you really think this is going to be the biggest worry we have to face?'

'How did I ever manage to marry such a wonderful woman? What did I do to deserve you?' He kissed her gently on the forehead and pulled her to him. They held each other closely.

Stephen watched with envy, hoping one day he would find a woman who looked at him the same way.

*

Ed and Stephen were waiting at the harbour when they pulled up in the sub. Jax, Mikie and Tammy didn't realise they were there until they opened the hatch.

'Oh dear,' Mikie muttered.

'Give the man some respect, Mikie, don't read his mind,' Stephen scolded him.

'Actually, I didn't. I just read his face,' Mikie replied.

'Please don't be mad,' Tammy said.

'Mad? I'm not mad, I'm worried sick! Do any of you realise that Mikie was caught on camera and anyone watching the news would see him?' Ed said, trying to stay calm.

'What?' Mikie exclaimed.

Upon seeing Mikie's startled face, Ed took a deep breath to calm his anger down. 'You will have to leave this island and keep your head down for a while. We cannot risk you being traced back here. I have some connections in the media and was able to trace every broadcast made that day, and we are fortunate that Jax and Tammy did not appear on any footage. It appears that Mikie was the only one caught on camera. It isn't safe for you to be here anymore.'

'What will we do? I don't want to leave Tammy,' Mikie said.

'We have no choice now, don't you see?' Stephen said sadly.

Ed started to walk towards the Jeep and then looked back over his shoulder. 'By the way, what you did was really good. You saved a lot of whales, no doubt about that. But later your behaviour was careless and dangerous.'

'Ed, you should hear what Jax did,' Tammy said.

'Tell me as we ride back,' said Ed with a smile.

*

When they arrived at the house, Jude, Dave, Ben and Crane were all there waiting for them, clearly unhappy.

'Oh great,' Mikie muttered. 'Here we go. We are heroes but I bet we get it in the neck! Do they look mad to you? I can't tell looking at their faces.'

'Take a chill pill,' Jax chuckled, 'nothing can take away what we just achieved, remember that.'

Tammy smiled at Jax and wondered how he was so positive all the time. Like her, his childhood had been problematic. Like her, Ed and Jude had changed his awful childhood into something special. It connected them.

'I'm so glad you are all right.' Jude smiled and hugged them in turn. 'You did an amazing job out there, so brave of you all.'

'It appears Jax has some special powers of his own,' said Ed with a smile.

'It's only because of what Crane taught me. Crane!' Jax gasped, as he noticed the large python around Crane's shoulders.

'I have overcome my fear and hatred of snakes at last,' he said laughingly.

'That's wonderful, I'm so pleased,' Jax exclaimed.

'And what did Crane teach you exactly?' Jude asked.

'Oh, a little bit about...' Jax began.

'Don't let him be too modest. He handled a lot of really serious wounds on the whales and saved every last one. He had all these medical supplies and got straight to work,' Tammy said.

'Is this true?' Crane looked at Jax.

'Yes,' he mumbled.

'Good lad.' Crane smiled and placed an affectionate hand on his shoulder. Jax looked up and smiled at him.

'You aren't mad I took the supplies without asking?' he asked.

'Not if you did that, no. Come and tell me all about it.' Crane and Jax went into the house.

'It was really scary and there was blood everywhere. I remembered what you did that time with the seal that was washed up by the port. Remember the one with the metal pole sticking out of his side?' they heard Jax say as he disappeared from sight.

The rest of the party followed and headed towards the kitchen.

'Who knows you came here?' Ed asked.

'No one at all, I made sure of that. Everyone I know thinks we went to France, even my housekeeper,' Stephen replied.

'That's good. That buys us some time. How easy do you think it would be for anyone to trace Mikie back to you?'

Stephen took a deep breath and looked at Mikie. 'I'm not sure, we have been pretty careful over the years, but I wouldn't like to risk going back home now.'

'I guess the idea of school is out of the question then?' Mikie smiled. Stephen shot him a look of warning. 'Only joking.'

'Well, while we were waiting for you, we all got together and came up with a few ideas. There is absolutely no connection from you to us, is there?' Ed asked.

'None at all,' replied Stephen.

'Well, I think it's essential that we find Mina and Diego. From what I've heard, I don't think they will be too hard for us to find, or for anyone else to find for that matter. We need Mikie to do this.'

'Of course,' Mikie said, nodding.

'You and Stephen must get away from here and lie low for a while to ensure no one traces you back to us, endangering Tammy and Jax. Once the coast is clear, Mikie can come back here for a little while and help me to locate Mina and Diego. It's essential that we find them. I thought perhaps you and Tammy might be able to contact them and ask them to guide you.'

'We can try,' Mikie said, and looked at Tammy. She nodded agreement.

'We just need to get you away from here first before we try anything like that. I don't know if anyone else can tap into your mind reading and trace you. We will double security around the island. Mikie, you must be more discreet than you have ever been before,' Ed warned.

'Discretion isn't his strongest point,' Stephen said.

'I know, that's what worries me.' Ed smiled at Mikie.

'Once we know it's safe for us, we'll get all the children together and go from there,' Ed said.

'I'll go home alone and ensure everything is taken care of there. I can't just disappear indefinitely, as it would draw attention. Can I leave Mikie here while I do that?' Stephen asked.

'Of course, I'll get Dave to take you to the morning hovercraft when it drops off tomorrow's visitors. Go and freshen up. After dinner, we'll plan exactly how we intend to go forward.'

'I don't suppose I could go in that sub of yours instead, could I?' Stephen asked.

'Well, I suppose I should check it's intact,' Ed said with a smile.

'It's in perfect working order,' Mikie said.

'Well, double-checking won't hurt,' Ed said.

'Can I…?'

'Yes, Tammy, go and stretch Sirocco's legs,' Ed said, smiling.

'Fancy a ride?' Tammy glanced at Mikie.

'On Sirocco?'

'Yes.'

Mikie gulped and followed Tammy. He wasn't good enough to go fast on Sirocco.

'You can hold on to me,' Tammy said. Mikie didn't look too reassured.

*

Dr Lloyd walked up to the hologram of the young boy on the news and stared at him, an unpleasant smile spreading across his face. He paused the image on the television and picked up the phone. He pressed speed dial number one.

'Colonel? I have some interesting news for you. You were right, they couldn't resist being show-offs and have started to draw attention to themselves,' he said with a smile. 'I know where to find one of them. I'll have him with you within the week.'

TWENTY-THREE

SEEKERS TRIUMPHANT

'Morning, Dave,' said Ed, as Dave approached the house.

'Morning all, and what, may I ask, are you doing?'

'Stepping back and repulsing the monkey,' said Mikie, laughing loudly.

'Eh?' Dave was puzzled.

'Tai chi,' said Stephen, appearing at Dave's side. 'They do it every morning apparently. They now have Jax and Mikie completely engrossed as new recruits.'

'I've occasionally seen Jude and Ed doing it but now it seems different,' Dave said. 'I prefer sub aqua myself, some nice dives along this island.'

'Oh, I love diving. I was planning on taking Mikie diving with me this year, proper UK diving, none of this fine water tourism equivalent!'

'I couldn't agree with you more. It's nice to meet someone who appreciates our underestimated ocean life,' Dave said with a smile.

'You'll have to take me on some of the dives around here.'

'I will. There are some strange things around this island, you'll be surprised.' Dave nodded his head, tongue in cheek.

'Why don't you go and stand very close to them and stay quiet? I think you'll be surprised at what you feel.'

'What do you mean? Feel what?' Dave asked suspiciously.

'Hard to explain but the air heats up something crazy and changes and you get all tingly and light. It's so weird. They just do something with the energy and it's like an electric current buzzing about you. I can't feel it at any other time – only when Tammy and Mikie are together. When they are close, they change the atmosphere around them. It's freaky.' Stephen said, nodding.

'Really?'

'Oh yes. Meanwhile, I'll load my bags into the Jeep. I think you'll be surprised at the heat you can feel radiating from the group, go check it out. I can't handle it for very long. Too hot.' Stephen returned to the house to collect his bags from the front step.

'*Scout on horseback – right – and kick with left foot,*' Jude instructed. 'Come on, Dave, join us. It's actually very different when Tammy and Mikie are with us, I've never felt anything like it. The energy is stronger and different in a way I have never experienced before.'

'I think I understand what Tammy feels inside sometimes,' Jax said. 'I never liked this much before, now I think it's cool.'

'We are surrounded by energy and constantly connecting with it, so it feels very powerful,' said Mikie, as he raised his leg and kicked out in turn with the rest of the group.

'Your martial arts work has done you credit, I cannot believe how quickly you have picked this up.' Jude smiled at Mikie.

'My hands are hot,' Jax said, wiping his hands on his jumper.

'Yes, I feel it too,' Dave said.

'See what I mean? I've lived with Mikie all my life and never felt anything like that. If this is what it is like with you both side by side, imagine how intense it will be with Mina and Diego at your side too. I'm not sure us normal humans can stand by you. My bags are in the Jeep, so I'm ready to go now,' Stephen said. 'Let's go.'

Ed, Jude, Tammy, Jax and Mikie stopped their movements, faced each other and bowed. The session was over. They turned to say their goodbyes to Stephen. Mikie went last, hugging his uncle as if he would never let go. His throat had tightened up and he couldn't speak. Fortunately, he was able to silently say, *'Be careful.'*

'I will, don't you worry about me. Just take care of yourself and learn some discretion.'

Mikie nodded. He watched, in silence, as his uncle jumped into the Jeep and Dave drove him away. He was unable to shake the feeling that this was the last time he would ever see his uncle. Sensing his concern, Tammy turned to Mikie and took his hand in hers. Mikie didn't take his eyes from the Jeep and gave her hand a gentle squeeze.

*

The black bubble-shaped taxi came to a rather abrupt stop outside Stephen's front door. The tinted window between the front and back seats prevented Stephen from seeing who was driving. Feeling incredibly tense after the nerve-racking journey from the coast, Stephen hurriedly climbed out of the taxi, grabbed his bags with shaky hands and paid the driver – who grunted and drove away at high speed.

Standing on his driveway, watching the taxi disappear, Stephen waited for his stomach to settle down. How that person could possibly have passed the test and become a taxi driver was beyond him. He wondered if he had deliberately wanted to disorientate him and make him feel sick. It had worked. He swallowed, took a few deep breaths and slowly came to his senses. Looking up, he saw his home, which had been a place of comfort all his life.

'Hmm, you don't seem so big now I have seen Brunswick House,' he said out loud. Still, he had that warm feeling that only being home after a trip away can bring as he lifted his bags and walked up the front steps. He opened the door, dropped his bags and looked around.

'Hello.' No one answered. 'That's strange,' he muttered.

Usually, his housekeeper greeted him. He closed the door and walked through the hallway. It was unusually quiet. Where were the dogs? No staff, nothing.

'Hello, anybody?' still nothing...

Hovering over a large portrait of Stephen's father on the wall, completely undetectable, was a *seeker*. The *seeker* carefully watched Stephen and studied his face as it was compared with the image stored on its microchip – it was a positive match. The *seeker* moved with startling speed as it shot from the portrait and jabbed its needle into the back of Stephen's neck.

'Ah...' Stephen didn't even have time to raise his hand to where he felt the sudden sting. His hand had barely moved an inch from his side when he fell, face down, onto the floor.

*

'Excellent, you are awake again,' said a vaguely familiar voice as Stephen tried to open his eyes. His head hurt. He groaned, went to touch his forehead and then realised his hands were tied. He went cold with fear as he remembered something being stuck in his neck. He looked in the direction of the person who had spoken.

'Remember me?' Dr Lloyd smiled, a nasty sneer upon his face.

Stephen stared with blurred vision at the face in front of him, contorted with hatred, close and intimidating. He knew that face from somewhere. Where did he know that face from? His mind was too foggy to remember. He shook his head, trying to clear his senses and squinted at the face once more. 'Peter? Peter Lloyd?'

'Yes, Stephen, although it's Dr Lloyd now,' he said, laughing. 'Feeling up to a chat?'

'What's going on? What happened at college was a long time ago. Don't tell me you've come for revenge on that?' Stephen shuffled until he was almost sitting up.

'Do you really think I would hold a grudge all these years just because you stole the girl I loved?'

'Yes – probably. Nobody knew you liked her, Peter. I was your best friend and even I didn't know you liked her, for heaven's sake.'

'You were always the ladies' man. Why would I point her out to you? I never trusted you. However, that's just the icing on the cake, really.'

'So, what's this about? What did you hit me with and where are all my staff?'

'Gone – dead to be exact.' Dr Lloyd chuckled nastily.

'Wh... what? Are you... are you crazy?' Stephen stuttered.

'Positively not,' he said, laughing. 'I saw a boy on the news the other day and it was remarkable how similar he was in looks to you – almost the spitting image of when you were younger – same cocky air about him. I have some friends looking for him and they are really keen to talk with you – now.'

Stephen glared at Dr Lloyd and was about to respond when he noticed something step out of the shadows. He held his breath as it moved towards him. Whoever, or rather, whatever it was, wore a ladybird-coloured army uniform. Stephen immediately recognised the outfit. It had been designed during the Pisces outbreak, designed to make the soldier strikingly visible, while at the same time hiding any signs of blood spilled. The suit was a vivid blood-red in colour and covered with round black dots.

There was a very small and sophisticated re-breathing device attached to the shoulders of the suit, which, in addition to air, supplied food and water. The entire suit was sealed and a black mask covered the wearer's face; a small glass area covered the eyes. The same air, water and food in these suits could keep a soldier alive for three months. Top-of-the-range technology-based weaponry was built into the outfit everywhere possible, providing each suit with capabilities equivalent to more than twenty standard equipped soldiers from the beginning of the century. Stephen had been approached by the army during Pisces and one of his factories was used to help design and make these suits, so he was well aware of their capabilities.

Attached to the re-breathing device and lying flat along the soldier's back were extractable laser guns. With a sharp pull down and across, they could be held in the hand and ready to fire in a millisecond. At the cuff of each sleeve were small pistols activated by merely raising the hand as if to wave. Soldiers had been killed during their training because they hadn't mastered the technique of saluting instead of waving. A fatal mistake should the soldier forget: fatal for anyone close by.

Knives and high-pitch sound devices (HPSDs) were deviously hidden into seams and pockets on the arms and legs. The HPSDs would emit various high-pitched tones not always heard by the human ear. Some tones would destroy viral and bacterial cells, the main reason they were invented, while others rendered humans temporarily immobile. The latter were designed to keep infected humans away from soldiers, since they could do little more than grab their heads in pain until the soldiers had passed by. The suits, obviously, protected the soldiers.

The final part of the suit was the belt, which held in small pouches most of the crystal ammunition required for the laser guns. The belt buckle had a quartz crystal designed into it that reflected the sun's rays when activated and burned anything in its path to cinders. On each side of the belt were clipped several seekers shaped like tiny flying insects. These small machines had a camera chip in the head that could capture an image of the intended victim. Using facial recognition, this *seeker* would then not stop until it had pierced its victim's skin. A soldier would use this while hidden and could select one of three settings: kill, render the victim unconscious for two days or paralyse them for four hours. Stephen now realised he had been paralysed for four hours.

The shadow moving towards him might have been mistaken for a soldier except for the way it moved –the languid cat-like walk reminded Stephen of Jet. As it neared him, Stephen saw the piercing black eyes encased in hollow white sockets. Stephen didn't want to speak or ask any more questions. He knew this was not a good situation to be in and when he saw those shining black eyes coming towards him, he could see his own death reflecting back at him. They had been waiting for him and he was well and truly caught, without so much as a fight.

'I am not going to talk or tell anyone anything,' Stephen hissed.

The alien was now kneeling by Stephen's side, so close that its mask was almost touching his nose. Those piercing eyes, still holding his death, were only inches away. It laughed – or at least Stephen assumed it was a laugh. It was more of a howl, yet not quite like the howl of a wolf – something far more unnerving – something else completely.

'Do you really think he needs your help in any way?' said Dr Lloyd laughingly. 'What he wants he will just take, with or without your permission.'

The alien took Stephen's head in his hands and probed deep into his mind, uncovering layers of information in a way that Mikie sometimes did; only this was far more intrusive and much more painful. Stephen's nose and eyes started to bleed, copious amounts of blood streaming down, and he shook as the alien continued to read his mind, taking all the information it required.

Finally, the alien dropped Stephen's head to the floor and stood over his body, moving his foot away from the increasingly large pool of blood.

'Vivacity Island,' the alien said in an inhuman growl to a group of similarly dressed figures standing behind it. 'Send a seeker there at once.'

'How could we have missed them? We sent more seekers there than anywhere else,' Dr Lloyd asked.

'That is what I intend to find out,' growled the alien.

Dr Lloyd leaned in close to Stephen's ear and whispered, 'When an alien takes too much information too quickly, the human mind cannot cope and collapses completely. You will go into shock and then slowly die – the pain will be excruciating.'

Stephen tried to open his eyes but there was too much blood and all he could see was darkness.

*

Sirocco cantered towards the house, where Tammy was eagerly waiting.

'Are you sure you're not coming?' Tammy turned to Jax, enquiringly.

'Sorry, I promised to help Crane with an operation on one of the monkeys. It's got a cyst and I've never seen one removed before, I can't miss out on it,' he replied.

'Okay then, we'll catch up with you afterwards. It looks

like it's just you and me, Mikie,' she said, as she swung herself, with ease, on to Sirocco's back.

'Uh-huh,' Mikie mumbled, as he climbed behind her.

Sirocco galloped away, with Jet not far behind, until they reached a small forest of trees where they slowed down to a leisurely walk.

'What's wrong, Mikie? You've been quiet since yesterday afternoon,' Tammy asked.

'I don't know,' he replied. 'I just have a really bad feeling inside that I can't shake off.'

'Perhaps you are worried about Stephen or the lack of enthusiasm Diego showed when we tried to contact him last night.' Combining Mikie's telepathic power with Tammy's manipulation of energy, they had both gained a little information from Mina and Diego, during the quiet of the night, albeit not enough to locate them precisely.

'Perhaps.'

'Mikie, at least we have some idea of where to find Mina and Diego. I'm sure Ed will have uncovered their exact locations from what we have told him.'

'Yes, it might be enough to go on. Otherwise, we'll just try to contact them again. Mina seemed pleased but, like you said, I don't like Diego's resistance.' Mikie frowned.

'Yes, he did seem a little reluctant to be found. Maybe that is what's bothering you.'

'It could be. This feeling is a new one to me, I haven't felt it before. I keep trying to find Stephen, but nothing is there.'

Just then, Tammy felt the heat in her chest and looked down to see her pendant was glowing bright red. 'Mikie,' she whispered, and turned to show him the pendant.

He turned his head sharply in each direction. What danger could possibly be lurking?

'Mikie, what could it be?'

'I don't know,' he said. 'I can't see or hear anything.'

'Where has Jet gone? I can't hear him,' Tammy realised, and looked desperately about her.

'I don't know, I haven't seen him for a while.'

'Look,' Tammy pointed to something in front of them. 'What is that?'

'It looks like a mechanical insect and I reckon it's watching us.'

At that moment, the *seeker* hurtled towards them at great speed.

'Run!' Mikie shouted.

Sirocco turned fast and galloped away from the *seeker*; Jet was still nowhere to be seen. The *seeker* was quick enough to catch any human and could have even kept up with the Jeep, yet it was no match for Sirocco. He sped away as fast as his namesake, and the *seeker* was barely able to keep them in sight.

'*We can't lead it back to the house,*' Mikie said.

'*What do you suggest?*'

'*Well, fancy trying out our pendants for real?*' he said with a smile as they raced through the trees. He felt amazingly calm – almost excited.

When the *seeker* was sufficiently out of sight, they found a tree covered in ivy and stopped to turn and face the *seeker*. When the *seeker* caught up, it paused, searching for signs of a trap, and detected nothing but trees. The *seeker* was about to launch itself forward when the ivy covering the tree suddenly reached out at great speed, rapidly wrapping itself around and around the *seeker*. As the *seeker* tried to wriggle free, the ivy tightened.

Sirocco charged towards the trapped *seeker*, Tammy flattening herself against Sirocco's neck, out of Mikie's way. Mikie reached for his pendant, pulled it from the clasp and in the blink of an eye, it had turned into a glowing sword. The ivy held the *seeker* tight as the sword came down and chopped it in half. It fell to the forest floor, in a shower of sparks. Mikie jumped down from Sirocco and used some dead leaves to pick up the *seeker*, careful not to touch it with his bare hands – just in case.

'You sure it's done for?' Tammy asked.

'Oh yeah, it's finished,' Mikie replied.

'Where's Jet?'

'I don't know.'

'Let's see if we can find him.'

They hadn't been riding long when Tammy saw a black figure lying still on the forest floor.

'Oh no,' she whispered, jumping from Sirocco and running to Jet. 'Jet! JET!' she screamed hysterically. 'Nooooo!'

'Is he all right?' Mikie asked, coming closer.

'I can't tell, I think he's dying. We must get him to Crane and Jax. Mikie, help me lift him onto Sirocco,' Tammy asked.

As they lifted Jet up onto Sirocco's back, Tammy called to the zebras to come. They started to walk towards the safari park.

Within moments, two zebras had arrived at full speed, one each for Tammy and Mikie. They mounted the zebras, lined up on either side of Sirocco to hold Jet steady, and cantered as fast as they could.

*

Crane held the stethoscope to Jet's chest and shook his head sadly. Jax placed a comforting arm around Tammy's shoulder as she watched.

'I have no idea what is the matter with him. He's breathing really faintly – it is as though he is in a coma, although I cannot see why,' he explained. 'I'm going to shave away some fur and see if I can find any bite marks. Ben, have you figured out what on earth that thing is yet?'

'No, it's nothing I've ever seen before. I reckon this is what got Jet.' Ben had been looking at the *seeker*, which lay broken on an examining table, with a magnifying glass. 'Look – there are three tubes in the body of this thing. One of them is empty, the other two are unused. It looks like they were once connected to this dart-like syringe at the front that has now been severed by… what did you use exactly?'

'Um, a stick,' Mikie mumbled. Ben looked at him and made it clear he didn't believe him. At that point, Ed came charging through the door with Jude close behind him.

'I got your message. What's going on?' Ed asked, breathlessly.

'Oh, my goodness, are you guys all right?' Jude ran over to Tammy and Mikie and looked them over.

'Yes, we're fine. It's Jet we're worried about,' Tammy replied reassuringly, pulling her head away from Jude's inquisitive hands. She bent over Jet and stroked his face.

'What's wrong with him?' Jude asked.

'Can't tell yet,' said Crane, still shaving Jet.

Jax followed Tammy, sticking to her side like glue. Tammy appreciated Jax's kindness and support, but it didn't stop her from feeling dreadfully sick and worried about Jet. She felt it was her fault and that she should have noticed he was in trouble sooner.

'You couldn't possibly have known,' Mikie said.

Tammy nodded. Jax took hold of her hand.

'What do you think of this, Ed?' Ben asked.

'What?' Ed asked, going to his side.

'This, it looks like some sort of poison, I'm guessing.'

'Can we tell what this is, Crane?' Ed asked.

'I can try; it isn't like anything I have ever seen. What about you, Crane?'

Crane finished shaving Jet and walked over to Ben. He looked at the small tubes and shook his head.

'Nope, not something I recognise,' he said. 'However, I do have a really good analysing machine I purchased last year, which will be able to give us a breakdown of the contents. That will help us figure out what's wrong with Jet. Come and look at his neck – I found the entry wound.'

There was a bruise the size of a thumbnail surrounding a very small puncture in the side of Jet's neck.

'It must have struck him almost as soon as we went into the forest,' Mikie said.

'Yeah, and we didn't notice for ages,' Tammy said, biting her lip, trying to hold back her tears.

'This thing is probably programmed to be quick. There was no way you could have done anything to stop it,' Ed assured her.

'Put some of that in here, Ben.' Crane passed him a test tube and watched as Ben carefully poured the contents of one of the tubes into it.

'Here you go.'

'Right, I'll just place this in here and wait for the results. Shouldn't take more than a minute,' Crane told them as he hit a button.

'That's a nifty piece of machinery, Crane, although I have to say it reminds me of my grandmother's old typewriter,' said Ed.

'Well, it's a little more sophisticated than that,' Crane said with a sniff. 'There, it's done already. Hmm, this is odd. It's a mixture of – oh.'

'What?' Ed and Ben said, at the same time, as Crane examined the printout.

'Oh dear, this is rather odd,' Crane said. He walked over to the *seeker* to examine it more closely, turning it over in his hands. He looked again at the sheet of paper containing the analysis results and then back at the *seeker*.

'Oh dear,' he mumbled.

'If you don't tell me what that little brain of yours is thinking this minute...' Ben started, and then stopped as Ed gave him a warning glance.

'This is military equipment,' Crane said. 'Oh dear, Ed, are you sure that it's not the army who are looking for the kids? That would put a whole different light on the matter.'

'No, I don't believe so. They would have contacted us first – not just sent out a gadget like this and started drugging animals and kids. It doesn't make any sense. I have contacts and can check.' Ed frowned, puzzled.

'Is it poison?' Tammy asked.

'I don't think so. I helped with injured patients during the Pisces outbreak and from what I can remember of this stuff, if it's going to kill, the effect is immediate. They can also carry doses that render the victim paralysed or unconscious for a specified period, which, I believe, is what has happened to Jet. We will just have to wait and see if he wakes up.'

'Oh, Jet,' Tammy soothed, moving close to him and stroking his head.

From the corner of her eye, Tammy noticed Ed as he glanced at Jude. It was only a brief glance, yet it was enough to catch Jude's attention and change the look on her face. Her eyebrows rose, questioningly, as if to say, '*are you sure?*' and Ed nodded in reply. Jude shrugged, as if to say, '*well, if you're sure then…*'

Tammy frowned and looked at Mikie, who had also noticed the silent communication that seemed almost like the telepathy they shared. Mikie smiled, knowing it was because Jude and Ed were so close and had been together for so long.

'*Some couples get it when they have a very close bond,*' he explained.

Tammy smiled, impressed, and was just about to ask what was going on when Ed started to speak.

'I never thought I would ever say this twice in my lifetime.' He stood tall, determined, in a manner that commanded the attention of everyone in the room. 'I am going to raise the shield around the island. We will monitor everyone and everything that enters and leaves. We will increase security and search every visitor who arrives from now on,' Ed said.

'Can I help you raise it?' Jax asked excitedly.

Ed nodded. Jax smiled at Tammy then, remembering Jet, quickly wiped the smile from his face.

'I want to work on these horrible little things and see if I can examine the programming within them better,' Jax said.

'Can you do that?' Tammy asked.

'Yes, I should think so.'

'Jax can do anything with anything technical,' Ed said with a nod of his head. 'What are you thinking, Jax?'

'Well, they'll be operating on some sort of wireless network, so perhaps I can use them to track any future ones and also to take them out and disable them remotely. I'll see what's possible when I get chance to hack into it,' Jax explained. 'Creepy little things.'

'Yes, they are,' Mikie agreed. He was looking at Jax and thinking he had met someone who really was a friend worth having. He was smart. Mikie was starting to feel like he was part of a nice big family he could fit in with.

'What do we tell people?' asked Ben.

'Terrorists,' Ed replied. 'Never fails. Dave normally manages these types of details but since he's leaving the island tomorrow, will you both take over and ensure the appropriate procedures are followed?'

Crane and Ben nodded.

'Tomorrow – did you find them then?' Mikie asked.

'Yes, I did. I was going to tell you tonight. Jude, perhaps you could pass on the much-needed good news.' Ed said, with a soft smile.

'We found Mina. She lives in Notting Hill with an MI6 agent,' Jude said.

'Mina,' Mikie said.

'I am assuming the woman she lives with was a friend of your mother's,' Jude continued, looking at Tammy. 'Anyway, Diego was a lot harder to find, wasn't he, Ed?'

'Yes, it seems he has a track record for trouble so there might be something in our earlier suspicions. His guardian is not someone I would have thought Sarah would choose. Perhaps she understood something I am not yet able to.' Ed shrugged. 'However, he has kept him very safe over the years. There is a history of school trouble with Diego. I'm not sure if I should share this with you. However, I figured Mikie would dig it out of me anyway.'

'I already have.' Mikie smiled, and blushed guiltily.

'I thought as much.'

'You aren't bothered?' Mikie asked.

'I don't have anything to hide, at least most of the time,' Ed replied, jokingly. 'I'll say it out loud for everyone else's benefit. At first, Diego was tutored privately at home until after a few complaints from upset tutors, the social care team went in and insisted he went to school. Then, last year, there was some kind of an accident in the school science lab – I am not sure of the details. It involved an explosion and the death of one young boy.'

'Oh no,' Tammy gasped.

'There was another incident after that, involving a potentially lethal nuclear incident that was fortunately turned around, and no major casualties were announced. However, Diego and Charles – his guardian – disappeared after that and haven't been seen since. However, going by the information that you two gave me and some research of my own, I am almost one hundred percent certain that he is hiding out in Peru, high in the mountains,' Ed declared.

'Peru?' Tammy asked.

'South America,' Ed explained. 'So, I have spoken to Dave already. He is pretty much ready to go.'

'Thank you, Ed.' Tammy rushed to give him a hug.

Mikie smiled and said, 'I just hope Stephen gets back soon.'

'Look,' Crane said, pointing at Jet. 'He's starting to come round.'

'Jet!' Tammy ran to his side. Jet opened his eyes, looked around the room then slowly started to move. He sat up unsteadily. He looked straight at Tammy, who held him close, whispering in his ears. Jet let out a loud growl that would have scared everyone in the room if it wasn't for the fact that Tammy was still hugging him.

'Thank God he's okay,' Jude said.

'Ben, Crane, come. There is no time to lose. Let's raise those shields as soon as the last visitors leave the island. Get all security and staff together for a complete island sweep – I want everyone available covering this island and ensuring we are all safe. Tomorrow, we make sure we, and nobody else, are in charge of who and what comes in. Understood?' Ed said.

'Yes,' said Ben.

'Yes, although we probably won't be able to detect something as small as this thing,' added Crane, nodding towards the *seeker*.

'I'm more worried about what is going to turn up when that thing is missed,' Ed retorted.

'I can ask all the animals to help, and if you can trust them to free roam, they will all help search the island,' offered Tammy.

'That sounds like a very good idea, as long as it's not on the same part of the island as the rest of the staff. I don't want to have to explain it to them all – the fewer people who know about the strange goings-on here, the better.

Ben, work with Tammy on where the staff and the animals go, okay?' Ed instructed.

'No problem,' Ben replied.

'Okay, guys, let's make this island perfectly safe for when Mina and Diego join us, so we can protect them all from whatever the hell is after them.'

Tammy smiled at Ed with pride as he spoke; he seemed magnificent, strong, powerful and completely in control. Only now did she understand why her mother had chosen such a guardian for her and, indeed, for all of the animals.

'Yes, he's amazing, isn't he?' Mikie said.

'Absolutely,' Tammy agreed.

'We know a war is coming but let us now be clear. As far as we are concerned, this war has already begun. Let's prepare and protect ourselves like we did before.' Ed took Jude's hand as she moved to his side. 'At least this time we will be able to see the enemy.'

TWENTY-FOUR

A CLOSE ENCOUNTER

Tammy sat next to Mikie alongside the pond, watching him restlessly throw small pebbles into the water. Jude sat in a lounger nearby, pretending to read a book. She couldn't concentrate, worried about Mikie and Tammy, and kept glancing over.

'I'm sure Stephen is all right,' Tammy said, once more smiling at Jude upon noticing her glance.

'I know something is wrong, Tammy. I can feel it – or rather, I can no longer feel *him*, so I know something bad has happened. I just don't know what to do,' Mikie said with a sigh.

'Look, here's Ed and Dave. Did you secure the island?' Tammy asked.

'Yes, we did,' Ed answered, wearing a frown. Jude was on her feet and beside him in an instant.

'Problem?' Jude whispered.

'I don't know. I'm probably just being paranoid,' he replied.

'Tell me.'

'I keep getting the feeling that I'm being followed, have done for the last two hours. Do you think we secured the island in time?'

'Hmm, I've trusted your Brunswick instinct for too many years to ignore how you feel. I'll go inside and get Security to come to the house as backup – just to be on the safe side.'

'That's a good idea. Any news from our friend in the know yet?'

'Yes, I'm not sure if it's good, though. As far as they're concerned, no one from the military is looking for Tammy.'

'Just as I thought,' said Ed, nodding. 'Not good news then. Where's Fudge and the other dogs? It seems awfully quiet around here.'

'Actually, I haven't seen them for ages. I'll make that call and see if I can find them,' Jude said, heading for the house. Ed turned to the others.

'Mikie is really worried about Stephen,' Tammy said.

'That's understandable. But I'm sure he's all right.' Ed smiled reassuringly.

Mikie was on his feet. 'I really don't think he is, Ed. I'm sure something has happened. I can always feel him, we are close and now he isn't there. I can't feel him at all.'

Ed put an arm around him. 'We'll go inside and call him, shall we? Jude is on the phone at the moment but when she comes back, we'll track him down, okay?'

'Thanks, Ed. I just don't think we'll be able to get hold of him.'

'Well, let's not think like that. We won't know until we call.' They watched the fish surfacing in the pond; eating, breathing and staring back at them.

Dave appeared on the other side of Mikie and smiled reassuringly. 'He'll be fine.'

Tammy gasped as the heat in her pendant burned and she looked down to see the red glow on her chest. 'Jude! Where's Jude?' Tammy asked. 'Something's wrong.'

'She should be back by now.'

Even as Ed ran to the house, he heard a growl. He spun around and felt something hard hit him in the face. He fell to the floor, unconscious. Dave, Tammy and Mikie quickly jumped up and backed away from the creature wearing a red and black-spotted suit. Nobody moved.

The alien stared at them, returning the retractable laser gun he had hit Ed with to its holster on the back of his suit. Another suited figure stepped out of the house, holding Jude close, a laser gun held to her temple. Dave took a step forward and the alien responded by effortlessly raising its wrist and firing a bullet from the pistol concealed within the sleeve into Dave's chest. Dave groaned, clutched his chest and fell heavily to the ground, alongside Ed.

'Dave! Oh my God, Ed,' Jude screamed.

'What should we do?' Tammy asked.

'I'm thinking,' said Mikie.

'I'm scared and I think Dave is dead. Do you think Ed is all right?' Tammy asked.

'I'm hoping so, I can feel them trying to listen to us and read our minds – it's very hard to keep them out of our heads.'

'How come we didn't hear them arrive?'

'I don't know.'

Just then, a man dressed in a smart suit came out of the house carrying Stephen's body over his shoulder. He approached the alien nearest Tammy, the one who had hit Ed. He smiled a horrible smile and looked directly at Mikie.

'I have a gift for you,' he said with a sneer.

He dropped the body on the floor and Mikie was shocked when he realised it was Stephen. He heard a groan as Stephen landed with a thud – at least he was still alive – barely.

'You animals,' Mikie shouted.

'Well, hardly,' Dr Lloyd said. 'Come with us quietly and we'll save his life for you. Otherwise, we'll let him die.'

'What do you want with us?' asked Tammy.

The nearest alien looked at her and took a step closer. Tammy took a step backwards and stopped when she reached the edge of the pond. It lowered its shiny black eyes closer to her face and stared at her, looking for something. Tammy stuck her chin out in defiance and stared back, daring the alien to come closer. She shook with fear; it was large and those eyes scared her. Then she saw something in them that she recognised – they were just like the eyes of a seal. Perhaps she could control these aliens like she could the seals or even the crocodiles.

She stared into its eyes and tried. The alien threw back its head and made a loud and horrifying howling noise. The sound echoed through the island and sent shivers of fear through Tammy and Mikie. It wasn't working.

'Leave them alone,' Jude screamed.

'So, these are two of them? Don't look like much to me,' Dr Lloyd said to the alien.

It nodded, raised a hand and, almost tenderly, touched Tammy's chin. Tammy pulled away sharply. She wobbled at the edge of the pond, regained her balance and had an idea. She looked at Mikie. He nodded, and they began. A column of water from the pond went hurtling towards the alien holding Jude. The column struck it in the face with such force that it had to let go. Blindly, the alien aimed the laser gun directly at Jude. Before it could fire, Jet appeared from out of nowhere and launched himself at the alien, knocking it to the ground.

In the same instant, completely undetected until now, Sirocco reared up and kicked Dr Lloyd in the back, sending him flying into the centre of the pond. As he surfaced, the water lilies rapidly wrapped themselves around him, forcing him to remain still or get a dunking under the water. He gasped for breath and every time he tried to speak, he was pulled back under the water by the lilies. Tammy looked at the alien nearest to her and watched in horror as it reached into the back of its suit, removed the laser gun and pointed it directly at Sirocco's head. Sirocco, not understanding the danger he was in, went to rear up and kick the alien. Tammy told him to remain still.

'Tell the cat to release him,' growled the alien.

Jet was sitting on top of the other alien – who was unable to move. As Jet released him, the alien got up, picked up his gun and seized Jude again. Tammy didn't panic – she was working on another plan.

Suddenly a heavy noise came from the jungle. A herd of elephants, zebras and rhinos burst into view, stampeding towards them. The alien holding Jude stared, not knowing where to shoot first. Tammy used this moment of uncertainty to send another jet of water at it, knocking the gun from its grasp. Jude pulled away and the alien was trampled by the charging animals. Meanwhile, Mikie stared at the remaining alien and took a deep breath. He focused all his concentration on the alien's mind, trying to take over its thoughts in the same way Tammy had done with the crocodiles. The alien seemed amused and stared back at him. They commenced a battle of minds.

'Help me, Tammy,' Mikie pleaded.

'I can't, it's taking all I have to hold the one in the pond. I can't hold him for much longer and I have to keep the other animals away,' Tammy said.

Mikie stared at the alien, scared for the first time that he was alone and trying to do something for which he was not strong enough. Jude watched him and saw the alien's hand start to shake.

'That's it, Mikie, you can do it,' Jude shouted. 'He's weakening!'

The alien tried to activate the gun; its fingers would not respond. It willed them to do as they were told – Mikie willed them not to do it. Its fingers remained still, its arm shaking more violently. Realising Tammy was struggling to hold the man in the pond – via the lilies – Jet plunged into the water and landed on top of Dr Lloyd. Jet glared at him and growled. Dr Lloyd froze, the lilies no longer needed.

Tammy told Sirocco what to do and just like in an old western film, Sirocco dropped to his knees and rolled onto his side as if he had been killed. The shot missed by centimetres. Mikie adopted a fighting stance. The alien went to back away and then hesitated.

'Let's see what you've got,' Mikie heard his opponent say.

Mikie threw himself at the alien and they started to fight. As Tammy and Jude watched, it was clear that Mikie was doing all the attacking and the alien was only defending. It was testing Mikie, seeing how good he was. Mikie spun around in the air and landed a hard-hitting kick in its face, causing it to stumble backwards, almost losing its footing. Mikie delivered a punch to the stomach and uttered a loud yell as he turned, leaned and aimed another kick to the face. The alien lost its balance this time and fell to the floor.

'*Very good for someone so young,*' it told him.

'Get up,' Mikie shouted, holding his fists in front of him. The alien stared into Mikie's eyes and uttered another terrifying howl before promptly disappearing into the surrounding trees.

'Where'd he go?' Jude asked.

'I don't know,' Mikie answered.

Dr Lloyd started laughing, loudly and uncontrollably. They tried to ignore him.

'Ed,' Jude exclaimed, and took her husband in her arms.

Mikie and Tammy looked around for the alien that had been trampled – it too seemed to have vanished.

'I saw the elephants trample him. He was definitely dead,' Mikie muttered.

'They did trample him to death, the animals also say he vanished just like the other one did. Why take its body?' Tammy frowned.

'I don't know, it doesn't make sense. Stephen…' Mikie whispered as he turned to his uncle, still lying on the floor.

Dr Lloyd was still laughing despite the presence of Jet, who leaned in closer and growled.

'You stay sitting there in that pond while we call the police,' Tammy told him. 'I'm going to call Jet off. The elephants, zebras and rhinos will circle the pond and trample you if you try to get out – understand?'

'Crystal clear, little girl. I'll be happy to do what you say, because they'll have me out of here in no time,' he said with a laugh.

'I'll get the ambulance and police on line. Mikie, see if Crane can help!' Jude said, gently placing Ed's head to the ground before running into the house.

Mikie squinted and focused on Crane. 'On his way,' he said, opening his eyes.

By the time Crane had made it to the house, Ed was almost fully conscious, resting his head on Jude's lap as she sat beside him, stroking his hair. Jax was close behind Crane, silent and ready to help at any command. He was gutted that he hadn't been here. He had, instead, been helping Crane complete the security on the island.

'You all right, Ed?' Crane asked.

'Yes, worry about those two. I think the dogs were hit by the same thing as Jet – they're in the house,' Ed replied.

Crane looked at Stephen first and saw no obvious wounds; he was deeply unconscious.

'What happened to him?' Crane asked Mikie, who was sitting at his side.

'I don't know. They brought him here like this, but I heard him make a noise once,' Mikie said.

'I'm sorry, I don't know what to do. It's better to wait for the air ambulance crew to arrive,' Crane said. He got up and went over to Dave. 'Now, an open wound I can deal with.'

Crane investigated the wound and smiled.

'Dave's going to be fine,' he told them. 'Fortunately no major damage has occurred. Nothing a few stitches and some rest won't cure.'

Everyone except Mikie breathed a sigh of relief; he was still staring at his uncle. Since they were isolated on an island, the ambulance and police arrived by air. By the time they landed, Crane had bandaged Dave's wound and moved the dogs to a place out of the way until they regained consciousness from the effects of the *seeker*. Ed was walking about with Jude's support. Ben had tied Dr Lloyd up and Tammy had sent the animals back to the safari park. Sirocco and Jet were out of sight. The scene almost looked normal.

*

A room had been made up for Stephen and Dave to share. Dave lay weakly in one bed while Stephen remained unconscious in the other. Ben, Crane, Jax, Ed, Jude, Tammy and Mikie surrounded the wounded men. The ambulance crew had agreed with Crane's diagnosis of Dave's injury and admired the work he had done. They had agreed that all Dave needed now was rest.

The police handcuffed and removed the hysterical Dr Lloyd. He was shouting for the aliens, as if he knew they could still hear him, furious that they had left him behind. Unable to find any trace of the other two intruders, the police assured Ed that they would learn all they could from the doctor about his accomplices. Stephen's condition had not changed. The air ambulance crew could not identify what was wrong other than that he was, undoubtedly, in some sort of a coma. They had transmitted blood and tissue samples through to the mainland hospital and the diagnosis was limited – undefined comatose condition. There was no apparent reason for the coma; his immense blood loss remained a mystery as far as they were concerned and all anyone could do was wait and see if he came out of it with time.

'Ed, I don't think Stephen and I will be going anywhere tomorrow.' Dave smiled weakly.

'What now?' Crane asked.

'I'll go,' Ed said.

'No, you will not,' Jude said, looking up at him sharply. 'At least not without Tammy and Mikie.'

'Are you crazy?' Ed asked.

'Ed, I love you too much to live without you and today they saved all of us. Tammy and Mikie can do things that make it clear it is us adults who need protecting, and that's just what they can do. They will protect you from these things, not the other way around.' She took his hand and held it to her lips. He sighed and nodded.

'I can't argue with that, can I?' he said. 'I was out of the game before it even began.'

'They're fast and strong,' Mikie said. 'They were just playing with us, finding out what we are made of.'

'Yes, I saw that,' Jude said.

'It's best if everyone leaves the island, at least for a while. I don't know what sort of powers these things have. They could be right outside our front door now and we wouldn't know about it,' Ed said.

'And next time they'll know what they're dealing with,' Jude agreed.

'They don't want to harm us, they want us for something else,' Mikie added.

'Yes, and I'm sure the rest of us are just unwanted baggage. We'll lock up the house for a while and make it clear we've gone, until they lose interest,' Ed said.

'I can make arrangements and take Stephen and Dave to the mainland, somewhere safe,' Jude said. 'I think you should take Jax with you.'

Ed looked at Jax and was about to ask why Jude would

suggest such a thing and then he realised why: Jax was good backup should there be any injuries to anyone. He was also probably safer with Tammy and Mikie than away from them – as long as they were hidden, of course. He regarded Jax and realised with pride what a brave young man he really was. Jax was still upset he had not been on hand to help fight. He showed no sign of fear over what had happened, just regret that he had not been there to help. Ed had to admire him for his courage.

'Can you both please help Jude and then take care of the island while we are gone?' Ed asked Ben and Crane.

'Of course, Ed,' Ben said, nodding his head.

'It goes without question,' Crane replied.

'Kids, we'd better get ready to leave. We'll go first thing.'

'We'll stay with Stephen a little while longer,' Mikie said.

'It won't take us long to pack, we'll do it later on,' Tammy added.

Ed could understand and ushered everyone out of the room to leave Tammy and Mikie alone with Stephen.

'*Ready?*' asked Mikie.

'*Let's do it,*' Tammy said.

They had silently been discussing how they might be able to help Stephen. If they used their combined powers, they might be able to speed up his recovery. They were seated on either side of his bed and placed their hands over his stomach and forehead. Dave watched, silently, from the other bed.

They searched his mind and could see brain cells, veins and the outline of his skull. Some parts of his brain were a healthy red colour. There was also what looked like a black cloud of smoke moving through the cells – this was the problem – they both knew it. Tammy pressed more heavily onto Stephen's forehead and creased her face up tightly as she concentrated on the bright white healing energy light and felt it coming down into her body and then through into Stephen. She sent the light around Stephen's brain, down his neck, all through his body, and could clearly see his organs and the dark grey areas of his brain where the damage was. Meanwhile, Mikie tried to activate Stephen's brain cells, calling to him, trying to activate and find memories and conversation, stimulating his mind by sheer willpower.

Dave watched and saw the deep concentration on Mikie's and Tammy's faces. He saw the light, too bright and strong to look at directly, and had to shield his eyes as the light encompassed Stephen's body. Eyes shielded, Dave watched for what seemed like an age before his eyes could take it no longer. The light grew brighter and the heat in the room made his body tingle as he was forced to stumble out of the room, barely able to see Tammy and Mikie any longer.

*

The following morning when Ed and Jude entered the room, Tammy and Mikie were lying across Stephen's body where they had both fallen asleep, exhausted. Jude gently stroked their heads, in turn, to wake them up. Sleepily, they rubbed their eyes, sat up and looked at Stephen.

'He is healing,' Tammy whispered gently, touching Mikie's hand and smiling gently. She could see the grey areas in his brain had almost completely gone and the rest were fading.

Everyone breathed a sigh of relief. Mikie swallowed with difficulty and had tears of relief in his eyes.

'I take it you haven't packed yet then?' Ed asked, deliberately changing the subject and trying to lift the mood.

'Oh, er...' Tammy began.

'Just as well I came to the rescue and did it for you then,' Jax said smugly as he entered the room, arms folded in a superior fashion.

'Thank you,' Mikie said.

Tammy walked over and touched his cheek and softly smiled. Jax blushed and looked at the floor.

'You get strong for when I come back,' Mikie told Stephen, tenderly touching his cheek.

As Mikie turned to leave, Stephen made a gurgling sound and grabbed Mikie's arm, pulling him back. Mikie dropped to Stephen's side, but Stephen was still too weak, and his mouth struggled to form any words as his eyelids fluttered open.

'Just this once, accept that I can read your mind and save your strength by not trying to talk. You mind has been horribly damaged and needs time to repair. But it will repair, Stephen. You aren't brain-damaged. You'll be okay,' Mikie whispered to him, tears in his eyes.

Stephen looked at him and nodded.

'Save your strength. We will be okay, and you're going to be fine, but it will take a while,' Tammy said gently, taking Stephen's hand into hers and sending more healing energy.

Stephen blinked, waiting for his eyes to focus, then looked at her. He was too weak to smile. Jude came forward and helped him take a few sips of water from a glass with a straw. He licked his lips after a few eager gulps and lay back exhausted. Before he fell asleep, he turned to look at Mikie and gave him an encouraging wink. Mikie smiled back.

As they left the room, Tammy could feel the guilt running through Mikie.

'*It's not your fault*,' she said silently to him as she took his hand and gave it a supportive squeeze.

'*Of course it is*,' Mikie replied.

'*It isn't, you can't blame yourself over this.*'

'*Tammy, I knew what was going to happen the moment he left. I felt it, but I didn't act upon my instincts. Damn it, even Ed relies heavily on his instincts and I failed with my powers. What good are they if I don't use them? I didn't even check up on him. I knew something was wrong all the time and should have gone after him sooner. Perhaps I could have intervened. Or even here, I was too big-headed and eager to prove myself and my fighting skills – I should have tried negotiating with that thing, not beating it, especially when it was only playing with me!*'

'*Oh, Mikie, you're wrong, you can't possibly...*' Tammy gave up, not knowing what words to say to make him feel better; she could too readily read the darkness of his thoughts. '*No one said this was going to be easy.*'

Ed came over to them with a heavy sigh. 'We need to get to Mina and Diego before they do. The Jeep is ready and Jax packed for you – we must go.'

Tammy followed. The Jeep was ready and Sirocco and Jet were waiting next to it.

'You all take care of yourselves,' Jude said as she hugged and kissed them one by one. First Jax, then Tammy, then Mikie and finally, for the longest time – Ed.

'It's all right, Jude, we should have a head start. I am thinking they will focus on coming back here and getting Tammy and Mikie first. I think they are still clueless as to where Mina and Diego are. Meanwhile, we will all be off somewhere else. I'm more worried about you. This place is dangerous now, especially if they appear and disappear like they do. The shield might be useless against them.' Ed held her tightly.

'I assume they got in before the shield went up?' Jude gasped, open-mouthed. 'Surely the shield will keep us safe?'

'I can only hope so, darling, I really don't know.'

'Okay, I'll be gone a few hours after you. Skeleton staff will remain to look after the animals. Just take care of each other. Find the others and get them to our hideout on the mainland.' Jude stood on tiptoe to kiss Ed's cheek.

'To your mother's?' Ed asked.

'Of course, the safest place on Earth. Not even an alien would take on my mother.' Jude tried to smile.

'Don't I know it!' Ed smiled.

Jude wiped the tears from her cheek as she watched Ed, Jax and Mikie drive away, with Tammy riding alongside the Jeep. She took a deep breath and put on a brave face when she felt Crane's reassuring arm around her shoulder. She waved with the best smile she could muster as they disappeared from view.

When the Jeep was out of sight, Jude, Dave and Crane turned and went back into the house. Jude led the way to the kitchen, Dave and Crane following.

Jude came to an abrupt stop, forcing Crane to bump into her and grab her for support. Then, he saw what she could see; the fear gripped him and held him rooted to the spot. He pushed Jude aside, behind him, trying to protect her from what he saw.

Jude was much calmer. 'I knew you were still here,' she said, taking a deep breath and holding her head high. 'It's no good, you won't find them now.'

The two aliens were seated at the kitchen table, laser guns aimed causally at their heads, a horrid growling laugh coming from behind their masks.

*

'Stop the Jeep now!' Mikie suddenly bellowed.

Ed stopped the Jeep abruptly and stroked his chin. Tammy came to a stop beside him, stroking Sirocco's neck and catching her breath.

'Ed?' she asked.

'Something is wrong,' he simply stated. 'What is it, Mikie?'

'They're here now, at the house, two of them!' Mikie gulped.

'But my pendant isn't...' As Tammy spoke, it began to glow bright red and her eyes widened. Jet whirled around and raced back to the house, followed closely by the Jeep and Tammy on Sirocco.

The Jeep had barely screeched to a jarring stop as Ed hurled himself athletically over the door and headed towards the house. Tammy was ahead of him and found the front door wide open. The unconscious bodies of both Dave and Crane lay sprawled out on the kitchen floor – there was no sign of Jude.

'Jude!' Ed shouted loudly. His voice activated a small metal gadget sitting on the table. It whirled to life; a small light flashed a couple of times, making everyone jump back nervously, then a medium-sized holographic image of Jude flickered before their eyes. She began to speak.

'They want you to find the other two, Ed, and exchange one of them for me. They've left a number in Canary Wharf for you to contact when you have them. That is all I am permitted to say, except that I love you and will miss you. Be strong. Goodbye, Ed,' she said with a faint and loving smile, and blew him a kiss.

Ed had his hand over his mouth, thinking desperately and trying to calm the anger that threatened to burst from him any moment. The way she had said goodbye had sounded so final. There was no way she would ever expect him to exchange her life for that of a child. He knew that. Jude's heart had been forever broken when the doctors told her she could never have a child of her own. She adored children. This was her telling him to forget about her and focus on the children.

'She means for you not to exchange them,' Tammy said, her heart racing in both terror and anger.

'I know,' Ed replied softly. 'She always was practical and fearless.'

'What do we do?' Mikie asked, feeling helpless and wondering if he should have seen this coming too, somehow. His confidence ebbed away like a receding tide.

'I don't know but we can't do anything until we've found Mina and Diego – then we will have something to bargain with,' Ed said. 'They will keep her alive until then.'

'We can't exchange one of...' Mikie began.

'Of course not,' Ed replied, reassuringly. 'But we'll still need them in order to have the bargaining power. They can read us as well as you, Mikie, and will know if we are lying. Jude will be safe as long as we are looking for them. That gives us time to think about how we get her back.'

'We'll get her back,' Tammy said, and stuck her chin out for good measure. 'I know we will.'

'Yes, we will,' Ed agreed. 'I'm not letting that woman go without a fight, and those things aren't getting their hands on any children either. We will find a way. Now, first things first, we need to locate Mina. Come on, let's get Crane on his feet and check Dave is all right.'

Jax was already stroking Crane's head as the others came to help lift him up. He groaned and slowly opened his eyes as they sat him in a chair. Mikie ran upstairs to ensure Stephen was still safe in the bed.

'Are you all right?' Jax asked.

'Yeah,' Crane grumbled dryly. 'Got a pounding headache, though. Cracked me over the head with something. I tried to stop them, but they were both so strong – I'm so sorry, Ed…'

'I know, don't worry about it,' Ed said. 'We have to find the kids and then we can negotiate the exchange.'

'I know, I know. I understand perfectly what needs to be done. Don't worry about me, I'll be okay. I'll call Ben in a minute to come and help me look after Dave and Stephen. Ed, you just go – find the kids. They won't be back for now so we can stay here. I'll see what I can find out about this number in Canary Wharf while you're away.'

'Good man, thank you, Crane. You're a good friend,' Ed said, resting his hand reassuringly on his shoulder. 'Look after yourself.'

Crane nodded.

The look Tammy gave Ed told him not all was well with Dave. Ed settled Crane out of the way so he couldn't see, and went over to Tammy.

'He is really hurt, Ed,' Tammy said. 'I am trying as best as I can.'

Tammy instinctively knew she had to do something and put her hand over the wound, feeling the damaged tissue and visualising the tissue and cells regenerating and rebuilding the injured organs. She understood that cells grow in number through a process called mitosis, whereby replicas of chromosomes in parent cells duplicate to form daughter cells and the prophase, metaphase, anaphase and telophase each happened in order to prepare for cell reproduction and healing. She could instruct, in intricate detail, each phase to happen rapidly. She also knew the different tissue types in the human body; epithelial, nervous, muscular, connective, areolar, adipose, lymphoid, yellow elastic, white fibrous, cartilage and so on. The knowledge was instinctive and embedded in her DNA. Tammy did not yet realise that she knew more about the human body than the best doctors.

Ed watched as the bleeding eased and the skin seemed to fast-forward into healing and closing. It seemed impossible, yet his eyes took it in and knew it was happening. Tammy breathed slowly and carefully; deep, long breaths; holding her breath for a moment before she released or took another breath.

'Crane and Ben can finish him later,' Tammy said, 'he will make it now.'

Nodding, Ed got up and went to make a call to Ben.

A few moments later, after Ed had told Ben everything,

he returned and sighed heavily. 'Ben can hold the fort as we go and find Mina and Diego and ensure they are safe.'

Tammy, Mikie and Jax nodded and followed Ed back out to the Jeep with their heads hung low. Tammy looked over her shoulder and took one last look at Jude's hologram, marvelling at how proudly she held herself, even in the face of such danger. Tammy admired and loved Jude more than ever.

'What are you thinking?' Jax asked.

Tammy turned and looked at him. 'I was just making a promise to myself.'

'What promise?'

'To get Jude back, safely, and to make them pay,' Tammy said, and stomped angrily out of the house.

'Oh, they will pay,' Mikie said.

'Yes, they will be sorry that they ever came after us,' Tammy said, so quietly that Jax barely heard her.

'She may not have been removed from the Island yet. I say we go and look for her,' Mikie said.

'I am with you,' Jax said. 'They can't be far.'

'Me too,' said Tammy. 'If anyone can find her, you can, Mikie. Scan for her now. I have a lot of anger I need to unleash.'

ACKNOWLEDGEMENTS

Glad to see you are still here! Or perhaps you are clinging to the idea that this is not actually the end of the story? You question if I would truly leave it there? I do not do it to torture you, it is simply that each book is more like a chapter in a bigger book, meaning that more excitement is only one page away. This had to end here for the next chapter to begin. The torture of a good book ending is just the fun part, right? That bittersweet feeling that it has ended. You must have read enough books to know this by now. This is only the beginning. Still don't think aliens are real? Let's see how you feel at the end of the series shall we. Mwahahahahaha.

How do we acknowledge those who have helped us put a book together – where does it start? With the parents we have battled with during our lives. What teenager agrees with their parents? I thank my family for making me who I am today.

What about the teachers who tell you you're not good enough? Did they make you fight harder to prove them wrong or crush your dreams? I forgive those who called me a day dreamer that would never achieve anything. One even told me smarter people than me had failed. I know they never understood all the stories I created in my mind during their class, whilst still learning what they had to say. I can multitask, you know. Telling me I couldn't do something just made me do it. I thank all the teachers for pushing me forwards one way or another – softly or harshly. Thank you to all the teachers, especially the great ones who told me I could do something incredible if I only chose to apply myself. Like Judith Cutler, my A-level English teacher, crime writer and surrogate mum. Thanks for all the guidance.

Thank YOU for reading this book. It is you who will help Tammy, Mikie and their family continue and grow and live in our hearts. You give them life. Thank you!

I thank my twin son and daughter for editing these in lockdown with me, at the age of 11, with brilliant feedback and from their friends. They helped make this book happen. Re-writing my fight scenes or dialog where needed. They certainly helped to grow and shape this story and the characters. Thank you!

This book is filled with spirituality and energy, as was Star Wars, with the Jedi knights in touch with the energy 'the force' around them and able to levitate and move objects just like the Children of Pisces can. I am an energy healer and thank the great teachers of this world for their precious secrets and teaching me how we can all be superheroes in our own way if only we know how. To Les Flitcroft, for showing me the priceless MCKS teachings, to you and Master Co for your teachings and precious free time online, you both kept me and many others straight and led the way during lockdown. And to MCKS for the sacrifice and genius you gave, also to all the great ones. To Eckhart Tolle for keeping me present and to all the many great people keeping us real in this world and reminding us of who we are and what we can be.

We are each important and special in our own way and not enough children, or adults, realise this. When we are truly balanced our creativity has no limits. Education focuses too much on academia and not emotional or spiritual intelligence and growth. Stay strong, never quit, and do more of what you enjoy doing. That's what I do. Thank you all who have helped the Children of Pisces come alive. Especially the animals.

Don't forget – turn that page for a sneak preview of Part 2…

READ ON FOR A
SNEAK PREVIEW OF
WHAT COMES NEXT...

PART 2:
CHILDREN OF PISCES:
THE CRYSTAL EARRINGS

In a moment of panic, which Mina would later come to regret, she brought a pile of cars crashing to the ground, forcing the men and aliens to take evasive cover. She raced from her hiding place, eager to put as much distance between her and them as she could. As she ran, she looked over her shoulder and saw that one of the aliens was holding up his hand, apparently stopping the falling cars in mid-air, while looking in her direction at the same time. He could see her. Mina touched her earrings and realised with alarm that they were no longer working - she was fully visible. No longer able to camouflage herself and hide from view.

'Oh no!' she moaned. Where had she left her skateboard.

Then she spotted it and as she ran past, started concentrating on the skateboard, which started to move towards her. She jumped on and skated away as fast as she could. But after barely a dozen yards the wheels fell off.

'Argh…' She screamed, as the skateboard skidded from beneath her feet and disappeared under a car. Her gymnastic abilities saved her from hitting the same car, as she flipped over the bonnet and landed on her feet on the other side. A perfect landing that would have gained applause in another situation. Meanwhile her pursuers had almost caught up, and she realised with horror that they could manipulate objects too; they had broken her skateboard.

'Oh no, what have I done?' she said, stumbling on, feeling her legs turn more to jelly with each step. All her life she had been the only person with powers, and it had never crossed her mind that anyone could overpower or beat her. This was indeed new territory.

As she ran, she chaotically sent car parts flying all over the place, desperately hoping that they would block the way behind her. Briefly looking back over her shoulder, she caught glimpses of the men ducking and avoiding the flying parts. Whereas the aliens merely moved the objects away energetically with a mere wave of their hand. No object thrown went near any alien. This wasn't going to work at all! They were gaining on her, and she was outnumbered.

She desperately looked around the scrap yard, trying to find inspiration on what to do next. They were almost upon her now. Heart racing, she pushed forwards. Then she saw the car crusher. It gave her hope and she headed towards it.

She climbed into the crusher and crouched down in the corner, behind an uncrushed car. She turned her earrings until she felt them working again. Feeling the usual tingling in her skin, as the crystal energy embraced her body, she felt the camouflage effect setting in. Now all she had to do was try to keep the crystals working and they wouldn't see her. If they did manage to find her, they would have to climb into the crusher after her and she could bring it down on them. Then, in that instant, the terrifying thought crossed her mind that they could do likewise to her. If they disabled her crystal earrings then she wouldn't be able to walk through the crusher and would surely die. She closed her eyes and felt the overwhelming feeling of fear and imminent defeat wash over her. She had never felt so powerless in her life. She should have waited at home as Lei had instructed. What had she done?

ABOUT THE AUTHOR

Rachael started writing short stories and poems young and had a poem published in America. She wrote her first novel aged 13, entered a few competitions, and then was distracted by almost 30 years of a successful IT Career and motherhood. She never stopped writing. Completing 7 books (5 for Children of Pisces) while she stayed home as a single mother raising her 1-year-old twin son and daughter and working as a childminder. During the covid 19 lockdown, she introduced her 11-year-old twins to this series, who fell in love with it.

She is at her happiest making up adventures in a quiet room with the fire crackling and cats jumping on the keyboard. Rachael loves to have fun, jumping out of a perfectly good plane, diving deep beneath the ocean, swimming with dolphins and taking her children in a hot air balloon over the valley of the kings in Egypt. They barely survived! She believes life is best lived to the full. Over the years she has broadened her experiences by becoming a holistic well-being coach for people and animals. Studying energy, aromatherapy and zoopharmacognosy, as well as helping nurture creativity in others, including her children. West Midlands born Rachael grew up surrounded by animals in North Devon, caring alone for over 60 rabbits when she was just 13 and now having 'not yet enough' pets, including 5 dogs and 8 cats. Rachael lives in a rural area on the River Thames, on the border of Berkshire and Oxfordshire. Once her twins have finished education, she aims to have a remote retreat where people and their pets come to heal and replenish while she and her children keep on writing. Say hello to her on twitter: @RachaelRuthH or Instagram: @rachaelruthholistic.